QUANTUM GIRL

TORN ASUNDER

BEING THE FIFTH BOOK IN
THE QUANTUM GIRL SAGA

BY

DONALD KIERAN AUSTEN

AND

PEYTON ELISE HERRON

INNER SPACE MEDIA
2024

QUANTUM GIRL—TORN ASUNDER,
Being the Fifth Book of the Quantum Girl Saga

Copyright 2024 by Donald Kieran Austen and Peyton Elise Herron

Published by Inner Space Media
10325 Donna Avenue, Porter Ranch, California 91326

Quantum Girl Resurrection / Donald Kieran Austen, Peyton Elise Herron
    p. cm.

ISBN: 978-1-7377812-8-8 (pbk.: acid-free paper)

Library of Congress Control Number: 2024905684

1. Science *Fiction*[1].   2. Superheroes 3. Alien Civilizations
4. Time Travel   5. Parallel Dimensions   6. LGBTQ
7. Bullying   8. Teen Suicide   9. Self-Harm

080424

Cover images designed by Donald Kieran Austen

Printed in the United States of America

---

[1] So stated as science *fiction* for the sake of Library of Congress Card Catalog classification and search engine visibility, though, most assuredly it is not.

to

Tenley

*who would make a perfect
Quantum Girl*

Quantum Girl Resurrection

FORWARD

What would anyone do if they could live their life all over again—if they had a second chance? I tried to kill myself once, but here I am, able to do things differently, able to choose my path in a different direction from what it was before.

Strange to say, I am not the first Peyton Herron. I suppose though, that I'm the last. All of my predecessors were good people—a lot like me in some ways and a lot different in others. I'm not a carbon copy of anyone but myself. All I can say is that I'm glad to be alive. I still marvel at the fact that I've been gifted with so many extraordinary abilities. And I am grateful for family and friends who have not only stuck by me through whatever adversity has come about but who have stuck by my mirror selves. This is the definition of love and love is what makes my life worthwhile.

Wishing everyone a second chance,

PEYTON ELISE HERRON

The Dryad Queen

Be gone, you whore-bent night, and with you lead
Your wretched host, that robs the purest
E'en of her name, and leaves, though woman borne,
The fruitless seeds, that reap their yield
In th' steadfast shame of her on whom they're blown.
Whilst witches must succumb to those chaste drifts,
For snowy vestures shroud their venery,
Here I, so muddied, see the unsunned snows
Resolve into a bountiful deep,
And drown my purpled heart in vestal tears.
How now this bawdy dark, that lays on me,
Conceals a bloodied fall, though `twere the bane
Of wedding sheets, that, newly washed, bespeak
Misfortunes of a rape. I am abused—
Defiled by fulsome breasts, so heavy hung,
That with each heated breath, they burden mine
To weigh my heart in sullied meat. Oh, Mother!
Are these the threads, that bandage open wounds
Just barely bled, so rudely torn to tatters,
And, like my womb, was worn, then torn asunder?

Meribeth Animous, 1837[2]

---

[2] *Maribeth Animous.1782-1846.*was the illegitimate daughter of English writer, Samuel Johnson and his chambermaid, Penelope Animous. The feat of her conception was miraculously accomplished by Johnson at the overripe age of seventy-two. Her illustrious progenitor succumbed to life's misery roughly two years later due to gout, barbaric surgery, and a stroke. Having received not so much as a stipend from her father's estate, she and her mother lived in abject poverty for most of their lives, for despite that her mother was an attractive woman in her youth, Meribeth was far from comely, having inherited most of her looks from her father, and so her matrimonial prospects were imaginary at best.

CHAPTER I

Peyton
*(the one who suffered brain
injury and then was cured)*

I was fifteen years old again. The life that had been stolen from me by my own hand had been restored—and yet the memory of my awakening in another reality so many years in the future remained in my head. My name is Peyton Herron. It was kind of strange. In the time before, I was an only child. This time around though, I had a non-identical twin sister named Ophelia. I called her Phee. When we were little, it was all I could pronounce of her name and it just stuck. Phee was *very* pretty—light blonde hair, blue eyes, and the heartthrob of literally every boy in school with a pulse. Sadly for all of them, she wasn't *into* boys, and, as for girls, there was just one in her life—Claire Salinger. Claire had dark brown hair with bangs and eyes you just wanted to melt into when she looked at you. Well, not me per se. I had a boyfriend—just not exactly at the time this story begins. His name was Mark and in the future that I came from, we were married and in love. Regardless that I was back in time, the in-love with him part never changed, though it was so strange when I saw him for the first time in his mid-teens!

Claire and Phee and I both went to Braxton which was a private, rather expensive, and somewhat prestigious school in Santa Monica, California. But I was also about to enroll at Massapequa. That was where Mark went. Massapequa was a public high school on Long Island in New York. I could do that—attend both—be in two places at once. That's because I had what was called a god-stone in my head that gave me superpowers. Like all the fictional comic book

1

superheroes, I wore a costume with a mask—well, truth be told, it was more of a cowl. My costume wasn't red or blue or anything like that. It was more of a window into outer space. As for me, I was not a comic book character. Truth, you know, can be stranger than fiction. I called myself Quantum Girl, a name that had endured through an infinite number of dimensions and realities.

It was the Peyton from the reality that preceded mine, who sacrificed her life to save me and who had merged all parallel dimensions together so that I remain the only Peyton Herron, with the exception of one who existed in the antimatter quantum fabric. Why it was called the quantum fabric escaped me other than that is what she must have named it—the other Peyton. I couldn't ask Phee. Her memory had been reset along with everyone else's but mine fortunately, which I say because the memory of what existed before had helped me set what I considered a righteous path—doing the right thing and doing it without expecting any sort of acknowledgment or reward. That's how I was brought up and although I, unlike my fervidly Christian mother, do not look upon the passages of the Bible as some undeniable truth, I wondered if somewhere within all that exists there is or once was a conscious higher power.

My mother's name was Katherine and she was a God-fearing, church-going, Bible-thumping woman. Come every week, come Hell or high water, she would drag me and my sister to church to listen to this sermon or that, always having us dress in our best Sunday attire. "It is the House of the Lord," she would always say, "and we need to look our best before Him." More times than not, my father would find some excuse not to go—there was the work he had to do that he had brought home from the office or how he was feeling under the weather and needed to lie down and rest and in furtherance of that, he explained, if he were coming down with something contagious, he wouldn't want to give it to any of the congregation and inflict his discomfort on them. Generally, my mother would shake her head to herself but let the matter stand where it was. Besides, she undoubtedly told herself, she still had her two lambs to offer up to pray to the Lord.

Dad worked for a large accounting firm at the time, or at least I was led to believe that was what it was. In any event, he was a CPA, which is short for Certified Public Accountant. But while Mama was devout Protestant, Papa was what one might have called a scorn-again Catholic, of the opinion that man created God and not the other way around. Just so long as they didn't discuss religion, they got along fine and I must say that there was a love between them that went unmatched. As for their daughterly affections, Dad tended to favor me while Mom leaned more toward "her darling Ophelia" as she put it. Phee and I were copacetic, but with me always having been a Daddy's girl and Phee Mama's little angel. That being said, our family structure had always worked out fine.

The last time around, though, after having been relentlessly bullied by Theresa Martinez, I wound up nearly brain-dead. This time I was stronger. I was Quantum Girl. I suppose I might have exacted some sort of revenge on my tormenter, but I knew the real cause. Theresa had been molested by her uncle for years. It changed her. It made her bitter and cold. Instead, I went back in time and phased her uncle to a monastery in Tibet high up in the Himalayas before anything had a chance to happen. Whether he found God or Buddha or set off in search of Shangri-La, I didn't much care. It allowed Theresa to grow up whole. The only problem was that when I got back things had changed. At school—at Braxton—Claire Salinger was locking lips with Theresa Martinez and Phee was off by herself getting books from her locker.

"Hey," I said to her. "What's with you and Claire?"

"Claire?" Phee replied. "Claire Salinger?"

"Yeah…" I said. "You two have a fight or something?"

"No," she answered. "Should we have?"

"I mean, I just saw her with Theresa Martinez. It looked like

3

you'd need a crowbar to pry them apart."

Phee just shrugged. "Not my affair," she went on. "Daisy's all up in arms, though."

"What for?" I asked.

"She and Claire were hot and heavy before Theresa enrolled last week." Phee shook her head. "Divers! And at our school! What *is* this world coming to?"

"Wait a minute!" I exclaimed. "What about Claire and you?"

Phee threw me a sour expression.

"You *are* kidding, Sis," she replied. "Ewww! Don't even go there! Why would you even say that?" She shut the locker door and spun the combination. "And don't you dare even repeat that to Connor or he might suggest a threesome with me and Myra. You know how guys are."

"Since when have you been sexually active?" I asked.

"Where have *you* been?" she replied.

"I have to go," I said and then phased back into the past. I needed to put things back or Jordan would never be born. It bothered me about what would happen to Theresa but this was a butterfly that I had to unstep on and let live.

I returned to find Phee back at her locker again, only this time Claire was with her. The locker door was closed. Phee had her back up against it and Claire was surrounding her with her arms propped against the steel, the two of them staring into each other's eyes and about to kiss when Mr. Chatterjee's Hindi-toned voice echoed through the hallway.

"Break it up, you two!" he ordered. "This isn't the Moulin Rouge!"

Phee's relationship with Claire was something kept under wraps as far as Mama was concerned—that is until Daisy spilled the beans at a PTSA meeting. This was immediately followed by Mama needing to be helped to a chair to recover from the revelation that her favorite daughter was a sapph. "For this cause, God gave them

4

up unto vile affections," she mumbled, "for even their women did change the natural use into that which is against nature."

Phee rushed over to her, squatting down and begging her to understand. Claire stood by her side. "It isn't *like* that, Mom," she begged. "Claire and I love each other. It's God's love, not the Devil's."

It took our mother nearly a month to accept the relationship, with constant interjections from me of a supportive nature. In the end, she came around, although her conscience was pitted between her love of God versus her love for Phee where the latter eventually tipped the scale. There was also the fact that I had a boyfriend and fostered neither any romantic nor sexual inclination toward the fairer sex. Thus, by the end of the moral month, we were a family again. Claire was even invited for dinner and both Mama and Papa met with her parents, who likewise found their daughter's love for Phee disconcerting but then they still had Chloë to serve out grandchildren to them one day. Oh, that my parents could have gazed into a crystal ball to have looked upon Jordan who was yet to be born from Phee and her interdimensional twin! As for my double life as Quantum Girl, that has yet to be revealed to them.

Among my several powers as Quantum Girl was the ability to duplicate myself an almost infinite number of times. Because of my family and Mark being on polar ends of the continent, I needed to be in two places at once. My family lived in California. Mark lived in New York and I was not one for long-distance relationships. Technically, once things began, I could have phased back and forth but to develop a bond with Mark that would eventually result in our getting married again. Even so, to start, I needed to attend *his* school as well as mine in order to meet him and create a friendship that would evolve into something more.

To accomplish this, I decided that I would divide myself into two and leave one of me at home with Phee and our folks while the other would phase to Long Island where Mark and his family were.

But I needed somewhere to live and at fifteen I couldn't very well sign a lease agreement or enroll in school without a parent or guardian. So—and perhaps you can give me points for thinking of this—I decided that when I turned thirty-five I would phase back in time to that precise moment, meet up with my younger self, and take on the role of my mother, which would make sense what with our *uncanny* resemblance to each other. And, *voilà*, there she was or I was right in front of me in my room.

"So, you're me?" I said with a nodding of my head as I circled around her, eyeing her from stem to stern. She was wearing a Quantum Girl costume sans the cowl that might as well have been spray painted on it conformed to our face so well. Not much naked to be seen, though, because as with my costume, every part of it— and hers was chin to skin as I used to refer to it[3]—appeared to be a window into the cosmos. "Not bad for someone approaching middle age."

"There is no middle age for us," she reminded me, "but I arrived on cue and protected my god-stone with a quantum field, so the two of ours won't combine."

"So," I said as I hopped back onto the surface of my dresser, "what's the future like? Do I marry Mark again? Do we have bunches of kids and live happily ever after? Enquiring minds need to know."

She smiled and shook her head to herself. "I'm afraid I can't tell you," she replied, "or it might change what will happen."

"Bummer," I said.

"Do you have your suitcase packed?" she asked. "I'd like to phase off in the morning."

"Packed and ready for launch," I told her, "though I'm going to need to pick up another hair drier after we arrive, as I assume you remember that Phee and I only have the one. Speaking of which,

---

[3] My costume or outfit as you know went from my shoulders to mid-thigh. Stockings and leotards were never my thing.

6

don't you want to say hello to her, though you might want to change first. You can borrow whatever you want from the closet. I mean, technically they're all yours anyway."

"Yes, they are" she replied, "but not necessary," and with that she phased into a sweater dress with knee-high boots.

I looked on in amazement. "How did you…" I started to ask.

"We have some powers you've yet to learn," she replied. "I'll teach you them when we get settled."

"Won't that interfere with the timeline?" I asked.

"No," she replied, "because I learned them from the older me when I was your age."

I stared at her perplexed. "But if you were taught by your older self, how did it get learned in the first place?"

"I've always wondered about that, too," she said then smiled. "Just think of it as Peyton's Paradox and confine it to the dustbin of the unsolved."

Just then, Phee walked into the room saying, "I just wanted to tell you that I'm spending the night at Claire's hou…se," her jaw dropping as she caught sight of the two of us or, rather, the two of me.

"What's going on?" Phee said, looking back and forth from the one of me to the other.

"I'm from the future," older me replied.

"She phased back in time to help me," I said.

"How so?" she asked.

"I'm going to New York to be near Mark," I replied.

"And abandon *me*?" she exclaimed.

I turned up my nose at her remark. "Of course not," I answered back. "You do remember that I can multiply?"

"You were dismal at math," Phee remarked.

"That was before I became Quantum Girl," I replied.

Phee stared at older me. "What year are you from?" she asked.

"2045," came the response.

"And what about *me* up then?" Phee asked.

"Happily married to Claire," older me replied.

Phee smiled with satisfaction but then pressed on. "You—younger you—said I'd have a child, a girl named Jordan."

"As you will," future me replied. "Would you like to see her?"

"Yes, please," Phee begged.

Older me seemed to focus on the air before her and then, all at once, it seemed that we were no longer in the room but in a meadow spattered with daisies. Phee was there wearing a sundress in her early twenties, and there was Claire with her, her same age. Beside them was Jordan who was no more than five years old, all of them radiating happiness.

The scene then changed. All of the background had disappeared and Jordan stood by herself. With every second, though, she grew and aged until she was a young woman who then turned to Phee and smiled.

"Hello, Mother," she said to her. "I'm so glad we both had a second chance." Then she vanished in a way that reminded me of the Cheshire Cat because what I most remembered about her was that smile. She vanished and we were back in our room, just the three of us again.

"We're leaving in the morning," I told Phee. "Well, one of me at least. Is it all right if she uses your bed," I asked, indicating older me, "as long as you're going to be at Claire's?"

"That's fine," Phee replied.

"And Clair's parents don't mind," I went on, "you're staying with her? I mean, they do realize that things can *happen* when the lights are out?"

"Her parents are cool about it," Phee said, "especially in view of the fact that neither of us can get pregnant."

"Yet," my older self chimed in.

"I mean by each other," Phee replied. "You know," she pondered, half to herself, "I never thought I could be attracted to another girl."

"Mama is worried," I said, "that the two of you might be 'just footsteps from Hell' as she puts it."

"Hell is just a manmade construct," she replied, "and unlike you, Quantum Girl, it's not anything I adhere to. I, dear sister—she glanced awkwardly at older me—sisters—am a God-fearing atheist."

"Mmm," came my thought-out reply.

Phee shook her head. "Well, that's a Calvinist response if ever I heard one."

I turned to older me. "We just started learning philosophy in our humanities class."

After Phee bid her adieus and went off to spend the night with her newfound love, older me and I hit the hay, though I remember continually breaking the dark silence with questions like, "Are Mark and I going to get married again?" or "Will we be happy?" or "Did it hurt giving birth to twins?" to which she replied, "Yes and go to sleep!" to which I responded, "Yes to which one?" to which she responded with a groan followed by her placing her pillow over her ear.

"I know you can still hear me," I said. "We both have quantum hearing," to which she repeated, "All of them. Now, go to sleep!" and so, at last, I did.

It was strange to dream of things that had never occurred—at least not in this lifetime—but my brain still held within it remnants of what had been in the reality before this one. I dreamt of death by strangulation and of how I was revived but with a mind half gone. I dreamt of Cleopatra, of not only meeting her but being her, and I dreamt as well of Khattaaara and how I when I was her caused planets to burn with their inhabitants— billions upon billions of them. I felt her heart race within her breast, not from the horror of it all but from the exhilaration of the wholesale carnage. My Christian spirit fought against her Gaaalthaaaran soul—against *my*

9

Gaaalthaaaran soul—against the countless orgasms that rippled through her nether flesh, down through the very tip of her *yaaargh* as she—as I in my former incarnation— took pleasure in the suffering of others, until at last I was awakened upon sweat-drenched sheets by my older self who stood over me, shaking consciousness back into my head.

"I remember the dreams that *I* once had," she said in softly spoken words as she sat on the edge of the bed stroking the hair that was plastered to my head. "I remember," she repeated as she stared off for a moment, "but I came to grips with them eventually."

"How?" I asked.

"The same way that Jesus did," came the reply.

"What do you mean?" I asked, sitting up in bed.

"I met him twice," she replied, "once when he was very young and once just before he was crucified. We spoke in Greek."

"What was he like?" I asked.

"Well," she replied, "when he was ten he was filled with doubt. His mother had assured him that he was the son of God, but he was bullied and beaten cruelly by other boys his same age who said he was just a bastard child. I broke up the violent moment I'd phased into and dried his tears. He said that no one believed him when he said who he was. I told him that it was only necessary for him to believe in himself. 'Who are you?' he asked. I told him that I was an angel and then phased us both to the Sistine Chapel in my time after it had closed for the night. He stared in awe at the frescoes on the ceiling. We must have spent several hours there but I returned him only a moment after we had left. Whether it was my words or the images he saw, he later said it had inspired him to become the man he was."

"Was he really the son of God?" I asked.

"If we can be Quantum Girl," she replied, "who's to say?"

"Mama said Jesus died for our sins," I reminded her.

"No," she said. "He lived for them."

When morning broke, the two of us filled ourselves with breakfast and then phased inside a house in Massapequa. I looked around, concerned that the owners would suddenly burst into the room, demand to know what we were doing in their house, and call the police.

"Where are we?" I asked with an abundance of concern, "and shouldn't we have phased to the outside and knocked before we went in?"

Older me smiled. "To our own home?" she asked.

"*Our* home?" I stammered.

"I took the liberty of phasing here a month ago," she said, "and bought the place for cash."

"Are we rich in the future?" I asked.

Older me shrugged. "As rich as we want to be," she replied. "Anytime I want diamonds or gold I just phase into the rocks where they are and take them."

"And we or I or you can do that?" I asked.

"I learned that trick from older me," she said, "when I was exactly your age."

"Wait!" I exclaimed. "Isn't that another paradox?"

"I suppose," she replied. "There must have been a beginning somewhere but I've never bothered to concern myself with it and, things being as they are, neither will you. Now, go upstairs and pick whichever bedroom you want, though I daresay I already know the one you'll choose."

I stared at her. "Kind of freaky," I said, "that you know everything I'll do."

"Only because I *am* you," she proclaimed.

"Still weird," I replied and then launched myself up the flight of long flight of steps.

The house was a wood-faced two-story that abutted the Massapequa Preserve. Just beyond within earshot, hidden by the autumn-colored trees was Massapequa Lake, though my quantum senses could smell its water's mist as it rose into the midday air. Needless to say, I took the room that looked out onto it all. This was a landscape unknown to those where I'd grown up. I could hear the chattering of squirrels and the drumming of woodpeckers searching for their meals. Knowing which room I would choose, older me had the walls painted pale pink which was my favorite color for walls. The furniture was pine with a thin wash of white over it and there was a four-poster double bed that was dressed in white with a canopy made from intricately woven lace. The floor was hardwood like the rest of the house, though there was a carpet covering much of it and there was a bathroom off to one side that connected to and shared with the bedroom that older me had taken for herself. In Massapequa, she was to be my mom—Elise Tenley Herron, recently widowed, her husband, my dear father, a casualty of the war in the Middle East.

After being officially enrolled at Massapequa High, I made it a point to seek out Mark, who, despite my previous effort, was still the subject of bullying by a neanderthal of a student named Garrett Wentworth. Garrett, who possessed a subpar IQ and attention span, had been held back twice. As a seventeen-year-old sophomore, he outweighed Mark by a good forty pounds and at some point in the school year had decided to make Mark his punching bag—no reason or rhyme to it—that's just what troglodytes do, even as teens. The fact, though, was that despite both Mark and I being only fifteen, past memories constantly reminded me that I was deeply in love with him and I was not about to let anything happen to him. And while perhaps I couldn't be his protector, Quantum Girl could.

"I thought you were just a dream," Mark said when he saw me again.

"I just enrolled," I told him. "My mother and I, we just moved here from California. The last time when we met I was just looking around to see what the school was like. We bought a house near the lake. Look," I said as the bell rang, "I need to get to class but maybe we could meet up after school—take a walk together through the forest. The leaves are all so beautiful this time of year. That is if you want to."

"Yes," he replied. "I'd like that."

"Well, then meet me out front," I said, "after school lets out."

I wound up getting in the classroom just as the second bell rang, went up to the teacher, and handed her a note. She nodded and then directed me to a desk toward the back. As luck would have it, there down the gauntlet to my desk sat Ugg Thump. His hand went up my skirt as I walked past him. Unfortunately for him, he received a jolt of quantum energy for his efforts.

"Ow!" came his response as I sat down behind him. "What the hell!" he whispered to me. "Are you, wired or something?"

"Force field," I whispered back.

"Yeah, right," came his response. "Just static electricity." He looked toward the teacher who had her back to the class and then turned back to me. "Hey," he whispered, "wanna make out after school?"

"Sorry, I'll pass." I whispered back.

"You'll be missing out on a good thing," he said.

"I said I'll pass," I replied. "I have a boyfriend."

"Don't tell me you're still with Four-eyes?" he said. "A girl like you deserves better."

"Meaning you?" I replied.

"Definitely," he whispered in return.

"In your dreams," I said.

"*Oh*, yes," came the whispered return. "with you naked and all over me."

"Garrett Wentworth!" The teacher's voice broke through the quiet air.

Garrett turned abruptly to face her. "Yes, Miss Barris?"

"Perhaps," she said, "you'd like to share your conversation with the rest of the class."

"Oh, um," he stammered. "I was just welcoming her to our school."

"No doubt," came Miss Barris's doubt-filled reply. "Class," she went on, ignoring him, "I'd like you all to greet our new student, Peyton Herron," to which the students gave a discordant hello. I just smiled in return. "Peyton is from California." That generated a few oos and ahs. "Where exactly in California?" That question was directed at *me*.

"Santa Monica," I replied. "It's on the Pacific Ocean next to Los Angeles."

"Well," she said, "I hope you'll find Massapequa just as interesting and make a lot of new friends."

"She already has a boyfriend," Garrett blurted out.

"How unfortunate for *you*," Ms. Barris replied. "Now, class, will each of you turn to page forty-seven of your textbooks."

And that is how my first day at Massapequa High School began.

Mark met up with me out in front of the school. The lawn was draped with hundreds of American flags. It was both patriotic and beautiful, so much in contrast to the browns and reds and golds of the fallen autumn leaves that served as a carpet beneath the masts which held the flags aloft.

We walked through the columns of stars and stripes to Merrick Road, half a mile or so, down to the lake where a raft of ducks made their way across the water. We had walked in silence most of the way with occasional glances at each other but it was as we made our way to the forest along the water's edge that I first took his hand in mine.

"Why do you let them do that to you?" I asked.

"I'm used to it," he replied.

"What do you mean?" I said. I stopped and looked at him, staring into eyes that shied away from mine.

"My dad," he muttered. "He drinks a lot. Sometimes he gets angry and takes it out on me."

"What about your mom?" I asked. "Doesn't she try and protect you?"

"She ran off when I was six," he replied. "Never even said goodbye. He used to beat *her*, too."

"What was she like?" I asked.

"She was pretty," he replied. "And a lot younger than him. I remember how she used to read me stories at night and then, afterward, kiss me on the forehead and say, 'I love you so much.' But what does that mean when she left me with him and never said goodbye?"

In all the time I'd spent with him back in the past, he had never mentioned any of this. It was like looking at a tree you've seen for years and only now realizing that something terrible had weakened its roots.

"Come on," I said, pulling him northward. "My house is just a few blocks from here. I want you to come home with me."

"What about the forest?" he asked.

"The woods can wait," I replied. "My mom said she was going to make something special for dinner. And you can stay the night. You can bunk with me." I looked at him. "No funny stuff, though. We're both too young for that."

"And your mom won't mind?" he asked. The expression on his face was beyond incredulous.

"She trusts me," I replied, "just like I trust *you*."

"But you hardly know me," he said.

"I know your heart," I told him, "kind and unwavering. You defended me last time I was here and you didn't even know me then."

"I didn't like what he did to you," he replied.

"You stood up for me," I said. "No one's ever stood up for me before."

"Can I ask you something?" he said.

"Of course," I replied. "Ask away."

He turned all shy for a moment and then half-whispered out, "I was just wondering if maybe you and I could be more than just friends."

"You mean like boyfriend-girlfriend?" I asked.

"Sort of," he replied.

"Well," I answered, "I don't know. I'm already involved with Justin Bieber. He wants to leave his wife for me."

"Sorry," he stammered out as disappointment seemed to crease his face.

"Hey," I said. "I'm just messing with you." I moved closer and kissed him on the cheek. "Yes, I'll be your girlfriend," I said in an a whisper in his ear.

We smiled at each other and then made our way back to the newly-rented house holding hands for the remainder of our trip. I led him to the kitchen where I demonstrated my culinary prowess by building two peanut butter and jelly sandwiches for us. As we sat at the table, however, older me phased into the room right in front of Mark who literally choked on his food.

"How did she…" Mark began to say.

"Shit!" That expletive came from me.

Older me, who was holding two bags of groceries in paper bags, stared from Mark to me and then back again. Mark was in the process of standing up, probably on his way to run out the door when I froze time and then went back in time and merged with my former self just as Mark and I had entered the house.

"Come on," I said. I took his hand and again and let him up to my room. Mark stared wide-eyed at the pink and white décor. "What do you think?" I asked.

"It's very…girly," he said awkwardly.

"It doesn't reflect who I am," I replied and smiled. "I just like pale pink. My mom decorated it though. She probably thinks I'm all frills and lace. Do I look all frills and lace to you?"

"I don't know," came the cautious response.

"Well," I proclaimed, "I'm not. If I were to choose to be anything it would be a superhero."

"Which one?" he asked. "You sure don't look like Thor!"

"I don't know," I replied. "Maybe Quantum Girl."

Mark looked at me with a furrowed brow. "Who's that?" he asked.

"Someone I made up," I replied. "She's my age and looks a lot like me except her skin glows kind of violet and the ends of her hair shoot out bits of light like optical fiber. She wears a costume that's like a window into outer space that shows stars and galaxies and nebula from different angles depending on how she turns or where you look at it. And her face is covered with a cowl to protect her identity so that no harm will ever come to those she loves."

"That's all great," Mark said, "but what kind of powers does she have?"

"Well," I replied, "she can phase through time and space, project force fields of quantum energy, and split herself into as many of herself as she wants."

"Sounds pretty cool," Mark said. "Better than Captain Marvel or Wonder Woman."

"Oh," I replied, "don't ever say that to Phee—about Wonder Woman I mean. She's totally obsessed with her."

"Who's Phee?" Mark asked.

I couldn't tell him she was my sister. How would I have explained her not being here with me? "A girl I knew back in California," I replied. "Her real name's Ophelia. Phee's just what I call her."

"I think you're kind of nuts," Mark said, "to leave California, I mean."

"My mom got a job out here," I replied. "Anyway, I got to meet you—boyfriend!"

Mark smiled—grinned might be a better word. But our attention suddenly shifted as a voice rang up to my room from downstairs.

"Peyton!" it called. "I'm home!"

"That's my mom," I told Mark. "Come on," and with that, I took hold of his hand again and led him downstairs to the kitchen.

Older me was there putting groceries away. She turned as we entered, taking special notice of Mark.

"Hello," she said to him.

"Hello," he said back.

"Mom," I said. "This is Mark. The boy I told you about who stood up for me."

"After *you* did the same," Mark replied.

Older me turned to him and smiled. Mark probably assumed she'd smiled to be friendly but I knew it was because it was so long since she'd seen him so young.

Older me extended her hand toward him. "I'm Peyton's mother," she told him, "but you may call me Elise."

Mark took her hand and shook it and then glanced from her to me and back again. "You two sure look alike," he said.

"That's genetics for you," I said with a smile.

"So, Mark," older me said, "will you be staying for dinner? I make a mean tuna casserole."

"That's my favorite, actually," Mark replied. "My mom used to make it for us."

Upstairs after dinner, when we were playing checkers on the bed, Mark said to me, "Your mom's really cool."

"I spoke with her while you were in the bathroom," I said. "I told her what's been going on with your dad. She's okay with your staying here. But she said that tomorrow she'll have to make a report with Children's Protective Services."

He didn't say anything. He just nodded. I beat him the first two games we played. Having a quantum brain allowed me anticipate every possible move and pick the best. I let him win the last one. I didn't want to shatter his ego. When it came time for bed, I retreated to the bathroom to change into my nighty. I think Mark's eyes nearly popped out of his head when he saw me.

"Sorry you have to sleep in your streets," I said. "Mom said she'd get you some jams and a change of clothes tomorrow to make due till we can pick up your things."

He got into bed awkwardly next to me, lying on his back, staring up at the cloth canopy. I lay on my side, facing away but I glanced over at him.

"Do you always sleep on your back?" I asked.

"Not really," he answered.

"Then roll over onto your side and cuddle me," I said. "Just cuddle. Those are the rules for now. But you can do *that* much in that you're my boyfriend and I'm your girlfriend now."

He moved into position, his arm wrapping me. I took his hand in mine and kissed it. I was back in time but I remembered what it was like when we were married and it was a lot like this.

CHAPTER II

Peyton
*(the one who stayed behind
with Ophelia)*

I had mixed feelings about being the one to remain in Cali. I mean, just because I divided in two didn't mean that only the one who was phasing to the East Coast had feelings for Mark. All that Phee knew about him was what I had told her. She had no recollection of what had happened in the future. Neither she nor Claire remembered the relationship they had had or the children they had borne, who were now my responsibility to bear—or her life on Rendenaaar that I had been told about by older her—or the beautiful girl she would one day give birth to and name Jordan—Jordan Katherine Herron—Katherine after our mother.

It seemed strange to me to now have a sister. I had merged into myself in the reality where Ophelia didn't die in our mother's womb but rather grew up to be my closest friend. So it was that I now had the memories of two realities in my brain. But my mind was still linked with *my* other self, and at night in bed, I could feel Mark's warmth against me. Phee was still at Claire's but I did not have to wonder what the future had in store for them.

It was strange though, because, in this new reality, neither Dhraaal nor Thara-Klo had found their way into this universe. Strange to say, I had come back in time to the very moment when I was about to place the noose around my neck. More than that, I had phased back with the god-stone already in my head. One might have labeled it a paradox, wondering where the god-stone had come from but the truth was that it had come from Dhraaal from Rendenaaar—just from another reality.

Dreams are curious things. Most of them go unremembered. Psychologists say that they are bits and fragments of what rests in the corners of our minds. Mostly, at that point in my life, my dreams had been nightmares, spanning from when I had first been bullied to the moment that I had stretched my neck at the end of a climbing rope. But that night it was different. I dreamt that I was standing on a barren plain with a galaxy of stars overhead. As I looked up, I saw what at first seemed like a meteor shower with a rainbow of colored sparks in the sky. Suddenly, though, the Earthbound projectiles all shifted course and headed straight toward me. I stood motionless, frozen in my footsteps, until one after another of them, reduced to the size of a grain of sand, slammed into my head. I felt no pain but with each impact, I saw what I could only describe as a ghostly version of myself emerge *from* myself and then dissolve into the nighttime air, each one a different color like the meteors or whatever they were that had smashed into my brain. Then, as the last ghost vanished, I woke up.

Phee was asleep in her bed, no doubt because it was still dark outside. I wondered what had happened to her staying with Claire. Had they gotten into an argument? I had hoped not. Claire and Phee were a good fit and I knew that deep down they loved each other to the bitter end. But as explanations could wait until morning, I just took a deep breath, rolled over, and went back to sleep, hoping for more peaceful dreams.

When morning dawned, Phee was already up, still in her pajamas, and in the bathroom brushing her teeth. I got out of bed and followed her in.

"Morning," she said through a mouthful of toothpaste that she afterward spat out into the sink. "I thought I'd let you sleep," she added, this followed by an influx of mouthwash, gargling, and another spit.

I pulled back the straps of my nighty, let it fall to the floor, turned on the shower, and then jumped in. "What happened between you and Claire?" I asked.

"Who's Claire?" she replied.

21

"Stop it!" I called out over the sound of the downpour. "What happened? Did you get into an argument?"

"I have no idea what you're talking about," she shot back. "I don't know anyone named Claire so I couldn't very well have had an argument with whoever she is."

I turned the shower off and stood there naked, dripping, and confused.

"Seriously?" I said. "I'm really not in the mood for jokes."

"What are you talking about?" Phee replied. "Wait! You don't mean Claire Salinger, do you? Why would I be friends with *her*? She's a solid sapphron and, from what I hear, totally committed to Theresa Martinez, though I'm not going to say which lips. But thank God that she did, so that Theresa would stop tormenting you."

I turned the shower back on, rinsed off, and then got out, grabbing and putting on my bathrobe, after which I caught my reflection in the mirror over the sink, noticing the monogram on the robe.

"Hey, Phee!" I called out. "What's with the monogram PJH?" then I walked barefoot into the bedroom.

Phee wrinkled her nose at me. "Peyton Jane Herron?" she replied. "Or don't you remember your own name?"

"So *both* our middle names are Jane?" I ask facetiously.

Phee sighed one of those, oh my fucking God sighs. "No," she said. "As you well know, my middle name is Elise. And why are you calling me Phee? What happened to Lia?"

It was then that my heart began to pound in my chest. What had happened to the world I wondered? This didn't seem to be the world I went to sleep in. As I stood there, I watched her fasten a silver necklace with a sterling woman's head that dangled from it. I walked over to her, raised up the head with my fingers, and stared at it. It was only about half an inch in length with the woman's eyes cast down, while on her head was a crown of thorns.

"Don't worry," she said. "It isn't yours. Yours is over on your nightstand. Besides, yours is gold."

I glanced over there. "Hey," I said. "What happened to my laptop? I always keep it next to my bed."

"If you mean your vag," Phee or *Lia* said, "I assume it's still between your legs."

"Ugh!" I growled. "I wanted to check something on the Internet. Where's yours?"

"My what?" she replied.

"Laptop!" I exclaimed with mounting frustration. "And why do we both have necklaces with severed heads on them?"

"Don't let Mom hear you say that," she replied. "You know how she is about Jesua."

"You mean Jesus," I replied.

"Good thing Mom isn't up here," she said, "she hates when anyone blasphemes her name."

I glanced around the room. "Where's the Bible Mom gave us?" I asked.

"Gave *you*!" she replied. "She's come to grips with the fact that I'm a lost cause. I think it's in your underwear drawer."

I went over to the dresser, opened the undies drawer, and scavenged through the *silk*. "Found it!" I said as I pulled out a small black leather Bible. Rifling through the pages as I walked over to my bed, I sat down and turned to the New Testament.

Sure enough, instead of Jesus, there was Jesua who was the Daughter of God, performed miracles, was eventually beheaded by the Romans, and then rose from her tomb three days later. Not only that, but the Apostles were all women!

Phee or Lia or whatever she now wanted to be called walked up to me and took the Bible from me.

"'Scuse me, Bible girl," she said, "but we need to get down to breakfast if we intend to get to school on time. She tossed the Bible in our wastebasket and walked to the door. "I'll be downstairs at breakfast," she said and then called out from the hall. "And you'd better cover up your laptop before you come down!"

It was frustrating—confusing to say the least. I decided to skip breakfast, just get dressed, and then phase over to the ocean to sit down in the sand and think. But when I tried, nothing happened. My attempt to phase into my Quantum Girl costume was just as futile as were my repeated efforts to duplicate myself. I found that I couldn't even listen in to what was going on in the kitchen. However hard I concentrated none of my powers worked. The realization came at last that they were gone. I was just Peyton Herron again. But, I wondered, how could that have happened?

Frustrated with disappointment, I went downstairs to find Phlia at the table with a plate of scrambled eggs and ham in front of her. I sat down across from her and was brought the same by my mother.

"Thank you, Mama," I said to her as she laid down the plate.

"Mama!" Phlia mocked under her breath.

"You hush up," Mama scolded. "I think it's endearing."

"Is endearing another word for weird?" Phlia said with more than a hint of sarcasm. She took a bit of her eggs and then went on, "I think Johnny Walters is going to ask me to the prom."

"Is he the boy," Mama asked, "who came up to you at church last Sunday?"

"No, Mom," Phlia replied. "that was Scott Berens. He's in my chem class. He just asked about the assignment."

"He seemed like such a nice young man," Mama said.

"Yes, Mom," Phlia replied, "and he's also a soc."

Mama sighed. "I don't see how in the name of Jesua," she said, "a handsome child like that could turn his thoughts to such ungodly desires."

"It's accepted today," Phlia replied. "LGB, no longer on the QT so they say."

"I could quote many passages in the Bible," Mama said back, "which condemn such behavior."

"Would you love Peyton any less," Phee came back, "if she

24

outright declared that she was of a mind to like other girls?"

"In your dreams!" I snapped back.

"Wet dreams, no doubt," she said under her breath.

"I'm not a lesbian!" I said.

"Whatever *that* is," Phee replied.

"Sapphron or whatever you called it!" I said. "Besides, I have a boyfriend if you must know. His name is Mark and he lives in New York on Long Island."

"You mean New Amsterdam!" Phlia shot back at me. "And how would you know anyone there, let alone have him as your *boy*friend? Seriously?"

"I just do," I said, "and why are you being so nasty to me? I thought you were my best friend."

"After you hid all my clothes," she exclaimed, "when I was in the shower in the locker room and forced me to go to class wearing just a towel?"

"Did not!" I exclaimed.

"Did so!" Phlia shouted back. "You're just a mean old bitch!"

Mama turned to face her from whatever she was doing at the stove. "Ophelia Elise Herron," she said with a stern expression on her face, "I will not have a daughter of mine speak that way in our home!"

"Sorry," Phlia replied.

"And that goes for you, too, Peyton," she said to me.

"What did *I* do?" I asked.

Phlia rose from the table with indignation. "Ohhhh," she pouted at me. "You can take off that fake halo from your head. It doesn't hide the horns!" Then she stormed out of the room.

She was different. *All* of this was different—even the family photos that were scattered against the walls. This wasn't the world I'd grown up in. The question was, if it wasn't my world, which world *was* it?

CHAPTER III

Quantum Girl Blue
(December 31, 1928)

I awoke on a sofa in the lounge of what turned out to be the Palmer Hotel in Chicago. I was in my Quantum Girl costume, but instead of my skin irradiating purple, it shone blue. There were people all around, all dressed to the nines, and there was gaiety. It turned out it was New Year's Eve in the middle of the Roaring Twenties with a small band playing the Charleston. The women— the younger ones at least—all wore calf-high beaded dresses and cloches that were beaded as well. These, I later learned, were called flappers. Long hair was out. Shorter hair with perms was in. And there were silk stockings on their legs with seams in the back. It was the Prohibition Era, so none of them had alcoholic drinks— supposedly. It was against the law that would eventually be repealed.[4] Beyond all that, the Palmer was viewed as a respectable hotel, often playing host to celebrities ranging from silent film stars to politicians to royalty and even kings.

I stared up with foggy eyes at a pretty twenty-something flapper in a blue beaded dress, her head adorned with a blue headband and blue-dyed ostrich feather, and who was a slightly older, nearly spitting image of Phee. The resemblance was so great that at first, I thought it actually *was* her.

"Love the glad rags and glitter," she said, staring down at me. "I'd never dare to wear anything that short, though. My guy'd think I was trying to take a ride with some egg."

I sat up, looking around. "Phee?" I asked, still groggy. "Where

---

[4] The Volstead Act, which brought about the Eighteenth Amendment, banned the manufacture, sale, or transportation of any alcoholic beverage. After having spawned widespread bootlegging and basically created the American Mafia with its reign of machine gun violence, it was repealed by the Twenty-first Amendment in 1933.

are we? Where is this place?"

"Geez," she replied. "Some guy slip you a Mickey or something? It's the Palmer, don't you know." She glanced at the small watch on her left wrist. "Ten to go till the New Year!" She turned her head in both directions, searching. "Scuse me," she said. "I need to go find my guy before the countdown."

There was a mirror across the room from me but I caught my reflection in it and realized how inappropriately I was dressed for the occasion. I assumed it was a costume affair, so I moved off to one corner and phased into something similar to what the other women were dressed in—a heavily beaded black dress with an equally heavily beaded black cloche. If I do say so myself, I was the cat's meow!

At the stroke of midnight, when the crowd had counted down to zero, confetti was thrown into the air along with paper streamers. People blew out rolled paper noisemakers and into horns as everyone began a chorus of *Old Lang Syne*. Suddenly, I heard one of the women scream and then the scream abruptly stopped. One man, dressed in a black tuxedo had a small device in his hand that he aimed, one by one, at members of the crowd and, one by one, whomsoever he aimed it at disintegrated. By that, I don't mean that they just vanished. I mean that their bodies were irradiated, the victims appearing tortured by the effect—and then they were gone. They each screamed in the beginning but then it became hollow and then there was no sound. I tried to freeze time. I tried to phase back in time to just before it had happened but something prevented me. Something was inhibiting my ability to alter time. As the man turned to the woman I had met, I turned into Quantum Girl, grabbed her, and then phased us both out of the hotel, just as the man who was with her was struck by the same energy beam.

At that point in time, I had no idea where I was—or when—or how I had gotten there in the first place, though judging from everyone's outfits and the décor I assumed I was somewhere in the

1920s and, from everyone's accent, still in America. But it was the not knowing specifically where that was my greatest handicap just then. I couldn't take the chance of phasing us into anything solid like a lamp post or a wall so I did the only thing I could think of—I phased us two thousand feet up in the air. From there, I had at least a perspective on where to go. The woman, though, couldn't understand what was happening. She looked down and began to scream hysterically and then, fortunately for me, she fainted dead away.

All around in the sky fireworks were going off in a spectrum of colors. Despite that it was now past midnight, yellowish lights dotted the landscape below due to the annual ritual of welcoming in the near year. From what I could see, this was a large metropolis, edged by a large body of water that reflected both the starlight and the Moon in its endless procession of waves that splashed rhythmically onto the shore.

My time travel ability gone, at least for the moment, I was at a loss as to where to go, until I noticed the enameled mesh purse that her unconscious hand still gripped. In it was a house key, a compact, lipstick, and an envelope with her name and address on it that had been sent to her from Baltimore. My newfound *traveling* companion's name was Mary Lindsey and she lived on West Estes Street in Rogers Park. Phasing both of us into the living room of the house in my previous flapper attire, I set her down into one of the easy chairs and then went to one of the several floor lamps that were there and pulled the chain to turn it on.

The room I had phased us into seemed cluttered by modern standards. There was a pair of red satin armchairs and a green sofa, all with braided fringe along the bottom edge, draping to the gray raised pattern carpet on which they sat, and what I felt was an excess of other furniture and knickknacks. Nothing there was really to my taste but I supposed that it was considered normal at that time.

Just after the lights went on, a woman's voice called down from the upper floor, "Mary?" it asked, "Is that you?"

It was an elderly woman who descended the stairs a moment later wearing a robe and slippers and looking concerned when she saw me squatted down in front of what turned out to be her granddaughter.

I stood up and greeted her. "Hello," I said, "My name's Peyton. I'm afraid Mary's a bit..."

"Sauced!" the woman said as she walked over and looked down at her granddaughter. "The word is sauced! If I told her once, I've told her a thousand times to stay away from those speakeasies. 'Mary, I said, 'you'll find yourself in trouble, especially if you wind up with the wrong man.'"

"It wasn't a speakeasy she passed out in," I assured her. "It was the Palmer Hotel. I think she just fainted from all the excitement. I thought it best to put us both in a cab and bring her home. I found the address in her purse. I don't know her that well."

"Well, thank you so much," she replied. "Peyton, you say? Well, I think you're an angel for bringing her home safe and sound. Lord knows the worry this girl has caused me, and my heart's not that good—not anymore. I'll go grab some smelling salts from the bathroom medicine chest."

A moment later the matronly woman returned with a long, white, silk-covered glass capsule which she snapped in half and then brought up to Mary's nose. Mary perked into consciousness with a start.

"For cryin' out loud!" she proclaimed. "What's going on?" She looked around and then at her granny. "How did I get back here?" she asked as she gathered her senses.

"Your friend, Peyton, brought you," her great-grandmother said, "And it's a good thing she did. Why some man could have taken advantage of you, gone to the world as you were." She looked at me. "I don't know how you managed, Dear, but I'm eternally grateful."

"The cabby helped me get her into the chair," I lied.

"I guess it was just a dream," Mary said, "I dreamt that I was floating thousands of feet up in the air with some girl in a strange costume that looked like a field of stars, screaming for my life that I was going to fall to my death."

Great Granny shook her head. Mary stared at me curiously.

"Who *are* you?" she asked.

"Why," Great Granny replied, "that's your friend, Peyton."

"Actually," I confessed, "I just helped get Mary out after all the shooting began."

"Shooting!" Great Granny exclaimed.

I shrugged. "Some mobster just started shooting up the place with a Tommy Gun. I have no idea why. I was there with my parents. I saw both of them gunned down. Then the same thing happened to the man Mary was with. As I knelt over the bodies of my parents, Mary urged me up and we both rushed into the lobby and then out to the street where Mary hailed a cab. After we got in, I guess it was all too much for her and she just fainted dead away. 'Drive!' I shouted at the driver. 'Where to?' he asked. 'Just go!' I screamed."

"Poor Fred," Mary sighed. "And to think he was the only support his mother had." She reached out and took my hands in hers. "Thank you so much for bringing me back here," she said. Then a thought crossed her mind. "But how did you know where I lived?"

"As the cab drove off, I searched your purse and found an envelope with this address." I took a deep breath and glanced at the front door. "Well," I said, "I guess I'd best be going."

Great Granny glanced at the clock that stood on the fireplace mantle. "It's nearly two o'clock," she exclaimed, "and you're how old?"

"Fifteen," I said. I thought as I spoke the word that I should have said that I was older but you can't take back words once they've been said.

"Oh, my word," Great Granny replied, "you're just a child, and now with your parents gone… I won't hear of you going off on your own at this late hour. You can sleep in William's old room—Mary's father's. He was killed in the Great War just after Mary was born, and then, not a year later, her mother passed because of cancer. Then my daughter and her Ralph left us back in Eighteen from the influenza. Seems we're all being taken, one by one." She left and trudged up the stairs. "Yes, sir, one by one, and more than likely I'll be next."

Mary rose from her chair. "I'm feeling better now," she said. "But that dream I had—it must have been a dream—just seemed so real." She stared into my eyes. "You must think I'm nuts to have believed that it happened, even for a second."

"No, not at all," I replied.

"I'm still kind of hazy about what all went on," she said. "I suppose that's all part of hysteria. We discussed all that in my class last semester. I'm studying to be a child psychologist."

"You like children I take it," I said.

"Oh, yes," she replied. "and I want my own someday. Hopefully a girl. I even picked out a name."

"Really," I said, "so soon?"

"I believe in being prepared," she replied.

"And what name did you decide on?" I asked.

"Jordan," she replied. "Great Granny thinks it's a silly name. 'You don't name a child after a river,' she said, 'let alone a girl.' 'But it *is* in the Bible,' I insisted, and besides, I told her, I like it. 'Well,' she said, 'if you ever have a little boy just I hope you don't name him Nebuchadnezzar!'"

"Is it just you and your great-grandmother?" I asked her.

"Just her and me for about as long as I can remember," she replied. "Funny, though," she went on, "I have a dream that keeps coming back about having a twin sister—not identical, you know."

She smiled. "Actually, she looked a lot like you. But the dreams are very distressing."

"How so?" I asked.

"They're always the same," she replied. "I'm with Lark. That's her name. And then all of a sudden, she changes into a monster with pointed ears and a tail that she wraps around my throat and I'm being strangled."

"And then?" I asked.

"I wake up," she replied. "Of course, it's all just a dream or, rather, a nightmare, as everyone assures me that I was and always have been an only child." She stared out into space for a moment and then went on. "It just seems so real—more like it's a memory than a dream." She took a deep sigh. "Oh, well," she said. "The mind can certainly play tricks." She looked back at me. "Hey," she went on, "Do you want something to drink? We've got milk in the icebox or soda pop if you prefer."

"Soda, please," I replied.

I followed her to the kitchen where she produced two bottles of Nehi grape soda, used a bottle opener to pry off the caps, and handed one of them to me. Then we sat facing each other at the table sipping our drinks.

"What are you going to do now?" she asked, offering up concern that I could see from the expression on her face.

"What do you mean?" I asked.

"Well," she said, "with your parents taken from you as it were, do you have other relatives you can stay with?"

I shook my head. "I'll figure something out," I replied.

"Don't be goofy," she said. "You're just fifteen. You can't make it on your own. Look, I don't mean to be forward or anything but we've got the extra room. You can stay here. You can earn your keep by helping around the house and sharing chores with me. Great Granny's getting on in years, you know, and can't keep up the way she used to when I was small. And regardless that I feel I owe you for bringing me back home and, to tell you the truth, I'd really like the thought of having sort of a sister who wasn't imaginary."

"I don't know," I said, though I had to consider the fact that I was stranded in this time with nowhere to go.

"It'll be fun!" she insisted. "In the evenings we can play records on the Victrola and on Saturdays we can go see a flicker. My treat. I hear there's a new Charlie Chaplin at the Diversey. I've never been there but Hildy Baxter—she works the make-up counter with me at Marshall Fields—well, she says they have at least a thousand seats and a full orchestra!" She stared at me with puppy dog eyes. "Please say yes," she begged. "You'll have more than a place to stay. You'll have a family and a home and I can see that Great Granny's already taken a shine to you. Please?"

"All right," I said. "We'll see how it goes."

"Yay!" she proclaimed. "You won't regret it."

And so it was settled. I figured as long as I was marooned in the past, I might as well make the best of it.

CHAPTER IV

Quantum Girl Red
(December 7, 1941)

I awoke in a pile of rubble and covered in dust. It was early morning and sirens were going off. People were panicked, running this way and that. Overhead was a squadron of prop airplanes with large red circles painted on their wings and fuselage that droned as they passed and dropped their payload of bombs that shrieked as they fell to the ground, striking buildings with devastating effect. The sounds of the explosions were deafening but the wake of destruction was tragic. People were running in every direction trying to flee the attack. Many didn't make it. There were the bodies of the injured and the dead everywhere. And then I heard her—a little girl—sobbing bitterly, screaming, "Mommy! Mommy!" with a sound that was packed with tears. I stood up and then phased a hundred yards or so in the direction of the sound. A sandy-haired girl, who appeared no more than six years old, lay on the ground clinging to the body of her mother. The woman was obviously dead. I could detect no heartbeat, there was blood on the side of her head, and her eyes were wide open, staring vacantly upward at the hostile sky. I went over to the girl, nudged her, and then urged her to let go of her mother and stand up, not giving a second thought to the fact that I was garbed as Quantum Girl, though, for some reason, a Quantum Girl who glowed red.

"Come on," I said. "I'll take you to someplace safe."

"I can't leave my mommy," she sobbed.

"She can't come with us," I replied.

"Why not?" the girl asked as tears flooded from her eyes.

"Your mommy's with God now," I said.

"I don't want her to be!" she wept. She dropped to her knees again and shook her mother's corpse. "Wake up! Wake up!" she

34

cried. "Wake up!"

I put my hand on her shoulder. "She can't," I told her. "Not anymore."

I urged her up and lifted her up in my arms. She looked at me, I think for the first time.

"Why do you look like that?" she asked, wiping her tears with the back of her right hand.

"Because," I told her, "I'm your fairy godmother."

"Like Cinderella?" she asked.

"Like Cinderella," I said.

Just then, a bomb from one of the Japanese Zero whistled through the air as it fell directly toward us. Immediately, I threw up a force field to protect us so that it exploded and dispersed twenty feet above our heads. Regardless, we needed to get to somewhere safe. I duplicated into ten more of me, each scouring the island for a place we could go and then merged back all in a split second. It seemed that we were on an island. Several blocks away was a hospital that hadn't been hit. I phased us then to the back of the building and then phased back into my Peyton self. The girl remained surprisingly calm despite the surrealness of it all. I set her down and then squatted down to face her.

"What's your name?" I asked.

"Margaret," she replied. "Margaret Fletcher."

My heart nearly stopped in my chest. Margaret Fletcher was the name of my grandmother. Phee and I used to visit her when she was in the convalescent home. I recalled hearing how she, as a little girl, had survived the Pearl Harbor attack. A million thoughts raced through my head. What sort of a guiding hand had led me to her at that particular moment, I wondered? Years before—or from now chronologically—Fate had brought me face to face with my great-grandmother on my father's side. Despite all that, I realized that my focus needed to be on that little girl for if something happened to her my mother would never be born and then I myself would cease to exist.

"Hello, Margaret," I said to her with a smile. "My name's—I was about to say Peyton, but then I thought better of it—Elise. Tell me something. Do you know where your daddy is?"

Margaret shook her head. "He's in the navy," she replied, "on a big ship."

"A big ship, huh?" I said. "Come on. Let's see if we can find him."

We went into the hospital which was in a frenzy with wounded everywhere. Medical personnel swarmed like ants from one makeshift bed to another. Some of the wounded lay on stretchers—some on the floor. Nothing like this had been anticipated when the place was built. The few beds in the emergency room had been filled by the first to have been brought in. I walked with Margaret over to one nurse who was putting an IV into the arm of an elderly man who appeared to be unconscious.

"Excuse me," I said, "but I'm trying to find this girl's father."

The woman glanced at me and then turned back to her work. "Good luck," she said as she taped the protruding part of the needle to the man's arm. "No one knows where anyone is. I just hope he wasn't on one of the ships."

"Why's that?" I asked.

"Last I heard," she replied, "the entire fleet was destroyed. From what we've been told, there weren't many who survived." She stopped what she was doing and shook her head. "This one's gone." She turned toward the center of the room, then and shouted, "Hey! Med assist over here!"

A man in scrubs rushed over. "We have to get this one outside," she told him. "He's gone and we need the bed."

As I turned to leave, I noticed my reflection in a mirror. I looked older than I was by several years, perhaps in my early twenties. I shrugged, wondering if it was an effect of the time travel phenomenon that had brought me here. Then I turned to Margaret whose hand I held.

"Let's go," I said. I led her to one of the offices that had been abandoned, set her in a chair, duplicated into a red Quantum Girl, and that one of me phased from there to the sky.

I hung in the air above the devastation. The harbor and the ocean nearby were littered with a wreckage of ships. Nineteen of them lay in ruin on their sides or sunken entirely, including eight battleships, but the Japanese air fleet was gone—back to the aircraft carriers from which they had launched their merciless attack.

Enraged by it all, irrespective of the timeline, I hurled out quantum blasts and destroyed as many of the Japanese fleet as I could including eight destroyers, thirty submarines, and one battleship. In school, I had learned about the history of the Pearl Harbor attack—how the Japanese ambassador was in Washington D.C. pretending to negotiate peace just before the unprovoked attack was to occur. More than twenty-four hundred Americans lost their lives as a result. *To hell with them!* I thought to myself. *To hell with them all!*

After that brief moment, I calmed myself and resumed my search. I soon found the ship that I was looking for and then phased to a hundred locations on it, within it, and around it in the surrounding water. Within seconds, I had found the man I was searching for—the man who was my great-grandfather—Michael Fletcher, an ensign on the USS Arizona. He was on one of the lower decks, his legs crushed beneath a dislodged torpedo. I quickly phased back into my Peyton self, though this time in a WAVE uniform. There wasn't much life left in him but he looked up at me. The water was rising around us. I had thought to phase us both out of there, but with his injuries, with the pressure from the torpedo removed, he would have bled out in seconds.

"Hey," he said in a weak voice. "Good to see a friendly face."

I managed to work up a smile and said, "Hey," back. "It's going to be all right," I assured him.

"Yeah," he replied. "That's what they told Mrs. Lincoln after her husband was shot. It's okay though. I knew the risks when I signed on." He reached into his shirt pocket, pulled out a folded piece of paper, and handed it to me. "This is for my wife and my little girl," he said. "I'd appreciate it if you could see to it that they get this. My wife's name is Laurel. Fletcher. My little girl is Margaret." He shook his head. "I always hoped someday I'd be able to walk her down the aisle. It seems someone else is gonna have to do that for me." He gave out a low moan, then, and he was gone. I took a deep breath, let it out, and then phased and merged back into my other self, note in hand.

I unfolded the paper and read the words that had been written in pencil. "To my darling Peyton," it said, "and to Fair Margaret. I don't think I have much time. I'm lying here with a torpedo on my legs, writing this on the back of a requisition form. The water's starting to flood in and so I don't know if this will ever get to you but, God willing, it'll find itself into your hands. All of us who signed up knew the risks when we did, though I figured that I lucked out having been stationed seven thousand miles or so from where all the fighting had been taking place. I don't know if you remember Billy Hawkins. I got word the other day that he was one of the casualties in Tobruk. I just want to say that you and Margaret are the best things that ever happened to me. I love you both so much. How we ever wound up crossing paths I'll never know—you and me both a couple of orphans with no one but ourselves until we had each other. I just hope the two of you find happiness. Tell Margaret that her daddy loves her and will always look down on her from Heaven to make sure she's safe. With all my love, Mike."

I folded the letter back up and put it in the pocket of my dress or, rather, a quantum fold that would remain close to me. Then I stared at Margaret, who now had no one in the world other than me—the granddaughter who had yet to be born. She was my responsibility now. There was no one else. There was no one for her but me. I had told her that I was her fairy godmother but it seemed that from that moment on I was to be her human mother as well.

CHAPTER V

Quantum Girl Orange
(August 8. 1951)

I awoke in a strange bed, stretching out my arms and squinting as the sunlight from what must have been an eastern sky struck my eyes, momentarily blinding me from its brightness. I pulled myself up a bit to somewhat of a sitting position and then looked around the room. I had no idea where I was or how I had gotten there. I found myself naked and, looking under the sheet that covered me, found that I had breasts that were strangely far more developed than they had been what I thought must have been only hours before.

It was as I was contemplating what could have happened, that a very attractive woman in her mid-to-late-thirties in a vastly out-of-style blouse, skirt, and hairstyle, walked over to the bed and sat down on the edge next to me, handing me one of the two cups of coffee she was holding.

"Bad dreams again?" she said, sipping her brew.

"What do you mean?" I asked.

"You've been having them again," she replied. "I can always tell. Those creatures again. The ones with the pointed ears and tails."

"I don't remember," I said.

"I thought…" she started to say. "There's no downside to us, is there? I mean, the sex is great—at least it is for me." She looked hard at me. "You're not having any second thoughts, are you?" She turned and stared out the window. Her auburn hair seemed to glow as the sunlight filtered through it. "I never loved anyone before. Not really. Not before you." She glanced back toward me just for a second. "My mother used to say to me, 'Tara, you're a strange one. You never look at boys. Why when I was your age they couldn't keep me away.' That's what she used to say. I never had the heart to tell her—not even on her deathbed. I wanted to explain to her, breathe out the words, 'Mom, I'm not *like* other girls. I *like* other girls. I just haven't met the right one, that's all—at least not yet. And then I met you and my heart raced a million miles a second from the moment I saw you and how impossible it seemed to me that you would like me in return." She turned back to face me. "I wish I could shout to the world that I *have* you but these are lonely times for those who feel like us. Those who have other perceptions of what should be normal look down their noses at us as though we are diseased. They'd lock us up in jail or in some asylum where we'd be drugged or perhaps lobotomized. But I was willing to risk it all for just one moment with you." She looked at the clock on the nightstand and then sighed, "Well, I'd better get a move on it. It's a quarter past six. I have to be at work in fifteen minutes and it's a ten-minute walk. Lucky you. You have an hour left to sleep." As she was almost out the door, she half-turned back and said, "Remember to lock the door when you leave. I'll ring you up later tonight."

After she was gone, I rose from the bed and looked around. It was a single-room apartment with kitchen attached. The kitchen table had a red marbleized Formica top with chrome steel legs surrounded by four matching Naugahyde-upholstered chairs. The refrigerator was a bulky, round-cornered monster with a cylindrical compressor on top and a freezer that was crusted with ice behind its lever-lock door. The furniture, lamps, and even the pictures on the wall were garishly geometrical with drab colors, making me convinced that I had somehow phased into the middle of the twentieth century.

I found my clothes folded on a chair near the bed. There was a white blouse, a poodle skirt, a padded bra, granny panties, bobbysocks, and saddle shoes. There was also a small black hard-sided handbag with a jeweled snap-over clasp. I opened it up and emptied it on the bed revealing a brass lipstick holder and matching compact, a white handkerchief with pink and blue embroidery, a house key on a brass ball chain with a blue rabbit's foot attached, and a blue leather wallet. In the wallet, there were some coins, none of which were newer than 1951, as well as several single dollar bills, a two, two fives, and a ten. There was also a paper student ID from Braxton that was handwritten with a date stamp of September 1, 1951, and a pasted-down black and white photo that looked sort of like me. But it was the name that struck me—Margaret Jane Fletcher, date of birth, February 26, 1935, which would have made her seventeen years old.

I stared at myself in the mirror over the dresser. The image that stared back wasn't me exactly but the resemblance was there, looking far more like me than Phee ever did. I thought to myself for a moment, considering the name on the identification card—Margaret Fletcher. That was my grandmother's name on my mama's side. I walked over to the dresser and really looked hard at myself. There were slight differences in my face and there was a birthmark near the underside of my right breast which was nothing I remembered. And, staring down downward at my reflection, it appeared that not only was I not shaved but not even trimmed. If this was truly 1951 that would account for it. No woman wore string bikinis back then. But how could I have wound up in my grandmother's body I wondered? I could duplicate into as many of me as I wanted and then merge them all back, but I had never been able to merge into anyone else. Then a human urge overcame me. I went to the toilet to pee and then got dressed.

I smiled to myself as I caught my reflection once again. I looked like Kathleen Turner in *Peggy Sue Got Married* and, like her, I was back in time—back in the body of my grandmother who was apparently having a lesbian affair with a much older woman—and still in high school it would seem. I never knew that about her. All I did know was that she'd married my grandfather when she was in her mid-twenties. In my time, the sapphic thing was fairly common, but back then it was pretty much kept in the closet. Still, I wondered how it had come about that my Grandma Margaret had gotten involved or why she gave it up.

According to the student ID, Margaret lived at 24946 Malibu Road in Malibu. It took half an hour to get there by bus but I made it with about a block's walk to a house that sat next to the ocean. I used my latch key to get in. Unlike the apartment, the house was decorated in more of what I would consider very modern and, as I thought, quite out of place for the time. It seemed very comfortable, I thought. There were French doors that gave way to a private beach and a view of the ocean that eventually melted into the horizon. Two bedrooms sat off to one side of the living room and I quickly found the one that was mine. Photos on the walls showed Grandma Margaret from a young age and there was a large painting over the fireplace of a woman who must have been her mother who looked even more like me though a somewhat older version—perhaps in her early thirties—reminding me so much of myself at that age, before I had merged into my younger body in order to find Mark when we were both in our mid-teens.

The walls in my room were painted a pale blue and, in addition to the bed, were a dresser, a desk and a chair, all of which, like the rest of the furnishings in the house, looked very expensive. The desk's surface rested on crossed bronze bars that were attached to bronze rods that ran in a perpendicular direction. On the desk sat several textbooks—high school level—and notebooks filled with writings, scribbles, and drawings in a hand that most decidedly was not mine. Forgetting the moment or my predicament, I found the voice of the waves splashing down on the beach almost hypnotic and irresistible. There was a bathing suit in one of the dresser drawers that I put on, then left the house through the French doors to scrunch my toes in the sand and make an imprinted path to the water's edge.

The water was cold but inviting. The waves drove hard against my calves, and then engulfed my thighs. At last, with a deeply held breath, I dove down into the chilling water and became one with the ocean from which life first emerged.

I was not as good a swimmer as Phee who at one point in another reality had set her sights on being an Olympic contender. Still, I was competent and able to cut through the surge of waves, swimming a thousand feet from the shore. It might have been risky for anyone else but I knew that if I tired too much to breaststroke it back, I could always phase myself to dry land. It was as I out as far as I chose to go, treading water and gazing back toward the shore that I first saw her—the woman in the painting. I tried to bring her features into focus but I could not. Nor could I hear her when she called out to me. *Why my powers should have failed me I did not know, unless,* I wondered *it was that the god-stone did not come with me when I traveled through timed or, perhaps, this brain could not control it.* It was some distance back to the shore and that frightened me having gone so far relying on powers I no longer owned. I was tired but I would have to steel myself to make the swim back.

The woman stood on the sand in a flowered sundress that flapped in the summer breeze. On her head was a white, wide-brimmed hat with a long, flowing ribbon that matched the pattern of the dress, her arm raised up, her hand pressed down on it so that it would not blow away. She stared into the distance at me and waved at me with her other hand. I waved back, dove headlong into the water, and then freestyled my way to where the water was shallow enough that I could stand. My arms were exhausted from the swim. I trudged the rest of the way through the briny water toward her, my brown hair clinging to my face, my flesh beaded with saltwater, the air chilling my skin to raise goosebumps as it blew in coldly from the west. When at last I came within earshot, she shouted at me.

"Hey!" her voice called out. "Why aren't you in school?"

"I overslept," I lied, "so I figured I might as well play hooky, considering I only had a couple of classes left."

"And cheerleading practice?" she asked as I drew close. She glanced at her wristwatch. "Come on," she said. "Get dressed. I'll drive you there."

As we began walking back toward the house I said, "I forget. Is my uniform here or did I leave it at school?"

Margaret's presumptive mom shook her head. "It's folded in your middle left drawer," she said. "As usual."

She wrapped one arm around me and pulled me close to her as we walked. "My dear Fair Margaret," she said. "What are we going to do about that scatterbrain of yours?"

I had to take a step back when I saw the cheerleader outfit. The pleated skirt which was knee-length and the long sleeves were Persian blue with Braxton embroidered in Cardinal red on the chest, outlined in white. The sweater was worn over the white blouse that was also there. The shoes were white with leather soles and there were white bobby socks and there were pompons made of yellow paper. Regardless of how conservative this would have appeared in my time, Margaret must probably have been the heartthrob of many a young man, few of whom would have imagined her leanings toward her own sex. As I stood posing for myself in front of the dresser mirror, I heard the woman speak.

"You look adorable," she said. "Who would have thought that the little girl I raised all these years would have grown into such a beautiful young woman?" She opened up her arms toward me with a proud smile. "Come here," she said.

I went to her and she embraced me. "No words for me?" she asked.

Not quite certain how to respond I said, "Thank you, Mama."

The woman pulled back a bit, held me by my arms, and stared into my eyes with sudden tears in hers.

"I'm so proud of you," she said. '

"For what?" I asked.

"For growing into the most wonderful daughter a mother could ever hope for," came the reply. She pulled me into her and hugged me again. "I love you so much," she said, then she let go of me, took a step back, and wiped away the tears that had dripped from her eyes.

But it all seemed strange. From what I'd been told, Grandma Margaret had been an orphan after both of her parents were killed during the Pearl Harbor attack. And yet here was her mother, alive and well it seemed. *What could have happened to have changed things?* I wondered.

"Did you have a good time spending the night with Suzie?" she asked.

"It was fine," I lied. "We just listened to records."

"I'm glad you enjoyed yourself," she replied, little suspected where Margaret had actually spent the night.

Having changed into my cheerleading outfit, Margaret's mother drove me to the campus in her bright red '47 Tucker and dropped me off at the edge of Charton Field where the school's football team, the Sky Hawks hosted their home games, cheered on by the squad Margaret was on —which I came to learn was called the Starlings—practiced their cheers.

"I'll pick you up in two hours," she said as I got out of the car after kissing her on the cheek, which I thought was appropriate, considering. Then I jogged over to where I saw the other cheerleaders had already gathered.

There were four other girls on the squad—Megan, Susie, Babs, and Jennifer. And there as well was Tara aka Coach Nichols, the woman with whom Margaret had been having a tryst.

"We were beginning to wonder if you'd show up?" Coach Nichols remarked as I joined the other girls.

I looked at her, surprised by her presence. So, it was the cheerleading coach who lured young girls into her bed—not a very Christian thing to do was my first thought. Suddenly, I felt very sad and protective of Margaret, even though I had no idea where *Margaret* went after my mind had been thrust into her physical form. But who was the worse culprit, I wondered—I who had usurped her body or that woman who had corrupted her soul?

Cheerleading was rather basic back then. There were no guys involved. There were no pyramids. No one was thrown up in the air. There were just us five girls. Regardless, practice proved an embarrassment for me since I didn't know any of the cheers. Feigning a headache, I sat through the first run and then learned enough that I was able to perform almost as well as the rest of the squad.

Coach Nichols stood in the shower room afterward, carefully eyeing each of us as we washed off all of our sweat. Once we had toweled off, the other girls changed into streets, but it hadn't occurred to me to bring a change of clothes along, and while there might have been some in Margaret's locker, the locker had a combination lock on it that remained a mystery to me. Thus, I was left with no choice other than to get back into my sweaty cheer attire.

It was as I was finishing dressing that I heard Coach Nichols off to one side talking with Babs. Babs—Barbara Torrance—was a very pretty girl with auburn hair, hazel eyes, and who looked much younger than her age. It became obvious that neither of them had noticed me.

"You don't have to worry," Coach Nichols told her. "It'll just be the two of us. My friend won't be there. Just come by after school tomorrow. I'll leave a key under the mat if you get there before me."

"I don't know," Babs said. "My mom is expecting me to go shopping with her."

"Just tell her you'll be studying at one of your friends' house like you did last time," came the reply. "I'm sure she'll understand."

"All right, I guess," Babs said. "But what about supper?"

"You can phone her from my place," the Coach went on, "and

tell her you were invited to stay overnight."

"But what if she asked to speak to my friend's mom?" Babs argued.

"Then I'll talk with her and pretend I'm her," Coach replied. "You want to stay on the squad, don't you?"

"Of course," Babs said, "but…"

"I think that's more important than shopping," Coach insisted, brushing back the strand of hair that had fallen over Babs's eye. "After school tomorrow. Okay?"

"He won't be there again?" Bab's asked.

"No," Coach replied. "I'll just be you and me."

"Zena Hadley got pregnant by some man," she said, "and her parents sent her off to a convent."

"It'll just be you and me," Coach insisted.

"All right, I guess," Babs replied in a timid voice.

Coach Nichols turned and walked over to the rest of us and blew into the whistle that hung from the chain around her neck.

"Girls!" she called out. "Next practice on Thursday! No one be late!"

The girls disbursed, including Babs, who walked slower than the others. Margaret's *mom* was already waiting in her car in line with four others. I caught up to Babs and walked with her to where our rides were.

"I know what's going on," I said to her.

"I don't know what you mean," she replied in a quiet voice.

"She's done it to me, too," I said.

Babs stopped and stared at me.

"She's not a good person," I told her. "You don't have to go. We can go to the police tomorrow, you and me."

"But then everyone will know," she said in a fearful voice.

"We'll do this together," I said. "It will all work out. You'll see."

But she didn't go with me the next day. Class let out early.

There was a quiet announcement at the school. Barbara Torrance, we were told, had taken her own life late the night before. The details were unclear but it later came out that she had slit her wrists and bled to death. There was no note to explain what had brought her to that moment but I knew the truth and so did our cheerleading squad instructor. I wanted to phase back in time but I couldn't. I wasn't Quantum Girl anymore.

When school was out, I decided to go to Coach Nichol's office and confront that monster face-to-face. I missed the school bus that would have taken me home but I figured I could always call Margaret's mom for a ride. I took a deep breath as I stood in front of the closed office door. "Tara Nichols," it read, "Girls Athletics Administrator." I thought to myself that it should have read, "Child Molester" instead. I took a deep breath, steeled myself, and knocked on the door. Little did I know what Fate had in store for me on the other side. The door swung open.

"Come in," said the now familiar voice.

Yes, it said, "Come in. Welcome to my house..." said the spider to the fly.

CHAPTER VI

Quantum Girl Yellow
(A.D. 1,219,064,261)

I awoke in what I thought might have been a room, but there were no walls—at least not as far as I could see—only a brilliant white light in every direction. It was also oppressively quiet—so much so that the sound of my own swallowing was the loudest thing I could hear. I tried to sit up but found that I couldn't. There was a barrier surrounding me—confining me. It was as though I were in some sort of an invisible tube—or a coffin. I tried phasing out of it to no avail. I attempted to move through time but couldn't. Neither was I able I hurl out a force field to shatter it. None of my powers worked. I shouted for someone—anyone—to let me out—but no one came. I pushed against the edges of my prison. I felt claustrophobic. Panic set it. My heart pounded in my chest. My breath became labored. Sweat encapsulated me. I lost control of my bladder. All of the strength and confidence I had as Quantum Girl had fled me. I prayed to God. I prayed to Jesus. I wept for my Mama and Papa to come save me. Minutes passed and then hours, but nothing changed.

Surprisingly, the air remained fresh, if somewhat tainted by the scent of the urine that had bled from me. Eventually, exhaustion overcame my senses and I either passed out or fell asleep. I dreamt of Mark and how for the very first time he held me in his arms and kissed me. My heart had pounded back then as well but in a different way. I felt something I had never experienced in my life. Blood had filled my capillaries and flushed my skin. I had felt a hitherto unknown ecstasy that I sensed from my breasts and from my loin while my quantum senses overwhelmed my nostrils with the unmistakable sense of musk—all of this from one kiss and an embrace—and I felt the warmth of his body, even through the layers

50

of our clothes. *Dear Mother Mary*, I asked in my head, *is this what it felt like when God came upon you, to impregnate you with our most Holy Lord and Savior?* But whatever it was or wasn't, I knew that this was love—our lips touching—inhaling in the very air that had at last breath been in his lungs. And what was more than all of this, I knew that he loved me back. And then I woke up—again!

This time there were *people* around me, although not exactly human. They were all dressed in some thin metallic clothing. None of them had any hair—not even eyebrows—and their craniums were substantially larger than any I had ever seen. When they spoke, their mouths never opened to form any sounds but I could hear their words in my head.

It has awakened, said one.

After a billion years, said another.

The Yellow Goddess, arisen for our salvation, said a third.

A billion years! I thought to myself. *That can't be right.*

Yes, revered Goddess, the first thought back, *a billion years.*

We have awaited your awakening for uncounted ages, said another voice.

I looked over to one side. This being looked slightly more female than the rest.

How is it that you know not our dilemma? she went on.

I reached upward to find that the barrier had disappeared.

You may sit up, she said, *We have removed the containment field.*

I did so cautiously and then swung my legs over whatever it was that I had been lying on. I looked up at her. "Where am I?" I asked. "Where *is* this place?"

Earth, she replied. *Does it matter precisely where? The world that you knew is no more. Nothing remains. Even the continents have changed.*

"Who are you?" I asked.

We are what remains of humanity, she said, *but doomed to extinction when the sun swells into a red giant in another thousand or so years. Ten million years ago, a rogue star plunged into the sun and accelerated its evolution. When it explodes, it will destroy the Earth and us with it. We have no means of escape. Whatever other planets there are that can support our life are far beyond our reach. Not enough metal is left to build starships, and, even if there were, the technology to build them is lost in the past. You and your sisters are our only hope. We have worshiped you for eons and prayed for your awakening.*

I looked at her with concern. "Sisters?" I said, questioning the word. "My name is Peyton Herron," I said. "Some have called me Quantum Girl, but I am not a god. I don't know how to prevent a sun from scorching the Earth or how to move an entire world."

The group stared at each other. I assumed that they were telepathing their concerns. Finally, the female turned back to me. *You need to come with us,* she said telepathically. *I will show you where your sisters sleep.* I followed her down a long corridor, similarly brightly lit, into one room and then another and another—five in all—each identical to the one in which I had awakened. In every one stood a bed of sorts and on each bed lay a different version of me as Quantum Girl—red, blue, green, violet, and orange—all in a state of sleep or coma or hibernation—and each, as I was told, had been in the unconscious state as I had been in for more than a billion years!

CHAPTER VII

Quantum Girl Green
(August 12, 39 B.C.)

I awoke unable to move—not a muscle—not even able to blink. My eyes were open but my vision was clouded. Everything was a blur. I could see shapes hovering over me and around me and I could hear some women chattering in a language I couldn't understand. After a few minutes, they left or else became extremely quiet—though I suspected the former—but as I said I couldn't move. The fact was, as I later came to find out, I had merged or been merged with someone who had the unfortunate luck to have been murdered and when someone is dead their nerves and muscles and all the rest don't perform very well or at all unless stimulated with an electric current—as Luigi Galvani proved in 1780—or through a god-stone, having the ability to regenerate tissue.

Little by little (or *un po' alla volta* as Galvani might have said) the quantum stone in my head healed the body I was in—resurrecting it from its lifeless state. Eventually, the body's heart began to beat again and blood once more surged through its veins. The flesh began to warm. My vision began to clear. After what must have been only five minutes, I was able to rise like Lazarus from the dead. I sat up and then stood.

Walking over to a table, I picked up a hand mirror with a polished gold surface. The reflection was of Cleopatra—my Cleopatra—the one who had stood by me in the future until her untimely demise. More than that, in the mirror's eye I saw two fang marks on my left breast that healed as I watched them.

If I remembered my history correctly, no one had ever found Cleopatra's tomb which meant that my sudden departure from Egypt wouldn't affect history or the timeline. I turned into Quantum Girl somewhat disturbingly to find myself radiating green rather than purple. I shrugged to myself but faced absolute consternation when I tried to phase back to my own time—and couldn't! Hearing people approach, I phased from the room roughly a hundred miles to the south to the Valley of the Kings where the pyramids and the Sphinx all stood. Cleopatra had told me of their magnificence but seeing them in person was quite different despite her vivid description or even from the photographs I had seen—each of them to presumably to deliver their architects to whatever afterlife they believed in. How ironic that all of that labor of carving and hauling stone culminated with them winding up, not in some great heaven but rather as a musty artifact on display in some museum. Still, it was a solemn moment for me, breathing in the past. I phased to the top of the Great Pyramid of Giza and looked across the drifts, illuminated by the moonlight. There I stood, hundreds of feet up, glowing like a lighthouse beacon in a sea of desert sand.

Morning would find me on the streets of Rome as Cleopatra. It was strange to see all the ancient marble buildings long before they had begun to crumble. Here marked the center of the supposéd civilized world, where just four years before the mighty Julius Caesar was assassinated in the streets by his own senators, Brutus among them—Brutus, whom he considered one of his closest friends. Throughout the city were the Vigiles who stood the night watch. Approaching one of them, I asked in Greek which, seeing through the eyes of Cleopatra I now understood, "Where is the house of Marcus Antonius?" I asked.

The Vigile, who refused to move, his eyes staring straight ahead, unwavering, replied, "Who art thou that seeks to know?"

"Cleopatra, Pharoah of Egypt, Queen of Kings!" came my reply. "Bring me to him," I demanded, "or I shall have thy head mounted on a spear!"

The man looked down at me with just his eyes, and then, as he appeared to note the royalty of me, he fell to his knees and bowed his head. "Forgive me, my Queen" he replied. "It is dark and I did not recognize thee."

"Rise then," I commanded, "and lead me to his house!"

The guard climbed to his feet but kept his head bowed so that his gaze would not meet mine. "This way," he said, then led me down several streets to a large house with a courtyard in front. The house or domus, as I later learned it was called, was made of stone with marble columns spaced about ten feet apart. At the door, we were met by two Pretorian guards who stood barring the entrance.

"Wake thy lord and master," said my escort. "Tell him that Cleopatra, Pharoah of Egypt, Queen of Kings, commands his presence."

One of the guards entered the house while the other remained vigilant. A moment later, the Pretorian returned with Mark Antony who was not as I had imagined. He appeared to be in his mid-forties, five-ten, with hazel eyes, and brown curly hair. His skin, tawny from the sun, he still stood a handsome figure of a man.

"Cleopatra!" he exclaimed with a smile. "Come inside."

I entered and then looked around the great room that was lit by oil lamps that were set on tables and in niches in the walls.

"Sit, sit," he insisted, then walked to a table where stood a decanter from which he poured two goblets of wine. "Forgive me," he said as he handed me one of the drinks, "but I have no pearl to add for flavor." He smiled and then sat down facing me. "To what do I own this pleasure?" he asked.

"I am in need of a place to stay," I replied. "The air in Egypt echoes with rumors of assassination."

"Of thee?" he asked with an expression of perplexity. "By whose authority?"

"Octavian," I replied from the tales the real Cleopatra had told. "He has his eye on both Egypt and Roman and it seems that you and I both stand in his way. Besides," I went on, sipping the wine, "I hear that his nostrils still flare since learning that the two of us have remained lovers despite your having wed his sister. She *is* a pretty thing if a bit obtuse."

He glanced to his back. "Better that she not hear you," he replied.

"Dear Antony," I replied. "It is not my intent to plague thy marriage, but I do require sanctuary until I can further the plans I have made."

"Of course," he said, setting his now empty goblet down on the table beside him. "Jealousy be damned! Thou shalt be my honored guest and nothing more. What phantasms fly through Octavia's brain are hers alone to console." He stood up. "I shall have my maids prepare quarters for thee. Thou must be tired from thy long journey. And thy stomach must rumble for food. A meal shall be prepared as well."

"I thank thee for thy kindness," I said, also rising.

"And I welcome thy kind face in these troubled times," he replied.

The room he led me to was spacious and elaborately decorated with purple draperies and marble busts which, oddly, were all painted to look human. It was an odd feeling to see what appeared to be two dismembered heads on pedestals, staring at each other—one of Julius Caesar and the other, as I later found out, of Octavian, who later became August Caesar, First Emperor of Rome.

The bed was stuffed with goose down as were the pillows. It was comfortable but my nerves were on edge. Here I was, fifteen years old—again—but trapped in the body of the thirty-year-old woman who was my former incarnation—or at least one of her—and I had no idea either how I had traveled back in time or how to return home.

I had a restless sleep that night. I dreamt that I was was Quantum Girl but had no clue as to where it was I stood. It was pitch dark other than the glow that came from me, only the light kept changing color—from purple to blue to green to yellow to orange to red, over and over again, faster and faster. Different torsos of me began to emerge, attached at my waist with each struggling to break free. Then, all at once, there were six of me, each those same different colors, facing outward in a circle, hurling out forcefields at some unknown threat.

"This can't go on," we all said at once. "There can't be six of us—not like this. We need to merge together again!"

I was awakened by Octavia, who had entered the room and gave out a blood-curdling scream. I opened my eyes to see that in my sleep I had phased into the glowing green Quantum Girl (or, rather, Quantum Woman).

She pointed at me like she was Lady Macbeth. "Demon!" she cried out.

As she turned her head back to call for her husband, I phased back into Cleopatra, so that when Mark Antony rushed into the room, there was nothing to see but his wife, clothed in hysteria.

"What has happened?" he asked.

"Thou hast invited a demon into our home!" she cried out.

"I see no one but Cleopatra," he replied, "who asked for protection from those who would do her harm."

"That is not Cleopatra!" Octavia screamed, with a rasp in her throat. "'Tis a lemure, sent by Hades to make murder upon our good house!"

"Madness!" Mark Antony proclaimed. "Does thou offer that I know not the woman who bore three of my offspring?"

"Husband," Octavia replied, "thine eyes are deceived. 'Tis a shapeshifter, no less. A moment before it was glowing verdant with a cowl upon its face!"

"Quiet now!" he ordered her. "'Twas nothing more than a dream! Get us now back to bed that Royal Egypt may rest undisturbed for the remainder of the night."

And so I was bid adieu and left to wonder what plans I needed to make once morning came.

CHAPTER VIII

Quantum Girl Violet
(April 22, 2025)

I remember being in outer space. I had duplicated myself a thousandfold to stem off an alien invasion. Their ships had appeared out of nowhere two days before. The Earth had no defense. All that anyone on the planet could do—whether civilian or military—was sit back and watch. The first attack came at 6:36 a.m. with a simultaneous onslaught on both the north and south poles, melting the ice caps and causing sea level to rise more than two-hundred thirty feet. Millions drowned. There wasn't enough time for evacuations. Most of the world—that which was not mountainous—lay under more than thirty-eight fathoms of ocean. Lakes and rivers drowned under billions of tons of saltwater. Whatever freshwater fish there had been, died with most of the land population. People clamored to the higher elevations to try to survive but with little food or water, death was inevitable. Meanwhile, the military had been reduced to its navies, but without the means to manufacture armaments, its supplies of weaponry were relegated to what was on hand. Even the concerted launching of nuclear missiles against the invaders proved useless as each and every one was destroyed by the enemy before it could even reach the stratosphere. It appeared that the only chance humanity had was me, Peyton Herron—Quantum Girl—a superhero whose presence on the planet no one knew.

It was a battle between the quantum forces that I was able to muster and the extraterrestrial technology. From what I was able to conclude, the invaders wanted to conquer the Earth because of its vast supplies of water—perhaps to colonize—perhaps to plunder. Where or when they had come from I had no idea. Their attack was unannounced and unprovoked. There was no communication. There was only an onslaught of their high-energy beams directed at Earth's polar ice caps.

Dividing into thousands, I had positioned each of my selves between their ships and the planet, hurling out forcefields en masse in an effort to stem the onslaught. But as the battle continued, I felt myself weakening. I could feel the quantum strength in me being drained until at last the power of their weapons broke through. The pain was excruciating, It was like a million knives had stabbed into me all at once. It felt like this was the end, but I knew that if I died, so would all life on Earth. The agony grew. I sensed that I was about to be dissolved into nothingness. I screamed—each of me all at once in the void of space where there was no sound. I screamed as I died. And then I woke up.

I was in a bed in a hospital room as it later turned out. The lights were off. It was night outside. I looked around the darkened room and then craned my head up just a bit. To my right, a chair had been drawn up to the edge of the bed, and in it sat Phee, asleep, leaning forward with her head cradled in folded arms that rested on the mattress. She stirred, then—I guess from my having moved—opened her eyes and stared at me.

"You're awake!" she said as her face lit up. "Oh, my God!" she exclaimed. "You're awake!"

"What's going on?" I asked. "Where am I? The last thing I remember was being blasted by the energy beams from the spaceships."

"So, you don't remember hanging yourself?" Phee said " Lucky for you the pipe broke. Water began shooting out of it. Everything got drenched but that didn't matter. I got to you and called 911. The paramedics worked on you for twenty minutes. The doctor said you suffered from a lack of oxygen to the brain. That was two days ago. We didn't know if you'd ever wake up."

"Where are Mama and Papa?" I asked.

"I made them go home," she replied. "I told them it was enough for *me* to be here with you." She looked strangely at me. "What's with the Mama and Papa?" she asked. "What happened to Mom and Dad?"

"Dunno," I replied. I pulled myself up to a sitting position. "Anyway," I went on, "why don't I phase us both back home? I'm sure *Mom* and *Dad* will want to see that I'm all right."

"What do you mean *phase us back home*?" she asked. "What's *that* supposed to mean?"

I shook my head to myself. "Apparently, I'm not the only one whose brain's been rattled." I extended my arm toward her. "Give me your hand," I said. "I'll get us back home."

She humored me—that in retrospect. She held out her hand and I took it in mine. But when I tried to phase us out of there, nothing happened.

"I don't understand," I said, perplexed. "Why are we still here?"

"Where are we supposed to be?" Phee asked.

"Home," I replied.

"What are you talking about?" she asked, bewildered.

"The god-stone isn't working," I said.

"What's a god-stone?" she replied.

I stared at her, incredulous. "God-stone," I said to her. "as in Quantum Girl."

She just stared back at me.

"Superpowers," I went on with emphasis but there was no response from her other than a blank stare. "I was trying to fend off the alien invasion. I'd duplicated into a thousand of me and projected quantum blasts at them but it wasn't enough. I felt as though I were about to die. And then I woke up here."

"You were dreaming," Phee insisted. "Dr. Tom said it could cause hallucinations."

"Dr. Tom," I repeated.

"The neurologist who's been treating you," Phee replied. She stood and turned toward the door. "I'd better see if I can get a hold of him and tell him you're awake and then call Mom and Dad."

"I need to call Mark," I said.

"Who's Mark," she asked

"My boyfriend?" I replied as though she should have known.

"Since when do sapphs have boyfriends?" she asked with a wide-eyed stare.

"What makes you think I'm sapphic?" I asked.

"What are you talking about?" she exclaimed. "You and Theresa have been together since school began. I didn't think a crowbar could pry you two apart. You hanged yourself over her."

"Because she bullied me," I replied.

"Because she broke *up* with you," Phee insisted, "over that shrew, Daisy McKenzie. I told you she wasn't worth it. I tried to fix you up with Myra Kartinova who is a million times hotter but you wouldn't hear of it, and then you go and try to end your life!" Tears flooded her eyes. "Seriously, what would I have done if you'd actually died? You're my twin sister! I can't even picture my life without you!"

She turned with drenched cheeks and left the room. I sat there dumbfounded. *What the hell was going on?* I wondered. And what had happened to the god-stone? *I couldn't have imagined all of it* was the one thought that raced through my head—my being Quantum Girl and all the rest—*I couldn't have!* Still, there was what she said—the lack of oxygen to my brain after I had tried to do myself in. I considered the possibility that Phee was right, that I had imagined all of it, and doubt began to creep into my mind. And yet, I thought to myself, it all seemed so real!

CHAPTER IX

Peyton
(the one in Massapequa)

True to her word, older me called up Children's Protective Services the next day when Mark and I were in school. When we got out, Mark insisted on carrying my books as we walked home. I thought that was really sweet. As it turned out, I was his first girlfriend and the first girl he'd ever kissed. The air was rather brisk as I recalled and I still remember the sound of the leaves as they crunched under our feet. It's funny how certain insignificant things can stand out in your memory, even if it is a quantum memory with total recall.

We walked down Parkside Boulevard, then cut across the baseball field to the reservoir where we sat down on the grass and watched the ducks for a while. Mark went into his backpack and pulled out a paper bag filled with popcorn and offered it to me. I shook my head.

"No thanks," I told him. "I don't want to spoil my appetite. Mama said we're having roast beef."

"It's not for you," Mark said with a smile. "It's for the ducks. I come by a few times a week and feed them. Watch!" That said, he threw a few pieces into the water and three ducks swam up to get them. "The one on the left —the black one—that's Mallory. The one on the right, the iridescent one—that's Galahad. And the white one in the middle—that's Guinevere."

I stared at him, astonished. "There must be fifty ducks here," I said.

"Fifty-four," he replied, correcting me, "not counting the eggs in the nests over on the other side—fourteen in all."

"And you named them all," I asked, "and you remember them?"

Mark shrugged. "It's not that hard," he replied, "once you get to know them."

I took a small handful of popcorn from the bag and hurled it into the water, watching as more of the ducks came to feast. Then I looked hard at him.

"You're amazing!" I said. There was just so much I never knew about him, the boy I was destined to marry one day. When the bag was finally empty, I stood up. "We'd better get back before it gets late." I extended my arm toward Mark. He took my hand and I helped him up. "This was fun," I told him, smiling, staring into his eyes. "We'll have to do it again."

As we walked back to the house I took hold of his hand, interlacing my fingers with his. I could hear his heart beat faster as I did. Regardless that I had displayed an affection for him, he still was very shy. I liked that about him—not that he lacked confidence but that he obviously really liked *me*.

When we returned home, though, we were met with a surprise. A woman social worker and a male police officer were in the kitchen with older me. The social worker, Mrs. Conroy, was sitting at the table. The police officer, whose name was Felon (which I thought was an odd name for someone in law enforcement) was standing. Older me was also on her feet, checking on the roast beef in the oven. All of them turned to the door when they heard us at the door, though I have no doubt that older me could hear us approaching from half a mile away.

As we entered, I stopped time and then unfroze older me. "You want to fill me in on what's going on?" I asked.

"I told you I was going to phone social services," she replied.

"Well, what's going to happen to Mark?" I asked with obvious concern. "If they're just going to stick him in some random foster home, I don't think that's right."

"Look," she replied, "I told them I'd be willing to have him live here."

"But wouldn't you need to be licensed as a foster mom?" I

asked. "That can take a long time."

"I know," she replied, "and that's why I phased back a year in time and applied and got approved."

"Wow!" I said. "I think of everything, don't I?"

"You will," she replied.

"Wait a minute," I said, giving it some thought. " If you're future me and you just told me about going back in time so that I'll do it when the time comes for me to come back here, who thought up the idea in the first place?"

"Another paradox," she said, "that we can try and hammer out together one day, but right now I think you should start time up again and settle things with the social worker."

"Okay," I replied and was about to unfreeze time when she stopped me.

"You do realize," she went on, "that you can't sleep in the same bed with him again."

"Duh," I replied. "I just let him cuddle with me last night."

"I know," she said. "I remember. I just want to set you straight because that's what I was told by *my* future self."

I shook my head and then looked her in the eye. "You know everything that's going to happen," I said. "Don't you?"

"Mmm hmm," she replied.

"But you're not going to tell me?" I asked. "*Are* you?"

Now it was her turn to shake her head. "Uh, uh," she replied.

"Stinker!" I said back.

"That's just what *I* said," she laughed, "when I was *your* age."

I stuck my tongue out at her. We repositioned ourselves to where we had been, and then I restarted time.

"What's going on?" I asked as though I didn't already know.

"Mrs. Conroy is from Children's Protective Services. She's here because I told them about the abuse from Mark's father."

"And?" I said, turning from her to the social worker and taking hold of Mark's hand.

"We need to conduct a full investigation," Mrs. Conway replied. "In the meantime, Mark can stay here." She glanced at Mark and then looked back at me. "Your mother's license as a foster mother has already been approved and I see nothing wrong with the living conditions here." She rose from her seat and then turned to older me. "I'll let you know the final disposition when our investigation is complete. It should take about two weeks. Please let me know if you need anything."

She handed older me her business card and then she and the officer left. I turned to Mark.

"So," I said, "what do you think?"

He took a deep breath. "I don't know *what* to think," he replied. "I've been so used to getting beaten."

"Well," I said, "All that stops from here on in."

Mark looked at older me. "Thank you," he said.

"You're most welcome," she replied. "Now you two go wash up before supper gets cold."

As we started to head toward the bathroom she went on, "Oh, and Mark, I emptied out my office for a bedroom for you. A bed and dresser will be delivered tomorrow, so I'm afraid that tonight you'll have to rough it on the couch."

"He can sleep with me again," I protested.

"That," older me replied, "wouldn't be appropriate since I'm now his foster mom."

I threw out my lower lip at her as Mark, who was still linked to me by our hands, tugged me on.

"Come on," he insisted, "I'm starved."

"Yes, husband," I replied.

He just shook his head to himself and pulled on my arm.

The door left open in the bathroom, we washed our hands at adjoining sinks. "Sucks that we can't share the bed anymore," I said with a frown.

"I don't know," Mark replied, "I think it's kind of for the best."

"How's that?" I asked.

"Well," he said, "It's not that I didn't like cuddling with you. It's just that…" and he broke off.

"Just what?" I asked as I turned my faucets off on my sink.

"I don't want anything to happen," he replied. "You know. Because I really like you and I want things to happen but not fast. Not that I wouldn't want them to happen or I wouldn't want them to happen with you. It's just that I…"

"Go on," I urged.

"If I say what I want to say," he hedged, "you're not going to think I'm weird or anything."

I twisted my mouth at him. "Why would I ever think that?" I said.

"Well," he went on, "ever since we started talking and then last night up against you, smelling your hair and all and feeling your heart beating and hearing your breathing, I kind of just knew."

"Knew what?" I asked.

"Just *knew* it is all," he replied as he half turned away as he hung up the towel he had just dried his hands with.

I grabbed a hold of him by his shoulders, turning him to face me and staring right into his eyes.

"Tell me," I insisted. "What did you know."

"That I'm in love with you," he spouted out. "Okay, I've said it. Now you can think I'm all weird and hate me."

"Oh, my God!" I said, and I pulled him toward me and kissed him on the lips. When the kiss ended, he just stared at me, half-frozen like a statue. "Now, if you'll excuse me," I proclaimed, "I'm going to the dining room to have something to eat." As I started to walk away, I added, "You can stand there like a damn statue all night if you like, or you can follow me there and pull out a chair for me to sit on which you would do if you actually really do love me." And he did.

CHAPTER X

Peyton
*(the one who stayed behind
with Ophelia)*

So, wherever I now was, I was Peyton *Jane* Herron, and Phee, who was now calling herself Lia and who apparently hated my guts, was Ophelia *Elise* Herron. Jesus had been re-gendered as Jesua, who it seems had not been crucified but, rather, beheaded. And, to top it all off, I had lost all of my superpowers and so had no way to get back home to what I considered to be a somewhat saner environment.

It seemed that wherever I was—assuming that I was not dreaming or dead in some weird version of Heaven—I wanted to know more about the reality I was in and, as there appeared to be no computers or Internet, I decided to go to the library between classes. Unfortunately, I had no idea where to go for them or for which period. I did not even know where my locker was, let alone know the combination and Lia was no help, lip-locked to Scott Berens at virtually every moment of the school day. I wondered how they even found the time to breathe!

"I think they'll need a crowbar to pry them apart," came a voice from just behind me.

I turned around and looked to see to my horror that the words had come from Theresa Martinez.

"Come on," she said, "Let's grab some lunch. I heard they're having pizza today."

There was a smile on her face as she grabbed my hand and pulled me along with her. *My God! I thought to myself. What is going on? Theresa was never friendly toward me. All she ever did was bully me and cause me to want to be dead!* But she wouldn't let go and dragged me to the cafeteria line.

"I'm buying!" she insisted. "Pick out whatever kind you want but I'd recommend the pineapple. Hey," she went on, "we're still on for after school at my place, aren't we?"

"I guess," I replied in a confused voice. "We're studying?"

She looked at me over her nose, her head slightly down. "You're kidding, right," she replied.

"I just thought," I said stumbling, "I mean, I'm kind of behind on history and…"

"Look," she interrupted, "my mom's gonna be gone all weekend and you said you already cleared it with your mom that you could stay over till Monday, so I figured we could…" She reached out her hand and stroked the dimple above my upper lip and then moved it down to flip my lower lip, all the while staring hard into my eyes. "*You* know," she went on.

I didn't say anything. We went through the line. We both asked for pineapple pizza and, true to her word, the Theresaurus paid. I didn't say much during lunch. I kind of just shoved the slice of pizza into my mouth a bit at a time and stared into space, lost in thought, as my former bully yammered on about this thing or that. It was mind-boggling—Theresa the Terrible being nice to me! My mama would have raised the roof if I ever voiced the words I was thinking but, really, this was some weird-ass fucking shit that was happening, like I was dead and this was some hellish purgatory.

"And then Daisy McKenzie started coming onto me," Theresa rambled on from whatever else she'd been saying as I tuned back in, "but I told her I was going with you and we were all hot and heavy and I'm sure I broke her heart but what choice did I have? The stars aligned me with the most beautiful girl in the whole fucking universe—with emphasis on the fucking part. Damn! I should watch my language!" Elbows on the table, her chin on her fists, she stared at me—lovingly, I think. "You are so fucking beautiful," she went on. "It hurts just to look at you!" Then the bell rang and we all got up—as did everyone else in the cafeteria—to head back to whatever

68

was our next class. "I'll meet you on the steps in front after school lets out," she called out to me and then headed out the doorway, blending into the retreating mass of students.

As I passed Phee or Lia in the hallway, I said, "Tell Mama that I'll be at Theresa's for the weekend."

"Whatever!" she frowned out, but brightened up as she caught sight of her erection-waiting-to-happen boyfriend. "Hey, Stranger!" she said with a smile as she went up to him and launched herself into his arms.

All things considered, the prospect of spending the weekend with the now-friendly Theresa Martinez didn't seem so bad. Despite that her bullying had previously driven me to hang myself—which, by the way, I do not recommend to anyone as a form of suicide—in this take on reality she actually seemed nice.

The remaining school hours took forever to pass. Each time, as the teachers were turned toward the blackboards, when I would look at the wall clock behind me, the second hand seemed to virtually stop and the face almost laugh at me and snicker, "Not yet! Not yet!" until at long last the final bell rang and everyone got up to leave for parts unknown.

"Peyton Jane Herron," the teacher's voice called out. That was Mrs. Fontanelli, dark hair, dark eyes, late fifties, a bit of a weight strain for the chair she sat in and the shoes she wore, dark-rimmed glasses, grating voice, she taught political science. "Please remain after class."

When the room had emptied, I went over to her at her desk. "Actually, it's Elise," I said.

"What?" the matron replied.

"My middle name," I said. "It's Elise, not Jane."

The rhinoceros of a woman glanced down at her seating chart. "It says that your middle name is Jane," she said back, "but no matter. The test you took just now. Yours, being the last to be handed in, was on the top. I glanced at the answer to your essay question about why you are proud to be an American and saw that you named our country the United States of America."

"And?" I asked.

"My dear," she replied, "you know as well as I do that it's been the United Socialist States of America ever since the uprising in 1962 when President Nixon was assassinated and the Great Insurrection took place."

"Of course," I said acquiescing, "I've just been tired the past few nights."

"I understand," she replied. "Just try and be rested by Monday."

"I will," I assured her and then I left the room.

Theresa was waiting for me when I finally made it outside.

"What took you so long?" she asked when I finally walked up to her.

"Mrs. Fontanelli kept me after class," I told her.

"What for?" she asked.

"She said I wrote down the wrong name for the country," I replied.

"What did you write down?" she asked.

"USA," I said.

Theresa rolled her eyes. "The old name," she groaned. "NCs get *so* offended by that!"

"NCs?" I repeated.

"New Comms," she replied. "Where've you been all your life? All my life? Come on. Let's get going."

She took my hand in hers and tugged me in what turned out to be the direction of her home.

"She is such a beast!" she said. "Mrs. Fontanelli. I could never do her. I wonder how her husband ever did. He's *muerto*, you know. Talk is that she murdered him and then buried his body in her backyard."

"Really," I replied.

"Of course," she went on, "it's all just talk but you never can tell. Seriously, though, can you imagine diving into her mat?" She shivered noticeably. "I cringe at the thought." She stopped dead in her tracks, turned, and stared at me. "There," she went on. "Icky vision all gone. Replaced by thoughts of you." She took a deep breath and then led me further down the path toward her home. "When did you first know?" she asked.

I glanced at her and then over at a homeless man who was shooting up on the curb. "Know what?" I asked.

"That you were a sapph?" she replied. "I didn't know until I saw you and then it was like *Holy Crap* and there was this throbbing in my vag and my nips got all hard and my head was, like, reeling. I couldn't think straight, no pun intended. And then I went up to you for the first time, my heart beating like it was ready to explode, afraid that you'd reject me but you didn't and here we are. So when did you know? Was it the same for you?"

It was at that moment that she interlaced her fingers with mine. I really didn't know what to say. Like, *Sorry, I have a boyfriend* or *I think you're nice, but…* or *I believe that gay sex is a mortal sin?* I decided to take the coward's way out with, "Definitely." I figured I could let her down easy later on. As she held my hand and pulled me closer to her, I wondered whether that was why she had bullied me in the other reality—because she felt that I had or would reject her.

It was another ten minutes before we reached our destination. Her house wasn't in the best of neighborhoods. There was a white picket fence around it with a creaking gate and there was loud Mexican music coming from the house next door.

Theresa checked the mailbox by the curb, removed whatever letters were inside, and looked at them. "Bills," she proclaimed, "and junk mail." She stuffed all that she had taken under one arm and then urged me to go with her with a motion of her head and "Come *on*," as she walked to the front door of the house and

71

unlocked it with her key. As the door swung open with a gentle nudge from her, she turned to me and said, "After you."

The living room was dark when we entered but Theresa immediately flipped a wall switch that caused a lamp to turn on. The house was a bit cluttered for my taste with furniture that looked old and out of date, but everything was neat and clean. Theresa set down the mail and her knapsack on one of the chairs and went into the kitchen.

"Want something to drink?" she called out. "We have tomato juice and Sgt. Pepper." She paused for a moment, then added, "Wait! There're a couple of bottles of Corona in the cabinet under the sink from way back when my uncle lived here."

She came out with the bottles in her hands. "They're kind of old," she said, "but I don't think they expire."

"I sort of need to use the bathroom," I said.

"Feel free," she replied.

"Where…?" I started to say.

Theresa looked at me with concern. "Down the hall to the left," she said, then, "Are you okay? I mean, you've been here a hundred times."

"I haven't been myself lately," I said. "A lot of things going on."

"*Entiendo mi amor[5],*" she replied. "You do what you gotta do. I'll be in my bedroom when you're done."

After finding the bathroom and taking care of business, I stared at my reflection in the mirror above the sink as I washed my hands. *What have I gotten myself into?* I thought to myself.

When I found her bedroom, there was Latin music playing. Theresa was sitting on the bed cross-legged in just her panties, sipping from one of the bottles of beer. "About time," she said. She patted the mattress a couple of times. "Make yourself comfortable and sit down by me."

---

[5] "I understand, my love."

I set down my backpack, took off my jacket and my shoes, and sat down facing her.

"Are you cold or something?" she asked. "I turned on the heat."

"Uh-uh," I said, "Why?"

She made a face at me and then extended her arm with the other bottle.

"No," I said, "I'm not supposed to drink alcohol."

"Since when?" Theresa replied. "Look," she said, "If you don't drink with me then you're going to make me feel strange, so please take it and drink."

I took the bottle from her and sipped some. I'd never had beer before. It smelled strange and tasted... different. "Bottom's up," she insisted. Not wanting to offend, I reluctantly drank it all down. At first, I didn't feel anything, but after a moment or so, I felt my head spin a bit.

Theresa made deliberate motions with her head to look around the room and then stared at me.

"What?" I said defensively.

"I told you my mom's gone until Monday. The front door's locked. No one's going to burst in."

"And?" I replied.

"This isn't a job interview!" she said. Setting down her bottle which was now empty, she thrust herself forward, grabbed a hold of my tie, undid it, and then pulled it loose. Then she attacked my blouse, one button at a time.

"What are you doing?" I asked.

"Getting you comfortable," she replied. She maneuvered the blouse off of me and then reached around me to unbutton my skirt, "Now lie back," she ordered as she threw me a commanding look. I obeyed and she pulled off my skirt and then tossed it to the floor. After I sat up again, I looked at her. "Satisfied?" I asked.

"Not yet," she said and again moved in toward me, reached around to my back, unhooked my bra, and took it off. That went to the floor as well. "Jesua, you're uptight today!" she exclaimed. "If you feel cold let me know and I'll turn up the thermostat." It was then that she had a sudden thought and she turned to her nightstand. "I got this from the guy two doors down. He thinks he's gonna fuck me. Is he in for a letdown." From the nightstand drawer, she produced two joints and a Bic lighter. She put one joint in her mouth, lit it, and then handed it to me. I waved it off.

"I'm not supposed to," I said.

She threw me a disparaging look.

"This isn't something anyone does by themselves," she said. "If you don't do it, then I can't and I really need this to get into my headspace. Okay?"

I took the joint from her as she lit the other one, inhaled as much as she could, held it in, and then let it out. "Come on," she insisted. "Take it in deep and don't you dare exhale until you absolutely have to. This stuff is the best. It's called the God strain—strongest fucking shit there is."

I stared back at her, brought the joint up to my lips, and inhaled as much as I could. I tried to hold it in but I coughed it all out.

"You'll get used to it," she said. "Try it again."

I did. This time I was able to hold the smoke in longer before I had to breathe it out. And then it happened. I began to laugh uncontrollably. "Oh, my God," I tried to say.

"What's wrong?" Theresa asked,

"I just realized something!" I laughed out.

"What's that?" she replied.

"We're both naked!" I said, nearly spitting out the words.

"Not totally," Theresa said.

"What do you mean?" I laughed. I was nearly hysterical by now.

"We still have our panties on," Theresa replied.

"Mine are too tight?" I laughed. "Are yours too tight as well?"

"Definitely," came the response.

"Then I think we should take them off," I said. My laughter had calmed down. At that point, I was just high.

"Good idea," Theresa replied.

"I have a *sudjestshun*," I said as though it were the greatest plan since the invention of the wheel. "You take mine off," I told her, "and I'll take off yours. That way we can each see what our *veggievages* look like." I cocked my head a bit and stared at her. "I always wondered what other *girlsiz* *veggievages* looked like. Once I looked at mine with a mirror. It looked like an oyster!" And with that revelation came another burst of spit-out laughter. "I've only eaten an oyster once. First, you have to pry open the shell and they're all pink inside and the oyster says, 'I don't want to be eaten,' and you say back, 'Oh, yes you do and then gobble, gobble, gobble and you're happy as a clam."

"You are *so* high!" I heard her say as the room seemed to spin in all directions. I fell onto my back and put my legs up and I could feel her pulling off my panties. When that was done, I sprang back up to a sitting position. "Now, you," I said and she fell onto her back as well.

Once hers were off, I stared hard at her vag. "I think yours is darker than mine," I said thrusting my head down and looking up close. "And your lips are different from mine." I pulled back and looked up at her, still holding onto her distanced knees. "It is so strange," I went on, "that they call the buttocks cheeks and the folds of the *veggievag* lips. So where are the eyes?"

"Up here," she said.

I pushed myself onto her and stared into her eyes. I thought they were the most beautiful eyes I had ever seen. She took a hold of my wrists and caused me to fall on top of her and then she kissed me—and then wrapped her arms around me. I could feel her breasts and the line of her sex against mine. My head was swimming—half from the alcohol, half from the pot—and there was just ecstasy. My inhibitions were gone. I lost sight of Mark. It wasn't that I didn't still love him but this was different. We must have made love for hours but afterward, it was all just a blur of flesh against flesh, the smell of musk, and the almost indescribable taste of applesauce with a tinge of salt.

Afterward, as the effects of the drugs wore down, I felt guilty and ashamed. Theresa was lying in bed beside me, clinging to me with one of her arms around me as she still slept. I tried to get up and out of the bed but my movement stirred her and, still half-asleep, she held me tightly and refused to let me leave.

"Stay with me," she moaned. "I need you next to me."

I relented.

"I love you, you know," she muttered. "You're everything to me." Her hold on me loosened. Her fingers danced on my skin and then gently crept their way down to the line of my sex where they found their way inside. She kissed the inside of my arm that was nearest to her and then spoke without opening her eyes.

"Five years ago," she said, "my uncle lived with us—my mother's younger brother. He was in his twenties. Anyway, whenever my mom left to go to work—she worked the night shift at an office building doing cleaning to support us—he would come into my bedroom and do things to me and make me do things to him. He said if I told anyone he would hurt my mama so I let him."

"For how long?" I asked.

"For around a year," she replied. "Then one day he and my mama had an argument and he beat her and gave her a black eye. I felt so stupid. After all I had let him do to me—after all he had made me do to him—he went and hurt her anyway. I just lost it then and I attacked him. I clawed at him with my fingernail. I would have ripped the dick right off of him if my mama hadn't heard the commotion—heard me yell—heard him screaming in pain. I told her in tears all that had gone on. She screamed for him to get out and he did. Afterward, she called the police and he wound up getting arrested and sent to jail. He's still there. They gave him twenty-five years or, I guess, took them away from him."

76

She opened her eyes to look at me. "All of that changed me," she said. "When I was a little girl, I used to dream of a beautiful wedding to some handsome man, but now all men just remind me of him."

I suddenly understood where all the anger had come from within her. I rolled over and faced her, put my arm around her, and pulled her against me. Her arm went around me again, with the tips of her fingers gently caressing the small of my back. I kissed her hair and felt her tears drip down onto my flesh as she remembered the times she could never forget. I had never understood why she had been so angry until that moment. Here, though, in this life, something had changed to have let us become friends to have led up to this one moment. I thought about her and about how gentle and broken she was inside through no fault of her own. But I also thought of Mark and I wondered if he would understand that although I had betrayed the sacred bond our futures held, it wasn't because I loved him less but that I had learned that the heart has room for more than one soul to love.

CHAPTER XI

Quantum Girl Blue
(January 1, 1929)

As time wore on, Mary and I became best friends. We went to the movies together. Most films were silent back then. Movies with sound had only first come out less than two years before. The film we saw was called *The Last Laugh*, about a doorman, so proud of his position and his uniform, who gets demoted to washroom attendant. He's so ashamed, though, that he continues to wear his doorman uniform when he goes home, pretending to his family and friends, until he's found out and put to shame. But wait! The final title card read, "Here our story should really end, for in actual life, the forlorn old man would have little to look forward to but death. The author took pity on him, however, and provided quite an improbable epilogue." In the alternate ending, one of his regular washroom patrons, a Mexican millionaire, dies in his arms and leaves him his entire fortune. I had never watched silent films before finding myself in the past. It amazed me how much could be said without words. For Mary, though, it was all just par for the course.

On weekdays I attended school—Lincoln Park High School to be exact—a large, three-story, red-and-white-brick building with four ionic columns at the entrance. There were no computers, of course, but there was a large library. Latin and Greek were taught as well as the Palmer Method of handwriting. There was home economics for the girls and wood and machine shop for the boys. The girls wore uniform dresses that fell just at the knees along with knee-high stockings. The boys wore pleated trousers held up by suspenders, white shirts, and neckties. Male teachers wore three-piece suits along with fedora hats that they took off before entering. And unlike the flappers of the day, the women teachers' dresses were considerably more modest. Some of the older kids would smoke in the bathrooms but that was strictly verboten, and anyone caught faced detention. The two books we were assigned to read and do book reports on were Main Street by Upton Sinclair and The Age of Innocence by Edith Wharton. Of course, with my quantum brain, I was able to read both books as fast as I could turn the pages. I was also quite good at geometry.

In my biology class, we learned about the Piltdown man, the supposedly missing link between humans and apes. Decades later, I remembered, that it all turned out to be a hoax but I had to listen to Mr. Abernathy, our teacher, go on and on about how this proved that man had descended from the apes.[6]

As her shift at Marshall Fields started at eight-thirty, Mary would always walk me to school, kiss me on the cheek for luck, and then take the train downtown that connected with the Loop, an elevated train that ran a circle around downtown Chicago with one of the stops at Randolph and Wabash, just a block away from her work. As school let out hours earlier than her work, I would either walk home with one or another of the other girls or else duck into a stall in one of the girls' bathrooms and phase back there.

It was just a month and a half later at around ten-thirty in the morning on Valentine's Day when everyone at school was exchanging colorful cards that I heard gunshots about two miles to the east. Excusing myself to go to the bathroom, I stepped out into the deserted hallway and phased to where I had heard the sounds. It turned out to be a garage at Dickens and Clark. Seven men lay dead near one wall inside in a pool of blood. The assailants, four men, two dressed as police officers, all saw me. One of the cops, who was holding a Tommy gun, turned to me and sprayed me with bullets.

---

[6] Six months later in Tennessee, a school teacher by the name of John Thomas Scopes would be put on trial for teaching evolution. The Monkey Trial, as it was called, pitted the ardently religious lawyer and former Secretary of State, William Jennings Bryan against the famous trial lawyer, Clarence Darrow. In the end, Darrow lost and Scopes was ordered to pay a one-hundred-dollar fine. But none of this had happened yet and this wasn't Tennessee.

Instantly, I threw up a force field that absorbed all of them. A confused look crept onto his face and then he and the two plain-clothed men hightailed it to their getaway car, a Model T that was parked on the street with its motor running and a fifth man behind the wheel.

"Come on!" the cop with the Tommy gun called out to the one who still remained. "We can deal with her later!"

The cop who had remained behind ignored them as they drove off, staring at me with an unflinching gaze. He pointed the gun he was holding at me but while he pulled the trigger again and again, it was his eyes glowing violet that caused me concern. There was power that radiated from them—power that began to weaken me. I could feel its strength and it took all of mine to fight against it. Instinctively, I became Quantum Girl but my sudden transformation failed to even make him flinch. As I felt him winning, with my last ounce of strength, I phased back to the school.

I staggered into the girls' bathroom and looked at myself in the mirror, supporting my weight by my hands on the porcelain sink. I was white as a sheet as they say as though all the blood in me had been drained from my skin. My heart was pounding and I needed a moment to catch my breath. It took what must have been five minutes for me to be able to leave the room and head back to class.

For the rest of the day, I was lost in thought. Who was the fourth man and how could there be anyone—especially back in 1929—who had a god-stone? Was it the same man from the hotel, I wondered, and if so he was definitely not a cop. A slew of thoughts raced through my head—*was Earth being invaded by an advanced civilization or had that one individual followed me back through time or, worse, was he the one who had sent me back and trapped me here? But, if so, what did he want from me? Why not just try and destroy me back home instead of sending me into the past?* These were questions that needed to be answered and soon!

I cursed myself for not having turned into Quantum Girl more quickly because all four men, including the quantum one, saw my face and my school uniform. I realized in horror that they could probably figure out which school I attended and so find out who I was. I wasn't so much concerned about myself. I had superpowers—but those around me didn't and I had lost the ability to phase back in time to undo what had occurred. I thought of just leaving, but if any of them went to the school to try and find me, their trail would lead back to Mary and Great Granny and I couldn't risk not being there to protect them from any potential harm.

I got back to the school without anyone taking much notice of my absence. In the end, I found that I'd received twenty-three cards, a rose from an anonymous admirer, and a box of chocolates from Bobby McFarland, a junior who would constantly eye me whenever we passed each other in the hall. The card was of a little girl and a little boy surrounded by embossed gold hearts. The boy held a butterfly net in one hand and a heart with wings in the other and there was an actual red cloth ribbon threaded through the card on the left side. The words on the card read, "With Love to my Valentine."

By the time I got home from school, it was on the news. Great Granny had her radio tuned to WGN as Phil Barnes broadcast the grisly details of what was being called The St. Valentine's Day Massacre. When she saw me, she quickly dialed to another station where Al Jolson was singing, *Why Can't You?* Ever so nonchalantly then, she turned to me and asked, "How was school today, Dear?"

"We all exchanged cards," I replied. "And I got a box of chocolates from Bobby McFarland. I think he has a crush on me."

"Is he one of the boys in your class?" she asked.

"No," I said. "He's two years ahead of me. Most of the other girls think he's the cat's pajamas. He's on the varsity wrestling team."

"Might be a little too old for you now," she replied.

"I know," I said. "Besides, I'm not interested."

"You just tell him," she replied, "that your old great granny said you're too young to be courted by a young man."

I struck a dramatic pose. "Oh," I said, with the back of my hand against my forehead, "I shall let him down most gently so that my refusal does not break his heart!"

We both began to laugh as Mary walked in through the front door, home from her work.

"What are you two howling about?" she asked as she took off her coat and hat and hung them up on the hall tree.

"Oh, nothing!" I said as I turned to her.

"By the way," she went on, "did you hear about the shooting near your school? Seven gangsters were gunned down with a machine gun no less."

"Where did it happen exactly?" I asked, pretending not to know.

"Over at the garage on Lincoln," she replied. "the cops say the place is owned by Bugs Moran, the racketeer. Isn't it exciting? It's the talk of the town. I bought the extra. I was going to use the nickel for a sundae but I just couldn't resist!"

She pulled out a folded paper from one of the large pockets of the coat she had just hung up, unfolded it, and then handed it to me. I looked at it, pretending to be amazed. The extra was from the Chicago Daily News Blue Streak. The headline read, "MASSACRE OF 7 MORAN GANG, VICTIMS ARE LINED AGAINST WALL; ONE VOLLEY KILLS ALL." It went on to read, "Assassins Pose as Policemen; Flee in 'Squad Car' after Fusillade; Capone Revenge for Murder of Lombardo, Officers Believe."

"Mary!" Great Granny called out. "I was trying to protect our Peyton from such grisly details."

"Oh, I'm sorry," Mary apologized. " I should have known better. It was a just so…"

"Amazing," I said, repeating her previous description.

Great Granny just shook her head. "Don't you think the girl's been through enough what with all that happened on New Year's

Eve at the hotel? And you, too, what with Fred having been gunned down."

Mary stared at me with obvious remorse. "I apologize," she said. " I hope this didn't upset you."

I shook my head. "It's all Jake," I said with a smile, relieved that I wasn't in any of the pictures.

It was strange to be back in time where I was, and I missed Mark and Mama and Papa and Phee, but it was as though I had found a new family here. There wasn't a day that went by, though, that I didn't try to travel back to my time. It seemed that I had all of my powers except for that one. The days and weeks and months fled by. No one had come looking for me—the gangsters or the man, I mean. Still, I remained on my guard, especially where Mary and Great Granny were concerned. And then it happened. On Tuesday, October 29, 1929, the stock market crashed following two days of heavy trading. Banks closed their doors. Businesses shut down. Men, who had been wealthy just a week before, leaped to their deaths from the windows of companies they had worked for. Mary lost her job. All of the money both she and Great Granny had in the bank was gone. There was no way to pay the mortgage or even pay for food. With the threat of foreclosure and starvation at our doorstep I had no choice but to be honest with the two of them. Peyton Herron couldn't help them in the misfortune they were about to face, but Quantum Girl could.

CHAPTER XII

Quantum Girl Red
(December 7, 1941)

After a few days, things at Pearl calmed down. Efforts were underway to clear the rubble and to reclaim and honor and bury the dead as the wounded still moaned from the attack and the widows languished in their sorrow. The waves of the harbor had calmed but the battered ships lay overturned and lifeless, awkwardly cutting through the water like iron caskets waiting to finally be drowned in Neptune's graveyard. Bodies of what were once living men, buoyed up to the surface, floating facedown, human flotsam, waiting to be pulled back to shore by men in skiffs armed with pike poles. There were no mass burials, regardless that two thousand, four hundred three men and women had lost their lives. Each was given the solemnity of a personal prayer before being lowered into a single grave dug just for him or her. Heads were bowed in reverence. The words of Franklin Delano Roosevelt, President of the United States, echoed over the radio. "No matter how long it may take us to overcome this premeditated invasion, the American people in their righteous might will win through to absolute victory."

The body of Michael Fletcher, ensign aboard the U.S.S. Arizona, was never found. The battleship was too badly damaged for any recovery efforts, and so it was left to sink to the bottom of the harbor. They named it Battleship Row, leaving more than one hundred men forever entombed more than six fathoms beneath the surface of the wave-encrusted sea.

Peyton Fletcher found her final resting place amid the cemetery of white markers. She and Margaret had only recently come to Pearl to meet up with Michael. As such, no one really knew her, so it was easy for me to take up her identity and her place as Margaret's presumably sole surviving parent. The issue for me to consider was whether or not to remain in Hawaii or return to the mainland. With war having been declared, there were no passenger ships to transport those who wished to relocate. Regardless that I knew from history that there would be no further attacks on the island chain, I felt it prudent to phase Margaret and me to San Francisco which back then was still a beautiful, sprawling metropolis.

There was money in the Fletcher bank account that I withdrew. The military didn't pay families death benefits back then, so what I took with me was all that there was to be had. I rented a bungalow in Piedmont. It was already furnished and I was able to put down two months in advance, though after that, our prospects were rather dim unless I found work. With the war in full swing and now on two fronts, most of the jobs were in factories with a good deal of women in the workforce. As working ten hours a day in noisy military production installations didn't suit my being a mother at the same time, I decided to take up modeling, though the only job I could find nearby was in Oakland at the Allen Art Studio, working for Albert Arthur Allen, whose specialty was nude photography and just women at that. Allen was a mild-mannered, slight-framed man with a receding hairline, fifty-five years old at the time and confined to a wheelchair since a motorcycle accident took his ability to walk back in 1923. He was, however, a man who took his profession seriously and was very meticulous about it. As it turned out, he took an immediate liking to me and hired me on the spot. Had he known my true age, perhaps things would have gone differently, but like I said whatever had thrust me back in time had caused me to look older than my years. Outwardly, I looked as though I were in my early twenties. My salary was $200 per week which was pretty good for the time. It was enough to pay the bills and place Margaret in a private school. There were half a dozen other models who worked there, all in the nude like me. Mind you, these were very tasteful, artistic compositions, nothing like the bondage shots that would one day favor Bettie Page in the 1950s. These were photos that were hung or sold in art galleries in both the U.S. and abroad.

When I had saved enough money, I bought a used cobalt blue 1938 Nash Lafayette sedan for $400. It had four doors. six cylinders, and running boards but no seatbelts. There was no safety concern back then. The fact that it lacked them didn't bother me as I knew that I could always throw out a quantum force field or stop time to protect Margaret if an accident was about to occur.

That I was no longer able to time travel bothered me to no end but the fact was that I was stuck in the past for the next twelve years due to my having to take care of Margaret until she was at least eighteen and gone off to college.

But I had no clue as to why as Quantum Girl I glowing red instead of violet. Logically, it seemed as though a red god-stone must have been traded for my purple one. But assuming that I was correct, I wondered whether my were powers all the same. Was it just a matter of color or could each stone endow its user with different abilities? After weeks of trying, I found that I could make myself invisible, but my power of X-ray projection was gone.

In time, Margaret accepted me as her mother, though a mother who appeared to be somewhat Heaven-sent. To her young mind, it was as though the woman she had seen killed at Pearl Harbor had miraculously been brought back to life as part angel. I guess that's just the nature of children. She would call me Mommy, climb into bed next to me at night whenever she had a bad dream, and cuddle up to me. She had seen me as Quantum Girl the day we met and she accepted me as both her mother and a celestial being.

"Can you see God when you're an angel?" she once asked.

"I don't know," I replied. "What does God look like?"

"He's big and old," she answered, "and he has a long white beard like Santa Claus."

"What if God *is* Santa Claus?" I said.

Margaret thought hard for a moment and then replied, "But Santa lives at the North Pole and God lives in Heaven."

"Hmm," I said, "You have a good point."

"You didn't answer my question!" she insisted.

"Well," I said, "I might have seen God once, but I think she's a woman."

Margaret laughed. It was the laugh of a child who hears something unexpected. "God's not a woman!" she proclaimed.

"How do you know?" I asked.

"'Cause," she said, "I saw the pictures in the Bible at church."

"And who made the pictures?" I asked her.

"I don't know," she replied.

"It was a man," I said. "And if you mean the same pictures as I'm thinking, his name was Michelangelo and he lived hundreds and hundreds of years ago in Italy."

"Where's that?" she asked.

"It's on the other side of the world," I said, "where everyone came from before they came here. And back then men thought that women were just there to cook babies in their stomachs until the timer went *Ding*! and then the baby pops out." And with that, I tickled her and she laughed uncontrollably, crying out "Stop! Stop!" and so I did.

"That's not how babies are borned!" she proclaimed.

"And just how *are* they borned?" I asked.

"You know," she said.

"I really don't," I replied.

"The stork brings them," she said. "He drops them down the chimbly."

"Ouch!" I replied. "That must hurt."

"Noooo!" she said. "The mommies catch them and then they love them and feed them and change their diapers when they make a stinky poop."

"I see," I replied. "Thank you for telling me."

"I would think that you would know all that already," she said, "seeing that the stork brought me to you." Then she took a deep breath and threw down her shoulders in frustration. "You still didn't tell me," she sighed out deeply, "why God is a woman!"

"Don't you think," I said, "that if God made people in *her* own image she would make sure that it was the mother who cared for the baby?"

Margaret thought hard again. "I suppose," she said.

"And wouldn't God be beautiful?" I asked her.

"Like you?" she asked back.

I smiled at that. "I guess," I replied, "if you think I'm beautiful."

"Oh, you *are*," she proclaimed. "You're the mostest beautiful woman in the world."

"Thank you so much!" I said.

"It's the truth!" she replied. And then she thought to herself for a moment. "So God is a woman! Wait till I tell Mary Anne Cox!"

"Oh," I said gently, "I wouldn't go around spreading the word."

"Why not?" Margaret asked.

"Because," I replied, "God wants it kept a secret—at least for now."

"But why?" came the response.

"Because most men," I told her, "couldn't handle the truth."

"I understand," she replied. "So it's just between us."

"Yes, it is," I said. "Just between you and me."

"'Kay," she replied and then added, "Mommy?"

"Yes, Fair Margaret?" I asked.

"Can we have dinner," she said. "I'm hungry,"

"Of course, we can," I replied. "What would you like?"

"A hamburger," came the unwavering response.

"Well, then," I said, "a hamburger it is." I stood up and held my right hand out to her. "Shall we go?" I asked.

"Are you going to magic us to a restaurant?" she asked back.

"Indubitably," I replied.

"Indubpably," she tried to repeat as she took hold of my hand. And then I phased us both to the White Castle in Queens, New

York. I ordered three sliders for us—one for Margaret and two for me—as well as two chocolate milkshakes. Sliders were small, square hamburgers that cost a nickel each back then. As we sat across the table from each other, Margaret looked at me with sad eyes.

"Are we ever going to see Daddy again?" she asked.

"I don't know," I replied.

"But couldn't you go back in time and save him?" she pressed on.

"I was there when he died," I said. "I told you. Don't you remember?"

"Uh-huh," she replied. "But what I meant was, couldn't you go back in time before the torpedo fell on him?"

"I wish I could," I said, "but I can't travel in time anymore."

"But you're Quantum Girl," she insisted. "You can do anything."

I took a deep breath and sighed. "I used to be able to," I said. "Just not anymore."

"Why not?" she asked.

"I don't know," I said, wiping some ketchup away from the corner of her mouth. "I just don't know."

It was at that moment that I caught sight of a man moving through a wall, as though the wall didn't exist, coming in our direction.

"Come on," I said, getting up and taking her hand. "We need to get back home." I led her in the other direction from the man and into the ladies' room. Two women stood at the sinks adjusting their makeup and jabbering about problems with their men being away at war. When they finally left, I phased us both back home and put Margaret to bed.

"I love you, Mommy," she said as I turned out the lights.

"I love you, too, Fair Margaret," I replied. "Sweet dreams." And then I left the room, leaving the door open just a crack, distracted by the thought of the sudden appearance of the man in the restaurant who had appeared out of nowhere. *Why would he have been there?* I wondered. *Was it just a coincidence or was he there because of me?* My heart beat hard in my chest—not out of fear for myself but for Margaret. I had grown to love her so much. She was my only concern.

CHAPTER XIII

Quantum Girl Orange
(September 9. 1951)

I tossed and turned in bed that night. I couldn't help thinking about Coach Nichols and Babs and then the next day when I learned how Babs had taken her own life, I went to confront the woman in her office at school.

"I suppose you've heard about what happened to Torrance?" she said in an ever so nonchalant voice.

"You mean that you fucked her and then she killed herself?" I told her.

"She was unstable," came the reply.

"She was fifteen!" I shouted back at her.

The cheerleading coach circled around me to shut the door. Then she looked at me. Her eyes went up and down my form. Her right hand reached up and stroked my hair.

"Stop it!" I demanded.

"Stop what?" she replied sounding innocent.

"Undressing me with your eyes!" I said. "I didn't come here to fuck you! I came here to warn you!"

"Warn me about what?" she asked.

"Going to the police," I replied. "I've already spoken with Megan, Susie, and Jenn and it seems that they've all managed to wind up in your bed just like Babs and just like me."

"And they all liked it!" she shot back, "as did you!"

"Not that I can remember any of it," I muttered to myself. "We're all your students," I went on. "We trusted you and you tricked us all into satisfying your sapphic desires!"

"My what?" she replied.

"Lesbian!" I proclaimed. "There were five of us. I was

Mondays. Babs was Tuesdays, and I guess the other three each had their assigned days of the week. Lord only knows what you did on weekends—probably raped a couple of ten-year-olds!"

"That's a cheap shot," she snapped back. "I've loved each of you!"

"'And then I met you,'" I said, repeating her words to me when I first woke up, "'and my heart raced a million miles a second from the moment I saw you and how impossible it seemed that you would like me in return.' Is that what you told each of us?"

"No!" she insisted. "Just you."

"Yeah, right!" I replied as I stared her in the eye. "I'm giving you till noon to resign." I turned and walked up to the door and gripped the doorknob. "If you don't, I'm going to the police."

It was as I spoke those words that I felt her behind me. Then something hard hit my head and everything went black.

I awoke in what turned out to be a laundry bag with a rag in my mouth and cloth tape holding it in place, wrapped several times around my head without regard for my hair. The bag was tightly tied at the end. Beyond that, it seemed that I was in the trunk of a car for it was its motion as it started to move that roused me from unconsciousness. To say that I was scared out of my wits would be an understatement. I could feel the motion. I could hear the occasional car as it passed from the other direction. I could feel the bumps and hear the crunching of small branches and soil under the tires as the car must have turned off onto a dirt road. Had I still been Quantum Girl I could have just phased out of the bag, out of the car, out of the ropes that bound my ankles and my wrists, and gotten away. But I couldn't. Margaret couldn't. And I wondered what would happen to me if Margaret died. My mother would never be born and then neither would I—or Phee. Poor Phee. She had nothing to do with any of this. Nor did Mama. But at least Mama had Jesus and I was certain that, no matter what, he would preserve her soul. She was a true disciple. Her faith was adamant and she saw the good in people before she saw anything else.

The gag in my mouth was made of rough cloth that had become layered in saliva as it pressed down toward the back of my throat and caused me to gag again and again. I tried to suppress the reflex response. I didn't want to throw up with the vomit having nowhere to go and I thought if it went up my nose how would I breathe?

The drive seemed to last forever. The occasional sounds of the oncoming cars had long since disappeared. The ride became rougher as I was bounced around in the sack until finally, it stopped as the car ground to a halt. I heard the door to the vehicle open and then slam shut again. There was the sound of footsteps and then of the truck lid being opened. One hand and then another gripped the bag I was in and forcefully dragged it out of the truck and let it drop down hard onto the ground without consideration or thought that I was inside. The impact hurt. My eyes teared up from the pain but I couldn't cry out. I couldn't scream for help. The rag was wedged in my now dry mouth.

I felt myself being dragged over a hard surface. I could hear the bag scraping against the ground. I could feel the rocks as they tried to cut through the thick linen. Regardless that the cloth was between me and them it still hurt. I prayed for Jesus to save me. I prayed for someone to come help me but my prayers were unanswered and no one came.

It was then that whoever did this opened the bag and for a moment I thought I was going to be released but that's not what happened. I could feel the cool night air as it rushed in. I could smell the scent of the ocean and hear the waves as they crashed against the shore. I tried to look up out of the bag but there was little I could see. I tried to talk—tried to scream—but the gag in my mouth prevented that. I wanted to plead with whomever it was to let me go—to let me live. And then I felt the cold hard metal disks that were being thrust into the bag with me—weight disks. I lost count of how many there were, filling the bag I was in. The steel felt cold against my skin and it was for the first time that I realized that I was nude. My thoughts were clouded but I knew it must have been Coach Nichols who had done this and that it must have been her who had knocked me out and done all of this to me and that it must have been her stuffing weights into the bag with me. The steel pressed down on me making it difficult to breathe. The last of them—she shoved them against my head without regard for how they would injure me. One pressed hard against my face. Another smashed against the back of my head. That one hurt the most but the bag was filled so tightly with the metal and me that I couldn't move. And then she tied it closed again and the air inside became thick and stale.

I felt myself being pushed, then, from the side—all the weight pushed into me—shoved or kicked, I don't know. I couldn't tell. The back was being rolled, because it had become too heavy to lift or even drag. And then I went over what must have been a cliff and I felt myself falling, faster and faster until the bag with me in it hit the water with a loud and foreboding splash.

But it was beyond the impact of hitting the water. The weights pushed into me like sledgehammers. And then the water— saltwater—began seeping through the bag as it sank deeper and deeper until it hit the bottom. The water was cold, freezing cold, as it embraced my naked flesh with its ripples of impending death. It washed over my face and soaked through the rag in my mouth. It stung my eyes and, despite me thrashing my head back and forth to avoid it, finally went into my nose, up through my nostrils, displacing what little air there had been. I thought about Mama and Papa and Phee and Mark. I thought about Cleopatra. I thought about how I'd been given a second chance by the other version of me sacrificing her own life to give back mine and how incredible it was to have been Quantum Girl with all of those special powers. But I realized I wasn't Quantum Girl anymore. I was Margaret Fletcher now and I was about to drown and die. I held my breath and fought with my lungs to not exhale. But the force of my lungs was stronger than my will and so at last I exhaled and there was no air left. Water filled my lungs. I choked on it. My head whipped back and forth in the throes of certain death. My tears intermixed with the ocean. I prayed to God again but God didn't answer. And then, I drowned.

CHAPTER XIV

Quantum Girl Yellow
(A.D. 1,219,064,261)

There were five other Quantum Girls and each of them was me! *How could this have happened?* I wondered. The last thing I remembered was telling Phee that I'd decided to divide so that one of me could go to New York to be with Mark. After that, everything was a blank. I stood in the fifth room that I had been brought into by the group of the beings mankind was to become whether through natural or unnatural means. *Homo futurus*—that was how I thought of them at the time. There before me in the center lay a red Quantum Girl, lying in an unconscious state—the same as the rest—the same state of hibernation that I must have been in before awakening only moments before. A strange feeling came over me as I felt my powers return. I phased from room to room, reexamining each of my other selves—blue, green, violet, and orange, and then back to red again—and I was yellow—each of us—each of me—representing the spectrum of colors of the god-stones. It was as I phased back to red that the woman telepathed me again.

We have prepared quarters for each of you, she said. *Would you like me to show you yours? And you must be hungry after such a long sleep.*

I only nodded but she must have read my mind for she added, *Indeed, we are human, descended from your race. We do not have names as you would pronounce them as we do not use words to speak, but you may call me*—and then she telepathed, not a name but rather what I would describe as a sensation or an emotion. For the sake of this narration, however, I shall call her Faaah.

Faaah led me down a long corridor that, to be honest, appeared endless and filled with blinding white light. Our journey came to an end after about a thousand or so feet when she stopped and faced the wall to her right. As if by magic, a doorway appeared and she led me inside. As I followed her through it, everything suddenly changed. It was as though I had stepped through a portal through both space and time. I found myself in what appeared to be the house I had grown up in, down to the small dark stain on the carpet in the living room where when I was ten I had accidentally spilled a few drops of India ink. Everything was as I remembered it. No detail had been missed. The only things that *were* missing were Mama and Papa and Phee. But if I were truly a billion years in the future, they were long dead and every bit of them absorbed back into the planet they had once called their home. "Ashes to ashes, dust to dust," came the words from the Book of Common Prayer, but even any copies of *that* would have been dissolved into atoms after all this time. I climbed the stairs to find my bedroom—Phee's and mine— and then looked out the window onto a street that must have been an illusion of what once had been. How strange to find all of my clothes hanging in the closet. Even the plumbing in the bathroom worked. I then went to my parents' bedroom. Everything there was the same as well, sans their presence. With a twinge from the sadness of knowing that I would probably never see them again, I phased back downstairs to face Faaah once more.

"How did you do this?" I asked her.

We pulled the images from your mind while you were in your unconscious state, she replied. *There are five similar houses—one for each of you.*

"But when will the others wake up?" I asked.

Faaah shook her head. *A day,* she replied, *a week, a million years, or perhaps never.*

"But," I said with concern, "you said you don't have a million years."

Such may be the fate of the Earth, she replied, *but perhaps you can awaken them.*

"I can try," I told her. "I *will* try. But first I need a little time to acclimate myself to all of this." I glanced at the television across from the sofa. "I don't suppose *that* actually works," I said.

It does, she replied, *but you may only view whatever you had watched in the past. All the libraries were erased by the great solar flare eight hundred million years ago.* She looked at me. *I shall leave you now to acclimate yourself as you desire.*

As she started to leave, I called out to her. "Wait!" I said. "How did we all get here? Wind up in hibernation, I mean?"

Faaah turned back to face me. *Legend has it,* she replied, *that it was the traveler who condemned all of you to eternal sleep.*

"The Traveler?" I asked. "Who is the Traveler?"

We do not know, she replied. *None who are living have ever met him. But it is said that he is you.*

"That makes no sense," I said.

Nevertheless, came the reply, *that is what the legend says .*And then she turned and left.

Alone in the house, I retreated to the kitchen. The fridge was stocked with foods I was familiar with. Cautiously, I smelled the milk which was still fresh. It even had an expiration date on it although *that* was from a billion years ago. I could only assume that whatever food there was had been created shortly after my awakening. *Or,* I thought, *perhaps all if this was just an illusion. After all, these beings were telepathic. What if none of this was real?*

But it was. I used my quantum powers to view the actual structure of all that was around me. There had been no deception. Whatever was here was the result of a billion years of technology. Regardless, whatever people were here in this time were stranded on a planet whose sun was about to destroy every shred of life on it. As it turned out, already parts of the Moon had been scorched by solar flares.

The present inhabitants of the Earth, whom I referred to in my head as the Zoron—don't ask me why—were the direct descendants of the humans of my time, though a result of deliberate genetic modification. That accounted for the physical differences but the telepathy was something else. The transmission of thoughts had come about as a result of an accident. In the latter part of the Twenty-first Century, the world government had ordered all new births to be *in vitro* so that the fertilized egg could be genetically modified. The explanation was two-fold. First, it was stated that it would give couples the ability to create designer children, allowing them to select such things as height, body structure, eye and skin color, features, etc. Second, it would help to eliminate genetic flaws such as a propensity toward cancer or Parkinson's disease, diabetes, and the like while even bolstering human immunity. The problem came when the computer program enabling this became sentient and decided on its own that humans would be better off as slaves. Thus, it modified even more of the DNA with an additional pair of chromosomes based on silicon rather than carbon. This had the accidental effect of creating a form of telepathy between individuals. But while the AI's intent had been to control the humans, the combined mental acuity of the species was eventually able to break free of its control and eviscerate it from the Internet and whatever computers it attempted to hide in.

Physically, the Zoron were quite different from the humans of my day. For one thing, there were no races to divide them as after countless generations, they had become an admixture of all three. Their skin was nearly transparent, which I had to get used to, as it was quite odd for me to witness muscles and in some cases organs and bone in plain sight. In terms of height, each stood between two and two and a quarter meters, depending on whether female or male respectively. Their eyes were wide-set and, as I had previously mentioned, their heads were proportionally larger than those in my time. None of them possessed any hair whatsoever—not even eyelashes—and their eyes were either hazel or blue. Meanwhile, their fingers were exceptionally long and thin with an extra joint on each one. The life expectancy of the Zoron was close to five thousand years. By comparison, Faaah was a mere child at only one hundred sixty-seven!

In terms of their social behavior, they existed in a free society without government. Due to the openness of their minds and the free distribution of necessities, crime did not exist. Neither did marriage, and those who wished to, practiced relationships, sexual or otherwise, of their own free will. From a young age, children were taught that jealousy is a behavior indicative of lower forms of life and that friendship triumphed over sex which might be had with anyone at any time, provided the parties were in need of release. And since disease had been eliminated long ago and pregnancy occurred only as a matter of choice, sexual interaction might occur between a couple or a throuple but never more. And while homosexuality in men had become nonexistent, bisexuality in women was considered natural and encouraged, the precepts of which had been handed down through the Book of Chloë, part of the Quantum Girl Chronicles, the holy scriptures that had been handed down throughout the eons subsequent to its writing. The Zoron spent their days creating literature, art, or, in some instances, scientific research. It should be noted that their literature consisted totally of thoughts and emotions that were made available for others to experience.

All of this I learned afterward. That first day, I fixed myself something to eat, took a long, warm bubble bath, and then watched The Time Traveler's Wife on the flatscreen TV in the living room. Sitting there as the blurry credits rolled up the screen, it suddenly occurred to me that I hadn't seen what was outside. Changing back into my now yellow Quantum Girl costume, I phased up into the sky.

Below me lay a sprawling city that appeared to be made of glass of the same six colors as each of my selves as Quantum Girl. In the center of the metropolis stood six glass statues, each of me—each with my arms folded across my chest, and each no less than one hundred feet tall. The statues surrounded a large building whose base was shaped like a six-pointed star with each statue positioned in the recess that reflected her color. That inner structure raised to a pyramid-like point from which six colored beams shot up into the sky like lasers. As I later learned, Quantum Girl and her history had become something of a religion to these people, no doubt because. with the sun soon to expand, she was their only hope of salvation. How strange it seemed to me that of everything that might have survived for so long, all of it related to me. The star-shaped building—the one in which I had awakened and where the other versions of me still lay asleep—was their temple—a holy sanctum, dedicated to the hexadic godhead.

The rest of the city radiated outward. Six avenues spanned seemingly endlessly into the distance. Meanwhile, dissecting them, were a series of streets in a pattern of concentric circles that grew larger and larger until they blended with the horizon, so large was the metropolitan area. Small passenger vehicles flittered this way and that on or just above the thoroughfares. Meanwhile, trees and gardens and small buildings threw patterns of color into what would otherwise have been a drab geometric landscape.

It was midafternoon as I viewed all of this. While the many leaves on the tree displayed themselves in various shades of red and yellow, my first thought was that it was sometime near the end of summer or early fall. But while the landscape is subject to seasons, the sky is immutable. White cumulous clouds billowed above my head forming pictures that could only be described by the imagination. As I considered what each one reminded me of, I wondered how truthful the individuals I had met were about how far in the future this was. A billion years was an awfully long time. I had to know for certain. Phasing into low orbit, I used my quantum vision to measure the distance from the Earth to the Moon to find that it was nearly four thousand kilometers farther than it had been in my time which corresponded with the year they had given me. It was an eon plus change.

Once that part of my curiosity had been satisfied, I phased back into the temple and examined the five other Quantum Girls one by one. None had any detectible heartbeat, respiration, or any other signs of life, and yet each was alive. I say alive but not in the traditional sense for the very atoms that comprised them appeared frozen in time. I tried to merge into each of them but found that I could not. It was as though a quantum barrier permeated every part of them.

Faaah walked into the chamber I was in. It was that of the blue Quantum Girl version of me. I glanced back at her and then continued to stare at Blue.

I see you have made attempts to stir them from their sleep, she telepathed.

"I tried to merge into them," I replied. "No luck."

Perhaps you can control the god-stones in their heads, she suggested.

"How do you know about..." I started to say and then realized the answer. "Oh," I went on. "I hadn't thought of that." I turned to face her. "It's been a long day. I think I'll grab a bite to eat and then get some sleep. I can try again tomorrow." I began to phase back to my house, then solidified again. "By the way," I asked, "do you know what caused me to wake up?"

We prayed to the Quantum Spirit, she replied. *For ten million years we have prayed.*

"Perhaps one more prayer wouldn't hurt," I said and then I phased out of the room.

CHAPTER XV

Quantum Girl Green
(August 13, 39 B.C.)

I broke bread with Mark Antony and Octavia when morning came. The woman eyed me with suspicion from the moment I entered the dining room for *ientaculum* which was the Roman name for breakfast that was eaten at sunrise. The meal, brought forth and prepared by slaves, consisted of salted bread, dates, figs, apples, pears, grapes, olives, and citron. For a beverage, the three of us were served wine. Octavia Minor, the two-year-old daughter of Mark Antony and Octavia, was held in the lap of a wet nurse off to one side.

"Didst thou know," Antony said, turning to Octavia, "that an assassination of Cleopatra was planned? These are troubling times!" he proclaimed. "And now with Rome divided as it were by the treacherous hand of Pompey!" He took a drink from his goblet and then went on. "May he be damned to Tartarus for all eternity along with his dog of a general, Sulla! How is it now that the Queen of Egypt needs to flee from her empire from barbarians in Roman attire?"

"Were she truly Cleopatra," Octavia said, "I would wonder, husband. But as she is not, my curiosity travels toward matters more salient to our house."

"Damn thy delusions!" Antony shouted back, pounding his fist down on the table at which Octavia jumped a bit from fright. "Is hers not the face of Cleopatra? When she speaks, it is not Cleopatra's voice that issues from her lungs? Dost thou think me a fool not to recognize her who I took to my bed and who bore three children from the seed of my cock?"

Octavia stood up. "It is a demon, not Cleopatra! My eyes did not deceive me, nor was I asleep!"

"Then I fear I must prove thee wrong," he replied. "Tonight I shall fuck our guest and shall for myself determine whether she be lady or dragon!"

"And what of me while you do?" Octavia wept. "What of me, thy wife whilst thou fucks this demon?"

It was at this point that Antony, too, stood from his seat. "I am a general!" he proclaimed, "and they husband! Thou mayest watch or else retire to the slaves' quarters for the night for all I care! I shall not be provoked with disbelief in my own house!"

Octavia stared at him and then fled the room. The wet nurse followed her. Antony banged his fist down on the table again. "Damn her insolence!" he shouted. "I married her to satisfy her brother, not to husband a madwoman." He looked up at me. "Knowest thou that is thee whom I love—whom I have ever loved with three children as proof. Indeed, my legions might have toppled the Egyptian empire but with thee upon her throne, my knees grew weak. Indeed, I would rather have sooner plunged my sword through my own heart rather than it prick the tiniest imperfection in thy fair complexion. Look you to the horizon where once all of Rome took root as far as the eye could see and tenfold farther still. Once, there was peace but for Brutus and his confederates who did take the life of my friend. Now, we must post sentries just to guard the parapets of stations but a day's march hence. Caesar could have held all of Rome together by the stripe of his clothes and yet I, despite my purple vestment, find it difficult to inspire the comradery he evoked by his mere presence. Oh, that they murdered him! No words could ever avenge that most foul deed!"

"You are as good a man as Gaius ever was!" I insisted, recalling my history. "Better in bed, I assure you." It was I who then stood up. "May we speak in private?" I asked. "I fear the walls have ears."

"I have another house," he said, "a mile or so to the west. I go there when I need some solitude to think."

And so we went, riding two horses to our destination and

bringing with us more bread, fruit, and wine for lunch later on, or *prandium* as they called it. The house was small—a single room with a table and four chairs and, to one side, a desk on which lay several scrolls and a map hand-drawn on papyrus. Across from that, against the opposite wall stood a narrow bed, more like a fainting couch that was made of exotic woods across which laid a down-stuffed mattress and pillow.

Antony removed the goatskin flask he had slung across his shoulder, took a swig, and then extended it toward me. "I'm afraid I can only offer thee just wine this time. My store of food was consumed by several guards I let stay here to watch for the advance of any garrison."

I waved away his offer but then asked, "Does thou truly fear for thy life?"

"These are perilous times," he replied. "One never knows what dagger might be hurled in one's direction." He looked at me in earnest. "Thou said thou wished to speak privately. What secrets hast thou with which to bend my ear?"

"Does thou believe in magic?" I asked.

"Shouldst thou consider the gods magical," he replied, "then I should believe wholeheartedly, having myself paid homage to both Jupiter and Venus. But why dost thou ask?"

"Beneath Egypt lies the dark continent of Africa," I said, "in which are lost civilizations with great wizards who invoke the powers of gods other than those of Athens or Rome. One such sorcerer appeared at my door not long ago—a wizened man. His name was Khofira and he insisted that he possessed powers that were supernatural. 'But why hast thou come to me?' I asked. 'Because,' he replied, 'I have again and again seen thou in my dreams, and, unworthy though I am, I have fallen in love with thee. Forgive me my words, my Queen,' he begged, 'but the heart knows only truth and the tongue follows the heart's command. The magic I possess is real but Death beckons me and so I wish to pass on that magic to thee.' Thus, with powders thrown, with rattles shaken, and incantations in a language I did not understand, he caused a small gem to explode from his head and enter mine. Then his eyes grew dark and, Death gripped his very spirit, and he dropped to the floor. I did not know what had happened. I attributed what he said to the ramblings of a demented old man. But then that same night, I was awakened from my sleep by a green light that lit up my room. How frightened I became when I realized that the incandescence had come from me. Truly, then, I trembled. Had this black wizard cursed me in some way, I wondered? Was I to die a most horrid death or, worse, be forever barred from the afterlife, never to see my children—our children? But as the hours and days wore on, nothing ill came of me. Rather, I found that I had gained certain abilities."

"And what might those be?" Antony asked, perhaps wondering if his lover of so many years had gone insane.

"This!" I said as I phased from one part of the room to another and then to another still, right before his eyes.

The man stared at me with his jaw dropped and took a step backward as though in fear.

"Or this!" I said as I duplicated myself once, then twice, and then again so that eight of me stood before him.

"'Tis the work of Hecate!" Antony stammered. "It will bring death to us all!"

"Nay, dear Antony," I assured him in a soothing voice as I merged myself back into one. "What is more," I said, "I have more powers still." I walked up to him, the greatest of all generals who now stood trembling before me. I took his hand in mine. "Thou are my greatest and forever love," I told him. "Fear me not." Then I led him outside where I pointed to a bolder that stood in the field nearby. Stretching out my arms, I caused it to rise into the air several feet, then, theatrically, I clapped my hands together and the rock glowed fiery red, turned into a liquid mass, then dripped like lava onto the ground from which it had been raised.

"Think what power I could wield against thine enemies," I told him. "*Thou* might be Caesar instead of thy brother-in-law, Octavius, who rumor says, boasts the name Augustus should he be crowned." The words came unwillingly from my lips as the thought of power surged through my veins. I shook my head to try and clear my thoughts but to no avail. The body I had usurped had taken over my mind.

"Fear not, my love," I insisted, as the itch of pleasure roasted my loins and surged its way up to the pinnacles of my breasts. I threw my arms around his neck and kissed him passionately. Then I stood back, undid the fastenings of my dress, let it drop to the floor, and stood before him naked and in want.

"Doth this portrait of me still frighten thee?" I asked. Then I split apart into two, each of me running my hands up and down his form until his fear had left and the maleness in him swelled as physical testament to his lust and desire.

The two of me embraced the man and then phased us all back to his bedroom at his estate. No matter that it was not even noon, we made mad, passionate love for hours, lost in our venereal desires. The Christian part of me had been overcome by Cleopatra's mind having supplanted my own. When the three of us were at last both sated and exhausted, I merged back into one and then we both dressed—I, though remaining naked, creating the illusion of clothing on myself—and then we went to the dining hall for *ceta*[7].

Octavia sat opposite me at the table, frequently glancing up at me from her food with an expression of both rivalry and fear. I pretended to ignore her as I placed bits of meat or fruit or bread into my mouth. Antony, it seemed, picked up on his wife's emotional malady and broke the silence that had ensued.

"How was thy day?" he asked her in a calming voice.

"I spent much time weaving," she replied.

"Octavia is masterful at it," Antony said to me. "I think she

---

[7] Pronounced *keta*, it was what the Romans called dinner.

might even come close to championing Minerva."

"Hold thy tongue, husband," she half-whispered, "lest Arachne's fate befall me as well."

I turned a curious look at them both. Antony bit some meat off the rib he held and then smiled and cast a glance my way. "It is said that Arachne boasted she could outperform Minerva as a weaver," he explained. "Minerva, angered by her words, changed her into a spider." He turned to Octavia. "I did not say thou wast better than the goddess," he went on, "only that you might come near to her skills."

"We have no such gods in Egypt," I remarked. "The closest is Tayet, the goddess of the bandages of mummification, though her skills are only summoned after someone has died or been killed."

There then came a smug expression on my face as I glanced at Octavia who replied,. "Is it not enough, husband, that she shares your bed after but one night's stay? Do not think I did not hear the sounds that rose from thy chamber just hours past? And in my own house by our guest who apparently favors your anatomy over my hospitality!"

Antony slammed his fist down on the table for the third time that day. "I will not have either myself or my dear friend berated by thy jealousies! It is I who command this household and not thee!" He then rose and turned to me. "Apologies for my wife's ill manners," he said. "Please forgive me as I take my leave to assuage the anger that now fills me." That said, he left the room.

Octavia glared at me. "Do not think that thou can steal my husband!" she snarled. "My brother would take umbrage at such an offense to his sister and war could ensue."

"Worry not," I said back. "I do not wish to take thy husband from thee—only to borrow him and his cock now and again." I smiled, half to her and half to myself, and then focused on the pomegranate seed in my hand that I put to my lips to suck out its tart red juice.

CHAPTER XVI

Quantum Girl Violet
(April 22, 2025)

Mama and Papa rushed to the hospital as soon as Phee called them with the news that I had woken up. Phee met them outside the room. I could hear her talking to them but I couldn't make out anything that was said. A moment or so later, all of them entered and Mama came up to me and took hold of my hands.

"Thank God you're all right," she said. "I prayed to Jesus to keep you safe and I see that my prayers were answered. The doctors said we can take you back home tomorrow." She looked over at Phee. "Isn't that wonderful, Ophelia? Your sister can come back home."

Phee smiled and then took hold of Papa's hand.

"But we need to watch her," she went on as though I wasn't even in the room. She reached out one hand and gently touched my neck with her fingers, then suddenly pulled her hand away. "Why would you do that to yourself?" she asked. "Jesus doesn't need to take you—at least not yet! You're only fifteen years old!"

"Perhaps this isn't the time," Papa broke in.

Mama turned her head toward him, her eyes filled with tears. "Do you know how I prayed to Jesus before our daughters were born that they come into the world safe and sound?" Then she turned back toward me. "You and Ophelia are all you and your father have that mean anything? What could have been so bad that you would want to try to take your own life? And on your birthday!"

"It was Theresa," Phee chimed in. "She broke up with her."

"I knew that girl was no good," Mama replied. "Love at so young an age and indecent love at that."

"Mama," I told her, "it wasn't like that. It wasn't like that at all. Theresa was bullying me. But that's over now. I don't want to die.

Not anymore. Really. I just don't understand what's going on."

"You just get some rest now, Sweet Pea," she replied. "we'll talk about things in the morning."

The next day found me back home, though confined to bed "by doctor's orders," fiddling with the meteorite Phee had given me supposedly yesterday. But how could that be, I wondered? It had been weeks since my fifteenth birthday. I remembered each day distinctly down to when I doubled myself so that one of me could go be with Mark. The problem was, if I were back in time, that event hadn't happened yet, so there wouldn't be an other self to come and rescue me from this insanity. And what had happened to all my powers, I wondered? *I couldn't have imagined it all*, I kept thinking. *I just couldn't have!*

I tried to explain it all to Phee but she only shook her head. "They say," she said, "that just before you die you relive your entire lifetime in an instant. Maybe it was something like that when you *almost* did."

"*They* don't say," I replied, "that you live out an imaginary life. I remember every detail. I was married to Mark. We had twins named Zhana and Samira. Mark Marsden. He goes to Massapequa High School on Long Island. But if you message him, don't mention that we were married but he won't remember any of that."

"Because it hasn't happened yet," she said, "because you went back in time and merged with your fifteen-year-old self because you're really a superhero called Quantum Girl who no one has ever heard of."

"I'm not making it up!" I protested. "How would I know about Mark if it wasn't true? He lives on the other side of the country. We've never been to New York—at least not in this reality. Look him up online. Maybe he has a social media account."

"Fine!" she replied half-heartedly. She went and got her laptop and began her search. "Ok," she went on. "I found a Mark Marsden on Facebook." She threw a strange expression at me. "Who uses

Facebook anymore? Attends Massapequa High School. Sophomore. Definitely cute." She stared over her laptop at me. "I thought you were only into girls?"

"That was the *other* me," I said. "The me before I merged into myself."

"Weird," came her response. "I'm strictly into boys. I could never get into any of that muff-diving stuff. I mean it's like so gross, no offense."

"Well," I said smugly, " apparently you haven't met Claire Salinger yet."

"What's that supposed to mean?" she asked.

"Nothing," I replied. "Just that you two eventually hook up and get married."

"You are cray-cray!" she insisted.

"We'll see," I replied.

"What?" she shot back. "I'm supposed to meet this Claire Schlesinger…"

"Salinger," I interrupted, correcting her.

"Whatever!" she replied. "And then I'm to fall madly, deeply, and irrevocably in love with her I suppose."

"Yes," I said.

"And eat her out on a daily basis?" she asked.

"I never asked," I replied, "but I wouldn't have put it past you."

"So disgusting!" she replied back. "Not in a thousand of your quantum lifetimes!"

"Whatever you say, Sis," I said and smiled.

"You're infuriating!" she snapped back. "You know that? And so what if there is a Mark Marsden who goes to Massapequa High? You might have seen him on YouTube or Facebook if you're *that* ancient and had not paid attention so that it became subliminal. I don't know what to think anymore. This is all driving me insane. Mom said you're to see a therapist tomorrow afternoon. Maybe you can wear your Quantum Girl costume and freak *him* out, too!"

The therapist turned out to be a psychiatrist named Dr. Edmund Scofield, who was in his late forties. I couldn't say how tall he was as he always sat behind his desk, but he was thin and slightly balding with blonde hair adulterated with aging gray. He had blue eyes, thin lips, and an Aquiline nose, the bridge of which served as a resting spot for the bridge of the frameless glasses that he wore. He had me sit across from him in a comfortable tufted leather chair that matched his own if slightly smaller and then, pen in hand, he began his line of questioning by asking me if I knew why I was there.

"It seems I remember things differently from everyone else," I replied.

"And what are those differences?" he asked.

"Well," I said, "I'm not sapphic—lesbian—at least I don't think I am. Everyone seems to be under the impression that I just got out of a torrid affair with Theresa Martinez. She's one of my classmates."

"But you didn't?" he asked.

"No," I replied. "The way I remember it, she'd bullied me to the point where I decided to end it all."

"By hanging yourself," he said.

"Yes," I told me. "I was pushed, called names, and even had a basketball slammed into my face by her."

"By Theresa," he asked.

"Yes," I replied. "It was anything but an act of love."

"And yet your family maintains," he replied, "that you had been intimate with her and that the reason you decided to end things was because she broke up with you."

"As I said," I replied, "I remember it differently."

The man scribbled something more in his notes and then looked up at me again."Tell me about Quantum Girl," he went on.

"It's a long story," I replied.

He looked up at the wall clock that was behind me. "We still have another fifteen minutes," he said.

I glanced back at it, then took a deep breath. "I guess there's time for the Readers Digest version," I replied. I took a deep breath and then began. "There was another Peyton Herron before me—in a different timeline. In the one I'm from originally, Phee—Ophelia, my sister—didn't exist and so I wasn't rescued in time after I'd hanged myself and so there was brain damage. It was the other Peyton who healed me with her god-stone—the one that Dhraaal gave her—by placing it in my head after taking it out of hers. Dhraaal was from Rendenaaar, which was a planet in a universe long before ours."

"If I may interrupt for a moment," he said. "You just said that the other Peyton had taken the…"

"God-stone," I said,

"God-stone," he repeated, "and that she somehow removed it from her head and placed it in yours. Am I to understand that there was some sort of surgery involved?"

"No," I replied, "she just willed it out of her head and into mine. Anyway, after the god-stone was in my head, my thoughts became out of control and I accidentally killed her with an energy blast. Then Cleopatra, whom Chloë Salinger had brought from the past, taught me how to use my powers, after which I met Mark and we fell in love and eventually got married—in the past, actually—1960 to be exact. Then the other Peyton saved the universe."

"The one whom you had inadvertently killed?" he said, questioning my story.

"Yes," I replied, "only it wasn't her per se but one of her duplicates that had survived. As Quantum Girl, we could duplicate ourselves into as many of us as we wanted. Anyway, after all of that had occurred and the universe had been, I decided to go back in time and merge with my teenage self as sort of a second start. But I desperately missed Mark and so I split into two. One of me phased over to where he was and the other stayed with Phee—that other being me. But then there was this massive alien invasion and it was

113

just me against them. My solution—at least it seemed the best at the time—was to divide myself into a thousand of me. After I did that, we all came face-to-face with the invaders, and then each of me began hurling quantum blasts at them while they were bombarding me with some kind of intense radiation—I don't know what."

"And where was your other self," he asked, "while all of this was happening—the one who went to be with Mark?"

"I don't know," I replied, "but I didn't have time to go and find her. I just knew that everyone on the planet who hadn't already been killed depended on me. And then I woke up in the hospital bed."

"How exactly had all the people who were killed died?" he asked.

"The aliens had melted the polar ice caps," I replied, "and the sea level rose. Most of them drowned, especially those who lived along coastal areas."

"But we're in Los Angeles," he said, "aren't we?"

"Yes," I replied.

"Which is next to the coast," he went on.

"Yes," I said. "And?"

"How do you explain," he asked, "that this office isn't underwater?"

"I can't," I replied, "unless this it's because this is a different reality where there was no invasion."

"Your powers as Quantum Girl," he went on, "do you still have them? Can you duplicate yourself here in front of me? Or *phase* to another part of the room?"

I shook my head. "I don't have my powers anymore," I said. "I don't know what happened to them."

Dr. Scofield glanced at the clock again and then picked up a pad from his desk and began writing on it. "I'm going to prescribe a medication for you," he said, glancing up at me. "Two milligrams of Risperdal to be taken daily in the morning. That should help with hallucinations." He tore off the small sheet that he had written on and pushed it across his desk toward me. I picked it up, glanced at it, and then placed it in my purse. "I'll see you again next Wednesday," he told me. "You can let me know then how things are going."

"So, you think I'm crazy?" I asked.

"We don't use that term in the medical field," he replied. "You have what we call a psychosis. Fortunately for you in this day and age, it's treatable. In a few weeks, all the delusions of your having been Quantum Girl will have gone away and you'll be able to lead a normal life. Perhaps you and Theresa can even get back together. Your sister informed me that she told her what you've been going through and she's willing to be there for you for as long as it takes. It's not everyone who's willing to make that kind of commitment, especially at your age."

And that was how it went—just take a pill and everything goes away. But was it all a delusion? I wondered. What about Mark? Was his love for me and mine for him a delusion as well? I couldn't just let it go, even with a pill forced down my throat before breakfast every day.

CHAPTER XVII

Peyton
(the one in Massapequa)

As the days and then the weeks wore on, Mark and I became closer to each other and Mark became more confident. Our walks through the forest and our feeding of the ducks had become a daily routine. When snow finally began to fall it was nearing Christmas. School had let out for the holidays. My older self took us to New Jersey for sledding. Despite that I could phase into outer space, being on a toboggan speeding downhill with Mark holding me so that I wouldn't fall off took my breath away. At the bottom of our exhilarating descent, I rolled onto my back, stared him in the face, and smiled. He moved closer and kissed me. This was the second time I'd been kissed by him but it wasn't like the first. He didn't have to say he loved me or I say that to him. We felt it toward each other and when at last our lips parted I smiled again—grinned is perhaps a better word—then pushed him up and over onto the snow where I rolled on top of him.

"You know I'm in love with you," I said.

"That's good to know," he replied.

I frowned at him. "I was expecting you to say that you were in love with *me*," I said.

"Girls!" he exclaimed with frustration.

"What?" I replied, wanting an explanation.

"I've been in love with you," he said, "since the first time I saw you when you stood up for me in the hallway. If only you could hear how my heart races a mile a minute whenever you're around."

"Oh," I said, "but I can. I have super-hearing, you see, among my many other powers."

"Really," he said. "So, you're like Supergirl."

"Oh," I said with a great air of confidence, "I'm much more

powerful than Supergirl, only…"

"Only what?" he asked.

"You're my kryptonite," I said and then I kissed him again after which I rolled off of him and onto my back so that we were both staring up at a sky that was filled with gray nimbostratus clouds that we'd learned all about in Earth Science class. Snowflakes fluttered down on us as we lay there and I took hold of his mittened hand in mine.

"They really are all different," I said.

"What are?" he asked.

"Snowflakes," I replied.

"How do you know?" he asked. "There must be trillions of them."

"More like septillions," I said. "That's a trillion trillion."

"I know what a septillion is," he replied. "But how do you know that none of them are the same?"

"Because," I said, "a typical snowflake contains ten to the eighteenth power of water molecules. It was suggested in 2121 by Jon Nelson, a physicist and formerly an assistant professor in the Department of Atmospheric Sciences at the University of Arizona, Tucson, that the odds of two snowflakes being identical are on the order of ten to the seven hundred, sixty-eighth 0power to one."

"My," he said back, "aren't you the brainiac."

"Another of my incredible superpowers," I replied, glancing at him. "So, tell me," I said ever so nonchalantly, "are you going to marry me when we grow up?"

"Don't you think we should at least start out by going steady?" he asked.

"Going steady," I repeated. "I didn't know anyone ever did that anymore."

"Sure they do," he replied. "They just call it something else."

"Like what?" I asked.

"Well," he said, "I think they just call it going together."

"I think then," I replied, "that we're going together. We've *been* going together for months!" I glanced over at him again. "You're not into that Jane Baxter girl, are you? I saw the way you looked at her at lunch the other day."

"You *are* kidding me, aren't you?" he said. "I mean she's got huge boobs which a guy can't help noticing, but did you ever try and talk to her?"

"Did *you*?" I asked.

"Before I met you," he answered defensively. "Seriously, she's got a brain the size of a pinto bean."

I stared him in the eyes. "The question beckons," I said, "do you *like* pinto beans?"

"Hell no!" he replied. "I like a girl with a head on her shoulders."

"Is that why you like me?" I asked. "Because I'm so smart?"

"You're more than smart," he said back. "You... special. And I don't like you. I love you. I told you. I've told myself that a million times. I don't think I could ever love anyone except you. So, yes, I want to get married to you someday."

"Someday," I repeated.

"Maybe when we're like eighteen," he replied and then glanced over at me. "Your mom likes me, doesn't she?"

"Definitely," I replied. "But there are things I need to tell you."

"Such as?" he asked.

"I'm just worried," I said, "that if I tell you, you won't love me anymore."

"As long as you don't tell me," he said, "that you used to be a guy, we're good."

"*Hell*, no!" I said back. "You haven't seen me naked—at least not yet."

He glanced at me again. "But I will?" he asked.

"Hell, *yes*!" I said back. "When the time is right. But first, we need to talk." I sat up and then turned toward him. " Come on. Let's head back home."

I stood up and then pulled on his arm as he pulled himself to his feet. Once his feet were firmly planted in the snow, I pulled him into me and hugged him. "I love you, Mark Marsden," I whispered in his ear. "I'll love you for as long as I live."

"I'm afraid I'm going to wake up and find out this was all a dream," he whispered back. I could feel his heart racing as his chest pressed against mine. I didn't need quantum powers for that.

CHAPTER XVIII

Peyton
*(the one who stayed behind
with Ophelia who's now in
the alternate reality)*

I had such mixed emotions. It was all so difficult for me. I was trapped in some alternate reality where Quantum Girl never existed and my best friend-sister hated my guts. As for Mark, even if he did exist in the world in which I'd awakened, he would be nearly three thousand miles away with absolutely no memory of me. To make matters worse, I had fallen in love with Theresa Martinez, and she with me, which might be hard for an adult to fathom since we were both only fifteen years old, but as Emily Dickinson once wrote, "The heart wants what it wants." Still, my love for Mark hadn't changed. With that in mind, I didn't know what to do.

I had spent the entire weekend with Theresa. Her mother having gone to visit her aunt, we had the reign of the place, though most of it was spent in the bedroom discovering ourselves. It was actually an incredibly sad moment for us both when we made our way back to school Monday morning. We walked hand in hand until the moment the bell rang and we had to go to our separate classes. I kissed her just then. It seemed to me that everyone watched but I didn't care if they jeered at us or turned up their noses. All I knew was that I had inhaled Theresa's breath and I would suffocate if I went without it for too long.

My first period was with—Oh, my God!—Mr. Chatterjee! If the word pompous applied to anyone, it was to him. There he was with his talk about the expanding universe again. *Dare I tell him how wrong he is?* I wondered. *He didn't take criticism very well. He would probably go into a cataleptic state if I told him what dark matter was.* I decided against any comment. *Best not to taunt the fire-breathing dragon.*

The day wore on languidly. I kept watching the clock until lunch break finally came so that I could meet up again with Theresa. She caught up with me at my locker on which someone had written in a florescent pink marker, "Muff Diver."

"Mine's just as bad," she said with a smile.

"What does *yours* say?" I asked.

"Carpet muncher," she replied, "which is definitely a one-up over what they wrote on Daisy's locker."

"What was that?" I asked.

"Cum sucker," she uttered with a hint of a snarl on her lip.

"Some people are just plain cruel," I replied.

"Don't knock it if you haven't tried it, I always say," she proclaimed and then turned with a scowl on her face toward a couple of boys who had their eyes fixed on us and were talking between themselves. "What are you staring at?" she shouted at them. "The only pussy you two are ever going to see is in your dreams!" As they walked away, she turned back to me. "Losers!" she said, shaking her head. "Come on. Let's go get something to eat. I'm starving!" She took my hand then and led me to the cafeteria.

We sat at the sapph table. There were two such tables, it seemed. That one was for lesbians. The other was for gay guys or socs as they were called there—wherever I was. Both were filled with what the quote-unquote *normal* kids thought of as lepers. Worse than that, there was one table filled with born-agains who decided we were fodder for Hell and were quite outspoken about it.

One of them, a junior named Lorna Parsons strode up to our table and said, "You do know that the lot of you are destined to live out eternity with Satan?"

Theresa looked at her with a serious expression on her face. "So, you're telling us that if we continue in our damnable ways we're going to have to spend the rest of existence with you?"

"That's not what I said!" she protested.

121

Theresa laid down her fork and stood up. "If that's the case," she said, "then I'm done with all this cum sucking shit. I'm going to find me some young man who can fuck my brains out so that when my time comes I can have an everlasting peace away from this Christian bitch!" She turned to me, took my hand, and pulled me up. "You want to come with me and find us some dude who can do us both in a threesome?" As we started to walk away she went on loud enough for her to hear, "Imagine having to spend eternity listening to her." Then she turned back to her with, "Are the rumors true that you actually superglued your vagina shut to avoid temptation?"

The girl just stood there with her jaw hanging, watching us as we left the lunchroom.

There were six other girls who generally sat at our table. Two were very pretty—Daisy McKenzie and Myra Kartinova being that pair. Two were Plain Janes but not unattractive. The remaining duo, who made claim on the Janes but probably secretly lusted for the rest of us, were what we used to call bull dykes who fancied themselves the non-girl versions of boys, and where boys all had a Y chromosome, theirs was a Y not? The two of them both had short-cropped hair and wore the same clothes as the boys all wore. At first, the school had forbidden that, but there came such a stir that the administration and the school board finally caved in to the demand.

"I heard that Ms. Hochul is secretly a sapph," Cora Mathers, one of the BDs said at lunch the next day. "I'd sure like to tap into that."

"Hey!" Raven Billow shot back. "I thought I was all that to you!" Raven was one of the PJs. Her name wasn't really Raven, though I never did find out what her real name was.

"Hell, no!" said the other Y not. "I'd much prefer to land Sweet Cheeks—her sister—Ophelia. Oh, ah feel ya, girl—every fucking part of you—with my tongue!"

"You're disgusting!" That from her gf and subdivide as she called her. "First, *Lia's* a diehard sparrow. Second, you're supposed

122

to be in love with *me*."

"And third," her dom shot back, "you're supposed to be grateful for whatever affection I throw your way." And with that, she threw her a sharp look, at which point the subdivide just hung her head and muttered, "Sorry."

The dom then looked at me as she disgustingly shoved an entire Twinkie into her mouth. "Word has it," she slushed out through the doughy mass, "your sister positively hates you." It was the word, "positively" that caused a bit of Twinky to be hurled in my direction which, fortunately for me, missed its mark.

"We're okay," I replied. "We just see things differently, I suppose."

"And so what does she think about your being a vagosaurus," she asked. "And I heard your mom's a Jesua freak."

"Lay off her!" Theresa shot back. "None of that's any of your fucking business!"

"Sorreee!" the dom, Lynette, apologized in a nonapologetic voice. "Just trying to make conversation."

"Well, make it about your *own* sister and mother," Theresa said in a commanding tone. "Oh, wait!" she went on. "Your mother left with some guy from the military just after you were born and your sister's in some psych ward for the mentally whacked!"

"Shut up!" Lynette said. "Just shut up!" Her subdivide, Rachel, reached over and placed her hand over hers. Lynette pulled her hand back and out from under with a quick, almost violent motion and then glanced up at Rachel. "When I want your pity I'll ask for it!" She pushed her lunch tray forward and then stood up. "I'm out of here," she said with the presence of tears in her eyes. And then she left.

"Not sure what I did wrong?" Rachel said.

"You didn't do anything. She just has issues." That was Theresa, trying to restore order.

The rest of our lunch was eaten in silence with occasional

awkward glances at each other.

"Maybe we should sit by ourselves next time," Theresa said to me as we emptied our trays into the trash and then set them on top of the bin.

"Probably for the best," I replied. "I guess it's hard for some people to be different when they don't know themselves."

"See you after school?" I asked.

"Of course," she said.

"Maybe," I said, "you could crash at my place for a few days." I smiled at her. "I believe in reciprocation."

"I'd love to but my mom's coming back this afternoon and I promised her we'd spend some time together. How about a raincheck, though? Maybe later this week."

"I don't know if I can survive that long," I replied.

"Oh, you'll manage," she assured me and kissed me on the cheek. "Mark my word."

"Sure," I said as she walked away, but what she had just said, the word she'd just used, caused my heart to stop for an instant. Mark. I felt as though I'd betrayed him but I'd fallen in love with someone else and yet... and yet I still loved him!

It was two days later at school, between fifth and sixth period, that I went into the girls' bathroom. The room was empty other than me. It was the bathroom in the basement that hardly anyone ever used but my next class was Chem and it was right up the stairs.

I had just sat down in the stall to pee when I heard footsteps and then scraping like someone was moving the trashcan. A moment later, I heard loud whispering. "Herron! Herron! Herron!" it repeated over and over again—male voices. I became terrified. I was in the middle of peeing when there was the sound of a thud against the door and looked up to see a teenage boy—a junior or senior—gripping the top of the door with his fingers and peering over the edge of it down at me. I quickly put my hands over my lap to cover myself.

"Get out!" I yelled at him, embarrassed and afraid.

My heart was still pounding as the boy jumped back down to the floor. I quickly wiped myself, pulled my panties up, and was about to pull up my skirt when the door was kicked in, hitting me, and knocking me back down to the seat, my elbow inadvertently flushing the toilet. The boy who had been spying at me over the door was now standing in the doorway glaring at me as I desperately grappled with my skirt.

"What do you want?" I asked, my voice trembling.

"What do you think?" he replied.

He reached out and grabbed my arm and pulled me out of the stall. My skirt fell to my ankles.

"Hey," he said to the other two. "Look what I found!"

The other two were definitely seniors. I didn't know their names but I'd seen them before and they were wearing varsity jackets—the kind with the school emblem on them and white leather sleeves.

"Herron," the one still holding my arm said in a low unnerving voice. "Peyton Herron."

"We heard you're a sapph," the second one said.

"We figured," said the third, "that the only reason you don't like dick is because you've never had it before. This is a school. We're here to educate you."

The class bell rang just them. I managed to pull away to rush toward the door but my skirt was still around my ankles and it tripped me up and I fell, hitting my head on the edge of one of the sinks. That had no effect on them. They pulled me up and held me by my arms. My head hurt. I could feel a trickle of blood run down the side of my face. As I looked up, I caught my reflection in the mirror over the sink. Where I'd hit my head, it was beginning to swell.

"Let me go!" I said, struggling, tears flooding from my eyes.

It was the third boy who walked up behind me, grabbed a hold of the top of my blouse, and ripped it open.

I started to scream but then then one who had ripped apart my blouse pulled a bunch of paper towels from the dispenser and stuffed them in my mouth.

"Try and scream now, bitch!" he laughed as he unfastened my bra in the front, then added, "Nice tits." He put his hands on my breasts, cupped them, and then rolled my nipples between his fingers. I could feel them getting hard. I could feel a sexual response but I fought against it, closing my eyes and trying to think of other things.

"It's show time!" he said as he pulled down my panties, bent down, and licked one side of my but cheek.

Then he slapped my bare butt really hard. I winced in pain but I couldn't scream because of the towels in my mouth. He forced my legs apart and then stuck his fingers into my vag. I was gagging on the towels all the while—choking on them. At one point, I threw up and it had nowhere to go but into my nose. I could barely breathe after that—gasping for breath. I thought I was going to die. I stared at my reflection in the mirror, half-naked, my eyes wet with tears. I tried to fight against them but it was no use. They were just too strong.

If only I were still Quantum Girl, I thought to myself, *I would send them to the edge of the sun!*

The two holding me pushed the upper part of my body forward until my forehead struck the faucet. "Ow!" I tried to cry out but with the towels in my mouth, it just sounded like a moan. Then one behind me, the one who had done all of that to me was the first to rape me. I would feel him inside me, forcing himself into me again and again until at last he withdrew and I would feel his semen drip down my left leg. My lungs let out a roar of fury that had nowhere to go. Then the other two had their way with me. The second one fucked my vag, but the third sodomized me. My lungs roared again when that happened. It hurt so bad. Tears gushed from my eyes. And they stopped. Finally, they stopped. And then they left, laughing amongst themselves, one of them laughing, "God, that felt so good! Excellent piece of saphhic meat! Guaranteed after feeling my cock in her, she'll never want pussy again!"

I pulled the paper towels out of my mouth and then seconds later vomited into the sink. Then I turned on the tap, cupped my right hand, filled my mouth with water, and spit it out. Lifting up my head, I stared at my reflection in the mirror. I felt dirty and cheap. I screamed out as loud as my lungs would allow and then smashed the heels of my fists into the glass as hard as I could, shattering it and cutting myself. Then I stood there, gripping the edges of the sink tightly with my hands, propped up by my arms, watching the rivulets of blood trickle down the drain mixed with my tears. And then I threw up again, so that my vomit covered it all, pink as my labia and equally vile after what had just occurred. That's what rape does to a woman—to a girl. If only I'd had had my powers. If only I could have been Quantum Girl for just a second, none of this would have happened. But I wasn't and it did. I couldn't go back in time. I couldn't change any of it. I could only let it change me.

Blood-drenched hands pulled up my panties and then my skirt. Blood-drenched hands did up the buttons on my blouse. I left my bra unfastened. I felt as though the walls were closing in. I had to get out. I had to breathe clean air. I left the room and climbed the stairs, leaving a trail of blood behind me—and then I passed out.

CHAPTER IXX

Quantum Girl Blue
(October 29, 1929)

"My goodness," Great Granny said when I told her and Mary that I was from the future. "I've heard some whoppers in my day but if that don't beat all!"

"Peyton," Mary said, "this is no time to tell wide-eyed stories. I mean, I read The Time Machine by H. G. Wells but that was all just fiction."

"Look," I said in the most serious voice I could manage, "I didn't want to say anything, but you don't have a job anymore. I don't want you to lose the house and have nowhere to go."

"Okay," Mary went on, "even if you *are* from the future..." and she took a deep breath and then let it out, "how is that going to help pay the bills?"

"Because I have superpowers," I replied.

"What are superpowers?" Mary asked.

"I think you'd better sit down, both of you," I warned them. "I don't want either of you to faint."

Reluctantly, they both sat, probably more to humor me than anything else. I mean, they had taken me into their home out of the kindness of their hearts, and then, suddenly, I sounded like a raving lunatic. Of course, they wouldn't know what superpowers were I realized. The first appearance of Superman. which came in the form of a comic book, wouldn't hit the stands for another ten years.

Not wanting to scare them out of their wits, I decided to start with something simple. As a blue Quantum Girl, I found I had an additional, different power. Not only could I phase from one point in space to another but I could phase objects to me. I chose one book from the shelf across the room. To both of their amazements, the book seemed to magically appear in my hands.

"Oh," Mary exclaimed in a dismissive tone. "That's just an old parlor trick. Great Granny and I saw something like that when we went to Riverview Park two summers ago. Didn't we?" she asked, looking to her great-grandmother for acknowledgment.

"Well," Great Granny replied, "it was sort of similar but it involved scarves and not books."

"Oh, you know," Mary ranted on, "that Peyton has about as much magical powers as I do! I just think it's not the right time to play tricks when we're in such a pickle with all that's going on right now."

"Don't say I didn't warn you," I replied and then phased to a different part of the room—once and then again.

"You must have done that with mirrors!" Mary exclaimed.

"Do you see any mirrors?" I said to her.

"Well, then," she went on. "It's hypnosis or something similar like that Austrian scientist, Franz Mesmer. We learned about him in school."

"Ugh!" I groaned. "Tell me if this is done with smoke and mirrors!" I duplicated myself so that there were five of me standing around them both. Looking at Great Granny, I thought a heart attack was imminent. "Would you like some water?" one of me asked her.

"I'd prefer a bit of brandy, thank you," she replied. "Over there in the decanter on the tea cart."

One of me brought her a glass of brandy while another one of me covered her with a shawl that I'd phased from her bedroom. Mary just stared at me aghast.

"So, what *are* you?" she asked. "You're not a Martian, are you?"

I smiled back at her as all of my duplicates merged back into one of me.

"I'm just an ordinary girl," I replied. "It's just that I have a small jewel in my head called a god-stone that's from another universe and that's what gives me my special abilities."

"How…" she stammered out. "How did you get it?"

And so I told them how I had tried to kill myself, only to wind up with a damaged brain unable to even take care of myself, how years later, another version of me helped me get better, how I met Mark, how we both fell in love, but then how I became curious as to what it would have been like to have grown up with a twin sister, and so I went back in time and merged into my younger self, and then, somehow, I woke up at the party nearly a century in the past.

"Why didn't you just go back to your time when you woke up?" Mary asked.

"I tried," I told her. "I really did, only for some reason I can't seem to time travel anymore."

"But in the future," Mary said, "you're called Quantum Girl."

"It's the name Phee and I came up with," I replied. "By the way," I added, "you look incredibly like her—just a few years older."

"Phee," Mary repeated.

"Phee is short for Ophelia," I told her."Ophelia Jane Herron. We're best friends—most of the time."

"How strange," Mary said.

"What is?" I asked.

"My full name is Mary Jane Lindsey," she replied, "and my mother's name was Ophelia."

"When we first met," she said, "you were dressed in a costume and a mask like Douglas Fairbanks did in The Mark of Zorro." She turned to Great Granny who was listening intently to our conversation. "You remember that picture, don't you? We saw it at the Biltmore over on Division for my eighth birthday." She turned back to me. "Great Granny was in love with Douglas Fairbanks. She positively hated Mary Pickford for having married him and stolen him away."

"You hush up," said Great Granny. "I was very happy that he found his one true love. I was just saddened by the fact that it wasn't me."

"Great Granny was quite the raving beauty in her day," Mary said. "She was born the very day the Civil War broke out—April 12, 1861—when Confederate troops fired on Fort Sumter in South Carolina's Charleston Harbor. Here," she said as she got up and went over to the mantle where there were several framed photos. She grabbed one of them, came back, and handed it to me. "Wasn't she just beautiful?" she asked.

I stared at the tintype, then glanced at Great Granny. Time had taken its toll on the nearly seventy-year-old woman. The photo reflected a beautiful young woman in her early twenties, wearing an embroidered white dress. What was most remarkable, though, was how much she looked like Mama. "Yes," I replied. "Very much so."

"I had my share of suiters back in the day," Great Granny remarked with somewhat of an air of pride in her voice. "Though there's not much of me left to look at these days—just gray hair and wrinkles."

Mary went over to her, bent down, and hugged her. "Oh," she said, " I think you're still beautiful."

"Don't you lie," Great Granny said back, "or your nose will grow like that Pinocchio marionette, though it *would* give the birds a nice place to perch."

"Great Granny," Mary said, interrupting the lament. "You still haven't seen Peyton in her costume." She turned to me. "You don't mind, do you?" she asked.

"Not at all," I replied and then phased into Quantum Girl.

"Look, Great Granny!" exclaimed Mary as she stood up, clapping her hands.

Mary stared at me, now for the second time but with the wonder of a child. Great Granny just stared. Mary then walked around me, enthralled by the iridescent glow and pattern of stars and galaxies and nebulae. Oddly, though, she pressed her index finger against my cheek which from my experience must have caused a bright spot to appear. She then backed up a few steps and looked up and down my form.

"What else can you do?" she asked.

"I can phase anywhere on Earth or outer space," I replied. "and I can project force fields."

"What does phase mean?" she asked.

"It means," I replied, "I can move from one place to another instantaneously." I changed back to my Peyton form and then looked her in the eye. "You're not afraid?" I asked. "You're taking this rather well."

"Afraid of what?" she asked. "Of you? Don't be silly! If you were going to harm either of us you would have done it long ago. Besides, we're best friends. Aren't we?"

"Of course, we are," I replied. "I think of you and Great Granny as family."

That was how it went and to my relief, it went much better than I had expected.

CHAPTER XX

Quantum Girl Red
(March 15, 1943)

It was the Ides of March, Margaret had just turned eight three weeks before, but there remained concern in me for the man I had seen in the restaurant the other day when I had phased the two of us to the White Castle in Queens.

I was in the middle of a nude photoshoot with Albert when not only that same man but seven others just like him suddenly materialized in the studio. Albert wasn't paying attention at the time, focused on me through his view camera, but I was facing the sudden appearance of the group out of thin air. The effect was the same as mine when I used my quantum abilities. They had not simply materialized. They had phased.

Just an aside about Albert and his camera—a large format instrument that he had used for more than a quarter of a century. It was made of red polished mahogany with a black accordion-like bellow, capped with a lens. The whole affair stood on a tripod made of the same wood and displayed an upside-down image on the glass back that could be clearly seen by him as he looked at it while draped under a black cloth hood. The camera had been his pride and joy and the tool of his profession ever since he had taken up photography at the age of thirty, back in 1926. Unfortunately, when one of the group had phased into the room, he had inadvertently bumped into Albert, causing Albert to bump into his apparatus, in turn causing it to fall crashing to the floor. The tripod broke, the bellows ripped, the glass back shattered, and how badly damaged the lens had become was never made known to me. Regardless that Albert was unable to duplicate, he was beside himself with grief at the sudden loss of what to him was not only a tool of his profession but an old and trusted friend. Albert turned around his chair to face them.

"What are you doing here!" he demanded to know, filtered through his veins and showed upon his face.

But Albert Arthur Allen in his sudden rage saw only a group of intruders as he stared around the room. In the heat of the moment, it never occurred to him that the men—all eight of them—were identical in appearance, each wearing the same black clothing that looked as though it were almost painted on. It was the face that echoed on each one of them that startled me—the same face that I had seen on the man in the restaurant who could have been—so close was the resemblance—an older brother to me. None of the men answered Albert Allen. It was as though he were incidental to why they were there. Instead, one of them held up his arm and stopped time. I felt the quantum effect as it rippled through me. I tried to fight against it—and failed! When time resumed and I could think again, all of them were gone. But there was something else. But there was something else. A double of me had been pulled out of me while time had been stopped. *How was that even possible?* I wondered afterward. *And who were those men?*

The fifty-seven-year-old man stared this way and that around the room, confused as to what had just happened. He glanced down at his broken camera and then turned to me.

"Are you all right?" he asked with an abundance of concern.

"Yes," I replied, looking from him to his shattered camera. "I supposed I should get dressed."

Before he could reply, though, I went over to where it was and stared down at it.

"I know how much it meant to you," I said in a consoling voice.

"It is, after all, just a thing," he replied, squatting down to examine the damage, "but I have its brother in the back room. It has not seen so much use but it will do until I get this one repaired—if it *can* be repaired." He paused for just a moment, then looked up at me. "Can you come by again tomorrow?" he asked. "I need to be with my family for a bit."

"Of course," I said.

He just sat there, staring down at the wreckage, his hands clenched into loose fists out of the shock of it all, remaining almost like a statue, as I retreated to the dressing room. "My wife makes delicious lasagna," he called out as I was dressing. "Perhaps you would like to come over sometime and have dinner with us. I have told her that you are my favorite model."

"I'd like that," I replied.

"And you must bring Margaret," he added. "I'm sure she would get along well with Edward. He's grown into a fine, handsome boy, you know."

I emerged dressed into the studio. "I'll see you back here tomorrow morning. You take care. I'm sure your camera can be mended."

I walked over to him, kissed him on the cheek, and then left. It was time for me to pick up Margaret from school. The problem was that I got there only to learn that she was already gone.

"Margaret?" I called out once inside.

Generally, she was waiting for me outside near the entrance. I looked both ways down the halls adjacent to the entrance. "Margaret?" I shouted in each direction. Children and teachers passed me as I pushed my way to the principal's office. I went to the front desk where a middle-aged woman sat. "I'm looking for my daughter," I said. "Margaret Fletcher. She's in second grade. Mrs. Halston's class."

It was at that moment that another woman walked into the office. "Is everything all right with Margaret?" she asked. "She such a sweet girl."

"And you are?" I asked in return.

"Miss Grady," she replied. "I'm Mrs. Halston's teacher's aide. But I don't understand. I saw you take Margaret with you when school let out not ten minutes ago." She sized me up with a strange look on her face. "Though you were dressed differently as I recall," she went on. "Did something happen? Did you and Margaret get separated? I can get security if you like."

My thoughts raced back to when the men had stopped time and realized what must have happened. "No," I said shaking my head. "That won't be necessary. I have a twin sister. It must have been her who picked Margaret up. I didn't know if I was going to be tied up at work. I should have called her. Margaret's probably already back at home. I'm sorry for the confusion." I smiled at her. "It's so nice to finally meet you. Margaret has only had the nicest things to say about you and Mrs. Halston. Anyway, thank you for your concern."

Miss Grady cast me a congenial look and then turned as one of Margaret's classmates caught her attention.

"Excuse me," she said and rushed off. "Gladys!" she called out, "I need to speak with you about your behavior in class today!"

Her exit gave me the opportunity to leave unnoticed. I made my way back to my car, got in, and then stared blankly out through the windshield wondering what to do. I'd wondered if—hoped that—the other version of me had not been in the control of the men.

As I was sitting there I had mental images of Margaret already at home in her room, playing with her doll. But I was also filled with anxiety. Nothing like this had ever happened before—nothing even close. I started the car and hightailed it back home—or tried to. As it seemed as though the trip would never end, I drove the car onto a side street and, after assuring myself that no one was around, I phased both myself and the car back home. But when I got out of the car and tried to go in the house, there was a quantum barrier surrounding it.

"Hey!" I called out. "Let me in!"

Then I saw her or, rather, me—the one that had been pulled *from* me. She looked at me and half smiled.

"I didn't mean to worry you," she said. "Sorry." Her eyes glowed red for just a moment and she smiled. "Come on in.".

As I walked inside, the other merged into me and I understood everything. When the men in black had somehow pulled a version of me out of me, another had pulled out of that one and instantly phased from the room. Concerned that they might go after Margaret next, she phased to the school, got her out of class, and then phased home with her, and placed a barrier around the house against any and all intruders. It was then that Margaret, having heard my voice, came out of her room.

"Is someone here?" she asked.

"No, Sweetheart," I told her, "just me—just talking to myself."

"Is supper almost ready?" she asked. "I'm hungry!"

"Almost," I replied. "I'm making salad and chicken with Alfredo sauce, and then for dessert, waffles with blueberries and strawberries and raspberries and kiwi."

"What's kiwi?" she asked.

"A delicious fruit," I told her. "And I had to phase to New Zealand to get it."

"Where's that?" she asked.

"All the way on the other side of the world," I replied, "where everyone is upside-down."

"Noooo!" she laughed.

"It's true," I said. "But if you were to ask them, they'd tell you that it's us who are hanging onto the ground by our feet, ready to fall up into the sky."

"That's silly," she replied. "How can anyone fall up?"

"Well," I said, "It's a thing called gravity that holds us down."

"How does it do that?" she asked.

"You know how our vacuum cleaner sucks things up?" I asked.

"Sort of," she replied.

"Well," I said, "it's kind of like that, only imagine that the vacuum cleaner is the Earth and everyone on it is the dust getting sucked in. Do you understand?"

Margaret shook her head. "Not really," she replied, "but I have a question."

"What's that?" I asked.

"Why are you wearing two sets of clothes?" she asked back.

I looked down at myself and realized that indeed I was.

"Did you become Quantum Girl again?" she asked.

"I guess I did," I replied. "I guess I'd better go to my bedroom and change."

"You know something?" Margaret said.

"Yes, Sweetheart?" I replied.

"It's really confusing sometimes," she said with a huge sigh, "being the daughter of Quantum Girl. It can be very zasperating, especially the phasing—one minute here, one minute there—but I kind of like it. It's just that…" and she paused.

"Just what?" I asked.

"That I can't tell anyone," she replied.

"You have to remember," I said, "but it's a special secret just between you and me."

"I know," she replied, "it's just zasperating, that's all. But I s'pose It's for the best. Besides, if I told any of the other kids, they'd all just think I'm a liar."

"Oh," I said, "we would never want that!"

"Or crazy," she said.

"You go wash up for supper," I said, "and I'll go get out of at least some of these clothes."

As I started toward my bedroom, Margaret asked, "Mommy?"

"Yes, Fair Margaret?" I replied.

"Am I ever going to get to be a Quantum Girl?" she asked.

"You never can tell what the future holds?" I replied. "But I do know what the future has in store for us right now?"

"What's that?" she asked.

"Chicken Alfredo and waffles," I answered. "Now, go wash up."

"Yes, Mommy," she replied. "I love you, Mommy."

"I love you, too, Fair Margaret," I said back and then went to my room to change.

I undressed but for one set of bra, slip, and panties. I'd taken off the garter belts and stockings as well. How strange it had first seemed to me that women had willingly worn all of this—and some had even worn a girdle—but having lived back then for so many years I'd gotten used to it. The garter belts were a bit of a hassle but it would be decades before there would be pantyhose to wear. Men still wore hats—either homburgs or fedoras—as did most women, though the women's hats ran the spectrum of styles and colors, some with feathers, some without, some sporting spotted black net veils, something which Marlene Dietrick was notorious for.

Anyway, once I had stripped down, I sat down at my dressing table and stared at my reflection in the mirror. There was still another one of me out there, but where I could generally sense one of my duplicate's thoughts, there was just dead air so to speak. There were only three explanations: one, that there was a quantum barrier shielding her thoughts; two, that she had been taken to a different time; or three, that whoever had taken her had killed her. The latter was unlikely, as I would have felt weakened by her demise but the first two were viable explanations, especially in that her abductors had demonstrated quantum abilities. My train of thought was broken by Margaret calling out from the living room, "Mommy, I'm really hungry!"

"Coming, I'm coming!" I called back.

Not wanting to get dressed again. I threw on a silk robe and some slippers and headed to the kitchen. Margaret was already at her place at the table. I served her her dinner and then my own and then sat down facing her.

"I was reading one of the comic books you bought me," she said, "and I was wondering. Superman saves people from bad guys. What does Quantum Girl do? I mean, you're just as powerful."

"I saved you," I replied, "from bad guys."

"But I've never seen any bad guys," she said. "At least not

here."

"That's because I'm very effective at what I do," I told her.

"What does effective mean?" she asked.

"It means," I replied, "that I'm very good at keeping the bad guys away from you."

"Mommy?" She said.

"Yes, Fair Margaret?" I said back.

"Why are there bad guys?" she asked.

"Probably because they didn't have mothers who loved them," I replied.

"Peter Pan didn't have a mother," she said, "but he wasn't a bad guy."

"Peter Pan is just a story," I said. "Now, finish your dinner and get into your pajamas and I'll tell you the story of Charlie and the Chocolate Factory."

"Is that another story from the future?" she asked.

"Yes, it is," I replied.

"Because you've been there," she said.

"Because I've been there," I replied.

"Before you met Daddy," she said.

"Before I ever met your Daddy," I told her, "and before I ever met *you*."

CHAPTER XXI

Quantum Girl Red
(the abducted one)
(Urth, 2038)

I had been pulled naked out of my naked self by one of the men who had phased into the studio. They merged together as we crossed into the quantum fabric and then flew out, over a planet that resembled the Earth but wasn't. It was called Urth, a blurred carbon copy of my world that existed in a different reality. He did not just bring me there through space, however, but through time as well— to what would have been my future by thirteen years—ninety-five years from where I had been in the past.

From the upper atmosphere, phased us to a penthouse apartment in Manhattan and then phased tennis outfits on us both.

"Where are we?" I demanded to know. "Who are you and what do you want from me?"

The man smiled as he went over to the bar and poured himself a drink. "Want one?" he asked.

"No!" I exclaimed. "I want to know why you brought me here!"

"In good time," he replied as he downed the Scotch from the glass in his hand. "My name's Peyton, by the way. Peyton Herron."

"*My* name!" I said back to him.

"Then that's something we have in common," he replied. "I must say, though, you do have a great figure—better than I remember. I actually hated covering it up with the tennis outfit but the sport is so difficult to play in the nude, unlike volleyball, especially for men. The ball can be positively lethal if it lands improperly, and then what would happen to all the children yet to be conceived?"

"You haven't answered my questions," I said with anger in my voice.

"You're quite a bit more testy than you used to be," he replied.

"We've never met before," I said, "unless you mean when you glared at me in the diner."

"The diner?" he said, shaking his head. "I wouldn't describe that as a meeting. I actually was about to offer to join you for dinner when you phased off with that lovely daughter of yours. No, I was talking about years before when the two of us were—how shall I put it—rather intimate with each other."

"I've never been *intimate* with you!" I snapped back. "Nor would I ever be!"

"Oh, but you did," he replied, "And you will be—rather soon I should hope. Pretty little thing, Margaret. We wouldn't want anything to happen to her, would we? As I understand, she's your maternal grandmother. That would mean, if she were to somehow be killed before giving birth to your mother, then your mother and you and that ravishing sister of yours would all cease to exist."

"You're a monster!" I yelled at him.

"One might say the same of you," he replied.

"You don't know me!" I said. "I always try to do the right thing!"

"Yes, you do," he replied, "Only trying and doing are two different undertakings."

"What are you talking about?" I asked.

"I'm talking about," he replied, "a shy, impressionable young boy whose first love and sexual experience was with the female version of himself. Unfortunately, although she must have thought of it as pity sex, he fell in love with her, and when she left his reality—all too abruptly, I might add—he never was able to put her out of his mind. Imagine if you will, someone offering you one taste of chocolate and then you sadly learn that you can never have anymore. That's how it was with you. The boy tried being with other girls but it was never the same. There was no recovering from that first experience. There was no way he could ever forget her—

the smiles she cast at him, the softness of her touch, the way he fitted into her so perfectly while they were making love. And then she was gone." He stared at me. "Do you have any idea how many years it took me to find you again—how many realities I had to cross? But here you are and here I am and, by the gods, I am not going to lose you a second time!" He paused and then continued. "I know you've been trying to phase from here but you can't. I set up a barrier around you."

"If you truly love me," I said, "you'll let me go. Besides, I need to get back to Margaret. If she dies on her own then, as you've said, I'll cease to exist and then you'll have nothing."

"Not true," he replied, "because there's still one of you back in your reality to take care of her. Tell you what," he said, picking up a tennis racket and a pink tennis ball. "I propose a tennis match. If you win, I let you go. If I win, you stay with me for good. Are you up to the challenge?"

"If I win I can go back home?" I asked.

"I swear upon my father's future grave," he replied.

He tossed me a racket and then he phased us up to the building's rooftop court. Once there, he bounced the ball he had in his hand over to me.

"I'll give you the advantage of first serve," he said.

I aimed and served. The match went on at quantum speed and took only a minute. I lost. I wound up winning the second match, though, and felt slightly relieved when I did. It went from fifteen-love to fifteen-all to thirty-fifteen to forty-fifteen to game, with him winning. There were six games total. We were on the sixth. I had won two. He had won three. This game would decide it all. It was thirty-love. I thought I had a real chance but then he scored two more points. Thirty-thirty. Then he scored two more and it was over—at least it was for me—game, set, and match.

CHAPTER XXII

Quantum Girl Black
(Date Unknown)

I awoke naked, standing in a pitch-dark room, pinned against a form-fitting recess that was cold against my skin. Concerned about both my whereabouts and how I got to wherever it was that I had found myself, with my last memory being in my bedroom asleep, I phased into Quantum Girl. But, from recent history, there should have been a purple glow, there was none—neither purple nor any other color. Regardless, having quantum vision, I could see in absolute darkness—cave darkness. Having said that, I stepped out of the form that I was in which turned out to be in the center of a room that had neither windows nor doors and with walls that described a twelve-foot diameter circle. Other than the form that I had been placed up against, there was nothing else in the room. I tried unsuccessfully to phase back home and then walked around the wall searching for some flaw in its design, only to find none. It was then that I discovered that I had a new power. I found that I was able to phase *through* the wall and literally walk out of the room. But what I discovered on the other side was the vacuum of outer space and that my prison was nothing more than a hollow metal sphere.

In interstellar space there is no air—no way to breathe—but the molecules that make it up can be created. Within every vacuum in the universe, dark matter exists—unpaired quarks and gluons that do not interact with matter. But I could change them. I could make them bond and so I did—all around me—and transmute them into breathable air—warm air—and surround them with a quantum force field to hold them in place. Once that much had been accomplished, I looked around. The universe is virtually endless—roughly ninety-three billion light years in diameter if one could find dead center with more than two trillion galaxies, each with hundreds of billions of stars, and each of them with its own system of asteroids, comets, and planets. Finding a needle in a haystack would have been child's play compared to finding my way back to Earth. I had no idea where I was or even which galaxy I was in.

As I hung in outer space, I looked down at what had been my prison. The outer surface was composed of neutronium. Thinking back, the original Peyton had said that the god-stones had been enclosed in a neutronium sphere, though far smaller. According to her, they served as a power source, not only for Rendenaaar but for the entire Gaaalthaaaran empire. And yet, there I had been in the center of this machine, connected in some way. Had I somehow been wired into that thing as a new source of limitless power? I wondered. But by whom and for what? Important as the questions were, my immediate concern was getting back to Earth.

I looked around at the obdurate sky. The universe was black in every direction with sprinkles of light from galaxies and nebulae and stars that each challenged the concept of nonexistence. Much of the light was billions of years old, remnants of what once was. My quantum vision, though, could bridge the length of time and see all that shone and everything that was reflected on as it was in the here and now. The sheer vastness of it all, though, was staggering and nothing looked familiar regardless of which direction I chose to look.

Twenty-seven light years away, I saw a planet with continents and oceans and carbon-based life but no civilization that I could discern. Still, as I needed a place to rest and think things out, I phased there, materializing in the midst of a verdant area with trees that were laden with hopefully edible fruit. The world revolved around a binary star system—one blue, the other green—that played host to twelve planets, this being one of them. There were two moons overhead, night having fallen where I was, although the light from the green companion star could still be seen at the edge of the of horizon, its light piercing upward, giving the sky an eerie, almost paranormal, look. Not far off from where I stood, I could hear a waterfall. The water rushed from a cliff above, dropping two hundred feet into the river it fed. Behind it, halfway down the descent, my quantum vision could make out through the falling water, a small cave that I decided would make a perfect place for me to rest and measure my thoughts. I phased there, thinking that there I would find a quiet spot, broken only by the sound of the water that endlessly caressed its mouth—but I was wrong.

Fate is not a cruel mistress but a curious one, for there at the heart of this small pockmark in the cliff stood a creature not so different from myself. She was a curious thing, dressed in metallic rags with dirt on her despite the preponderance of millions of gallons of water a second just outside. She had dark hair and violet eyes. The grim hid much of her face, but, regardless it was not hard to tell that she was not quite human—neither in face nor in form. Two pairs of breasts spanned the breadth of her chest—one just below the other, arranged (if that is the right word) so that the upper pair draped upon the lower. Neither was really hidden. I suppose that modesty is not a priority when one lives in isolation. Her ears were pointed, but it was the tail—a tail tipped with fur—that nailed shut the coffin of doubt that hers was a totally different species. Looking at her, she reminded me of what the other Peyton had related about the inhabitants of Rendenaaar so many universes in the past. But how on earth could that be? I laughed to myself at the irony of the expression. Of all in existence, wherever the Earth was, it was nowhere near here.

The girl, if I may call her that, appeared frightened by my presence. I held out my hands as a gesture that I meant to do her no harm, realizing at last that it might have been my costume that frightened her. I phased it off and turned back into my Peyton self. She stared at me curiously, circling me, never taking her eyes off me for a second. She stopped, though, when she was fully behind me, slowly approached, then slid her hand down my dress from the small of my back to the extent of my derriere. Then she walked around to face me, staring, speaking words that were indecipherable to me, though strangely, I could hear her thoughts.

What manner of being are you? she questioned. *Where is your yaaargh? Are you an outcast? Was it excised for insurrection?*

It was then that she noticed something else. Cautiously, she lifted her left arm and pulled back the hair that covered my right ear. Upon seeing it, she jumped back a step. If that were not enough of a shock, her eyes bent downward to my breasts. Even through the cloth of my dress, she could see that mine were not the same as hers. As though in a heat of emotion, she reached toward me and tried to grab hold of what she thought was my dress, not realizing that it was only an illusion. She grabbed at it several times but her hand just went through it, grasping only empty air. Finally, she seemed to grasp the fact that there really was no dress. Instead, her hand went up to my breasts and felt them up and down through the illusion of cloth to assure herself that I only had one pair and not two. She looked at me bewildered, her eyes traveling up and down my form. I shook my head to myself and then just phased off the *clothing*, leaving myself totally nude. At first, she just stared at my breasts but after half a moment, her eyes drifted down to my vag. Mind you, I had never seen a naked inhabitant from Rendenaaar but it was my understanding that their reproductive system was through their tail, so I assumed that what she saw was new to her. Cautiously, she reached out with her left hand, at last making contact with the line of my sex. She ran her fingers up it and then stared at it bewildered. Then she squatted down. Her other hand came up and she spread it apart just a bit. It was when her fingers tried to enter it that I slapped her hands down.

"That's quite enough," I said.

She gave a start, stood up, curiously sniffed the air several times, brought up one of her hands to sniff her fingers, and then looked me in the eye as though uncertain what to make of it all.

"There are certain lady parts," I said, "that are considered private baring intimacy between two people, and you and I have barely met."

She shook her head as an indication of her not understanding anything that I had just said, so I projected the meaning of the words into her mind. It seemed that I could do that as well.

She smiled at first and then outright laughed. Her voice was strange and her words in her language even stranger.

You are an off-worlder, her thoughts said. *Which planet are you from? I have never seen a species such as yours. Or are you perhaps a mutant? I would not put it past our scientists to do such a thing.*

No, I voiced into her head. *Such anatomy is natural to my kind. I am from a planet called Earth.*

I am from Pragthaaar, her thoughts voiced back even over her alien words. *It is an outpost of the Gaaalthaaaran Empire. I was marooned on this world when the god-stones became mute.*

How long have you been here? I asked.

Long enough for me to want to leave, she replied. *It is a lonely, harsh existence here. I was the only survivor of a crew with a compliment of more than two hundred. My name is Laaadra-Taaagh.*

Peyton Herron, I thought back at her. I think she had realized by then that our communication was by telepathy as she became silent and her thoughts more focused. *But if Rendenaaar exists here, then I'm no longer in my universe,* my thoughts voiced out. *Have you heard of someone named Khattaaara?* I asked.

I would be a fool if I did not, she replied. *Princess Khattaaara is heir to the royal throne.*

I thought it best not to reveal that I was her reincarnation, especially not knowing her loyalties at that time. My ability to read minds at that point was not yet fully honed.

Laaadra-Taaagh stared at me, smiled, and shook her head. *I fear*

148

that I have damaged your apparel, she thought at me. *For that I am sorry.*

No need to be, I replied and phased back to into my costume sans the cowl. *It is all simply an illusion.*

How are you able to transform yourself thus? she asked.

Where I am from, I replied, *I am also known as Quantum Girl and I have many powers.*

Do you have perchance, she asked, *the means to create a starship to take us from this godsforsaken world?*

Such is not necessary to take us away from here, I replied, *but I need to know where to go.*

Unfortunately, she lamented, *our guidance system was destroyed in the crash.*

Alas, I find myself marooned here with you. But we can discuss it later. For the moment I need to rest as I have neither eaten nor slept in some time.

Then follow me to my home, her thoughts spoke into my head, *and I will provide both sustenance and a bed on which you may rest.*

She led me out of the cave and across a narrow path that made its way to the top of the cliff where flowed the river that fed the waterfall. Night had already fallen by the time we got there. The raging waters glistened, reflecting the light from three moons that hung bright in the purple sky. The wreckage of her ship was not far from where we had marked the end of our ascent. The downed vessel loomed large and foreboding against the distant horizon, perhaps a thousand meters in length, half as wide, and as tall as a five-story building. Regrettably, as it turned out, it was the wreckage of an interstellar vehicle that had been built for transportation and not for comfort. And to think that of all the crew that must have manned it, she alone was the only one to have survived.

We entered through a hatch that opened near the ground. She climbed in first and then I followed. Panels of light lit up the interior. Metal pipes lined metal walls. Water dripped down almost everywhere through cracks in the hull where the ship had been wrenched apart so violently, taking with it all hands that had been on board but one.

Her room was somewhat small with a steel door that gave me the impression that its original purpose was for something other than as a sleeping quarters. The entire floor, though, was covered in a forcefield that served as a mattress.

You may take repose here, she said, *and I will bring you some food.*

Where will you sleep, I asked.

Here, she replied and then added, *Do not worry. I will not kill you in your unconscious state. And I expect the same from you.*

I do not kill, I told her. *It is the commandment of my god. "Thou shalt not kill."*

Which god is that? She asked.

The god of Israel, I replied. It seemed, though, that the name Israel was not understandable to her through telepathy.

Our people, she said, *have many gods. Mine is called Urthaaag who is the god of war. I am a soldier, trained to be a soldier from when I was a child.* And then she left.

Well, I thought to myself, *I am now stranded in another universe, the one so far from mine that, as the other Peyton had once said[8], that there were more between ours and this than there are grains of sand in all the deserts and all the beaches on Earth.* And yet there I was, brought back to that same infinity where my past incarnation had lived and breathed and committed genocide on a galactic if not intergalactic scale. But, for the moment, I was worn out—at least emotionally—and quite hungry. Laaadra-Taaagh brought me some indigenous sweet fruit which I ate with a ravenous appetite that sated my hunger and quenched my thirst. There was also a bit of meat apparently from a deer-like creature whose species

---

[8] The one who had saved the universe from collapsing and not the one who had sacrificed herself for me.

frequented the forest nearby and which tasted like salted pork. Once my stomach had been filled, the weariness of the day crept over me, and so I laid down on the virtual bed and soon fell fast into dreams.

In my dream—or, rather, nightmare—I was Khattaaara. I stood on a world with a giant red star, so large that it filled up half of the sky. At my feet and all around me as far as the eye could see lay the bodies of what must have been the inhabitants of this planet, red-skinned beings, humanoid in form but with what looked like gills for ears, a fin-like projection that ran from their foreheads back to their necks and with unusually long delicate fingers—three of them—on each hand. I say *had* because they were all dead. There were children among them and infants as well. I surveyed the landscape of alien carnage without the slightest vestige of concern. Then, suddenly, I felt two arms wrap around me but I experienced neither shock nor fear—rather, a sense of warmth and sexual excitement coursed through my veins.

"What must I do with thee," a male voice said in a language much like Laaadra-Taaagh had spoken—the same guttural sounds, the same almost reptilian hiss to his words, which, oddly enough, I could understand. "Thou hast killed every one of them." His hands cupped my lower breasts, clenching my nipples with the sides of his fingers causing them to swell in response.

"Because," I said, "they refused to worship me—as thou dost!" I tilted my head back to fall against the curve of his neck. "Why must life be so hard?" I sighed.

"Pity them for pity's sake," he replied as his *yaaargh* intertwined with mine.

"How many worlds does this make?" I asked him.

"Far too many to dwell upon," he replied. "Perhaps next time we should give them a chance to realize the majesty within you."

"I have little patience," I said, "as thou well knowest."

"I made thee a goddess," he replied. "Gods need to show mercy sometimes."

"And who would show mercy to me?" I asked.

"I would," he replied, "always and ever."

It was then that he plunged his *yaaargh* into mine. I felt my mind grow numb as the pleasure of it saturated my brain.

"My dearest Khattaaara," he said when he had at last withdrawn his *yaaargh* from mine, "if only thou wouldst place love over the hatred that comes from thy quest for power."

"My dearest Dhraaal," I replied, "if only words were wishes."

And then I woke up to find Laaadra-Taaagh beside me, her back toward me, me fast asleep, the end of her *yaaargh* furring at my face, which is probably what had awakened me. Gently, I moved it off of me, turned my back to her, and drifted off again. If there were more such dreams I did not and do not remember them.

CHAPTER XXIII

Quantum Girl Orange
(September 9. 1951)

Death is not what the pious believe it to be. As I died, there was indeed a white light but it was not a gateway to Heaven. It was the dying gasps of the cells in my brain as they flickered out one by one. There were no angels that came to welcome me to some glorious kingdom. There was just the release from the pain of the water having filled my lungs. The struggle to exist came to an end. My body went limp, and then everything around me went dark.

I don't know how long it was or how it happened or why but it seemed that my demise had reactivated the god-stone in my head. The stone regenerated my cells and brought me back to life. My eyes, still open, saw the cloth of the bag that scraped against my face but this time it was different. I could see the warps and wefts of the linen fabric and, when I focused really hard, the molecules of which they were comprised. The ocean water had saturated and filled the bag. I could taste the briny liquid that had drowned my mouth after it had filtered through the cotton duck. I phased out of the bag and then stared back at what had been the instrument of the murder that had been committed upon me. It was night in the world above and so the water around me flowed darkly with its currents, but being Quantum Girl once again, I could see everything around me as though it were the brightest day.

My heart nearly stopped, though, as I caught glimpse of the others along the bottom in the sand. There had been reports of several girls gone missing over the last several years but there they were, each in their own linen chrysalis—never to emerge—the promise of butterflies broken, never to spread their wings. My X-ray projection revealed their various states of decomposition. I was no forensic scientist but I could tell that one had been there for what must have been years, as little was left other than her bones and, yes, I could tell that all of them were or had been girls. One was still dressed in a cheerleading outfit from our school—desiccated flesh, sockets without eyes, long blonde hair that made mockery of the life that had once caressed it with a brush—drowned souls, each of them, buried without even a prayer in a watery grave. There were three in total. I phased to the surface leaving my unfortunate companions behind. I stood dripping on the cliffside from which I had been pushed. I coughed out the water in my lungs in an explosion of salty liquid that spewed out into the air ten feet or more and then fell back into the ocean like forgotten rain. I would call the police later—perhaps in the morning—but for the moment, I both wanted and needed to get home. It was late and Margaret's mother would be worried and with good cause.

It was well past midnight when I phased just outside the front door to the house and then went in. There was a police car outside with its Mars light still flashing. Inside, in the living room, were two uniformed officers standing with Margaret's mom. Seeing me, her face went white. She rushed to me and hugged me.

"Oh, my God," she wept. "I didn't know where you were." She let go of me and took a few steps back. She stared at me, my hair and clothes that were both still wet. "What happened to you?" she asked.

"Coach Nichols," I said. "She tried to murder me."

"Coach Nichols?" she repeated. "Your cheer instructor?"

I nodded.

"How?" she asked. "Why?"

And so I told them what had happened, ashamed of what had gone on between me and the coach—Tara. When I got to the part about how I had been rolled off the cliff, how it had felt, and how I had noticed the three other bags, she sank into a chair. I had to lie about how I had escaped, of course. Somehow, I said, I had gotten my hands free and had managed to push off the knot at the top of the bag, then swim to the surface, and make my way back home on foot.

One of the cops asked if I could take them back to where it all happened.

"I think so," I replied, "but if you don't mind, I'd like to change into some dry clothes."

"And get some supper in you," Margaret's mom insisted. She turned to the officers. "You don't mind waiting, do you?"

Both of them shook their heads. "We can come back in an hour if it's all right. I know it's late but…"

"I understand," Margaret's mom interrupted. "She won't be going to school tomorrow and definitely not until you arrest that monster. To think that there'd be another Ted Bundy teaching at her school!"

"Who's that?" the other cop asked.

Margaret's mom suddenly looked flustered. "Oh," she said, "some serial killer I heard of years ago."

"What's a serial killer?" the first cop asked.

"Someone who murders for the hell of it," she replied.

I stared at her more closely than I had ever done. She couldn't have known about Ted Bundy's killing spree. In 1951, Ted Bundy would have been a small child and the term *serial killer* hadn't been coined until the 1970s as I recalled. She was from the future just like me. Looking closer I realized she *was* me only older. But how would I tell her that my mind had somehow supplanted Grandma Margaret's? For the moment, I decided, I would keep that fact to myself.

After I had showered and changed into dry clothes and then gotten some food in my stomach, Margaret's mom (who was older me) and I got into our car with the patrol car just behind. I guided us to the cliff that I had been thrown over. As we stood at the edge, with me being held in older me's arms to prevent me from falling, I pointed down at the ocean below.

"The other bodies are down there," I said against the updraft of

155

wind that challenged us. "There were at least three of them, all in cloth bags like the one I was in."

"We'll get a dive team here in the morning," one of the cops said.

"Do you need us anymore," older me asked.

"Not for now," he replied, "but she'll need to come down to the station, maybe in the afternoon. We'll need to take a statement."

"We'll be there," she replied. Then she took hold of my hand. "Come on, Margaret," she said "Let's you and I go home."

The drive back was met with silence. I watched her as we drove. It seemed that her mind was a million miles away. *How had it come about that she'd become Margaret's mother?* I wondered. *Margaret was our grandmother. And how far back in time had she gone for it to have occurred?*

At long last, we pulled into the driveway. I was the first to get out of the car. She just sat there, engine running, staring off into the night. I walked around the car and knocked on the window. She turned her head and looked at me.

"Come on, Mom," I said through the glass. "Let's go inside."

I took her hand, helped her out, and then guided her into the house. It seemed as though her heart had been taken from her. I brought her to the sofa and urged her down onto it and then knelt down facing her.

"I'm all right," I told her. "I just got a little wet is all."

I smiled and took her hands in mine.

"You could have died," she said, "with all those other girls. I don't think I could have gone on if that had happened."

"But it didn't," I insisted. "I'm fine and soon that horrible woman will be behind bars."

She stared into my eyes. "You don't know how much I love you," she replied.

"Of course, I do," I said. "And tomorrow we'll go to the police station and I'll give my statement and then we can put it all behind us."

The next morning, a team of four divers recovered the bodies of six girls. Three had drifted several hundred feet from where I had found myself. Two had been killed from blunt force trauma to the head while the other four had drowned. The victims were later identified as Rachel Sparrow, Colleen McGuire, Donna Gibbs, Amy Penrose, Moira Thatcher, and Linda Spire. All had been students at Braxton. Two had been cheerleaders. All four had Tara Nichols as their gym instructor. Their deaths spanned over the past fifteen years. All of them were assumed to have been runaways. In fact, each of them had left a note to that effect, which forensics, given recent circumstances, determined to have been forged. Two days later, four police cars showed up at the school. Coach Nichols was taken away in handcuffs to the Lincoln Heights Jail. On Monday, November 27, 1951, trial began at the Criminal Courts Building in downtown Los Angeles. The proceedings lasted eleven days with the jury deliberating for just under five hours. The verdict was guilty on all six counts of first-degree murder, one count of attempted murder, one count of contributory manslaughter—that was because of Babs—and, per the defendant's testimony, fifty-four counts of aggravated child molestation, all of which culminated in the defendant being sentenced to death. The subsequent appeal that was filed by her attorney was denied. On Monday, January 5, 1952, Tara Nichols, age thirty-seven, was placed in the gas chamber at San Quentin Prison where her execution was carried out. Los Angeles County Sheriff, Eugene W. Biscailuz and twelve men and women watched as the former gym coach was led in tears into the green steel chamber, begging for mercy. Strapped to her chair in the bathysphere-like compartment, cyanide gas was released. The witnesses observed convulsions in the condemned that finally stopped from the heart attack that had been caused. Half an hour later, electric fans sucked out the lethal atmosphere, whereupon two orderlies, wearing gas masks and gloves entered the chamber to make certain that death had occurred. Neither Margaret's mother—older me —nor I nor any of the victims' parents were allowed to be present, but this is what we were told after it was done.

It was an emotional time for all involved but at least it gave closure to the murdered girls' parents. Shortly after the bodies had been recovered and the county coroner had completed the autopsies, six funerals were held and there was a memorial service at the school. Some of the students stood in disbelief. Some cried for the sake of the lives that had been lost. Megan Charles and Suzie Dubois, two of the other cheerleaders on Margaret's squad, sat on either side of me, each taking one of my hands throughout the ceremony. It was a half day at school because of it. When we were let out, Megan, Suzie, and Jennifer insisted that we all go to one of the malt shops the kids hung out at. Older me had already arrived to pick me up, but I told her that I'd been invited to go with the girls for just a bit. All of them came with me to the car.

"She'll be in good hands, Mrs. Fletcher," Megan said.

"Would it be all right if you picked me up in an hour at the malt shop?" I asked.

Older me smiled. "Of course," she said. "I think it'll do you good." Then she drove off.

"Your mom's really neat," Jennifer said.

"Yes," I agreed, "she really is."

At the malt shop, each of us had burgers, French fries, and malted milkshakes. All three of the girls admitted that Coach Nichols had come on to them but that they had rebuffed her advances.

"What about you?" Suzie asked.

"She came onto me, too," I replied.

"And?" Megan asked.

"And what?" I asked back.

"Did you and her ever, you know?" she asked, pressing the question.

I just shrugged.

"No way!" said Jennifer in a low voice.

"That's enough!" commanded Suzie. "You know what happened to Babs." Then she turned to me. "It's all right," she said. "It won't go any farther than this table. Isn't that right?" and she glared at the two other girls who nodded. "We're here for you. Anytime you need to talk, we're here."

True to their word, none of them ever said anything to anyone. Older me picked me up afterward.

"How did it go?" she asked after I got in the car.

"Fine," I said. That was all I said. It was a quiet drive home.

When we got back, I excused myself and went to my bedroom to lie down. Quantum Girl or not, it had been a long event-filled day.

CHAPTER XXIV

Quantum Girl Yellow
(A.D. 1,219,064,261)

It was the question of all questions—could I control the other god-stones through mine? I decided to divide into five of myself and then merge simultaneously into each of the sleeping versions of me. This was something I had never attempted before. Beyond the need to try and rejuvenate the dying sun, there were questions that I wanted answered, such as how it had come about that I had split into six Quantum Girls and why each of me had a different colored god-stone in my head. I myself—meaning this version of me—had no recollection of when I had fallen into that eternal slumber. Nor could I fathom how any of me was able to have survived for so long. If the god-stones were able to make us live forever, why then were all of us—or all of me—unconscious for more than a billion years? Immortality is of no use if consciousness does not go with it hand in hand.

When I did merge, though, it wasn't as I had expected. I had thought that *my* mind would simply combine with theirs but that's not what happened. I awoke in a strange dimension in outer space only it wasn't space that I found myself in. Everything was liquid. I could see galaxies and planets and stars, but it was as though I were in an infinitely large fishbowl. And then I realized it wasn't just the one of me staring at all of this but all six, each radiating a different color. I tried to ask the others if they knew where we were but we all uttered the exact same words at the exact same time, as though we were speaking from the same mind which, as it turned out, we were. But then something worse happened. We all began to drown, swallowing and breathing globs on the spacetime of which this universe was comprised.

Suddenly, simultaneously, each of us was enveloped in bubbles of air. Each of us, as though in syncopation, spat out the water that had gotten into our lungs and then caught our breaths. Then the bubbles were pulled together and then merged into one, and all of us were pulled together and merged into one. Staring down at my hands, I watched as I radiated a rainbow of colors. But there was more to it than that. I was growing younger by the second until I was a fetus in my mother's womb in an amniotic sack. There was another fetus next to me in an amniotic sack of her, the two of us head to tail with her facing down. The other—soon to be named Ophelia—began to push away from me. It was odd that I could hear our mother's heartbeat and hear the rush of the blood as it flowed through her veins. A moment later, I could hear her scream as my sister, about to be born, began to push her way through the birth canal. When she was gone and I was alone I felt myself being turned around and then, like my sister, forced out from the womb. I know now why it is that babies cry just after they're born. The act of birth is a painful ordeal for the infant as well. Having one's still soft head being forced through an opening not quite large enough for the task is like having an elephant sit on your face. There is pressure from that. Your umbilical line is cut. You now have to use your lungs for the very first time. The warmth of your mother's womb is gone and your skin is suddenly cold. You've gone from a comfortable ninety-eight point six degrees to seventy-two with bright lights glaring all around you and noises of what you will later learn are people, their voices droning in your ears with sounds you cannot understand.

And then it all reversed—back into the womb—this time drowning in the amniotic fluid only to wake up in the liquid of that strange outer space. Once more we were in separate bubbles of air that began to collapse or, perhaps, deflate is a better word. Each one of me was face to face against each other, gasping for air as the membranes of the bubbles began pressing against our faces. We watched each other in horror. We watched each other suffocate. We phased a bubble of atmosphere around us, tearing away the sticky membranes that clung to our faces and refused to let go. And then we watched as a liquid star exploded, enveloping the protective sphere we were in. There was intense light and heat and the pain of being boiled alive in that liquid space until the hurt was too much and we all in one same instant passed out with the welcome beckoning of impending death.

I had no conception of how much time had passed, but I awakened to find myself lying on the floor in each of the five rooms. As I climbed wearily to my feet, each of me wondered if what I had just experienced held some hidden meaning. I reintegrated my selves in the purple room as I called it and then went off to try and locate Faaah.

I found her in her room having sex with another female who was nowhere to be found. I supposed that when someone is telepathic they could mindfuck another telepath who isn't even in the same room with them. Faaah, having sensed my presence, oddly not at all embarrassed by my discovery, simply ended her telepathic connection and sat up.

I connected to the other versions of me, I thought into her head, *but nothing made any sense. It was more like a dream than anything else. None of the other of my minds were awake.*

The liquid you were drowning in, she telepathed back, *that is the nature of our universe now. It came about as a result of our scientists creating artificial gravitation waves that affected all of the dark matter that permeates interstellar space. In turn, it changed the physics of everywhere.*

So, you are responsible for what will happen? I asked.

No, she replied, *it was your people. In their quest for knowledge, they disturbed the equilibrium of the universe. Our ability to telepath is just one result.*

But how did I wind up in your chamber or whatever it is, I asked.

We found you—all six of you—eons ago—deep inside the

mountain (I could not make out the name) *on the continent of* (again, no word could I discern through the telepathy but I felt through her thoughts that it was not far from where we were). *The six of you were all trapped within the rock. We discovered you because of the radiation from the crystals in your heads.*

But why have you kept us here? I asked. *How do you know we can help?*

Because, she replied, *our legends speak of a girl with powers over the universe, though they did not tell that there were more than one of you.*

Legends are seldom true, I said.

Perhaps not, she answered, *but you are more to us than merely a legend. You are the center of our religion. You are the resurrection. It is told that when all of you awaken from your sleep you will use your powers to save all of creation including us.*

In my time, I replied, *we had a similar prophesy, only ours told of the end of days where all would die and ascend to Heaven.*

As you can see, she replied, *such never came to be. We are just hopeful,* she went on and then abruptly stopped. She was staring at me but it wasn't *that* she was staring. It was the *way* she stared. There was a frightened look on her face.

What's wrong? I asked. *Why are you looking at me like that?*

It was as I looked down at myself that my question was answered. Something was happening to me. I was phasing in and out of existence, though from my perspective both she and everything around us were blinking on and off like a strobe until it all vanished—until I vanished from the room.

Wait, her mind shouted at me. *Don't go!*

But it was too late. Those were the last words of hers that I heard in my head as, suddenly, I was in poised outer space, high above a planet with an atmosphere and clouds, and there were buildings that I could see and lights that flickered from the night side. But then I turned and looked behind me. There were five others—five quantum others— all identical but for their colors—those same colors as the sleeping Quantum Girls only these were aliens with pointed ears and two pairs of breasts and tails—Gaaalthaaarans. A pulsation of terror gripped me with the thought that suddenly invaded my brain. I stared down at myself. I, too, had twin pairs of breasts and a glance behind revealed that I, like them, had a tail—a *yaaargh*—that was it. That's what it was called. And my ears! They were pointed as well. *Dear God,* I thought to myself. *I'm back in the Rendenaaaran universe, and each of us—each of me—is Khattaaara! What the hell,* I thought to myself. *What the hell is going on?*

CHAPTER XXV

Quantum Girl Green
(August 13, 39 B.C.)

My plans with Antony were twofold. To the first, I would help him accede to the throne of Rome. To the second, I would myself regain my place as Pharaoh with death as the reward for any who got in my way. But for Antony to accede to the throne, Caligula, Rome's then-present emperor, needed to be killed—perhaps assassinated is a better word. This, of course, could not be done in one night as the eyes of Rome would look with suspicion on the pairing of a sudden death and a sudden ascension. And with the ears of Octavia at my door, I thought it best that I depart the comfort of Antony's bed and infiltrate the house of Augustus Caesar.

As it turned out, Augustus was a rather handsome man, who had recently married his third wife, Livia, a rather ordinary-looking woman with a round face, a low brow, and a somewhat bulbous nose. As was the case of most of the noble Romans, and despite his marriage vows, Augustus had his share of women, adolescent girls, and teenage boys. Thus, it was not difficult to gain his audience when I, Cleopatra, just *happened* upon his doorstep one night and begged his company.

Deciding to avoid the Praetorian Guard, I simply phased into his bedchamber. Augustus was standing staring out the doorway to the inner courtyard—standing there naked I might add, with there being present a naked young girl, who could not have been more than twelve years old in his bed. I don't know if he glanced back when I turned my head to look at the other or if he saw me through his peripheral vision but he spoke to me, still staring outward.

"Cleopatra," he said. "How nice of thee to come visit. I'd been meaning to get to Egypt but one crisis after another always arose—the curse of the mighty." He then turned to the naked young girl.

165

"Cassia," he told her, "please allow Her Majesty and myself some moments in private to discuss the politics of the day."

Without so much as a word, the girl rose naked from the bed and obediently scampered from the room. When she was gone, Augustus turned to me.

"Pretty young thing," I commented as I watched her leave. "It would seem that plucking flowers extends beyond the landscape of your garden."

"Her parents sent me her as a gift," he replied. "It seems that her father wishes a position."

"Such a dutiful daughter," I said. "Girls of age that must be incredibly agile in bed."

"And yet not so well versed," he replied, "as a woman with thy legendary experience." He stared at me, cocking his head just a bit. "However didst thou make it past my guards?" he asked, "or were they so blinded by thy radiant beauty that they could not see their way to stopping thee?"

"You flatter me, Your Eminence," I replied as I glanced down at his naked form, "but I see thou are more than blinded. Indeed, thou honors my presence with the attention of thy sex."

Augustus glanced down toward his lap and then stared into my eyes without the slightest hint of embarrassment. "My dear lady," he said with the boldness of a Caesar, "would thy beauty be offered before all the legions of Rome, my men could throw down their swords and slay the enemy with no less than their manhood."

I laughed most heartily at his remark which conjured up images that even the Circus Maximum would not and could not entertain. "Thou dost flatter me to no end," I said. "But please," I invoked, "either dress thyself befitting thy station or else plunge thy weapon into the heart of my passion and slay the beast inside me."

"Given the choice, Madam," he proclaimed, " I would choose the latter."

That so spoken, I undid the fastenings of my dress and let it fall to the floor, leaving me naked before him. Augustus stared at me with gluttonous eyes.

"Thy beauty," he proclaimed, "hath been sold short. Antony was a fool to have allowed thee to escape his clutches for even a second."

His eyes not letting go, he approached me, took me into his arms, and then mated his desire with mine. A normal woman would have felt pleasure, no doubt, but I was Quantum Girl and so the sexual urge was intensified to a level beyond human comprehension. My mind shivered in that moment of ecstasy, even more than when I had been with Antony, for this man came upon me like a ravenous wolf incensed by the heat of his mate. Falling into his bed beneath him, I screamed out my passion until the ending came for both of us at once and he collapsed beside me, weakened by the vehemence of it all. Sweat had gathered upon us both and the scent of our combined passion wafted up into my nostrils and filled my brain with even greater desire. Was it minutes or hours that we enacted our lust? It was difficult for me to remember, so blurred was my brain. But, afterward, we drifted into sleep in each other's arms and did not awaken until the sunlight of a new dawn bled into the room.

What neither Antony nor Augustus realized was that each of them had one of me. It was very disconcerting, though, when having a discussion with Antony about the politics of Egypt, that I was feeling everything transpiring in Augustus's bed. In fact, the sensations were so distracting that I needed to excuse myself to my room, lie down in bed, and do everything I could to prevent myself from vocalizing the pleasure that my other self was experiencing. Isolating my mind from that of my other selves was something I had not learned how to do.

Concerned for my well-being, Antony came to my room to inquire.

"I grew concerned about thy sudden departure from our

conversation," he admitted.

I looked up at him. "I am in need," I told him. "I cannot contain it." My voice trembled. Beads of sweat had gathered upon my brow. My hands that had labored on my sex suddenly fled up to my head. My fingers intertwined with my hair and then tightened their grip. "Please, take me!" I said, struggling with the words.

Antony glanced behind him. "Octavia is in the house," he replied.

"Shut the door then," I said "Bar it if thou must, but be thou my lover again! Quickly!" I begged. "For the love of Venus herself, act thou quick!"

Antony shut the door and then turned its latch. Removing his toga, he climbed onto the bed to try and satisfy my urgent needs. It was a strange event in retrospect, having two men in two different places make love to me at the same time. It seemed that my powers in this regard were worth more to me than all of the other advantages they gave and that sometimes they were meant just for me. This was my reasoning at the time, for, despite that my brain still held all the thoughts and memories of Peyton Herron, the lust-filled heart of Egypt's queen had become the master of my flesh and the coxswain of my soul.

The campaign to restore me to my throne was mapped out on two separate fronts but with singular lines of deception on my part. My conversations with Antony involved strategies wherein Augustus would be deposed one way or another, either by prison or poison.[9] Meanwhile, my plans with Augustus were for Rome to cede Egypt back to me, as, after my presumed death, the Roman legions invaded and all that had been under my command became a Roman province. For this favor, I pledged eternal loyalty to his crown. This last plan proved triumphant, and, within a year, Egypt was mine once again. How this would affect the timeline, I did not

---

[9] As Fate would have it, the man survived another fifty-three years until his natural death at the age of seventy-five.

know or care. As Cleopatra, I did my best to see to it that the gods I worshiped remained active within the temples. And, with knowledge of the future, I did one more thing. I had Augustus agree to have executed the man named Pontius Pilot when he appeared half a century thence. Thus was it written down upon royal decree and carried out decades afterward. Whatever else he might have been, Gaius Julius Caesar Augustus was a man of his word. With Pilot out of the picture, Christos, as the Romans had named Jesus, was never crucified, but rather lived on to practice his teachings and was quite successful in converting both the Romans and the Greeks to the monotheistic religion of the ancient Jews. Only in Egypt did the old gods remain.

All of this came about some seventy years later well past my hundredth birthday, celebrated as and named *Dea Immortalis* or the Immortal Goddess. I met Jesus some years after what would have been his crucifixion. He was not a tall man, perhaps five and a half feet tall at best, which was somewhat average for that day and age, looking somewhat older than his years, worn down, perhaps, by his endless travels under an unforgiving sun. At my invitation, he stayed a guest in my palace for several months, during which time we had many splendid conversations about his God and mine, although he argued that to consider the existence of both together, coexisting, challenged reason. "Why should gods have mortal attributes?" he argued. "A god should be above all the frailties of man." The Christian soul of me nodded in agreement, but the pharaoh in me denied his reasoning. Regardless, he became fascinated by the theory of special relativity and the possible existence of other universes. He scoffed at first at my suggestion that the universe we were in had a breadth of more than ninety-three billion light years, and that one light year was nearly a trillion miles in length. Heaven, he said, lay just above the dome over the Earth that he insisted was the center of everything. The sun and the five planets, he told me, traveled their course across the firmament that was the sky and the stars were but holes poked through it revealing the light from Heaven. All that changed for him when I became Quantum Girl in front of him and phased us both into outer space.

"What is this?" he asked, his heart trembling as he witnessed the panorama of stars in every direction.

"This is but a fragment of the universe," I replied. "The Earth exists in what is known as the solar system and the solar system, in turn, exists in the Milky Way, a galaxy of hundreds of billions of stars."

I then phased us into intergalactic space where we could clearly take in the endless fields of galaxies. Back and forth to this one and that we went—to this star system and that and into the heart of colorful nebulae. We watched as a star went nova. I phased us back through time and stood upon Earth's soil as dinosaurs roamed the planet. We witnessed from outer space as an asteroid crashed into the Gulf of Mexico, throwing up a cloud of dust and debris that would cause an extinction-level event and give rise to the age of mammals.

Phasing four and a half billion years further back and then forward a hundred million years at a time, I showed him how the Earth had been shaped from a cloud of stellar dust and how the Moon was formed when a planet the size of Mars crashed into the Earth four billion years ago and hurled massive amounts of rock into orbit to eventually coalesce by the forces of gravity and become the Moon. We saw then how thousands of comets, over the course of tens of millions of years had bombarded the Earth with their melted ice that filled the planet's immense valleys to becoming its oceans.

Traveling further ahead in time, I went on to reveal to him how ape-like creatures slowly evolved into modern man and how man learned the trick of fire that set him on a path toward civilization. When we had at last returned to my chambers, he stared at me like someone suddenly awakened from a dream.

"But where were Adam and Eve in all of this?" he asked.

"Written in scrolls like other fabulous legends," I replied.

"And Noah's flood?" he went on. "What of that?"

"Caused by the rapid melting of glaciers that covered much of the upper latitudes," I replied.

The man was obviously shaken by all that he had seen and heard. His hands trembled. His voice faltered as he spoke.

"And what of God in all of this?" he asked. "Where is my Father and where lies Heaven?"

"I do not know," I admitted. "Perhaps in the quantum fabric." I stared hard into his eyes. "Eshu," I said in a most gentle tone, "Thou art my friend so I do not wish to destroy thy faith. I do not know that which underpins existence. Somewhere there must have been a beginning and even the scientific explanation for creation affirms that in the beginning there was light." I took his trembling hands in mine to calm him. "But there is one thing more," I said. "For years thou hast preached to men how to live but thou hath never thyself lived as a man. To do so, thou must know all the ways of men, not just some of them. Take thee a wife. Bring forth children into the world. Learn for thyself the true meaning of the word *father*. Thou dost know a kind woman named Mary Magdalene who is a fellow traveler and who believes in thee more than any other. She would make a fine wife and bring forth sons and daughters to which thou could impart both morality and faith. Thou couldst give to them the true meaning of love and plant in their hears the seeds of thy wisdom. Even a god must walk in the shoes of men to understand their hearts."

"I shall consider thy words," came the reply.

And consider he did, for within a year he had wed the woman I had named, who soon bore him a beautiful daughter they named Maryam Cleopatra who had dark eyes and hair, and a smile so bright it could light up the darkest room.

My affair with Antony had never led to much. Augustus had given me what I wanted but both of them had lived their lives and had long since become fodder for the grass. Nero then became emperor, a mad little man with a penchant for power—Nero, who sat back helplessly as Rome burned for six days straight. One could see the pillars of black smoke rise like atom bombs into the air, even from across the Mediterranean. It was around that time, that I saw the man, oddly dressed in strange black, tight-fitting attire. With an outstretched hand, he sent a blast of quantum energy at me. Immediately, I projected a force field to protect myself but some small portion of the energy struck me in the head. As I was losing consciousness, I phased more than six thousand miles away to a beach on the Pacific Ocean, not far from where I, as Peyton Herron, had grown up. And while the blow from being hit by the beam hurt like hell, it served to free my mind from the hold that Cleopatra had on it. I watched the sun as it set in the west, greatly relieved that after more than a century, I was myself again.

CHAPTER XXVI

Quantum Girl Violet
(April 30, 2025)

With everyone certain that I was batshit crazy, I figured that I would have to get proof in order to convince them that I was not. After careful consideration, I decided that I needed to find my way to New York and hook up my other self. She would remember everything and, hopefully, still have her powers.

I didn't want to tell anyone before I left because I knew they'd try and stop me. I changed my mind, though, and told Phee what I was about to do.

"You can't be serious?" she said.

"No one believes me," I replied.

"That you had superpowers, battling alien invaders in outer space" she asked. "What if I suddenly told you that I was, I don't know, Cleopatra in a former life? Would *you* believe *me*?"

"No," I replied.

"See?" she said.

"I wouldn't believe you," I replied, "because *I* was. Cleopatra was one of my reincarnations after Khattaaara."

"Oh, my God!" she exclaimed.

"We've been together since before we were born," I said. "I know it all sounds insane. If I hadn't lived through it, I wouldn't have believed it either. But I need to do this and I need to know that you... maybe you don't believe that I was ever Quantum Girl... but I need you to believe in me. If I'm wrong, I'll come back and accept any treatment. But I need to do this. I need to find the other Peyton Herron and I need to find Mark. This is the most important thing I've ever asked of you, but I need you to trust me."

"If I let you go," she replied, "I need you to promise that you'll text me every day."

"I promise," I said.

"What am I supposed to tell Mom and Dad?" she asked.

"Tell them I went to stay with Myra Kartinova for a couple of weeks," I said, "that I just needed to think things out."

"How are you going to get to New York?" she asked.

"I used my debit card to purchase a plane ticket," I replied. "I schussed an Uber for four a.m. to take me to the airport."

The alarm on my cell phone went off at three-thirty. Phee was already awake.

"I didn't want to miss saying goodbye," she said with tears in her eyes. "You take care of yourself."

When my ride showed up outside, we hugged and then I left. It was about twenty minutes to the airport. I made my way through security and to the terminal and then boarded the plane. The flight I had booked was the cheapest one I could find which was early morning and on a Wednesday. Actually, Wednesday was better for me, as I figured that it would be easier for me to find Mark at school rather than trying to figure out where he lived. The trip was to take a little over eight hours, leaving from LAX and arriving at LaGuardia. I only took a carry-on bag that I put in the overhead. In the seat next to me sat a woman in her mid-thirties with a pale complexion, blue eyes, and freckles, who was ever engrossed in her laptop. Beside her near the aisle sat a fidgety boy around ten that she kept telling to "hush," whom I assumed was her son. Just before the plane began to move, a voice came over the intercom.

"Hello, everyone, this is your captain speaking. Welcome to Spirit Airlines, flight 167 to Las Vegas, Chicago, and then onto New York. Please place all seats in the upright position for takeoff, fasten your seat belts, and enjoy your flight."

I had a window seat and stared out the window as the plane took off. The plane took off over the ocean and then circled around to head east. The lights of the city glistened from below and then there was only an occasional light here and there. As the plane became engulfed in clouds, I thought about all the times I was able to phase into the upper atmosphere and beyond. I just wondered, both frightened and concerned, at who or what might have taken away my powers and dropped me headlong into this mundane reality.

I managed to fall asleep for about an hour but then was awakened by a message from Phee at half past eight. *Mom and Dad are very upset about your disappearing act,* she said.

Tell them I'll be fine, I wrote back.

You don't have to deal with them, came the reply. *I do! Mom virtually interrogated me. "Why didn't you tell us?" she said. You seriously owe me on this one!*

Definitely, I said. *I'll do your chores for a month when I get back. That is if they don't lock me away!*

Text me after you land, she replied.

I will, I told her. *I love you, Sis.*

Love you back, she replied. *Take care of yourself and don't take any candy from strangers!*

I messaged back, *lol,* and then tried to go back to sleep but failed.

Wending my way through the airport after disembarking from the plane, I became aware of the airport smell that was caused by the jet fuel. For some reason, I hadn't noticed it as much when I was in L.A., perhaps because my mind was so concerned about Phee breaking her word and telling Mama and Papa that I'd left and them calling the police to prevent me from getting on the plane.

I took another Uber to the school which brought me there close to noon. I figured I'd do that before checking into a motel. That way I could find Mark and perhaps my other self.

It was both daunting and exhilarating at the same time, going into the school, I mean—Massapequa High School. That's where Mark went. He had never talked about it a lot. He said there were bad memories. I wondered which class Mark would be in, but then the lunch bell rang and I didn't have to wonder. I caught a glimpse of him as he was herded down the corridor amidst the throng of other students exiting their various classes.

"Mark!" I called out to him, though it became apparent that he couldn't hear me above the din. Then I lost sight of him as the crowd stopped and turned in his direction. Some of them laughed. As for me, I pushed my way through. When I got to where he was, he was on the floor as were his glasses, a few feet away from him. Another boy, the same one I'd seen last time I was here, had one foot on top of Mark's chest and shook his head to himself.

"Loser!" he spat out at Mark. Then he saw the glasses, turned, and stepped on them.

"Hey!" I shouted at him. "You leave him alone!"

The brute turned to me and gave me the once-over. "Well, well, well," he said. "What have we here? I haven't seen *you* around before."

He grabbed me by the shoulders, pulled me into him, and forced his lips on mine. I could feel his tongue trying to push its way through my lips. I pulled back in disgust.

"Take your hands off of me!" I said and then kneeing him in the groin.

His face turned red with anger. He slapped me hard across the face. I have to admit that tears came to my eyes. Everyone watching suddenly became silent.

"What?" he said to his audience as though he were innocent of any wrongdoing. "The bitch kicked me in the balls!"

Mark struggled to his feet and then stared at the boy like a bull about to charge, and he did. Down went both of them, Mark on top. The older, larger boy tried to fight back but Mark now had the advantage and was so incensed that he kept punching him in the face until the bully lost consciousness. I got in back, took hold of Mark's arms, and gently urged him off the now bloodied aggressor. "That's enough," I said softly in his ear.

Hearing my words, he stopped and got off the other boy. Then he looked around the floor, bent down, and picked up what was left of his glasses. As he was getting up an older male voice broke the silence. All eyes were then focused on a fortyish man in his shirt sleeves. The man looked at the boy on the floor and then at Mark.

"Who started it?" He demanded to know.

"Marsden did!" one boy shouted. "Garrett was just standing there when he attacked him."

"That's a lie!" I shouted back. "Garrett, or whatever his name is, attacked Mark and then broke his glasses!"

By this time, Garrett was coming to. He shook his head to awaken himself, wiped his bloodied face with the back of one hand, and then dragged himself to his feet, whereupon both he and Mark exchanged dirty looks.

"All right, all right," the man said. "Wentworth, you get down to the nurse. Marsden, you come with me." Then he glanced in my direction. "You, too," he said. "I don't recognize you. *What's* your name?"

"Peyton," I replied. "Peyton Herron."

"Well," he said, "It looks like someone got you, too. That's quite a shiner."

I turned to Mark who looked at me and nodded. I put my hand to my left eye and winced. Then I reached into my purse, pulled out my compact, opened it, looked at myself in the mirror, and frowned.

"Hey," Mark said to me in a low voice, "it's not so bad. You're still beautiful, whoever you are."

I smiled at his words. We followed the man to administration and then into his office. "Charles Gilford, Principal," the door to the room announced, the name having been painted backward on the reverse side of the glass window in black, edged in gold. There was one chair facing the desk. Mr. Gilford pulled up a second and then told us both to have a seat which we did. After we all sat down, he looked at both of us, taking note of my black eye.

"Are you all right?" he asked.

"I'm fine, I guess," I replied.

"Just the same," he said back, "we'll have the nurse take a look at you when we finish up here." He then turned to Mark. "Mr. Marsden," he went on, "you and Mr. Garrett seem to have an ongoing situation."

"He's the one that always starts things," Mark replied. "I never did anything to him before today, but he hit her." He glanced at me, then looked back at Mr. Gilford. "I mean, look at her," he said. "Who does that to a girl?"

Mr. Gilford looked from him to me. "Miss Herron," he said, " I try my best to know all of the students at the school but I don't recall ever seeing you here before."

"I'm not enrolled here," I replied. "I just came here to see Mark."

It was at that point Mark turned and stared at me.

"So," Mr. Gilford said, "I take it then that you two are friends."

"No, Sir," Mark replied, turning his head to stare at me. "But I'd like to be."

"I guess we'll deal with all that later," the principal said with somewhat of a sigh. "In the meantime, Miss Herron, would you tell me what you saw?"

"Well," I replied, glancing at Mark, "there were a lot of kids in the hallway as the bell had just rung. I saw Mark and called out to him but he didn't hear me because it was so loud there. Then the students who all had been going off in their separate directions suddenly stopped. I heard some of them laughing and wondered what was going on so I made my way through them until I saw Mark on the floor and the other boy's foot was on his chest. There was a trickle of blood from his nose and his glasses were on the floor a few feet away. I assumed they had gotten knocked off when he was knocked down. Anyway, the boy who had his foot on top of him called him a loser and then went over to the glasses and stepped on them. I shouted at him to leave Mark alone but then he turned to me, looked me over, and then forced a kiss on me. I pulled away and then kicked my knee into his privates at which point he punched me really hard in the face. Everyone became really silent at that point but the boy acted like I deserved it. That's when Mark attacked him to try and defend my honor, I guess." I turned to Mark. "Thank you for that," I said with a smile and then turned back to Mr. Gilford. "That's when *you* came along."

Mr. Gilford turned to Mark. "Is that the way you remember it as well?" he asked.

"Yes, Sir," Mark replied. "I know I hit Garrett pretty hard but he deserved it. No one has a right to hit anyone for no reason, especially a girl."

There was a knock on the door and a woman entered, said something quietly to Mr. Gilford, handed him a note, and then left. The man unfolded the note, glanced at it, and then frowned. He looked up at the two of us.

"It seems," he said, "that Mr. Wentworth has an orbital fracture, a possibly detached retina, and a broken jaw." He took a deep breath and let it out. "While I agree with you, Mr. Marsden, that what Mr. Wentworth did was totally wrong, it is the school policy that the only physical force that is justified is one of self-defense and not retaliation. That being said, I'm going to need to suspend you until all of this can be sorted out. Beyond all else, your actions have placed the school in a precarious legal position."

"What do you mean?" Mark asked.

"Mr. Wentworth's father," he replied, "has already threatened to file a lawsuit."

"That quick?" I said.

Mr. Gilford looked at me and shrugged.

"But Garrett was the aggressor!" I insisted.

"That's something the courts may have to decide," came the response. "As for you, Miss Herron, I'm going to insist that you see the nurse."

"All right," I replied.

"I'll take her," Mark said.

Mark rose from his chair and I followed suit. Then we both turned for the door.

"Mr. Marsden," the principal said, "if it's any comfort, if I were your age, I probably would have done the exact same thing."

And then we left. Mark walked me to the nurse's office. The nurse had me sit down on the examination table and then looked at me. She touched my face where it was swollen. I flinched from the pain.

"How bad is it?" I asked.

"It may get worse before it gets better," she replied. "How did it happen?"

"She got slugged by Garrett Wentworth," Mark broke in.

The nurse glanced at him and then looked back at me. "Mr. Wentworth was in here just a few minutes ago," she said. "An ambulance is bringing him to the hospital. That was quite a bit of damage you did to him."

"That was Mark," I replied. "He was defending me." I glanced at Mark and smiled.

"Well," the nurse said, "you have what in medical terms is called a periorbital hematoma."

"That sounds serious," I replied.

"In layman's terms, a black eye," she said.

"Will it leave a scar?" I asked.

"No," she replied. "It will be black for about a week, turn purple and yellow, and then begin to fade. But you can cover it up with make-up. The swelling should go down in a few days. In the meantime, I'm going to give you some ibuprofen for the pain. You might also experience a slight headache and some nausea for a while." She then turned to Mark. "I trust you're going to watch over her while she heals."

"Yes, Ma'am," Mark replied.

"All right, then," she said. "The two of you can go. Just try not to get into any more fights."

"Yes, Ma'am," Mark replied again.

"Yes, Ma'am," I echoed.

Mark and I then walked to his locker where he got his jacket, his backpack, and the rest of his books.

"I have a question," he said staring into the metal. "How do you know me?"

"We're friends on Facebook," I lied.

"We are?" he asked. He shut the locker and then leaned back against it. "But," he went on, "why did you come to see me?"

By this time, I kind of realized that I was not going to find my other self—that this was a reality that she wasn't in, so I lied again.

"I liked what you posted," I replied, "and I think you're kind of cute. So, I thought that we should meet."

"Which school do you go to?" he asked.

"Braxton," I replied.

"Where's that?" he asked.

"California," I replied.

"Really!" he said, stunned. He stared this way and that across the hallway we were in. "This is some kind of a joke, right? Roger put you up to this."

"Who's Roger?" I said.

Mark stared hard at me. "You're not messing with me."

"Not yet," I replied and then smiled.

"You really came two thousand miles," he said, "just to meet *me*."

"Two thousand, four hundred, fifty-nine point four miles to be exact," I said. "What's the matter? Haven't you ever gone out of your way to meet anyone?"

"I went to see Chris Evans at the Comic-Con a couple of years ago," he replied.

"There you go," I said.

"But that was here in New York," he replied.

"Still…" I said and then paused. "Who's Chris Evans?"

Mark gave me an exasperated look. "Captain America?" he replied. "I take it you're not into superheroes."

"Not made-up ones!" I said.

His mouth twisted into a frown. "Are you here with your parents?" he asked.

"Nope," I said. "Just me."

"And you came all this way," he said, "just to…"

"Stare into your pale blue eyes?" I asked. "I have a question for you. Do you think I'm pretty?"

"Definitely," he said, "even with that circle around your eye." He reached out to touch it and then pulled back, remembering my reaction when the nurse pressed against it. "Is it painful?" he asked.

"Not a lot but I do feel a headache coming on," I replied. He walked me to one of the water fountains where I swallowed one of the pills the nurse had given me, then I stood up and wiped my mouth with the back of my right hand. "I think maybe I should've ducked," I said.

Mark shrugged and then we both laughed.

"Ow!" I said.

"What?" he asked with concern.

"It hurts when I laugh," I replied.

"So," he asked, "where are you staying?"

"Nowhere at the moment," I replied. "I was planning to take the next flight back, only I'm not really feeling well. My head is starting to hurt and I am feeling a bit nauseous. So, I was just wondering…"

"About?" he asked

"Whether it would it be all right," I replied, "if I stayed at your place for a day or so before I went back home? Till I'm feeling better."

Mark's face twisted up again. "I suppose I could ask my dad," he replied, "only…"

"Only what?" I asked.

"He kind of has a drinking problem," he replied. "Sometimes, when he's drunk, he gets angry. I just don't want anything more to happen to you."

I smiled and kissed him on the cheek. "I can take care of myself," I assured him. "Besides, if I'm there, maybe it'll calm him a bit."

We walked the mile or so to his house, though I had to sit down when we got to the lake.

Mark's face took on a mien of concern. "Are you all right?" he asked.

"It comes and goes," I replied. "I just need to sit here for just a bit."

There was a raft of ducks in the water. One of them, a mallard with a green feathered head, swam up to us.

"*Hey*, Tristan," Mark said, taking some popcorn from his jacket and squatting down to feed it.

"Did you *name* some of them?" I asked.

"All of them," he replied. "Do you see the one across the lake with the brown head and white wings? That's Guinevere. She just laid a brood of eggs. And that one over there near the tree. That's Lamorak, totally fearless. He'll attack strangers."

"You certainly know your ducks," I said.

"Ever since my mom ran off a couple of years ago," he replied. "they've kind of become like family." He stood up. "Well," he said, "I guess we'd better get going. I like to be there before my dad gets home. He gets upset when I don't have supper fixed."

I stood up and took his hand in mine. "I'll help you with that," I told him. "I'm a pretty good cook."

And so off we went, with me ignorant and unprepared for all that lay ahead.

CHAPTER XXVII

Peyton

(the other one in Massapequa—
—the one with quantum powers)

Nothing good lasts forever. That's what they say, whoever *they* are. More than a month had passed and Mark and I were getting along like two peas in a pod when, late in the afternoon, there was a knock on the door. The three of us were eating supper and we all turned sharply toward the unexpected interruption. I was the one who rose from my seat.

"I'll get it," I said and went to the door.

A woman with sandy hair and glasses stood on the other side.

"May I help you?" I asked.

"I was told that Mark is living here," she replied. "Mark Marsden."

I looked at her with caution. "And who are you?" I asked.

"I'm Mark's mother," she replied.

She suddenly looked past me. I glanced back to see older me had also come to the door and was standing just behind me.

"Won't you come in," older me said.

"But Mom!" I protested.

Older me gave me a sharp look and then gently took me by the shoulders, urging me out of the way.

"Mrs. Conroy phoned earlier," she said. "She told me you might be dropping by. We just sat down to supper. Perhaps you'd like to join us."

"No, thank you," the woman replied. "I just came to take Mark back with me."

Mark had joined up by this time, curious as to who was at the door and, perhaps, wanting to make sure that I was all right. As I looked back at him, I saw him staring almost in terror at the woman

184

who said she was his mother.

"What's wrong?" I asked him.

"It's not possible," he said, not taking his eyes off of her.

"What's not?" I asked.

"I told you that my mother left us," he replied. "What I didn't tell you was that she was killed in a car crash not long afterward. I saw her body at the morgue. I don't understand."

"*I* do," older me said. "She's Thara-Klo. Take Mark. Phase anywhere but here. I'll deal with her. Trust me."

I took hold of Mark's wrist and initiated a phase from there. As I watched older me and the woman who had introduced herself as Mark's mother, I saw her transform into what must have been a Gaaalthaaaran from the descriptions I had heard from the original Peyton and Phee. A second later, we were back at school. It was deserted but we were safe.

Mark's reaction to the sudden change in our location was not a good one. His face instantly grew pale and he turned this way and that, letting go of my hand and backing up until his retreat was thwarted by one of the lockers to his read and met with a clang that was amplified and echoed in the empty corridor.

"What happened?" he stammered. "How did we get here? What's going on?"

I held out my hands toward him, palms out. "Calm down," I replied. "I can explain."

"Explain?" he repeated. "How do you explain that one second we were in your house and the next second we're here?"

"I phased us here," I replied.

And then he threw up.

"Sorry," I said. "Just a side effect."

"How is this possible?" he asked, staring at me.

"I explain everything," I replied, "but I need to go help her first."

"Who?" he asked, " Your mom? Why would she need help other

than the fact that we left her alone with a dead woman?"

"That wasn't a woman," I replied. "And it wasn't your mom. It was a Gaaalthaaaran female from a planet called Rendenaaar and she wants to kill me."

"And I'm Luke Skywalker," he said, "waiting for Darth Vader to kill *me*."

"This is *not* science fiction!" I exclaimed, exasperated. "Thara-Klo is my daughter from a previous incarnation and she wants me dead!" I paused, then went on. "And that wasn't my mother back home. That was a future version of *me*! I came back in time to help me get to know you."

"Why would she or you do that?" he asked halfheartedly.

"Because," I said, "in the future, you're my husband—at least in the timeline I left. And because…" and I hesitated. "And because I'm in love with you!"

"Okay, okay," he replied. "So how are you able to do all this stuff?"

"Because I'm Quantum Girl," I said.

"Quantum Girl," he repeated.

I rolled my eyes and then phased into my costume. I thought he was going to faint. Fortunately, he didn't.

"Anyway," I said, "I need to go help my future self. Even though Thara-Klo may not realize it, she has the mother stone in her head, and it's a lot more powerful than the god-stone in mine. Hang on. I need a moment."

I took that moment to divide into two of me. Mark sank down to the floor and just stared. Then one of me vanished—phased off to help future me deal with Thara-Klo. Then I phased back into my street clothes.

"My luck," he sighed. "First girl that actually likes me and she turns out to be an alien."

"I'm not an alien!" I protested. "I'm just the reincarnation of one."

"That's certainly comforting to know," he said.

I went over to him, extended my hand toward him, and helped him up to his feet.

"I won't let anything happen to you," I told him. "You just need to trust me."

Meanwhile, back at home, older me was doing battle with Thara-Klo who, as I said, had dropped her disguise to initiate an all-out attack. When I phased there, the place was in shambles. Both of them were hurling quantum blasts at each other, though it appeared that Thara-Klo was winning, as the point of intersection was nearing older me. That's when I intervened, phasing behind her and sending a bolt of quantum energy to her *yaaargh*, technically a low blow, but effective. The alien being winced in pain, then turned and saw me. A rope of energy shot toward me and wrapped around my neck. In another moment, I was pulled up to her, whereupon she raised up her *yaaurgh* and stung me with it. Everything around me began to grow dim as I dropped to the floor. I passed out, then, but not before I saw older me tower with rage and hurl a blast at the intruder so devastating that the Gaaalthaaaran screamed and then disappeared.

Back at the school, I turned to Mark. "I need to get back home," I said. "Something's happened to the other me. She's gone."

"Take me with you," he replied.

"I don't want anything to happen to you," I told him.

He looked at me all so seriously. "You said that in the future we were married," he replied. "If my place is beside you then, it's beside you now. That's how it works."

"I can see where the stubborn came from," I said. "Give me your hand." He did. "Now, take a deep breath and let it out. It'll keep you from having to vomit after the phase."

"I wish you'd told me that before," he replied.

I took his hand, made sure he exhaled, and then phased us back to the house. "Oh, my God!" I said as I saw the ruin. And then I saw her—the other me—on the floor.

"She got stung by Thara-Klo," older me said. Then she collapsed.

"I'm going to try and merge us back," I replied. I went up to her and made several attempts but nothing worked. I turned to older me. "What did *you* do when you were me?" I asked her.

"This never happened," she replied.

"How is that possible?" I asked.

"I don't know," she answered. "It would seem that the timeline is being interfered with."

"By whom?" I asked.

"No idea," she replied.

"What do we do about the other me?" I asked. She had begun to tremble. Her skin was clammy and cold.

"I'll phase her to the hospital," she replied. "You stay with Mark. Protect him. His future and ours depend on it. Maybe you can try to hide in a different time."

Then she lifted the other me—the possibly dying other me—into her arms and was gone.

"You know this is freaking me out," Mark said.

"I can imagine," I replied. Suddenly, I felt myself collapsing but Mark caught me.

"What's wrong?" he asked.

"It's my injured other self," I replied. "I think she's dying."

Mark looked at me, our eyes only inches apart. "What happens if she does?" he asked.

"I'll grow weaker for a while," I replied. "She's one-third of me."

He looked at me, puzzled. "But you divided in two," he said. "My math may not be the best, but wouldn't that make her half?"

"There's another of me back in L.A.," I said. "I'm all right now. You can let go." I thought for a moment and then said to him, "Look, I need to get back there and warn her. I hope you don't mind coming with."

"Just so long as I can get frequent quantum miles," he replied. "I'm hoping one day to make it to Mars."

"Oh, I can take you a lot further than that," I said. "Come on." I took hold of his hand, reminded him to exhale, and then I phased us back to my parents' home.

CHAPTER XXVIII

Peyton

*(the future Peyton who went back
in time to help Peyton meet Mark)*

The ER was swarming with doctors, patients, and staff. I had phased my younger self to the Mayo Clinic in Rochester. I held her in my arms at the ambulance entrance. I had phased on the appearance of a paramedic uniform but she was still in her Quantum Girl costume. I stopped time and let go of her. With time stopped, she just hung mid-air. I dissolved her costume, grabbed a hospital gown, put it on her, laid her on a gurney, and caused time to resume. Then I turned to one of the nurses.

"I have a fifteen-year-old, possible cardiac arrest," I told her.

The nurse called out, "Code Blue!" and a team of doctors and nurses rushed over and wheeled her over to one of the ER stations. I then went into the ladies room, phased into street clothes, turned my hair dark, and then went over to admitting.

"My daughter was just brought to the ER," I told her.

The admitting clerk glanced at me. "Let me go check," he said and then got up, went there, and returned a moment later.

"They're working on her," the clerk said as he sat back down. "Would you mind filling out a form? It would be helpful."

"Of course," I replied.

Name, address, date of birth, preexisting conditions, allergies, emergency contact, person responsible, if a minor. I filled it all out and then handed it back. A moment later, a doctor in his late thirties emerged from the ER and went over to the admitting clerk, who in turn pointed at me. I stood up from the chair I had taken as the doctor walked up to me.

"I'm Dr. Collins," He said. He glanced down at the chart in his hands. "You're Peyton's mother?"

190

"Yes," I said. "How is she?"

"We got her heart started," he said, "but that's all we've been able to do so far. Her pupils are nonresponsive."

"What does that mean?" I asked.

"She's in a coma," he replied. "It could mean that there was brain injury. What happened to her? There appear to be burn marks on the left side of her head that even singed part of her hair."

"There were men working on a high-voltage line," I said. "The line fell near where she was standing and a flash of electricity jumped from the cable to her. Then she just dropped."

"I'm going to order a Functional MRI of her brain," he said. "That should give us a picture of what's going on."

"Will she be all right?" I asked.

"It's hard to tell," he replied. "Just don't give up hope. She's young—strong. We just need to find out if there was any damage and the extent of it."

"Can I see her?" I asked.

The doctor nodded. "Just for a moment," he replied. "I want to get the MRI done as soon as possible."

I walked into the ER and went over to one of the nurses.

"I'm looking for my daughter," I said. "Peyton Herron. Dr. Collins said I could see her."

The nurse led me to her bed and drew back one of the curtains. She was lying there like she was asleep, but she was anything but. There were wires hooked up to her for her heart rate and pulse. I just stood and stared. I stopped time around the curtained-off area we were in. I pulled what I called a *Ka* out of myself—a ghostlike part of me. I then levitated it to a horizontal position over young me's body and merged the two. I should have been able to hear her thoughts—even feel any pain she was experiencing—but there was nothing. Reluctantly, I withdrew the *Ka*, shook my head to myself, squeezed her hand, and left. A few minutes later she was wheeled into the MRI room. After half an hour had passed, the same doctor approached me.

"I don't know how or why," he said, "but halfway through the imaging she opened her eyes. They'll be bringing her back to the ER in a few minutes. I'd like to keep her overnight to continue to observe her. She's a very lucky girl. To be honest, I didn't expect her to ever wake up."

I saw her afterward when she was brought back. She smiled at me. It was a weak smile but she was all there.

"Did we get her?" she asked.

"We got her," I replied, "at least for now. I'm just glad you're awake."

"It must have been the god-stone," she replied. "I guess the MRI activated it when my brain couldn't."

"Lucky for you," I replied.

"Lucky for us," she said. "When can I go home?"

"Tomorrow," I replied. "Then, when you're back to full strength you can merge back with yourself. She and Mark are on their way back to L.A."

"Thank you for all you've done," she said.

I smiled at her. "One day, you'll do the same."

"I know," she replied, "but I appreciate it nevertheless."

CHAPTER XXIX

Peyton

*(the one who stayed behind
with Ophelia who woke up in
an alternate reality)*

I awoke to find myself in a speeding ambulance, sirens wailing, with two paramedics on board. There was a needle stuck in my left arm and clear fluid flowing into it from a bag that was suspended from a metal pole. Both of my hands and wrists were bandaged and an oxygen mask covered both my mouth and nose. The paramedics must have given me something for the physical pain but there was still the emotional trauma from what I had been put through. I felt so violated. I'd never had anything like that done to me before and I didn't know how to handle it. I felt my muscles trembling and my eyes were bleeding tears. I tried to raise myself up but I was strapped down on the gurney. The paramedic who was riding with me, a woman, gently put her hand on my shoulder.

"You need to stay still," she said. "You've lost a lot of blood."

I turned my head away to one side, tightly closing my eyes.

"It's going to be okay," she went on. "When we get to the hospital, we'll get someone to talk to you about what happened. A lot of people feel like ending things but it'll get better. You'll see."

"I didn't try to kill myself," I said. "I was raped. I smashed the mirror out of anger."

"What happened?" she asked.

"There were three of them in the girls' restroom," I replied. "They jumped me and then raped and sodomized me."

"I'm so sorry," the woman replied.

"It hurt so bad," I told her, "but there was nothing I could do. They were too strong and they didn't care what they did to me. They

193

didn't care!"

The woman put her hand on my shoulder. "The school contacted your parents," she said. "They're going to meet us at the hospital."

The trip from when I had awakened probably only lasted five minutes, though it seemed like forever as I stared blankly at the equipment that lined the inside of the vehicle. At last, though, the ambulance slowed, turned off to one side, backed up, and came to a stop. It was the driver, one of the paramedics, who opened the doors from the outside, and then he and the woman rolled the gurney out of the rear door and into the emergency room. Several orderlies and the attending physician rushed over.

"There are lacerations to both hands and wrists," the woman paramedic told the doctor. "Possibly some glass. And you're going to need to do a rape kit."

"How deep are the lacerations?" the doctor asked.

"One is pretty deep," the woman answered. "I had trouble stopping the bleeding."

"Prep her for surgery," the doctor told the orderlies as they transferred me to one of the wheeled hospital beds. Another man came over to me and asked if I was allergic to anything. I told him no. A few minutes later I saw him inject something into the tube going into my arm and then I guess I must have fallen asleep.

When I woke up again, the surgery was over and my hands and wrists had been rebandaged. Mama was sitting in a chair in the hospital room I was in. Papa was staring out the window.

"Mama?" I said in a weak voice as I saw her.

She turned to me and smiled, although it was a smile diluted with the worry she felt. "Hello, Sweet Pea," she said. "How are you feeling? Do your hands hurt a lot?"

"Not so much," I said. "I'm sure they have me on pain medications. But it's not that. I was raped by three boys in the girls' bathroom."

I could see my mama's expression change to one of both

confusion and concern. Meanwhile, Papa had overheard what I said. His reaction was just anger.

"Which boys did this?" he demanded to know.

"James," my mama said in a quiet voice, "we need to give her time. She's hurting right now—emotionally. Let the authorities handle it."

"Anyone who would hurt her deserves to be sent straight to Hell, even if I don't believe there is such a place."

"Papa," I said with tears in my eyes, "Mama's right. I know you want to protect me but I just need you to be here *with* me. I need both of you."

Papa frowned. "I just can't believe that anyone would do such a thing to you," he said. Then he shrugged. "I'd reach out and take your hand but you're all bandaged up. Do you mind if I kiss you on the forehead like I used to when I'd put you and Ophelia to bed?"

"Will it heal me?" I asked with a smile.

"I don't know if I have any such powers," he replied, " but one can hope." Then he bent down and kissed me. "Now that you're bigger," he said, returning the smile, "I don't have to aim so hard. You know I can't see up close without my glasses."

That got a slight chuckle out of me. It was just then that a woman in her thirties in a jacket, blouse, and skirt entered the room. She flashed a badge. "I'm Det. Jeffers with the Santa Monica Police Department." After glancing at Mama and Papa she looked at me. "You're Peyton Herron, I assume."

"Yes," I said.

"I'm going to need to get a statement from you," she went on, and then looked at Mama and Papa; "I think it best if I conducted the interview in private."

"We're her parents," Papa protested.

Mama took his hand. "James," she said to him, "I think our Peyton might feel uncomfortable describing all the details with us in the room."

Papa looked at me and I nodded. It wasn't that I felt ill at ease taking in front of them. I just didn't want Papa to go off and do something stupid after hearing all that I'd been put through. Papa shrugged, with great reluctance it seemed, but he and Mama left the room.

"I know this sort of thing can be difficult," Det. Jeffers said. "but we'd like to be able to catch the young men who did this to you."

"I was raped," I replied. "You don't need to mince words."

"Can you tell me what happened?" she asked.

"The school allows boys to use the girls' washroom if they claim they're really a girl. It's been that way at a lot of schools the past few years. Most of the girls raised objections to it but nobody in charge cared about anything they had to say. Anyway, I was the only one there in one of the stalls with the door latched shut. I saw one of the boys watching me. He's pulled himself up to look over the top of the stall door. Then he kicked it in. I was thrown back and hit my head really hard against the wall. Then I was dragged out. One of the boys ripped open my blouse and fondled my breasts. Then I was held down by two of them at a time while the other one raped me. They took turns. The third one—he sodomized me."

"You didn't consent to any of it," she asked.

"No," I replied. "Why would you even think such a thing?"

"It's just a question I'm required to ask," she replied. "Do you know any of the boys' names?"

"One of them was Perry Dunbar," I told her. "I didn't recognize the other two boys but they were older—seventeen, maybe eighteen."

"Do you know if any of them used condoms?" she asked.

"No idea," I replied. "They raped me from behind. They had me bent over one of the sinks. All I know is that I was a virgin before. And now I'm not. I don't know what I did to deserve any of it."

"You didn't do anything," she replied. "You didn't ask for any of it and you certainly didn't deserve it. Maybe Perry Dunbar and

196

his two friends think they'll be able to get away with what they did, but they're wrong."

"It's going to be my word against theirs," I said.

"We'll get them," she replied. "The rape kit showed evidence of semen. When it comes back we'll have their DNA."

"They'll just say I was willing," I said.

"The doctor who examined you," she replied, "said you had massive abrasions and tears to your tissues. That's proof that you *weren't* willing. It's evidence of a rape. Trust me. We're going to make them pay for what they did."

When evening came, an unexpected visitor arrived. It was Phee or, rather, Lia in this iteration of reality.

"Hey, Sis," she said. "Mom and Dad told me what happened to you. I'm really sorry."

"I'll survive," I told her.

"I can't imagine what it was like," she replied. She sat down on the edge of the bed, facing me. "Look," she went on, "I know we've kind of gone our separate ways for the past few years, but I'm hoping… I'd like that to change. I mean I know you think I've been a total bitch and you're probably right but I'm your older sister…"

"By five minutes," I said with a smile.

"Hey," she replied, "in biology, we learned that there is a type of mayfly that only *lives* for five minutes. Anyway, I'd like us to be friends from now on." She reached out to take my hands but then, seeing the bandages, pulled hers back. I looked down at my hands and then up at her.

"I got mad after it happened," I said, "and smashed the mirror over the sink."

"Who did it to you?" she asked. "Who raped you?"

"Perry Dunbar and a couple of other guys," I replied. "I've never seen them before. They looked a little older. College maybe. Does Perry have an older brother? One of them kind of looked like him."

"Brett," Lia said. "Goes to UCLA."

"The policewoman said they were going to arrest Perry after the rape kit results come in," I said.

"And then what?" Lia replied. "They always get off."

"Not always," I said.

"Oh," Lia said, "they'll take them to trial and put them on the witness stand and they'll deny everything. Then they'll put you up there and ask you if you let them and how much you enjoyed it. Maybe they'll admit that you told them to stop but that it was too late. All that'll happen is they'll do their best to humiliate you."

"The detective said it wouldn't be like that," I replied.

"And you believed her," Lia said. She shook her head. "You don't want a trial," she went on. "You want justice."

"What does that mean?" I asked.

Lia rose to her feet and went to the door. "It means," she replied, "they'll never be able to rape anyone again. Take care, Sis. I'll stop by again tomorrow if you're not already home."

"Lia, wait!" I called after her, but she didn't turn back.

It was a week later that I heard on the news that Brett Dunbar and a Fred Terrell, a freshman at UCLA had both been castrated in the Dunbar home and that Perry had been found dead in the Dunbar living room with multiple stab wounds to his chest and castrated as well. That evening, the doorbell rang, followed by a banging on the door. It was Papa who answered it. There were two uniformed police officers on the other side.

"We're looking for Ophelia Herron," one of them said. "We have a warrant for her arrest."

"On what grounds?" Papa demanded to know.

"Two counts of felonious assault," came the reply, "and one count of murder."

I watched in horror as they entered the house and put Lia in handcuffs. She'd been standing on the stairs, watching, but then tried to flee up to the second floor. She didn't make it far. One of the officers tackled her, pulled her arms behind her, and snapped the cuffs on her. Then he pulled her to her feet and urged her out the door. She was barefoot and in her robe.

"Don't say anything to them," Papa warned her. "I'll call a lawyer and go down to the station. We'll get you out."

The cops put her in the back seat of their unit and then drove away. Mama turned to Papa.

"What's going to happen to my baby?" she asked him in tears.

Papa already had the receiver to the phone up to his ear and was dialing a number.

"Bill," he said. "I need you to find a good criminal defense attorney. No," he answered, "It's for Ophelia. She's been arrested."

It was a rough night for all of us, but to this day I can't imagine what Lia must have felt. My heart went out to her.

CHAPTER XXX

Quantum Girl Blue
(October 29, 1929)

"So, tell me," Great Granny said to me, "how is your being Quadruped Girl going to help us in our situation?"

"Quantum Girl, Great Granny," Mary corrected. "it's Quantum Girl."

"That's what I said, isn't it?" she replied.

"No," Mary answered, "You said Quadruped Girl She's not a horse, you know, though she would probably make a beautiful centaur."

"Well," Great Granny answered, "she knows what I meant. Now, how about letting her tell us?"

I reached into my pocket, took out a penny, stared at it, transmuted it to gold, and then I turned to Great Granny and handed it to her. "This should pay for food right now," I said. "Later, we can pay off the house."

"I should think so," Great Granny said, weighing it in her hands. "Thank you, Peyton."

"So, what's in store for the future?" Mary asked.

"What just happened," I said, "will be known as the Great Depression. A lot of people are going to be homeless and hungry. Men will wait for hours in line just to get a job for the day. Some businessmen will jump to their deaths out of windows. But in a few years, FDR will help take us out of all of this."

"Who's FDR?" Mary asked.

"Franklin Delano Roosevelt," I replied, "a distant cousin of Teddy Roosevelt. He'll put in place what he'll call *The New Deal* to provide jobs and insure bank deposits so that what just happened can never happen again."

"And so everyone lived happily ever after?" Mary asked.

"No," I replied. "In a little over two years, a German intelligence officer named Adolf Hitler will rise to power to become Chancellor. Then in 1939, Germany will invade Poland and begin World War II. The war will last nearly seven years and take the lives of upwards of seventy-three million people, including six million Jews who will be starved and gassed to death in concentration camps. Italy and, later, Japan will side with Germany and become known as the Axis, while Great Britain, the United States, and France will bond together as the Allies. The war will take a major turn in Europe when Germany and Italy begin to run out of fuel and when the U.S. drops two atom bombs on Japan."

"What are atom bombs?" Mary asked.

"They're bombs that can destroy entire cities," I replied. "Two will be dropped on Japan—one on Hiroshima and one on Nagasaki. The blast will kill hundreds of thousands and cause Japan to surrender. Five years later, the Korean War will begin, followed in another five years with a war in Vietnam that will last until 1975 and take the lives or more a million people, half of whom will be civilians. In 1990, Americans will enter into a never-ending war in the Middle East."

"It seems that all men are good for is war," Great Granny commented.

"Were you in any?" Mary asked. "Any war, I mean, As Quantum Girl."

"No," I said. "Never."

"What about just saving people?" she pressed on.

"From what?" I asked.

"Well," she said, "like from getting murdered or burned to death in fires."

"I wouldn't know where to begin," I replied.

"Maybe you could work with the police," she said.

"I think that most people," I replied, "would be afraid of someone with superpowers—especially the police."

"I'd be willing to vouch for you," she said. "I'm sure Great Granny would too."

"I think that Peyton should do what she thinks she should do," she Great Granny replied.

I stood there, not knowing what to say. I phased off my Quantum Girl costume and looked at them both, one at a time.

"I just know what I would do if I had all of your powers," Mary said. "I mean, you just told us about millions of people that are going to die, probably just because of the decisions of a few. If they were killed, all the rest would be saved."

"You're right," I admitted, "but what about the millions or tens of millions who won't be born because of it? What if I could go back in time and sink all of the slave ships so that no negro person would ever be brought to American? None of their descendants would ever have been born. It would be as though I had murdered all of them. Which is the better morality?"

"I'm not talking about the past," Mary argued. "I'm talking about the future. Even if you ignore all the wars you said will happen, what about the future in your time?"

"I suppose I could try," I said, "but there are nearly a hundred years between now and then and I don't know if I'll ever be able to get back."

"I understand," she replied. "It's just seems such a waste. What good are such powers if they're only really good for parlor tricks?"

"Someone should tell that to Harry Potter," I replied.

"Who's that?" Mary asked.

"A fictional character in the future," I replied.

"Enough of all this talk and hypotheticals," Great Granny broke in. "I don't need any more miracles just now. But I would appreciate my afternoon tea."

Mary and I both looked at her and then at each other and smiled.

CHAPTER XXXI

Quantum Girl Red
(March 14, 1943)

I gave a lot of thought to what Margaret in her innocence had said, comparing Quantum Girl to Superman. *What did I do for the world?* I asked myself as I lay in bed that same night. The world was at war for the second time in just two decades. Despite that I knew that it would end in two more years, the carnage would continue until then.

Few on the side of the Allies knew what was being done to the Jews in the concentration camps—the starvation, the gas chambers, the depravity. Hitler had risen to power on a message of hate. The Germans had been a defeated people, impoverished by the war that they had fought and lost—"The War to End All Wars" it was claimed at the time. The *Deutche Leute*, as they called themselves— the German people—had been starved out by the brutal politics of the time. Hitler blamed the Jews, many of whom had survived destitution through their control of financial institutions. He labeled them victimizers and said the true Germans needed to rise up against them, take back the Fatherland, and so they did. Each and every person of Jewish descent was rounded up, tattooed with a serial number on their arm, made to wear a Star of David on their coat, and either sent to a ghetto or to a concentration camp. The phrase at the onset, *concentration camp*, only meant that many would be housed in a relatively small area, but with Nazi politics, it came to represent a prison of starvation and death. This was the onset of the Holocaust, the method by which Hitler chose to exterminate the Jewish race in favor of what he described as those of pure Aryan blood. But what was I to do? If I rescued any I would alter the timeline. It was bad enough that my presence in the past must already have done things to change what was meant to be. But those who had died were already long dead in my time. What else could I do but stand by and watch, helpless to change anything for fear that millions who were born as a result of what the world became would cease to exist? This was my kryptonite—the knowledge that if I did anything to help, I would, in the long run, do more harm than good. And so I sat on the sidelines and watched the horror that was taking place.

Out of morbid curiosity, I guess, I decided to divide into two and then phase off to Germany (one of my having to stay with Margaret) in order to witness the Jewish men, women, and children who were reduced to near skeletons and then herded into what they were told were showers, told to strip, and then murdered with cyanide gas. Nazi dentists then went, one by one, among the bodies to extract any gold from the mouths of the victims, after which soldiers dragged the naked corpses to nearby massive trenches that had been dug, and rolled the bodies into them. Afterward, steam shovels plowed the excavated dirt back into the trench that had been transformed into a mass grave.

The Auschwitz concentration camp consisted of thirty-two red brick barracks for prisoners plus there was the administration building and the guard compound, the latter two enclosed by a barbed wire fence. Prisoners were forced to work ten hours a day constructing new barracks, paving roads, or laboring in the mills, mines, and factories of neighboring towns. There was little food or water given to them and there were rats everywhere which when caught at least supplemented their meager diets. Those who had been there for months or years took on the appearance of skeletons with little more than skin drawn over them. I walked among them, dressed as the wife of a German officer. They stared at me with desolate, hungry eyes. In one of the barracks, I came across a little girl who could not have been more than six years old, attired, like all the rest of the prisoners, in what looked like pajamas with thick blue and white vertical stripes. I spoke to her in the German that my quantum brain had quickly absorbed. Her name, she said was Hannah—Hannah Liebermann. Her parents were dead, not from the gas chamber or from being shot, but from giving all of their food rations to her. Still, she was undernourished and pale, with sad, blue eyes. As I phased ahead six months, I learned that she, too, had died. No one mourned her death. No one mourned any of their deaths. There was no one left *to* mourn. But for the scant survivors who would be rescued at the end of the war, the shadow of death hung over each and every one of them.

Tears came to my eyes as I thought of her—of Hannah—her small and naked body in one of the mass graves nearby, there to rot with the thousands of others until nothing would be left of her but the bones she wore in life.

"Fuck that!" I said to myself.

I went back in time to the day I had met her, to just after I had left, took her in my arms, and then phased us back to my parents' home. My mother was in the kitchen cooking dinner when Hannah and I suddenly appeared. She looked at both of us, but more at me.

"Why do you look older?" she asked. "And who is this little girl?"

"It's a long story, Mama," I said, "but I've had to stay back in the past to raise Grandma Margaret after her parents died. As for this little girl, her name is Hanna Liebermann, but from this moment on, she must be Hannah Herron, your niece."

"But where is she from?" Mama asked. "Surely, her parents will be looking for her."

"Her parents are dead," I replied. "They died trying to save her."

"Save her?" Mama asked. "Save her from what?"

"From starvation at Auschwitz," I said. "She's six years old, but she was born in 1937. She wound up in the concentration camp with her parents by the misfortune of being a Jew." I gently took Hannah's arm and showed my mother the numbers that had been tattooed on it. "If I hadn't rescued her," I told her, "she would have died. I need you and Papa to be her parents. I need you and Phee to teach her English. And I need all of you to love her. I would have kept her myself but I'm concerned about interfering with the timeline." I looked at my mother with the premonition of tears. "Will you do this for me?" I asked.

Mama stared at me and then at Hannah and then she squatted down in front of her and gently placed her hands on her shoulders. "*Wie geht es dir, meine Hannah?[10]*" she asked her in German, which surprised me.

"*Nicht gut,*" she replied in a sad voice, "*Meine Mutter und mein Vater sind gestorben und ich bin ganz allein.[11]*"

"*Nun,*" Mama replied, "*du wirst nicht mehr allein sein.[12]*"

Hannah smiled at her and then looked up at me. I smiled at her and nodded.

"I didn't know you spoke German," I said to my mother.

"Four semesters in high school," Mama replied. "A foreign language was required."

"I need to go back," I said as Phee entered the room. "I'm curious as to how the Holocaust could have ever happened and what sort of monsters were behind it."

"Be careful," Mama cautioned.

My face twisted into an *Oh, please!* sort of expression. "I'm Quantum Girl!" I said. "I'll be fine."

I glanced at Phee and then phased back in time, with her words, "Who's the kid?" echoing in my head.

I had thought to go back to when I left, but, after a quick trip to Phee's and my bedroom to glance at the Internet, I decided instead to phased to April 30, 1945, to the bunker in Germany where Adolf Hitler and Eva Braun had fled.

"*Was bist du?[13]*" he kept repeating as they saw me appear out of

---

[10] "How are you, my Hannah?
[11] "Not good," she replied. "My mother and father are dead and I am all alone.
[12] "Well, you're not going to be alone anymore."
[13] "What *are* you?"

thin air as Quantum Girl. Eva Braun simply fainted.

"*Ich bin der Messias*," I said, "*der Rächer der Juden.*[14]"

Hitler pulled out a Luger pistol from the holster on his belt and emptied it at me but the bullets dissolved in the quantum field I created between us. I stared at him with glowing eyes and transformed his uniform into that of a concentration camp victim. The man reached out to strangle me but as his left arm passed through the quantum field, numbers became tattooed on it. I did the same for the unconscious Eva Braun. One last thing was to phase off all of the hair on their heads, including Hitler's iconic mustache. That done, I phased them both back in time to 1940 and into Auschwitz. There, a Jewish madman would claim to be Adolf Hitler. There, he and his wife would be starved. Their clothes would turn to rags, though it would be Eva who would eventually wind up dying in the gas chamber. The Führer himself never visited Auschwitz, but Adolf Eichmann did on Christmas day, 1944. It was then that the now *Jewish* Hitler, emaciated and in rags, forced his way to the gate where Eichmann and several officers had gathered, as I stood by, invisible, watching.

"*Ich bin Adolf Hitler, ihr dummen Idioten![15]*" he yelled. Eichmann and the officers casually walked over to where the former Chancellor of the German Reich was standing and laughed heartily. "*Ich bin Adolf Hitler!*" the man screamed out at them, his face blood red. Eichmann's face suddenly turned serious. "*Sie sind also der Führer?*" he said back. "*Nun ja, zufällig habe ich gestern Morgen mit Herrn Hitler gefrühstückt... in Berlin![16]*" Then he pulled out his pistol and shot him in the head—turnabout was fair play for the man who had decided to play God.

Still curious about Nazi politics, I phased back a week or so and attended a few of the clubs that the S.S. and ranking officers

---

[14] "I am the Messiah," I said, "the avenger of the Jews."

[15] "I am Adolf Hitler, you stupid fools!"

[16] "So, you are the Führer?" he said back. "Well, it just so happens that I had breakfast with Mr. Hitler yesterday morning... in Berlin!"

attended and caught the eye of one *Oberleutnant* Wilhelm Schlass, who commanded an air squadron in the Luftwaffe. I was sitting at a small table in a corner of the room, nursing a glass of cognac. He approached nursing a drink of his own.

"Is this seat occupied?" he asked, glancing down at the one other chair at the table where I sat.

"Not that I know of," I replied.

"Then I'm welcome to join you?" he asked.

I nodded and he sat down. He was tall and good-looking with blonde hair and blue eyes—Aryan from head to toe and, no doubt, uncircumcised.

"*Bitte*,[17]" he replied to my nod. "I haven't seen you here before," he went on.

"I just arrived from Frankfurt," I replied. "The train ride to Berlin was miserable. I had to share my cabin with a woman and her screaming little monster." I fumbled with the cigarette I was smoking, then put it out in the ashtray on the table. "I came to see my husband off before he left. They assigned him to the Russian front. *Generalfeldmarschall* Brauchitsch."

The officer stared at me. "You are the wife of *Generalfeldmarschall* Brauchitsch?" he said, astonished.

"You have heard of my husband?" I asked, nonchalant in my tone.

"We have all heard of him," the *Oberleutnant* replied. "But I never expected him to have such a beautiful young wife."

"And I did not expect to have such an old man for a husband," I replied. "These are difficult times. Sacrifice and necessity sometimes go hand in hand. But now that I have missed him in Frankfurt, my sacrifice will have to wait."

I reached into my handbag and took out a package of cigarettes that was empty. Wilhelm—for I shall now call him that—immediately produced a blue guilloche enamel cigarette case from

---

[17] "Thank you," he replied.

his pocket. The case was encrusted with diamonds. He opened it up to offer a cigarette to me. I reached out and took hold of his wrist with one and took one cigarette with the other but not letting go. I placed the cigarette in my mouth and lit it with the lighter on the table. Then, glancing down at the case, I stared up at him.

"Faberge," I said, taking a drag on the cigarette and then exhaling the smoke. "Where does an *Oberleutnant* come upon such a thing?"

Wilhelm shrugged. "It was in the house of one of the Jews we put on a train," he replied. "They will not need such luxuries where they were sent."

"The Jews!" I bemoaned. "Filthy, disgusting creatures! One had the nerve to spit on me as I walked down the sidewalk with my husband." I stomped out the second cigarette in the ashtray as I had done the first. "My husband had him dragged off and shot."

Wilhelm looked down at his wrist and at the hand that was still holding onto it. "Perhaps," he replied, "since you have missed your husband, you will permit me to show you some of the sites of Berlin?"

"I would like to see the Chancellery," I told him. "Walther had promised he would take me there and show me around, perhaps even introduce me to the Führer."

"I cannot make such promises as to introductions," Wilhelm replied, "but I can take you on a tour of the building. Perhaps afterward we might go dancing or back to your hotel."

"I have not had the time to find one yet," I replied.

"Then I must insist that you stay at my flat," he said.

"And would your wife be comfortable with that arrangement?" I asked, turning his wrist to reveal a gold wedding band.

"My wife," he replied, "is comfortably at our home in Stuttgart where she crochets doilies and talks endlessly about the weather."

"Any children?" I asked.

"The doctors said that she is infertile," he replied, "or that I am."

He paused and then admitted, "I would have liked to have had a child to carry on the Schlass name."

"What if it was a girl?" I asked.

"Then, I guess," he said, "the Schlass name would be a casualty of the roll of the dice."

"But your bloodline would still go on," I replied, "unless diluted by some Jew she might fall in love with."

"The blood of Aryans and Jews do not mix," he replied. "It would be like trying to mix oil and vinegar. Come on," he said as he rose from his chair.

I looked up at him. "The Chancellery?" I asked.

"The Chancellery," he replied and then walked around behind me and helped me with my chair.

We took a cab to the Nazi headquarters. It was a large three-story white stone building with a dozen columns in front that rose staunchly over eleven arches that gave way to the inside. Two uniformed guards stood outside the entrance. After Wilhelm presented his papers, we were permitted to go inside where we were greeted by a large lobby with walls that were carved out by more than sixty or seventy arched windows and a visible open hallway on the second floor. The floor of the main floor, visibly boasted a rather busy pattern of predominantly white ceramic tiles, edged in black with a double-edged black tile boarder that held a similar albeit larger pattern to that which I just described. My overall impression was that it was a stark although expensive design that I would define the modern gothic style.

"Welcome to the Ernst Reuter House," Wilhelm said as we stood beneath its massive ceiling. "It is just a building like many others—brick and stone. But here, unlike similar structures, lies the brain and heart and soul of the Third Reich. Here is where the Führer gathers with other members of the German High Command and makes his decisions so that the human race will be purified in the eyes of God."

It was just then that two men entered the great hall. Wilhelm came to attention, thrust out his right arm, and said, "Heil Hitler!" The men in question, quite coincidentally, were Hitler and Eichmann. The salute was acknowledged with a slight wave of the head by Eichmann and a glance by Hitler. The men passed by us and then exited the building. As they did, Wilhelm lowered his arm and relaxed a bit.

"Have you any idea the men who were just here?" he asked.

Did Hitler, I wondered, *have any idea that in just a few hours, Eichmann would take a train to Oświęcim, Poland where Auschwitz was located, and shoot him in the head?*

"Adolf Hitler and Adolf Eichmann," I replied. "My husband has their photos over our fireplace mantle. But I have not seen either of them in person until now."

"It is the greatest of honors," Wilhelm assured me, "for from the ashes of a defeated Germany, they will have the Fatherland conquer the world."

"And what will be your place in this new world?" I asked. "Perhaps as Führer yourself one day."

Wilhelm turned pale at my words. "One must not speak such things," he said in a quiet voice. "There are those who take note of the slightest echo and pass them up the chain of command. With such words, I could be sent to the Russian front with your husband." He took a hold of my hand. "Let us go back to my flat," he said. "I have a bottle of schnapps that will take the chill from my bones."

CHAPTER XXXII

Quantum Girl Red
(the abducted one)
(Urth, 2038)

z

I was trapped. I had played his game hoping that I might win, hoping that if I did he would let me go but he hadn't and that was that. I would risk Margaret by trying to escape and I knew that my other self would take care of her for as many years as she needed care just as I would have done.

The male Peyton Herron was more of a sad figure rather than evil. The fact was that he was desperately and irrevocably in love with me based upon some incomprehensible belief that when we were younger we had *been together* which I say as an allusion to our having had sexual relations. None of that or any similar event was part of my memory and I often wondered whether it had been the previous version of me or one of her interdimensionals who had mated with him in his past. If that were the case I could partially understand his great attraction toward me. Still, whoever it was who had had with him, it most certainly wasn't me.

I cooperated. I had no choice. He was kind to me—loving might perhaps be a better word. There was sex between us every night except when I had my periods—sex with no love—at least not from Often times, he would take me places such as to the theatre, the opera, and museums—even through time into the past or future on his world. me. It came as odd to me that his parents recognized me at once and were both very loving, cordial, and accepting of the fact that the two of us were together as a couple. The problem beyond all else was that Peyton and I were different versions of each other. That felt strange to me, though I remember having been told about Liam, who was Phee's male counterpart—about them falling in love and everyone accepting it at the time—and that made me feel a little better. Mark was still on my mind but I knew that while he was gone from my life forever, at least, perhaps, he might be with the other one of me—the one with Margaret—the one on my Earth.

It was arranged that Peyton and I would marry due to the fact that I had become pregnant. It was not by choice but encouraged because he said there were other versions of him out there who had each gone in search of me who were "not as nice" as he was. It was a quantum wedding. On this world, in this reality, all of the adults had god-stones in their heads. The ceremony took place on Titan with Saturn and its rings large and impressive in the sky. The terrain of the satellite was mostly rock and pebbles but Mr. Herron—who was the male version of my mother as all the sexes here are reversed—had phased there earlier and carved out a flattened plain and then phased seating and an altar, while Mrs. Herron—Jane— had taken upon herself to phase flowers, tables, and food. About fifty relatives and guests were present including a male version of Phee and his husband, Clark. I was dressed in a Michelle Cinco gown with a twenty-foot train, encrusted with thousands of Swarovski crystals. A female minister conducted the ceremony. The *I do* I spoke was particularly difficult considering the circumstances but the words came out and a moment later, I was Mrs. Peyton Herron, matriarch of the Herron household with two little boys on their way to being born.

We named them John and Samuel. Peyton chose the names without any knowledge of their counterparts in the other reality. It was a hard delivery but the two came into the world unscathed— John with a swath of dark hair and Samuel, sandy blond. I couldn't help but love them and in the next five years that passed, they grew into smart and loving children.

It was a rainy March, however, when one of Peyton's duplicates returned. This one had been searching all this time without success and he became angered at the thought that his other self had been with me for the years he had been alone.

"Merge back into me," my now husband said, "and share my memories."

"Memories of what you had while I was gone are not the same," he cried out, "as having lived through it, having touched her, having fucked her! It is time for me to be with her and not you, especially since I sense that we have changed much from our time apart! You have grown soft and weak, doting on her like a dog to its mistress!"

"She is my wife now," my Peyton said, "ours if you so choose. Recombine with me."

"To hell with you!" the other said and then blasted him with quantum energy.

My husband flew twenty feet backward. When he recovered, a battle ensued—one quantum man against another. No one else was around. No other adult, I should say. But the clash awakened the twins from their naps and they wandered out together to see what the ruckus was all about.

"Stay inside!" I shouted at them.

I tried to project a quantum field around them but it was too late. Both were hit by splattered rocks and instantly killed. I rushed over to their now-dead bodies.

"Murderers!" I screamed at both of my husbands. "Murderers!"

I took my children into my arms and wept the most bitter tears of my life. Silence ensued after they were killed. Moments later, I looked back over my shoulder to see my husband take hold of the other and force him back into himself. Then he turned to me and shook his head.

"You may not know it," he said, "but I've already gone back in time more than a thousand times to try and change things. No matter what I do, they always die." He paused briefly and then went on. "There is still one more of me out there," he said. "I love you too much to risk you as well. I have removed the barrier around you. You are free to return home. I cannot live with you for fear you will be harmed. And I cannot live without you."

Suddenly, his body began to glow as bright as the sun, and then he was gone. The next day, after a brief ceremony, we buried my twins and I returned back home. My other self was nude in the studio, having just finished a photo shoot. I stayed hidden in a pocket dimension watching until Arthur had left to go in back to his darkroom.

"You're been gone a day," my other self said, "but you look older."

"More than five years," I replied.

"The men who abducted you…" she began.

"One man," I said. "One strange man who loved me, who held me and then let me go."

Then I merged back into her, fully dressed as Arthur wheeled himself back into the room.

"I forgot to ask if you could come back tomorrow," he said.

"I need a few days," I replied as I broke down in tears.

"What's wrong, my dear?" he asked.

"Nothing," I replied. "I just remembered something that had happened. I'll be back on Friday if that's all right."

"Of course, it is," he replied. "If you need anything let me know."

"I'll be fine," I said. "I just need some time,"

I rushed out of the door and phased back home, leaving my car behind. I phased into my bedroom, threw myself down on the bed, and wept and wept until I had no tears left. I looked at the clock. I needed to pick up Margaret from school. I phased back to my car and drove there just as she was coming out the entrance doors.

"Mommy, Mommy!" she cried out as she raced to the car and got in. "I got an A in art for my drawings!" Then she looked at me and asked, "Mommy, what's wrong?"

I took a deep breath and then pulled away from the curb. "Nothing," I said. "Fair Margaret," I went on as I tried to regain my composure. "Did you know that you once had two brothers?"

"Uh-uh," Margaret replied, shaking her head.

"Someday I'll tell you about them," I said with a smile as a single tear dripped down my cheek. But I never did. I just held the memory of them in my heart.

CHAPTER XXXIII

Quantum Girl Black
(Date Unknown)

As the days progressed, Laaadra-Taaagh and I worked together to find and gather food as the ship's supplies had been depleted long before my arrival. I began to teach her English and she began to teach me Gaaalthaaaran. It seemed, though, that my quantum brain was far quicker to learn. I found out from her that the god-stones had been used for teleportation and for interstellar colonization. Then, suddenly, all of that stopped. No one knew why. More than that, communication ended between Rendenaaar and its colonies, some of which were on planets in galaxies billions of light years away.

"Shep saaastem saaatop duraaang laaandng," she said. "Shep craaach on plaaant. All killett jaaast noaaat me. Bhut me baaad huraaat. Tayaaak longuh tium Laaadra bettur."

I had never known an alien before but we became the best of friends. Her command of English became better but was hindered by her pronunciation. There were all too many ahs and hisses and clicks in her native tongue and she was not one to mimic the intonation I lent to words when I spoke. Try as she might, she retained an almost indecipherable accent and it became the brunt of humor between us. We would laugh about other things as well. Humor and companionship kept our spirits aloft. Once when we were bathing naked in a pond, she used her *yaaargh* to splash water on me.

"No fair!" I called out at her in her native tongue. "I have no *yaaargh* with which to strike back at thee!"

But I had two hands and did my best to retaliate. She did the same in return. Back and forth it went as a water fight between us, both of us laughing uncontrollably until, at last, she took hold of my forearms with her hands and cried out, "Enough!"

I caught my breath as did she, but then she pushed forward against me, thrust her lips onto mine, and kissed me. Her arms then wrapped around me and mine around her. I could feel the pairs of breasts pressed upon my one, all six aroused by the moment. Then her *yaaargh* went between her legs and the wetted fur of its tip gently stroked my vag until it found its way inside to churn back and forth, bringing such ecstasy to me as I had not felt in so long. I shared the sensation telepathically with her. I could feel the heart inside her beat rapidly, almost in rhythm with mine. And when the full effect of the crescendo of passion had been achieved, we both held each other tightly, shivering to ourselves until, at long last, we released the holds we had on each other and lay on our backs, floating mindlessly, trying to recover from the pleasures we had achieved.

That was the first time for us but it would not be the last. Days would pass and then years. I could have taken us both off of the planet we were on but without a map to guide me, I knew of no other place to go that would support life. But beyond all else, I had found peace and contentment with her.

It was early one morning that Laaadra-Taaagh shook me hard to awaken me from what seemed like a drug-induced sleep, it had laid so deeply upon me. I could hear a heavy rain outside as it pounded on the hull of the wreckage of the spacecraft that we called our home.

"What is it?" I asked her, moaning from the dregs of sleep that still drowned my conscious mind.

"A ship," she said. "I have already established communications. It was headed to Rendenaaar when it intercepted the distress call I had set up before we ever met. The ship will arrive in less than a day, but, unfortunately, it will take countless lifetimes to get back to Rendenaaar, even at near-light speed. Ever since the god-stones ceased working, our ships are no longer able to travel beneath outer space.[18]"

"Getting to Rendenaaar should not be a problem," I assured her. "if I am provided with star charts, I should be able to move the entire ship there instantly. Admittedly, though, I had never phased anything quite so large. *Perhaps,* I thought to myself, *if I multiplied myself a thousand times it might work.*"

The ship arrived that same evening with a compliment of nearly six hundred Gaaalthaaarans, as it turned out, who had been headed for a planet in a distant galaxy when the power of the god-stones failed and the ship and its crew were thrust back into normal space.

The starship, which was named *Straaaghtraaan* was akin to a small city. The intent was to phase the entire vessel to the planet to serve as a permanent base for the colonizers. When the god-stones stopped working because Khattaaara had stolen them, the ship stopped dead in space and was only able to propel itself at space-normal speed. That meant it would take over two hundred thousand years to make the return trip.

The members of the crew looked upon me with curiosity and disdain. I was of a species they had never before encountered. But it was when they saw me transform into Quantum Girl that apprehension was added to their emotional mix. And there I was, surrounded by aliens and not the illegal kind—actual extraterrestrials who in my time had been dead for trillions upon trillions upon trillions or years, and yet there they were, untouched by the ravages that time and space would eventually inflict upon them.

The captain of the ship was named Puhraaagrahn—a large Gaaalthaaarans with orange hair that ran from his head down his back and then blossomed like fire at the end of his *yaaargh*. He stared at me in my glowing black costume when we first met.

"What manner of demon art thou?" he asked in a burly voice

---

[18] Such was how the Gaaalthaaarans described faster-than-light motion through the quantum fabric.

that sounded like the serpent he likened me to.

"I am," I said, "called *Zhaaagur Scraaa*,[19], from a planet called Earth."

"And where is this Earth?" he asked.

"In another universe." I replied, "far into the future."

"There are no other universes," the captain said, "Only this one with Rendenaaar as its center."

I just shrugged. *Let him believe whatever he wants*, I thought. But aloud I said, "I can take thy ship and all of thy people to Rendenaaar, but I need to know the path to get us there."

With some persuasion from Laaadra-Taaagh, Puhraaagrahn led us to the bridge and activated a map that appeared to be made of particles of metal that rose and fell, forming the shapes of galaxies, and revealed our position in relation to the galaxy where Rendenaaar spun its course around its sun. With but a sweep of his hands, the stars grew larger and larger until the Rendenaaaran system was revealed.

"There!" the captain said as he pointed. "There hangs the beginning and end of all that exists. Behold Rendenaaar, the world where Khii, having created the heavens, first sparked life!"

So, Khii was their representation of God. *Had God created this universe as well,* I wondered, *and, if so, who would die for their sins?* Laaadra-Taaagh and I had discussed our separate religions. The Gaaalthaaaran idea of creation was similar to that of Christianity, but they had no Savior to redeem them. I spoke at length with her about Jesus but even so, she was filled with doubt. "If Jesus were truly the Son of God," she said, "why would God have let Him be tortured and killed?"

"So that He could wash away our sins," I replied.

"How would his death do that?" she asked. "Sin is not something tangible. It relies on the actions of each individual."

---

[19] As explained in Quantum Girls and Quantum Girl Nexus, *Zhaaagur Scraaa* means Quantum Girl in Gaaalthaaaran.

"His crucifixion," I explained, "redeemed mankind from the sins each of us is born with."

"But thou hast said," she replied, "that because of the transgressions of Adam and Eve, which thou hast called Original Sin, all women thenceforth, should bear pain and hardship in childbirth. And yet even after His death, with their sins supposedly washed away, women giving birth still suffer. Why then should the curse of Eve not have been lifted as well?"

I thought about that long and hard. This was the rote my mother had drilled into me since I was able to speak. "And why," Laaadra-Taaagh had said, "should knowledge be considered a cursèd thing to be reviled? Thou hast named so many men and women in thy history honored for their intellect. Why then should the first two have been banished from their garden for the sake of noticing that they were absent clothing? Even Jesus, thou hast claimed, possessed wisdom. Did then his death rob them of their percipience?"

I had no answer. Not once in all my Sundays at church was I taught to ask questions as bold and perhaps blasphemous as those she had laid at my feet.

"Stories!" she finally exclaimed, "Yours and ours! They are all but mythologies to coax our people into submission. Thou canst not fathom how everything that exists came from nothing. But neither canst thou explain the concept of love of one being for another that is born not of any gods but of disparate thoughts and emotions. Perhaps in our love, I would sacrifice my life for thee and perhaps thou might do the same for myself, but to contend that one person, whether being or god, by his actions could remove some intangible commodity such as sin, to me appears the same for us to think that the universe shall cease to exist when we die because we are no longer a part of its perception. Thou told me that the other Peyton combined all dimensions so that there remained only one. Where then would rule thy God? Where then would one find thy Heaven?"

"Perhaps within the quantum fabric," I replied.

"There to find the Silver Goddess," she answered, "who, by your telling, is the other Peyton Herron, a version of thee. Art thou then God, the Creator of Everything?"

"Nay," I said, "I am just one girl."

Laaadra-Taaagh stared hard at me. "I think," she said, "thou art perhaps more than thou dost realize. Still, I should pray for *thy* love rather than to some fabulous deities whether from thy people's writings or those of the most holy of Rendenaaar."

In the days and nights and years I had spent with her, Laaadra-Taaagh's presence had filled my heart with love, but her words made me doubt those beliefs that had for so long been ingrained in me by the religion I had been born into.

Regardless of the confusion that wracked my brain, it was now my task to phase the ship back to that world where my past incarnation had lived in all of her wickedness. How or why I had been brought back to this past I did not know. I put that thought from my mind, though, as I contemplated the means by which I would phase such a massive vessel back to its world of origin.

CHAPTER XXXIV

Quantum Girl Orange
(March 18, 1951)

There was something that had disturbed me ever since I had awakened in the body of my grandmother. Where had *she* gone? Where was *her* mind? Had mine replaced hers or was hers simply repressed? Not knowing how it had happened in the first place, there was no basis upon which for me to figure things out. And there was another issue that concerned my older self, who had raised Margaret since the Pearl Harbor attack, more than eleven years prior. Should I tell her who I really was, I wondered, or should I keep up the pretense? I opted for the latter.

My older self had encouraged me for some time to attend an Eastern college. Her personal preference was Smith in Massachusetts, ostensibly because it was "a good all-girl school," but in reality because that was the college that Grams had attended, where she had earned a master's in mathematics.

"I'm not sure if Smith is the right choice for me," I protested. "I mean, I don't know anyone who'll be going there and I'll be thousands of miles away from you and all my friends."

"It's important that you go," she insisted.

"Why?" I asked. "What's so special about it? It's just a college like all the rest."

"Because that's where you need to go," she said.

"Why?" I demanded to know. "You act like you can see into my future. If so, perhaps you can tell me what my GPA is going to be."

My older self looked at me curiously. "Your GPA," she repeated.

"Yes," I replied. "Grade point average. And?"

"Who calls it a GPA?" she asked.

"Everyone," I said, "Why are you interrogating me? I just said I didn't know whether I wanted to go to Smith or not. What the fuck!"

"Who are you?" she asked, her face becoming more and more serious with each second.

"What do you mean?" I replied. "I'm your daughter!"

"Who uses expressions," she said, "that won't come into use for another fifty years!"

I was caught. I shrugged. "If you must know," I said, "I'm you. I don't know how or why but I suddenly wound up in Gram's head in the past."

"How long?" she asked. "How long have you *been* in Gram's head?"

"About a year and a half," I replied.

"Jesus!" she exclaimed. "And in all that time you didn't think to tell me—to trust me?"

"You mean," I said, "I didn't think to trust *me*. Seriously, I didn't figure out that you were me until you mentioned Ted Bundy to the cops. Before that, I just thought the resemblance was some genetic thing."

"Well," she said, "now that the truth is out, we're going to need to find some way to get you out of there."

"And figure out," I replied, "where my or our actual body went."

CHAPTER XXXV

Quantum Girl Yellow
(The Rendenaaaran Universe)

I was Gaaalthaaaran! Somehow, I was back in time, not only in Khattaaara's universe but in her body as well. The problem was, I was not in control. I was just a passenger in her head, able to see through her eyes, hear through her ears, and experience whatever sensations she did but only as an observer. The worst part of it was that I truly believed that she was insane.

I shared consciousness with all of them. They were each eerie reflections of her evil—Khattaaara multiplied by six. There they were in outer space telepathing each other rather than her simply combining into one. It was as though she needed approval and reinforcement for her actions, even if the encouragement was derived from different versions of herself. Each one, no matter which color, spoke to the others as though she were a unique and separate individual. It was schizophrenia carried out to the extreme.

I could hear the conversation between them:

There is nothing to stand in our path!

We need to destroy it all!

Not before we take as much as we can first!

We need to take slaves for our pleasure first!

Why should anyone have what we want?

We need to act now!

Suddenly, there came the realization to all of them at once that they were not alone.

Someone is listening in!

How is that possible?

Hush! I can hear its thoughts!

It's not Gaaalthaaaran!

What if it wants what is ours?

Where is it?

Inside us, I think.

We need to know now!

We need to focus our thoughts!

Each of them turned their heads and searched around themselves, their *yaaarghs* held high. When nothing was to be seen, the thought came to each of them that the intruder had invaded their minds. I tried to mask my thoughts but that proved futile. I could feel their telepathic minds enveloping my own with voices that strangled my consciousness.

Peyton Herron, I heard them say in a chorus of reptilian sounds. *Peyton Elise Herron. Thou art not from this universe. Thou art… indeed… a reincarnation of ourselves! How far into the future hast thou come? Give forth thy secret to us! How do we find thy home? We see images. There are billions of our future kind waiting to be enslaved!*

Get out! I thought. *Get out!* I could not let them find Earth! *I just need to wake up!* I thought to myself. *Wake up! Wake up! Wake up!*

But it was all too late. Khattaaara began to merge herself together. I could sense her delving further into my thoughts, trying to learn where I had come from. I tried to block her out. I tried to think of something else—anything else! I thought of Mark and Phee and Mama and Papa and home but despite all that, I could feel Khattaaara's thoughts invading mine. And then it was as though they had a grip on my conscious mind, suffocating it.

CHAPTER XXXVI

Quantum Girl Green
(September 30, 39 B.C.)

As night drew down upon the land I had phased to, I took note of a glimmering of light far off in the distance and decided to investigate. This I did as Quantum Girl, an emerald figure in the moonless night. The light turned out to be a large campfire in the center of a large village of Indians whom I later learned called themselves the Chunwa, the distant ancestors, I later learned, of the Chumash tribe. All around were hundreds of huts that looked like igloos but for the fact that they were constructed of thatched palm fronds.

Most of the tribe lay asleep within their dwellings, though an old, crippled man wended his way across the open space in a cross-legged, sitting position, moving himself a foot or so at a time with the aid of two wooden crutches by which he lifted and then rocked himself forward. As he saw me, he mumbled some words to himself and then called out in a loud voice, *"Hutash! Hutash!* [20]*"*

All at once the village awakened. As its inhabitants emerged from their huts, those that saw me dropped to their knees and fell prostrate in supplication.

Assuming that my glowing Quantum Girl presence terrified them, I phased back to my Cleopatra self, though the transformation appeared to frighten them even more. I saw one young woman

---

[20] Hutash was the name of their Earth goddess and was married to the Alchupo'osh or Sky Snake, who could breathe out lightning bolts from his tongue. The tribe believed that Hutash created the first people from the seeds of a magic plant on Limuw, now known as Santa Cruz Island. When the island became too crowded, Hutash made a rainbow bridge over which the people could safely cross to the mainland—from the tallest peak on the island to the tallest mountain near what would later be named Carpentaria—warning them to tread carefully. Those who fell into the ocean she turned into dolphins to prevent them from drowning. That in turn led to the kinship between dolphins and men.

trembling as though the world was about to end. I went to her, bent down, and urged her to her feet. Still, she refused to look up into my eyes. I reached under her chin and, with my fingers, gently coaxed her head upward so that her eyes met mine. I smiled at her and then she, feeling a bit eased, smiled back. She offered me her hand and led me to a hut much the same as all the rest. She stopped at the entrance and then urged me to go inside with a gesture of her hand. I entered into a dark room that was impossibly larger than the structure outside. I turned and looked in all directions wondering how this could be. In the distance, I caught sight of a faint purple glow. As I approached it, the glow resolved into the figure of a man perhaps thirty years old, perched on an ornately carved wooden throne and wearing a costume similar to mine but with no cowl. Staring at his face, I thought it odd that he bore a strange resemblance to me.

"Good evening," he said as he stared back at me. "A little older than I expected, but quite beautiful nevertheless."

"Who *are* you?" I asked.

"Peyton Herron," he answered.

"Really," I replied.

"Peyton Eliot Herron," he went on.

"A male version of me," I said. "Is that what you want me to believe?"

"Believe whatever you want," he replied. "That's up to you." He rose from his seat, stood, and strode up to face me. "Do you think that just because you merged all of the dimensions you got rid of all of the realities?"

"That wasn't me," I said. "It was my predecessor, an alternate version of me."

"Interesting," he replied. "I myself was in a somewhat vegetative state until I was rescued by a predecessor of my own who I, unfortunately, and quite accidentally, killed. It appears we have quite a bit in common."

"I find it interesting that we're both here at the same time?" I asked. "Don't tell me you were secretly Mark Antony."

"Nothing of the sort," he replied. "I phased here from my reality because I knew you'd be coming."

"How?" I asked.

"By your trail through the quantum fabric," he replied.

"Just how long have you *been* here?" I asked.

"A few days," he answered, "to get acclimated."

"So, you can see quantum trails that haven't happened yet?" I asked.

"No," he replied. "I watched your trail and then went back in time to arrive ahead of you." He paused, turned back toward his throne, and then spoke again. "Out of curiosity," he went on, "what are your memories of your life on Rendenaaar, assuming that you have any?"

"Nothing," I said, "Only I heard that Khattaaara was a monster."

"And that," he replied, turning back to face me, "is where the similarity ends and the disparity begins. I myself have full recollection of my existence as Khattaaar, the bleeding heart emperor of Rendenaaar and its colonies. Anyway, I'm glad we've now found each other so that we can move on together."

"What do you mean?" I asked.

"Why as man and wife, of course," he said.

"You're joking," I replied.

He sat back down on his throne. "Whatever makes you think I would joke about that," he said. "I distinctly remember half a lifetime ago when the two of us had sex. I fell in love with you back then and have never quite recovered."

"Again," I replied, "that wasn't me."

"Then perhaps it was your predecessor," he said. "Either way, it's basically still you."

"I don't have feelings for you," I replied.

"Give it time," he said. "After all, you're not going anywhere."

"I can phase away from here anytime I want," I replied.

"I don't think you will," he said.

"And why is that?" I asked.

"Because then something unfortunate might happen to your dear Mama and Papa, and Phee," he replied. "As you may have discovered, you've lost your ability to travel through time, but I have not."

"If you expect me to share your bed…" I said

"As you did before," he replied.

"Again," I insisted, "that wasn't me!"

"It doesn't matter which one of you it was," he replied. "You're here now, you're mine, and you have no choice."

I felt helpless, trapped in the past, unable to protect my family. I had no idea what to do other than go along with his demands.

CHAPTER XXXVII

Ophelia
(March 14, 1943)

I wondered what was going on with Peyton. The part of her that left to go to New York to be with Mark had gone incommunicado. Meanwhile, the one who had stayed behind had totally disappeared. I didn't worry about that one of her too much, thinking the two had just merged back together and remained in New York, though I wondered, *What about her school attendance here?* The truth was that I missed her and wondering if she was all right sent my anxiety level through the roof. But then she appeared in the kitchen with Mom, dropping off a little girl named Hannah. I only caught a glimpse of her before she phased off back to parts unknown but she appeared several years older. Mom said the same. That piqued both of our curiosities. Regardless, I had no clue as to whether *that* Peyton was the missing one or the one who had gone to New York. Just thinking about it made my head spin. Things like that were difficult to fathom—especially at fifteen—when you had a sister who could duplicate herself an infinite number of times.

But despite that Peyton was gone, she left off a replacement sister in Hannah. Hannah was only six years old and didn't speak a single word of English which I took it upon myself to teach her. She was a bright and pretty girl but with sad eyes. Within a few weeks, though, we were able to communicate at least a little bit. She laughed riotously whenever I made an attempt to pronounce either German or Yiddish words. I apparently had a horrible accent when I did.

It was one night during the fourth week that something odd and frightening happened—Hannah briefly phased in and out of the bedroom we were in. She noticed it, too.

"What just happened?" I asked with grave concern.

231

"I was in the camp," she said with a terrified look in her eyes. "I don't want to go back there."

She stared at me and then threw herself against me and wrapped her arms around me as tight as she could. I held her gently, trying to comfort her.

"I don't know what's going on," I told her. "But I've got you."

And then it happened. She began to phase in and out again, only this time, holding her, I was phasing with her. We went from the bedroom to a dark room filled with ghostlike shapes people. When the fluctuations stopped it was the latter place we were in. It was night and the place was dank, filled with the stink of sweat and human feces. It appeared to be a barracks of some sort filled with people. I would hear their whispers and their moans. Of the ones I could make out in what light there was that had crept through the windows, most were emaciated, dressed in ragged uniforms with dark and light horizontal stripes. A number of eyes fell on us both. I didn't know if it was because he had appeared out of nowhere or if it was because we were nicely dressed and seemingly well-fed. One middle-aged woman came over and looked down at Hannah,

"Channa," she said, *"vau bistu geven? Mir hobn shoyn kukn far ir."*

I turned to Hannah. "What did she say?" I asked.

"She asked where I had been and said they had been looking for me. What should I tell her?"

"Say that I've been taking care of you," I replied.

"Mayn fraynd, Ofelya," she said, *"hat genumen zorgn fun mir. zi iz Amerikaner."*

"Amerikaner!" the woman exclaimed, staring at me with astonishment.

"Vos tut an *Amerikaner froy in aoyshvits?"* she asked.

"She wants to know," Hannah said to me, "What an American woman is doing in Auschwitz? What should I tell her?"

"Tell her," I began to say, and then said, "I don't know."

"*Zi veyst nisht,*" she told her.

The woman looked at me and then shook her head. "*A mshugene froy!*" she proclaimed. "*Nu, di gardz veln handlen mit ir.*"

"What did she say?" I asked Hannah.

"She said you're a crazy lady," Hannah replied, "and that the guards will take care of things. Can we go back home now?" she asked.

"I don't know how," I said. "It must have been something that Peyton did wrong that pulled us both back to your time."

"I don't want to be back here again!" she said with tears in her eyes.

"I'll protect you," I assured her.

"How?" she cried. "You're just a prisoner like everyone else!"

"We'll see about that," I said.

Hannah led me back to the triple bunk bed where she had spent her nights before Peyton had rescued her. Her bed had been at the bottom but there was a man already asleep there.

"*Shtey aoyf fun meyn bet!*" she insisted, pushing at him to wake him up. This was her telling him to get out of her bed.

The middle-aged man looked up at her with half-awake eyes, saw that it was her, and wearily rose from the bed and climbed to the top bunk, mumbling something under his breath. Hannah took my hand and urged me onto the bed with her. The straw-filled mattress was old and filthy and stank from the man's sweat. Regardless, as there was nowhere else, I got onto it and she followed. Hannah pulled a thin, moth-eaten wool blanket over us that smelled worse than the mattress, and spooned herself against me. I put my arm around her and held her. As my eyes gradually adjusted to the darkness, I stared into the night at the victims of this God-forsaken place. Looking up at the ceiling and hearing the muffled sounds and the creaking of the cots, I realized that there was at least one floor above the one I was in, filled with just as many Jews.

Morning dawned with one guard calling out, *"Aufstehen! Beeil dich! Schnell! Schnell!"* which Hannah said meant, "Wake up! Hurry! Fast! Fast!"

Everyone got out of bed and then we were all herded outside to use the latrines, men, women, and children alike with no regard for privacy. The stench was indescribable. After that, everyone was told to line up for the morning count. The problem was that there were two more prisoners than there should have been. One of the guards, a man in his mid-thirties, first walked up to Hannah and stopped in front of her.

"Also, Hannah, du beglückst uns noch einmal mit deiner Anwesenheit[21]," he said.

Hannah stared down at the ground.

"Ja," she replied.

Then he looked at me. *"Und wer, darf ich fragen, ist deine kleine blonde Freundin[22]?"*

"Ihr Name," she said, *"ist Ophelia und sie ist nicht klein. Und ihre Schwester ist Quantum Girl, die das alles mit einem einzigen Gedan-ken zerstören kann![23]"*

"Ach so" he replied, *"Antwortete er. Und wo ist ihre Quantum-Girl-Schwester jetzt? Wird sie wie Superman vom Himmel herabfliegen oder wie General Patton in einem Panzer?[24]"*

"Und du!" he shouted at me. *"Warum trägst du keine Uniform? Warum ist dein Kopf nicht rasiert?[25]"* He grabbed my arm and pulled back my sleeve. *"Und wo ist dein Tattoo? Komm mit mir!"* he ordered, yanking me from the line.

"Ophelia!" Hannah shouted after me.

---

[21] So, Hannah, you choose to grace us with your presence again.

[22] "And who, may I ask, is your little blonde friend?"

[23] "Her name is Ophelia and she is not little. And her sister is Quantum Girl, who can destroy all of this with a single thought!"

[24] "Ach so," he replied. "And where is this Quantum Girl sister of hers now? Will she fly down from the sky like Superman or in a tank like General Patton?"

[25] "And you!" he shouted at me. "Why are you not in uniform? Why is your head not shaved? Come with me!"

If she said anything else, it was drowned out by the distance, as the man pulled me forcibly toward and into the commandant's office.

The room at least was clean and warm. The commandant was an angular-looking man around fifty. Engrossed in paperwork, he glanced up at me for just a second.

"*Name?*" he said.

"Ophelia Herron," I replied. "I'm an American."

He stopped writing and looked up at me. "*Amerikanisch,*" he said with a look of distain. "*Und wie erklären Sie sich den Aufenthalt in einer der Baracken?*[26]"

"I'm sorry," I replied. "I don't speak any German."

"*Sie hat kein Tattoo*[27]," the guard said, yanking my arm up for the Commandant to see, at which point the Commandant stood up.

"I could have you shot as a spy," he said in a thick German accent, "but I'm feeling generous. The air is brisk. The birds are singing. And since you apparently like our facilities, I'm going to invite you to stay." He gave glances to two of the guards in his office. "*Verarbeite sie!*[28]"

The guards grabbed both of my arms from behind.

"Wait!" I insisted but to no avail.

I was taken to another room and ordered to remove my clothes by a stocky German woman. At first, I refused, looking at each of the guards. The woman threw a sharp glance at one of them, who came up to me and then slapped me hard across the face. It hurt really bad, but I tried my best not to show it. Not wanting to be hit again, I undressed down to my bra and panties, the woman ordered, "*Ziehen Sie Ihren Büstenhalter und Ihr Höschen aus!,*" by which I inferred from the way she stared at the undergarments I still had on me, that she meant for me to strip down entirely,[29] Reluctantly, I

---

[26] "And how do you explain being in one of the barracks?"

[27] "She has no tattoo."

[28] "Process her!"

[29] It's strange how the memory of spoken words comes to you once you've

did. Then she had me sit down on the table, spread my legs, and examined my vagina. It was humiliating, especially as the guards looked on and traded smiles with each other. But it was when the woman took out an electric clippers that I backed away and shouted, "No!" I tried to resist, but the men held me down.

Tears came to my eyes as the woman shaved my head. I watched through blurry eyes as all of my beautiful, long blonde hair dropped to the floor to be swept away later or gathered up for some rich *Frau's* wig. The woman then approached me with a rag, doused in alcohol and rubbed it on the inside of my upper left forearm, returned to her desk, and then came back with an electric tattoo machine with two needles that branded a serial number onto my skin after shoving a dirty rag into my mouth so that my screams would not be heard. A piece of white cloth adhesive tape was placed over the numbers, presumably to prevent infection—like these monsters cared! I was then taken outside where I had white powder thrown on me and then handed my new striped clothes—a shirt and pants, no underwear, thin-souled leather shoes, and given a used woolen blanket, similar to the one that had covered Hannah and me during the night. After that, I was shoved back into the barracks. It was Hannah who found me and led me back to the bunk bed. I threw myself down onto the mattress, buried my head in the blanket, and wept more bitterly than I had ever done in my life.

learned them.

CHAPTER XXXVIII

Quantum Girl Violet
(April 30, 2025)

Mark's father was already home when we got to his house. He was gaunt with graying hair, sitting hunched over at the kitchen table, a bottle of gin in his left hand, a glass *of* gin in his right.

"You're home early," Mark said to him.

Mr. Marsden turned his head slightly toward us. "I was told that my services were no longer required." He turned back to his glass and took a drink. "Who's your leggy friend?" he asked. "I don't recall that you *had* any friends."

"My name's Peyton," I said. "Peyton Herron and I'm pleased to meet you. Mark has told me so much about you."

"Nothing good, I take it," he replied as he poured more gin into his glass.

"I told Peyton she could spend a few days here," Mark said to him. "She missed her flight back to Los Angeles because she was helping me."

Mr. Marsden turned around and had an eyeful of me, head to toe, taking particular notice of my black eye.

"Looks like you found yourself a fighter," he said, still staring at me.

"That was Garrett Wentworth," Mark said.

"The boy you've been tangling with?" he replied, his gaze fixed on me, practically undressing me with his eyes.

"I try my best to ignore him," Mark said. "*He* tangles with *me*."

Mr. Marsden glanced at Mark and then stared back at me again. "And so how did your friend…" he began to ask.

"Peyton," Mark interrupted.

"How did Peyton," he went on, "wind up with a mule's kick to her face?"

237

"He threw me to the floor," Mark replied. "She kicked him in the um…"

"I get the picture," Mr. Marsden said. "And then he decked her. Feisty little thing, ain't she?"

"It's all right if she stays here?" Mark asked. "She's got nowhere else to go."

"I suppose," came the reply. "Put her up in Miller's room—what used to be Miller's room. Now, go and leave me be."

After we had left him—Mark and me and my overnight bag—he called after us, "Tell her not to mess with anything!"

Mark showed me to the room. It was fair-sized but with the footprint of his brother that included a lot of football memorabilia including a New York Giants helmet and jersey that were hung on one wall.

"Miller was into football," Mark said. "He was five years older than me—died from heart failure last year during one of the college home games. The doctors said it was from one of the Covid boosters he'd received. My Dad's never been the same since."

"Were you close with him?" I asked. "With your brother, I mean."

"Not so much," Mark replied. "He was the jock; I was the joke—the bookworm who never got into sports. Funny, Dad was so into football even though he was a drama coach. That's how my mom and dad met. She used to be his student and one thing led to another and she got pregnant with Miller and one thing led to another and they got hitched. I came as a surprise later on. I guess *he* took after my dad and *I* took after my mom. She was pretty good at writing like me. Anyway, Miller used to keep Dad in check. He had a violent streak in him as long as I've known him. I guess that's why my mom eventually left. After Miller went off to college, it all got worse, especially the drinking, and I became his punching bag. I guess that's just my place in life, considering what went down at school today."

"Hey," I said in a gentle voice, placing one hand on his cheek, "it's going to be all right. You'll see."

Mark shook his head. "You don't know my dad," he replied. "Not like I do."

During our time together in our future life, Mark had told me how his father used to beat on him, especially after he had too much to drink which I guess was a lot of the time. Without his brother there to protect him, he said it got pretty bad.

It was a long day, though, and so Mark went off to his room and I tried to settle in a bit. I got undressed and jumped into the shower. The warm water felt good as it poured down on me. I thought I heard something but I dismissed it. Then, all at once, the shower curtains were pulled back and Mark's father was on the other side. His eyes went up and down my naked form. I was about to scream when his fist came at me and hit me in the face much harder than Garrett had. I didn't lose consciousness but close to it. Everything was a blur. As I collapsed, I guess he caught me because I felt myself lifted and brought into the bedroom and dropped down on the bed. But that wasn't the end of it. He got on top of me. He spread my legs and then he entered me—I who at that time was still a virgin. I felt a sharp pain as he ripped through my hymen and then mercilessly attacked my womb. Still in a daze, I managed to scream. A moment later, I heard Mark's voice.

"What are you doing?" he yelled.

He tried to pull him off of me, but his father was far stronger than he was. And then I heard a crash and the man went limp, his full weight on top of me. Mark pulled him off, pushed him to one side, and then stared me in the eye.

"Are you all right?" he asked.

"No," I sobbed.

There was no regard to my being naked—not by either of us— not a solitary thought. Mark helped me sit up. He was breathing heavily and I was beyond myself in tears. Then I glanced over at his father. There was blood on the bedding—a lot of it—that had gushed from his head. And there was shattered glass from the small round fishbowl that Mark had smashed over his head.

"I think he's dead," I told Mark, my voice trembling.

Mark went over, felt the pulse in his neck, and then rolled him over onto his back as I moved out of the way. The man was in fact dead. Vacant eyes stared upward. There was neither breath nor life left in him. Mark looked at me and shook his head.

"What are we going to do?" I asked him.

"We can call the police," he replied.

"And tell them what?" I asked. "We both just got in trouble for fighting. They won't believe the truth."

"So, what's left?" he asked.

"Get rid of the evidence," I replied. "There's a huge ocean right next to us and a lot of hungry fish." I glanced at his father's corpse. "He's already dead," I went on. "The dead don't care what happens to them—only the living do. There's no need to ruin both our lives over what he did."

"I'm the one to blame," Mark said. "Just me."

"Trying to save me," I replied. "He knocked me out and then began raping me. I'm fifteen years old and he knew that. The thing is that the law sees life through a different lens. There will be questions—suspicions. There'll be blame."

Mark didn't have words to answer. He just nodded his head in silent assent. I looked down at myself. The first thing I needed to do was to put on some clothes. Once I was dressed, the two of us attended to the gruesome task at hand. We wrapped the now late Mr. Marsden in the bedcover and then tied it around him with some rope that Mark found in the garage. Then we carried him to the car that was *in* the garage and loaded him into the trunk, which was not exactly easy for me, struggling to lift my half of one hundred eighty pounds of dead weight. That done, Mark slammed the trunk lid shut and turned to me.

"Okay," he said, "now what? I don't know how to drive."

"I do," I replied, "but where's the best place to get rid of the body?"

Mark took out his laptop and began to search. "There's a small lake off of Narrow River Road on the east end, about an hour and a half from here. There aren't any houses around but the road goes right up to the shore. We'll need the rowboat. I can strap it to the top of the car. And we need to bring some weights."

The rowboat was about ten feet long and had two wooden paddles, all of which were leaned up against the back wall of the garage. The car already had carriers on it. With a little bit of effort, I helped Mark get the boat onto the car roof so that he could secure it in place. Then we got into the car with me behind the wheel, backed out, and were soon on our way.

We didn't say a whole lot during the drive. It all seemed kind of creepy. I mean, it did to me. I can only imagine how Mark felt. Abuser or not, rapist or not, drunk or not, this was his father who in better times had actually been a decent sort of guy—at least that's what Mark had said. But time and tide change people, I guess, and Robert Marsden was a prime example. Some might have argued that his wife's abandoning him changed him, or that his son's dying left him hard, or that the alcohol took its toll, but the truth was that while adversity can distort who we are, deep down the good or bad in us is pretty much set in stone. Hard times just tip us in the direction we were meant to fall and Robert Marsden's character in the end was just who he was all along.

The night air was chill and quiet with just a thin sliver of moon to reflect any light from the sun that had hours ago disappeared from the western sky. It must have been two a.m. when we finally arrived. Mark unfastened the boat, then we dragged it to the shore. We did as much with the body in the trunk and then lifted it into the small craft. Moments later, our feet and legs wet from launching the boat into the water, Mark paddled out to the middle of the lake.

Throwing a hundred, eighty-pound body overboard is not an easy task, especially when it has another sixty pounds of weights fastened to it. The end result was that the boat heeled over, began to take on water, and sank as its cargo spilled into the black watery depths. Mark and I had to swim to shore. The problem was that Mark did not know how to swim. He began to kick wildly and swallow water. I had to calm him down, get him to trust me that if he just stretched out on his back he would float, and then I towed him back to shore. Phee could have done a better job of it. She was the competitive swimmer but Phee was nearly three thousand miles away.

We lay breathless on the land when we finally reached it, then hiked over to the car and drove back to Mark's home. It was nearly morning by the time we got there. We took separate showers, put on our night clothes, and then went to bed. Mark climbed into his. I didn't want to sleep alone after all that I had gone through that night. It was my call. I got into his bed after him and snuggled up next to him. As we lay there under one blanket, the only words that were said came from me.

"Thank you," I said, "for saving me."

And then we went to sleep.

CHAPTER XXXIX

Peyton
(the other one in Massapequa—
—the one with quantum powers)

Having said goodbye to the older version of me after we all had supper, I phased Mark and myself back to my bedroom in Santa Monica. It was three hours earlier and still light outside, not because of any quantum effect but because of the time difference. After rushing to the bathroom and vomiting in the toilet from the phase shift he still wasn't used to, he returned to find me with a look of consternation on my face.

"What's wrong?" he asked.

"There are supposed to be two beds here," I said, "not one."

"Maybe they moved one out because you left," he said.

"They wouldn't do that," I replied. "Besides, like I told you, one of me was still here."

It was at that moment that the bedroom door opened and a tall, blond guy peered in. "Dinner's ready," he announced. "And, by the way, it's your turn to do the dishes." Suddenly, he noticed Mark. "Who's your friend?" he asked.

"Who's my friend?" I spat back, bewildered. "Who the hell are *you*?"

He just smiled, shook his head, and strode down the hall toward the stairs. "And, need I remind you, you need to keep your door open when you have boys over! House rules!"

Mark turned to me, curious. "Who *was* that?" he asked.

"I don't have the faintest," I replied, "but I definitely need to find out. Come on."

We went downstairs to the dining room where the table was set for four, though Mama apparently had been told that there would be a guest, and so she was in the process of setting an extra place. Papa and the blonde guy were already seated. I looked at him with growing concern.

"Where's Phee?" I asked.

Mama glanced up at me. "Who?" she replied.

"Phee!" I repeated. "Ophelia. Your daughter?"

"You're the only daughter of mine I know about," Mama replied. "And I wish that you would give me a heads-up before you bring one of your friends to dinner." She looked at Mark. "Not that you're not welcome…"

"Mark," he said. "Mark Marsden. I'm very pleased to meet you, Mrs. Herron." He turned to Papa. "And you, too, Sir."

"Mark's from New York," I broke in. "Massapequa." I turned, then, and stared at the blonde guy. "I guess it's not your turn to introduce me to *your* guest."

"Whatever do you mean?" Mama replied.

At this juncture, the blonde guy stood up and extended his hand toward Mark. "How do you do?" he said. "I'm Payton's ne're-do-well twin brother, Liam."

"What the fuck!" I unwittingly said.

"Payton Alise Herron!" came Mama's sharp retort. "I will not have that language used in our home or have it come from your mouth ever for that matter! We are Christians!"

"Yes, Mama," I replied, "but I *don't* know who *he* is!"

Liam (so that was his name!) just shook his head, glanced at his cell phone, and then turned to Mama and Papa. "I'm sure it's a wonderful meal as usual, but I just got a text from the Kremlin. They want me to broker a peace deal in Ukraine." Then he turned to me. "You can come along if you want."

"That's okay," I said, totally confused. "I need to stay with Mark just now."

Liam then transformed into who I later learned was Quantum Lad, a glowing orange version of me, and then phased off to parts unknown.

I looked at Mark and then at Mama and Papa. "I don't understand any of this," I said. "Where is Phee, who is Liam, and how in God's name did he get a god-stone?"

Mama and Papa looked at each other with concern.

"Liam is your brother," Mama insisted, "and as for the god-stones, your father and I passed them onto the two of you when you turned fourteen or don't you remember?"

"Could you fill *me* in?" Mark asked. "I'm in the dark about all of this."

Papa was the one who spoke. "Payton and Liam's mother and I both had god-stones. I was Quantum Man and she was Quantum Woman. It was the stones that pulled us together. That's how we met. What we did, we did in secret. We felt at the time that the world wasn't ready for real superheroes. But times have changed and now Quantum Girl and Quantum Lad, having revealed themselves have become revered icons. As for us old fogies, it was time for us to retire and live peaceful family lives."

"But that's not how it happened!" I exclaimed.

Papa glanced at Mama and then looked at me. "What you're thinking," he went on, "is probably just an aftereffect of the god-stone. It should pass in a day or so and then you'll forget all about that Ophelia girl."

"It's just a temporary delusion, Dear," Mama said comfortingly. "You're father and I both had them after the god-stones went into our heads. You just need to take things easy for the next few days."

"So," said Papa, staring at Mark, "what are your intentions with our daughter?"

"I'm in love with her, Sir," he said.

Papa turned to Mama and then shook his head to himself. "I hope her tailor doesn't mind," he whispered in her ear.[30]

"She's a grown girl," Mama said. "She can do what she wants. It's a woman's prerogative to change her mind." She then looked at

---

[30] At least that's what I thought I'd heard.

the both of us. "Please remember to use protection if the two of you have sex," she said. "and by that, I mean a harness. I remember one time I was having intercourse with a lovely young boy and the moment I had my orgasm, the quantum force shot him backward clear across the room and slammed him into the wall. The poor thing broke his collarbone and two ribs. He was in the hospital for months afterward."

"We'll try and remember that, Ma'am," Mark replied, massaging his right shoulder with his left hand as he spoke.

We ate dinner pretty much in silence with glances back and forth between Mark and myself. It was meatloaf and mashed potatoes and gravy with salad on the side. Mama always liked to include the salad with the meal rather than making it a preliminary. Dessert consisted of chocolate ice cream with hot fudge sauce. When it was over, Papa suggested that I take Mark back to my room.

When we were in the room, Mark and I began to laugh uncontrollably. "I keep picturing the guy being thrown across the room," he laughed.

"Oh, my God!" I laughed back. "But those aren't my parents!"

"What do you mean?" he asked.

"My parents never had quantum powers," I said. "I don't have a brother. And my being Quantum Girl is still something I've kept hidden from the world. I must have phased us into some batshit crazy alternate universe."

"Just one question, then," Mark asked.

"What's that?" I replied, still trying to contain my laughter.

"Well," he said, "if we're in some alternate universe, where's the other you—the one who actually is from here?"

We didn't have long to wait for the answer as a moment later, a Quantum Girl phased into the room, stared at the two of us, but mainly at me demanding to know, "Who the hell are you?"

CHAPTER XL

Peyton

*(the one who stayed behind
with Ophelia who woke up in
the alternate reality)*

The trial for Lia was held at the Clara Shortridge Foltz Criminal Justice Center in downtown Los Angeles, an eighteen-story rectangular building that resembled a white honeycomb with the appearance that it was all balanced on dozens of tall white columns. The deputy/bailiff opened the doors at 8:30 a.m. and court convened half an hour later. All of this took place six months and four days after her arrest.

Aside from courtroom staff, lawyers, and the jury, there were the families of the victims, two of the victims themselves (the two who had survived), several witnesses, and a number of reporters and sketch artists. Lia sat beside her lawyer at the defendant's table, dressed in a white blouse and tweed skirt. At a few minutes past nine, the judge entered the courtroom, a man in his fifties with a pale complexion and graying hair.

"All rise!" the bailiff called out, "Department 347 of the Superior Court of the State of California for the County of Los Angeles is now in session, the Honorable Lawrence J. Pierce, judge presiding." When the judge sat down, he went on with, "Please be seated."

The judge looked toward Lia. "Will the defendant please rise," he said. Lia stood. "The defendant, Ophelia Elise Herron, a minor, is charged with one count of murder in the first degree and two counts of mayhem under California Penal Code Section 203 wherein it is alleged that she did willfully and with aforethought and malice, murder and castrate one Perry Dunbar, age seventeen, and castrate one Brett Dunbar, age eighteen as well as one Fred Terrell, age twenty. The jury has been sworn." He glanced down at some paperwork on his desk and then looked up again. "Is the prosecution ready for its opening statement?"

The assistant D.A. stood and spoke, "Yes, your Honor," she replied.

"Proceed," said the judge.

Marion Beckford, an attractive woman in her thirties, turned to the jury. "Despite the defendant's young age," she began, "what we are dealing with are some of the most heinous crimes that have come across my desk in the seven years I have been a prosecutor—three young men castrated and one murdered with no less than twelve stab wounds to his chest. The two survivors will never be able to have children—perhaps never to marry due to how the defendant mutilated them. To look at her, one sees a beautiful young woman, outwardly innocent and demure. But look inside her heart, for therein lies a vicious animal that destroyed the lives of two brothers and their friend. It is therefore our intent to prove that the defendant, Ophelia Herron, did, with malice and aforethought, murder and maim her victims."

She then sat down. A moment later, Lia's defense attorney, Aaron Milner, a decent-looking man in his early fifties, rose to his feet and walked out into the well.

"All of us are human," he said. "Every man and woman eat and drink, breathe air, and know both love and hate, but each to a different degree and to a different purpose. The Bible tells us, 'Thou shalt not kill,' but in war, soldiers are told *to* kill, and in twenty-seven states, including this one, there exists the death penalty. 'Thou shalt not kill,' except, apparently, with good reason. After 9/11, we went into Afghanistan and we killed, not because we had to, but because we could not allow the nearly three thousand who died on that day to have perished in vain. The defendant, Ophelia Herron, has a twin sister—not an identical twin, but a twin nonetheless, who is sitting just behind her."

The jury and everyone else in the courtroom all turned and looked at me.

"For nine months of their lives," Aaron Milner went on, "they shared a womb, and, for the decade and a half that followed. they shared their lives. The prosecution told you that Ophelia Herron viciously murdered and castrated one young man and then castrated two others. But what she did not disclose was that those same three young men had cornered her sister in the girls' bathroom at school and brutally raped her, each one of them taking turns, one of them sodomizing her—all of this after shoving a dirty rag into her mouth so that she couldn't scream. Eight years ago, the slogan that went viral across the nation was 'Believe All Women' who said they were victims of sexual assault. Ophelia Herron believed her sister when she told her how she had been gang raped by the two men who now sit in this courtroom and by the one who paid the ultimate price for his sin. Ophelia Herron, fifteen years old, now sits in judgment for crimes committed not out of malice but out of the immeasurable love for her twin. Ophelia Herron could not let her sister be raped and sodomized in vain. Perhaps she didn't have the maturity of those in government to decide what is right and what is wrong. She is fifteen years old. Ophelia is no monster and I intend to prove that what actions she took were predicated on both the belief that further harm would come to her sister and from a preponderance of love."

After he sat down, the judge said, "Is the prosecution ready to call its first witness?"

"Yes, Your Honor," Marion Beckford replied. "We would like to call Det. Peter Mortimer to the stand."

Det. Mortimer rose from his seat in the gallery and walked to the elevated chair beside the judge's desk. The bailiff then approached.

"Please state your name," he said.

"Det. Peter Robert Mortimer," came the reply.

The bailiff went on. "Please raise your right hand. Do you solemnly swear to tell the truth, the whole truth, and nothing but the truth so help you, God?"

"I do," Mortimer answered.

"Det. Mortimer," Beckford said, "Would you describe the three crimes to us?"

"Objection, Your Honor," Milner chimed in. "Vague and ambiguous as to which crimes."

"I'll rephrase," Beckford said. "Det. Mortimer, would you describe for us the three crimes alleged to have been committed by the defendant?"

"I was first called to the Dunbar residence," he replied, "the same night as the incidents occurred, at approximately ten-thirty p.m. Perry Dunbar was already deceased with twelve stab wounds to his chest. He was on his back, his trousers were open, and there was blood around his pubic region as a result of his genitals having been severed. The genitals of his older brother, Brett had also been severed but by the time I arrived he had already been taken to the hospital by an ambulance."

"Were the genitals of any of the victims ever recovered?" she asked.

"Just those of Perry Dunbar which were found near his body," he replied.

"What do you believe happened to those belonging to the other two victims?" she asked.

"We concluded that they were flushed down the toilet," he replied, "based upon the trails of blood leading from the upstairs hallway to the upstairs bathroom."

"And did you find anything else?" she asked.

"Yes," he answered, "we found the defendant's fingerprints on a kitchen knife that one of the surviving victims had wrestled from her hands before she fled."

"Did either of the surviving victims," the prosecutor went on, "identify their assailant?"

"Yes they did," he answered. "They identified the defendant,

Ophelia Herron."

"No further questions," Beckford said.

The trial went on as most trials do, calling the victims to the stand, the victims who lied, insisting that the rape was consensual. The county coroner testified as to how the knives were used and, in the case of Perry Dunbar, which wound caused the fatality. She demonstrated with a forensic mannequin how the first stab occurred while he was standing and showed that from the angles of the remaining eleven wounds, he was already dead on his back on the floor. Lia sat phlegmatic through it all without anger or tears. Even her fists remained unclenched and calm. Finally, on the third day, she was called to the stand. The defense went first.

"Miss Herron," the defense counsel said, "did you commit the crimes that are alleged?"

"Yes, Sir, I did," she replied.

"Can you tell the court why?" he asked.

"Because of what those three did to my sister," she replied.

"And what did they do?" he asked.

"Objection!" Beckford said. "The victims are not on trial."

"Goes to the defendant's state of mind at the time of the incident," Milner said.

"I'll allow it," the judge ruled. He turned to me. "You may answer the question," he said.

"They raped her," she replied, "and one of them, he sodomized her. They stuffed paper towels into her mouth so she couldn't call for help. The doctors said that after all that had happened, she might never be able to have kids."

"Why did you take it upon yourself," he asked, "to do what you did?"

"The rape kit didn't prove anything," she replied. "They must've worn condoms and so the police weren't going to do shit." She looked out toward the jury. "My mother is a Christian and she taught me to be one, too. In the Bible, it says, 'An eye for an eye,' not 'An eye for a sigh.' She read me passages about Jesua and about how the Romans mocked her as the Queen of the Jews and made her wear a crown of roses with the thorns still attached and how they raped her one by one until she could take no more and cried out, 'O Mother, O Mother, why hath Thou forsaken me?' Well, Peyton, she couldn't even cry out to God because of the towels down her throat. After it all happened, she smashed her fists into the mirror, shattering it, cutting herself so badly she might have bled to death if someone hadn't found her in time." She glanced at me and then stared toward the jury. "The fact that someone did find her in time was just luck. When I broke into the Dunbar home through the back door in the kitchen, I heard them all laughing about it."

"Did you go there to kill them or castrate them?" he asked.

"No, Sir," she replied. "As I said, my mother taught me the Bible and about forgiveness. But for people to be forgiven, they need to know remorse which obviously they didn't. I'll admit that I became very unchristian at that moment. That's when it came to me what I had to do. I took off all my clothes, even my underwear, and walked into the living room where all three of them were. None of them needed any prompting as to what to do next. All of them dropped their trousers and their tidy whities, while I went over to a bureau and faced it and spread my legs. What none of them saw, though, was the kitchen knife in my hand. Perry was the first to try and fuck me and when he actually began to put it in me, I wheeled around and stuck the knife into him all the way to the handle. He looked at me with terror in his eyes and then fell down onto his back. Meanwhile, the other two ran half-naked up the stairs and I followed them. I was waving the knife around when Fred Terrell, who came at me from behind from one of the bedrooms, grabbed one of my arms and Brett tried to take the knife away but I got him in the crotch. It went right through and cut it off. I saw it fall to the floor and there was blood gushing and he was holding himself trying to make the blood stop and then Fred spun me around and yelled,

'I'm going to kill you, bitch! I'm going to kill you!' forgetting, I guess, that I still had the knife and so I did the same to him and he started screaming as well. Then both of them rushed back downstairs to get away from me, forgetting their junk on the floor, which I picked up and flushed down the toilet. After that, I followed them downstairs. Perry was already dead, but there was so much anger bottled up in me about what they did to my sister that I just kept stabbing him and then castrated him as well. Only with him, I didn't flush anything. I heard the dog in the yard barking and I threw it to him as a treat. After that, I got dressed and left the way I came."

After final arguments, the twelve men and women who had been selected to decide Lia's fate deliberated for a little more than six hours. When they were once again seated in the jury box, the judge turned to the foreman.

"Has the jury reached a verdict?" he asked.

"We have, your honor," the foreman replied.

The bailiff took a slip of paper from the foreman and handed it to the judge, who unfolded it, and then looked at it.

"As to count one," the judge said, "mayhem as pertains to victim one, Brett Dunbar, how do you find?"

"We find the defendant not guilty," the foreman said.

There was a noticeable sigh of relief from Lia and Mama and Papa and myself, though a murmuring on the prosecution's side of the gallery.

"As to count two," the judge went on, "mayhem as pertains to Frederick Terrell, how do you find?"

"We find the defendant not guilty," the foreman said.

I could see Lia breathing easier.

"As to count three," the judge continued, "mutilation of a corpse, how do you find?"

"We find the defendant not guilty," the foreman said once more.

"As to count four," the judge asked, "how do you find?"

I could see Lia noticeably tremble. She turned to her lawyer who patted her hand and said something quietly to her after which she nodded her head.

"We find the defendant guilty," the foreman said.

Lia turned white upon hearing those words. Then, to the bailiff, the judge said, "The deputies will remand the defendant back into custody. Court will reconvene in two weeks for sentencing. The jury may be excused. We thank you for your service."

Mama, in tears, tried to go to Lia but one of the deputies held her back as Lia was taken away. Papa went over to Mama. She fell into his arms. I had no power to change anything. If only I did, the rape would never have happened. If only I could have gone back in time to prevent Lia from doing what she did. But I wasn't Quantum Girl anymore. I was just me, and so all I could do was watch, helpless to change anything that had occurred.

CHAPTER XLI

Quantum Girl Blue
(December 14, 1929)

Mary and I were playing checkers in the living room while listening to Amos 'n' Andy on the radio. It was our third game and I'd won the last two.

"Your move," I said to her.

Mary glared at me, noting the grin on my face.

"What are you smiling at?" she asked. "Am I about to lose *again*?"

"No," I said, "it isn't that, even though you *are* going to lose… again. It's the radio."

"What about it?" she asked.

"Amos 'n' Andy," I said.

"And so what?" she replied. "Everyone I know thinks it's hilarious."

"It's so politically incorrect," I said.

"What's that mean?" she asked.

"It means," I said, "that in my time, they'd be condemned for airing it."

"Because?" she asked.

"Because it's so racist," I told her. "Two white guys pretending to be two stupid black men, implying that all blacks are inferior."

"You mean negroes?" she asked. "Well, they *are*, aren't they?"

"No," I replied.

"Well," she said, "that's not what we were taught in school. In fact, it's in the Encyclopedia Britannica. I remember looking it up for a report I had to do in high school. Wait. Let me show you."

She got up and went to a tall thin cabinet where the books were all lying on their sides. She opened the door and slid out one of them.

"These were my father's," she said. "He taught history at Loyola." She flipped through the pages and then found the passage she was looking for. "Here," she went on, reading, "'Mentally, the negro is inferior to the white. The arrest or even deterioration of mental development [after adolescence] is no doubt very largely due to the fact that after puberty sexual matters take the first place in the negro's life and thoughts. The mental constitution of the negro is very similar to that of a child, normally good-natured and cheerful, but subject to sudden fits of emotion and passion during which he is capable of performing acts of singular atrocity, impressionable, vain, but often exhibiting in the capacity of servant a dog-like fidelity which has stood the supreme test.'"

"But none of that is true," I replied.

"Are you telling me that you know more than the Encyclopedia?" she asked.

"I'm telling you," I replied, "that the understanding of the races will change over the next hundred years. In fact, in exactly eighty years, a black man will become President of the United States."

"You're joking!" she exclaimed. "A negro President."

"Well," I admitted, "he was—or will be—only half black. His mother was—or will be—white."

"A mulatto?" she replied. "You do know that's against the law?"

"Not where I come from," I replied. "Blacks and gays have as many rights as everyone else."

"What are gays?" she asked. "I've been gay many times. Do you think that rights are taken away when someone is happy?"

"No," I replied. "In my time, the word gay means homosexual."

"So," she said, "in your time the government allows men to have sex with men and women to have sex with women?"

"It even allows them to get married to one another," I replied.

Mary took a deep breath and then let it out. "I don't know if I'm ready for your kind of future," she said. "But on the bright side, by then I'll probably be dead and gone to Heaven." She shook her head

256

and then looked me in the eye. "May we resume our game of checkers?" she asked. "I need something to distract me from all of the confusion you've thrust into my head."

I jumped three of her red checkers and then looked up at her. "King me," I said with a smile.

"Oh," she replied, "I'm just too distracted by all of this future talk. Are you sure you're not winning because of your quantum brain?"

"Well," replied with a smile, "if I could give you my god-stone I would."

We both laughed heartily, but then I grabbed my head. My eyelids clenched. My fists tightened. My throat let out a scream. The lights in the room turned dark all at once, each exploding their glass bulbs. And then, as if by magic, the god-stone flew from my head and into hers! The pain was gone but my breath was labored as I tried to regain myself. I lifted my head, then, to see her, garbed as Quantum Girl, in full costume, glowing blue in the blackness of the room.

Mary stood tall as though her body surged with immeasurable power, her back arched, her arms down and out at her sides. She raised her hands and stared at her glowing palms. Then she looked at me, my face illuminated by her quantum glow.

"What just happened," she said, her voice echoing as she spoke. She walked over to the mirror above the mantle and stared with awe and what she had become. "Why do I look like you?" she asked.

"I don't know what just happened," I replied. "The god-stone that was in *my* head is now in *yours*."

"So, now *I'm* Quantum Girl!" she exclaimed. "I can save the world from hunger! I can stop every war that might occur!" Then, suddenly, the exhilaration left her and she looked at me again. "I'm sorry," she said. "I guess this means that you don't have your powers anymore. I shouldn't have them. They belong to *you*. But I don't know how to give them back. You'll have to tell me."

"I don't know either," I admitted. "The other Peyton gave me the stone from her head but I don't know how she did it and she died just after she did."

"We'll figure this out, I'm sure," she said, going up to me and gently taking hold of my shoulders. "You've been like a sister to me. We'll get that thing out of my head and back into yours." She dropped her arms to her sides. "But please," she begged, "can you tell me how to change back to me?"

"Just think about changing back," I told her. "Clear your mind and command the god-stone to do it."

Mary did as I said. She closed her eyes and held her breath and in another moment, the costume and its glow were gone and she was back to being herself.

"Thank goodness," she exclaimed as she stared down at herself with only the streetlamp from outside casting a faint light into the room. "I didn't want to have to go out into public looking like that! Now, if we can just make our way around in the dark to find the spare lightbulbs, we'll be able to bring back some small semblance of normal. They're in the pantry on the upper shelf as I recall."

CHAPTER XLII

Quantum Girl Red
(March 14, 1943)

Wilhelm's flat was rather plain in that it just served as a temporary abode while he was in Berlin. It seemed that many officers shared the same building and most probably graced their living room walls with the exact same framed photograph of the Führer.

As I looked around at the trinkets he had on display, Wilhelm poured me a drink and then walked over and handed it to me, cradling the one he had poured for himself.

"Thank you," I said as I took the glass from him. I brought the glass to my lips and drank a small bit. "It is very good," I remarked. "Very sweet."

"It is all right," he replied, "but I will tell you, once I was in the Black Forest where they have many distilleries. There the schnapps is magnificent!"

I walked over to the window and stared out.

"If you look far over to the right," he said walking up behind me, "You can see the Berlin Cathedral. It was built at the beginning of the century by order of Emperor William II, designed by Julius Raschdorff in the Renaissance and Baroque styles."

"You seem to know a lot about it," I replied.

"It interests me," he said. "I was not always a soldier. I studied at the Bauhaus-Universität Weimar to become an architect. But then the war broke out and here I am. To be honest, I would prefer to sit at a drafting table with a pencil instead of having a pistol strapped to my side."

"Do you not revel in the dreams of our Führer?" I asked.

"I'm afraid my dreams are far more modest," he confessed.

I turned to face him. "And what *are* your dreams?" I asked.

"Not to conquer the world," he said, "but to find personal contentment."

"Surely you have that at home," I said, "with your wife?"

Wilhelm shook his head. "I married her," he replied, " because she told me she was with child but time proved she was not."

"She lied to you, then?" I asked.

"Perhaps," he replied, "but she is Catholic and doesn't believe in divorce so I am stuck with her. Regardless, for the moment, she is in Frankfort with her apron and I am here with you. It is a shame that you are married to *Generalfeldmarschall* Brauchitsch."

"To be honest," I confessed, "I am but his mistress. He divorced his wife a year before the war began."

"And how did he meet you?" he asked.

"The same as you," I replied. "He was strong and impressive at the time, but the war has aged him these past five years and he does not perform so well in bed as he did when we first made love."

I appraised the man with my eyes. It had been more than a decade since I had been with anyone and to have sex with him allowed me to have pleasure without emotional attachment. Regardless of the dreams that belabored his thoughts, he was a Nazi in his current walk of life and that was someone I could never even lend my heart to.

"Do you find me somewhat attractive?" I asked him.

He stared at me. "To ask such a question," he replied, "would be like asking Pope Julius II whether he found the ceiling of the Sistine Chapel somewhat interesting."

"Then despite your matrimony," I asked, "you would wish to have me in your bed?"

"Even should the Führer tell me no," he replied, "I would still say yes, at risk of being shot. You are more beautiful than any Fräulein I have seen."

"Then have me you shall," I said.

I walked over to the small bed at the side of the room, sat down,

260

and took off my shoes as Wilhelm watched me with bated breath. Then I stood up once more and removed my outer clothes, slip, and panties, my eyes never straying from his. All that remained were my black lace bra, garter belt, and stockings. He walked over to me and gently ran his fingers up the line of my sex.

"I have never met a woman," he said, "so smooth down there other than in statues."

"Then you must think of yourself as Pygmalion," I replied, "and me as Galatea." I looked him up and down. "But regretfully," I went on, "I see that you still wear your sculptor's clothes."

At once, then, *Oberleutnant* Wilhelm Schlass began to quickly and eagerly undress in front of me like a schoolboy about to have sex for the first time. How strange he appeared in his nakedness, uncircumcised as he was. I had never seen that before other than in photos of Michelangelo's David, which was ironic in that David in real life would have been circumcised as he was a Jew. Regardless, David's member as I recalled was quite a bit larger in that the statue stood more than thirteen feet tall—a frightening challenge for any woman I would think.

I reached behind me, unfastened my bra, held it out with my arm extended, let it drop to the floor, sat down again, and then unhooked my garter clips one by one. Next, I rolled down my stockings, reached down, and gently laid them beside my bra. Then I pulled down the garter belt lifting myself up just a bit, brought it over my now bare feet, and tossed it on the small pile I had just made. Finally, I laid down on the bed, my eyes never leaving his. I sunk the back of my head down on the pillow, raised my knees, and spread my legs invitingly, placing my hands behind my head as a sign of want and submission. The man climbed on top of me and then, at last, entered, moving rhythmically back and forth, groaning and sweating, especially toward the end. When it was done, he laid down on his back next to me, glanced at me, and then stared up at the stark white ceiling.

"Would that I could flee this wretched war," he said, "and take you with me, but there is nowhere to go. In another year, Hitler will have conquered the world, you will be at Brauchitsch's side, and I will be back in the arms of that wretched woman who wears my ring. Such is life. It is, as they say, the cross we all must bear."

"I must go," I said to him, getting dressed. "I have a train to catch."

"You go to the husband who is not your husband?" he asked.

"No," I said shaking my head. "I go home. I have a daughter that I need to take care of, who comes before the love of any man."

I rose from the bed, dressed myself, and then left with a bit of regret. *We are all*, I thought to myself, the *victims of whatever circumstances we find ourselves in.* Once I found myself alone in the hall outside the apartment, with an inward sigh, I phased back to my house in Malibu, just a few short moments after I had left.

CHAPTER XLIII

Quantum Girl Black
(Date Unknown)

A thousand of me breached the hull of the ship and then stood in space around it. My hands pressed against the cold metal surface of its skin, shielded from the radiation of its sun by the planet itself; not that it would have mattered as my god-stone would have protected me from the fiery surface of the very star the planet circled. I had been shown the star charts in order to be able to phase the entire vessel and its crew back to Rendenaaar, though I had made several preliminary jumps there ahead of time as a precautionary measure. When the time came, the legion of me phased the craft into low orbit around the planet and then accelerated it in order to keep it there.

It was an exhausting feat—moving a ship that weighed more than a million tons a distance of more than a billion light years—and all in less than a blink of an eye. Once done, one of me phased into the ship and then the rest phased into that one, which probably to anyone watching looked like a virtual tornado of blurs that finally resolved into a single Quantum Girl.

"We're here," I said, though only Laaadra-Taaagh could understand me, and then I collapsed, or at least began to. My costume wavered and then vanished, leaving me as Peyton again and naked for all of the crew who were in the room to gawk and sneer at. But she caught me and helped me to a chair. Then she looked around at my audience and shouted at them in Gaaalthaaaran. My command of the language was poor, but I still could read her mind as she spoke.

"How dare you laugh at her!" she yelled. "She has just saved all of your lives and brought us all back to our home world!" She turned to one young woman and commanded her, "Fetch a dress for

263

her to wear so that she will not shame these *chraaaghtaaa*[31] with her beauty!"

A dress was brought a moment later. Laaadra-Taaagh helped me put it on. It was made of a gossamer-thin blue metallic fabric that would have provided a normal human little warmth but served to guard my modesty until I recovered my strength. Another young female brought me an amber-colored drink that proved both refreshing and sweet, tasting a bit like grapefruit with a hint of lime. When I had finished, Laaadra-Taaagh walked up to me and extended her hand toward me.

"Come," she said. "The captain has offered his quarters for the night as a token of his gratitude. I fear that you are in great need of rest."

"I am," I replied.

I took her hand and she helped me to my feet. Then she led me to a cabin near the bridge of the ship, a large room with a window that looked out into space. Through it, I could see half of Rendenaaar, grand and majestic, as it orbited its orange star alongside its companion world with their moons. There I had been birthed in a previous existence, dropped from my mother's *yaaargh* into her *plaaaghnar,* the marsupial-like pouch in which I grew until I was ready to be born. And yet I had no memory of this planet or any of those who had tread upon its soil.

The room, which was neither rectangular nor round, was paneled in an ebony-like wood, while in each corner, also wooden but of a lighter shade, were carvings of trees whose branches hung over a bed, fitted with jewels of seven colors—hundreds of them— reminiscent and perhaps in homage of the god-stones that had empowered the Gaaalthaaaran civilization for thousands of their years.

I laid down in the bed and stared up at them, each with a faint glow from within. Laaadra-Taaagh snuggled beside me, glanced at

---

[31] A Rendenaaaran animal, similar to a slug.

me, and then followed my upward gaze.

"They're like stars in the sky," I said, "and yet each the color of a god-stone."

"Do you have god-stones where you are from," she asked, "other than those that came from here?"

"We have many gems that are both rare and beautiful," I replied, "but none wield such power as those of Rendenaaar."

"What will you do," she asked, "when at last you set foot on our soil? Will you plant your feet and make it your home or must I dread the threat of your absence one day?"—this as her fingers played with a strand of my hair.

"I don't know," I admitted. "This universe is alien to me and I to it."

When, several hours later, morning dawned on that part of the planet the spacecraft held orbit above, I decided to phase down to view the place of my incarnate's origin. I went with Laaadra-Taaagh, standing mid-air amidst the orange-tinged clouds, small beads of moisture gathered upon us from the billowing masses. My cape flapped in the wind that licked our ears with its vociferous breath. Below us was the capital of the Gaaalthaaaran empire with roads that disappeared into the horizon in every direction like the spindles of a spiderweb attached to trees so far in the distance that they were invisible to the naked eye.

It was disturbing, however, to witness the wreckage of the beauty that once was. Buildings that had once been held aloft by the god-stones lay in broken ruins on the surface, many having crashed into those that had stood firmly on the ground, all casualties of the theft that had been committed by Khattaaara and her confederates without regard for the consequences of their act. How many thousands just in this city alone had perished as a result of their plunder was heartbreaking—males, females, and children, their lives lost as a result of her quest for immortality and power. As I glanced at Laaadra-Taaagh, I could see threads of tears stream across her cheeks only to be swallowed by the atmosphere's hungry breath. She pointed toward one large and regal structure in the center of it all that had miraculously escaped the decimation.

"There!" she announced in defiance of the deafening blasts of air. "There stands the Palace of the Emperor!"

"Then, I guess," I shouted back to her, "that's where we'll need to go!"

I phased us down into what was the Great Hall. The empty room was round and as near as I could tell one hundred feet or more in diameter. The walls were marble that was embedded with the skeletons of ancient creatures the size of dinosaurs, the ceiling translucent with thousands of gems that, similar to those in the captain's quarters, the same colors as the stolen god-stones. Our footsteps betrayed our presence as we made our way toward one of the seven doorways. We both heard her at our backs as we were about to enter one of the passages and we both turned around to see a Gaaalthaaaran standing in the arch of the doorway on the other side of the room.

"Who dares to breach the sanctity of the Great Palace?" came a female voice, its source still hidden in darkness, spoken in the Gaaalthaaaran tongue which for some odd reason I could now fully understand.

I had expected her to emerge from the shadows a step or two but that did not happen. Instead, she phased to where we stood and sized us up. As expected, she was Gaaalthaaaran, but there were two things that struck me. One was the jeweled crown that she wore. The other was the resemblance. Despite that this being was Gaaalthaaaran, there was an uncanny resemblance in features to me! Laaadra-Taaagh noticed it at once, glancing back and forth between the two of us. This was not an ordinary member of this civilization or even a random member of its royalty. This was Khattaaara!

How could that be? I wondered. How could someone and their reincarnation meet each other? Then I remembered Cleopatra who

266

was also me in the past. I also considered the fact that as it would be possible to meet yourself in a different time, there would be nothing special about this, although the fragmentation of the soul in either circumstance would probably have given many a theologian or philosopher something to ponder over.

"Who are you?" Khattaaara demanded to know. "And how did you manage to find your way in here?"

"The same way," I replied, "as thou didst when thou spanned the distance from the doorway to here."

My words appeared to take her aback. "Only a god-stone can allow one to accomplish that! Didst thou murder one of my companions to acquire it for thyself?"

"Nay," I replied. "'tis my own, given to me long ago. Nor do I know ought of thy companions."

She stared at me and then walked around me, noticing my rounded ears and the shape of my breasts, apparent through my form-fitting costume.

"What manner of creature art thou," she asked, "absent *yaaargh*, with but one pair of *khalthraaam*[32], and with ears most suited for our males? Methinks thou must be a deformity of Nature."

"Not so!" I said in my own defense. "I am human, from a universe so distant in time from this that were this one as a grain of sand at thy feet, mine would be so far as all the grains of sand on this world laid end to end." I phased off my cowl and revealed my face to her. "My name is Peyton Herron and I come from a planet called Earth."

"And on thy planet Earth," she replied, "do all of thy people possess god-stones such as thine?"

"Nay!" I said and shook my head. "I alone possess one."

She stared hard at me. "Thy face is familiar," she said, "almost to make mockery of us."

"Apologies," I replied, "but there is reason behind such

---

[32] The Gaaalthaaaran word for breasts.

resemblance, for although I now stand before thee, I am the reincarnation of thyself, forced to relive all at once the memories of what thou hast done and of what thou yet shall do. I have just now witnessed the wreckage caused by thy theft of the god-stones from the vault where they were held."

"Why should one care about the weaknesses of others?" she shot back. "Like myself, thou hast inhaled the *braaactrum*[33] to know both power and immortality."

"Apparently, there is no immortality," I replied. "Otherwise, I would not exist. Sometime in the future, you will die like all the rest of your kind."

"Thou doth claim," she said with defiance, "that thou art my reincarnation, and yet there thou doth stand before me with but half the *khalthraaam,* each one filled with its own separate milk so necessary to suckle the babe; thou with rounded ears, unable to waft forth the scent of our sex to attract and hold our mates; and thou absent the *yaaargh*, so necessary for both pleasure and reproduction. Thou standest before me, then, a poor reflection of myself—thou who cannot in truth be the product of the royal blood that flows through my veins."

"May one speak before thee?" Laaadra-Taaagh asked.

"If it be thy wish," Khattaaara replied. "Blow forth thine errant wind in hope that one or two words may find their way into my ears."

"It is true," Laaadra-Taaagh said, "that Peyton Herron is different from Gaaalthaaarans, each of us created in the image of Khii, but she is whole in her own way. For lack of a *yaaargh*, she has a fold that to touch gives as great a pleasure to her as do our *yaaarghig* and from which wafts a similar aphrodisiac as perfume our ears. As for her *khalthraaam*[34], her kind finds two sufficient to

---

[33] An atmospheric effect on Rendenaaar similar to the Aurora Borealis, though used as a simile for intimate knowledge.
[34] Pronounced K'*hal* tah rahm.

nurse their young. Apologies for my admission, but I have bonded with her and I have found no equal for the pleasures that fold and her human tongue have enacted upon me."

"Show me then thy human form," she said, "that I might judge whether such should one day be suited for my royal self to own."

Laaadra-Taaagh looked at me and nodded, and so I phased off my costume and stood naked before them both.

Khattaaara surveyed my form, then raised her left arm and made a circular motion with her fingers for me to turn around, which I did. I felt her hand as her fingers slid down my back where a *yaaargh* would have been had I been one of her kind.

"Turn to face me once more," she ordered.

I did as she directed. She cupped one of my breasts, lifted it just a bit to look beneath its slight fold, and then placed her fingers upon my vagina, ran up it, and then entered it with one. I pulled back.

"That is quite inappropriate," I said, "as would be the case if I, with one of *my* fingers, entered thy *yaaargh*!"

Khattaaara scowled at me. "Thou has said that thou art my very self born into another form. Why then should I be hindered from examining that which is already mine?" She then turned to Laaadra-Taaagh. "What pleasure, sayest thou may be experienced from my other self?"

"Many, my Liege," she replied, "beyond what anyone could hope to experience with our own kind."

Khattaaara stared me in the eye. "Thou shalt show me," she demanded.

"Again," I replied, "'twould be inappropriate for we are in spirit if not in form one and the same."

"Thy tongue betrays, thee," she said. "If in spirit we are one and the same then it would be no different than when I by myself gratify my sexual desires." She glanced at Laaadra-Taaagh. "Or would you rather I phased her to the center of the orange globe that lights our sky?"

I glanced at Laaadra-Taaagh who appeared to tremble at the thought.

"I shall do as thou asks," I told her. "The life of my friend is worth far more to me than the humbling of myself."

"Come, then," she said. Her purple eyes grew bright like stars and she phased us both into her bedchamber.

How strange it was, then, to find myself naked and in bed with the woman my soul had evolved from. In her face in part, I could see my own, but the spirit that wrestled with her flesh and bone was merciless and evil. She only knew want—nothing more.

From my time with Laaadra-Taaagh, I had learned the pleasures that might be found by pressure and caress, by cunt and by tongue upon *yaaargh* and *khalthraaam*, and such I enacted upon Khattaaara, in my mind pretending it was Laaadra-Taaagh and not her. At last, her heart beating like a metronome set to its lowest point, her *yaaargh* spraying out the blue liquid that bursts from its tip when a female's satisfaction occurs. Her nipples peaked their most, her back arched to its full, and her lungs deluged the air with a scream of ecstasy that might have echoed the very walls of the palace and shaken them down to their foundation. When it was over, she turned her head toward me and said, "Your slave doth not lie."

"She is not my slave," I replied, "but my equal and my friend."

"But thou shalt be a slave to me," she said, "and I a slave to you."

"I do not seek to be indentured" I replied. "I only wish to find my way back home."

"Then we shall find it together," she said.

"But if you leave here," I replied, "what effect will that have on the future?"

"That matters not to me," she proclaimed. "Besides, I have an ability unknown to thee."

"*That* being?" I asked.

"Try using your powers," she replied. "Try phasing from this room."

I tried but could not.

"The god-stone in my head," she went on, "now commands the one in yours. Such is the power of the mother stone. Tomorrow we shall seek to find your universe, your world, and your home. You are mine, Peyton Herron, from this moment on and for the rest of eternity!"

CHAPTER XLIV

Quantum Girl Orange
(March 18, 1951)

I could say that we put our two heads together, but the reality of it was that it was the same head in two different bodies. There were three separate questions we needed to resolve. The first was, how did we get divided and wind back in time? Second, where was Margaret's consciousness whilst I was in her body? And third, where was my body while I was in her head? To make things clear and simple, we both had absolutely no clue. Most theoretical physicists would have just ascribed it to a quantum effect and left it at that. They have a tendency to do that. If one can't explain something, they call it quantum. We called it being in a quandary. To make matters worse, although older me could travel through time, I couldn't, and try though she might, she couldn't move me even a split second, backward or forward in either direction. Anyway you looked at it, it appeared that I was trapped. But what about Grams? I obviously wasn't her in the future. But when would my consciousness leave her?

"What am I supposed to do, then?" I asked my older self as she sat next to me along the counter at Schwab's, each of us gnawing away at the Sundaes we had ordered. Schwab's Pharmacy was the iconic drugstore and soda fountain where actress, Lana Turner was discovered. "Am I supposed to marry Gramps and have sex with him? Gross!"

"Well, if you don't," she replied, "Mama will never be born and then neither will we or Phee. If you have any suggestions, I'm open to hearing them."

"Is there some divine plan in the quantum fabric," I asked, "that insists that all Peyton Herrons are doomed to lead batshit crazy lives? Seriously, for being *blessed* with superpowers (and I used air

272

quotes) what the fuck is going on?"

"I will not have you using that language," she replied.

"Really!" I shot back at her as I plunged my spoon into the vanilla mass. "You're not my mother, you know!"

"I'm Margaret's mother," she replied, "and have been for quite some time."

I glared at her. "How old are you anyway?"

"Twenty-seven," she replied.

"Well, that explains it," I said, bringing another spoonful of ice cream drenched in hot fudge to my lips.

"Explains what?" she demanded to know.

"Why you're so grumpy," I replied through a mouthful of sundae.

"What's that supposed to mean?" she said.

"You're at that age," I replied, "where hormones take over. Your body craves sex every waking moment but there you are virginal as the day you were born."

"What makes you think I haven't had sex?" she said.

I grabbed hold of the maraschino that had topped the sundae by its stem and stared at it. "This isn't the only cherry in the room!" I said.

"And I suppose you've done better?" she said with scorn.

"I'm not nearly twice as old as me," I remarked back.

"Just to let you know," she replied, "I've had sex many times!"

"You mean with that dildo I found in your drawer?" I said smugly.

"You just try raising a six-year-old child," she snapped back, "from when you're just fifteen and see how many relationships you find time for!"

"Chill out, *Mom*," I replied, " I was just messing with you."

I stirred my spoon, gathering up the melt at the bottom of the glass. "By the way," I said casually, "I was thinking of starting a comic book collection."

"Because?" she asked. "I wasn't aware that we liked comic books."

"Because," I said, "they're going to be worth a shitload of money someday."

"That's well and good," she replied, "but I already beat you to it."

"No way!" I said, staring at her with a dropped jaw.

"Thousands of comics from the Golden Age," she replied, "all bagged and boarded, which they didn't use to do. I had to phase back to the future to get the supplies."

"You *will* show them to me when we get back home?" I demanded and then thought for a second. "Where are they?" I asked. "I thought I'd searched everywhere."

"They're in a vault under the house," she replied.

"Wait!" I said, "There's an actual vault under the house—like a room?"

"Uh huh?" she replied.

"And just when were you going to tell me about *that*?" I asked.

"Well," she replied, "I wasn't going to tell Margaret anything." She paused and then turned serious. "I've been meaning to ask you, when you were kidnapped, why didn't you immediately escape?"

"Because," I replied, "when I first woke up as Margaret, I didn't have my powers. They only returned to me after I died."

"Interesting," she said.

"And fortunate for me," I said, then glanced in her direction. "You about done?"

"I am," she replied.

"Then let's get out of here," I said. "Unlike you, I have homework that needs to be done. Plus there are two tests I have to study for, for tomorrow."

As we both rose from our seats, she replied, "I'm sure that with your quantum brain, it'll all be a snap."

"You'd think," I said, "but with my quantum brain, I need to dumb things down. I don't want to be sent off to some school for the brilliant—like to Smith!"

"Back to that again," she replied. "You need to go there because Grams did and, for the time being at least, you're Grams."

"Okay, okay!" I said. "At least I can phase back home whenever I want."

We went to the cash register and paid, leaving a tip on the counter. Then we walked to our car, got in, and drove home.

CHAPTER XLV

Quantum Girl Green
(September 30, 39 B.C.)

I had to comply. I had to sleep with him with the Sword of Damocles hanging over my head. If I didn't, my parents and my sister would be killed. He was the male version of me physically, but emotionally we were lightyears apart. He used—or, rather, misused—his abilities. He had set himself up as divine ruler to these people from the moment he arrived and trapped me into being his whore. I often wondered how things would have gone had Cleopatra's presence not left my mind. What was worse was that his supposed love for me became compromised by our sexual routine. After a while, he became bored with *just me*. More than that, he became dangerous.

He drank the native alcohol to the point where he was drunk much of the time. For sport, he would destroy things—trees, huts— whatever irritated him. As a result, the villagers feared him. If I threatened to stop him, he reminded me of what he could or would do to my family. He would sleep with the native woman, regardless of whether or not they were bound to some other man.

"You need to leave them alone!" I said to him one day when we were both outside with the native prostrate before us as was his command whenever they were near. They feared him more than death for he had proven more than once that he was fully capable of inflicting insufferable pain.

"Who are you to order me?" he said with a grain of arrogance and the scent of alcohol on his breath.

"You're just weak," I replied, "a coward who pretends to be a king!"

"Kings are cabbages with crowns!" he proclaimed. "I am a god—their god!"

"Then I am their goddess!" I replied.

I phased into the air in my Quantum Girl attire. "I don't like what you're doing to these people," I shouted back, my quantum voice thundering in the balmy air, "and I don't like my family being threatened!"

He stared hard at me, seething with newfound anger. His eyes began to glow bright—violet—violent it would seem! Circular waves of force projected from him and hit me hard. It was odd, though. I myself remained unmoved but as the energy struck I felt something leave me and I turned and saw *her*—Cleopatra—hanging in the air just behind me, naked, her eyes wide open, her mouth formed into a scream. And then all at once, she began to age or perhaps rot is a better word! This was the corpse I had entered—taken possession of—reanimated—but now that I was no longer a part of it, the six weeks or so that the natural process of decay should have taken place began happening at an accelerated rate. Its eyes turned white, its lips shrank back, its abdomen expanded, its hair and teeth fell out, the skin turned gray and fell off of it like moths fluttering to the ground, and, what was left—all of the muscles and organs—began to liquify, leaving the skeleton exposed. It was hideous beyond belief. Finally, all of it fell from the air and went crashing to the ground, tearing apart into a discordant mass of broken bones with a jawless skull staring up at me as though to ask me, *How could such a grandiose life find such an ignominious end?* I stared at it from my perch in the sky. My stomach heaved and I threw up a pinkish, paste-like mass that hurled from my mouth and then fell down upon the calcified remains of what had once been the Queen of Egypt—of the majesty that had once been me! I wiped my mouth with the back of my hand and then turned to where Peyton should have been but he had vanished, phased off perhaps to continue his debauchery of one or more of his nubile supplicants who mistook him for their god.

It was by chance that I enacted a power that was perhaps unique to the green god-stone. It happened after I had phased back down to the village and came across a woman who was scolding her young daughter and was about to slap her across the face. As I raised my hand to take hold of hers and prevent her from harming the child, I inadvertently merged into her, becoming her as I had into the corpse of Cleopatra. Immediately, I held back striking the girl, whose eyes were red from tears, and took her in my arms and hugged her. The crying slowly stopped and the girl dried her cheeks.

"What is wrong, Chihara?" I asked in the native tongue, inexplicably knowing the girl's name.

"I don't want to share my bed with him!" she wept. "I do not care if he will kill me! I do not want him and he is cruel!"

I continued to hold her and gently kissed her head. "You do not need to, my daughter," I said in her mother's voice. "He is an angry devil who needs to be stopped."

"But what can be done?" the girl asked. Her eyes begged for an answer.

"There is another," I replied. "She will do battle against him. Her name is Peyton Herron."

"What sort of a name is that?" the girl asked.

"Peyton," I said, still holding her, "means noble. And Herron is like the bird." It was serendipitous that not far off stood a flock of blue herons wading near the shore. I released her from my arms and then turned her around to look. "Those are herons," I told her.

"I thought they were called *rhorhora*?" she replied.

"That was their old name," I said. Then I stopped time, emerged from the woman, and phased up in the air over where the birds had gathered.

The girl pointed toward me. "Look, Mother!" Chihara said. "It is the Herron! She has come to save us!"

Her mother looked and stared at me in awe. "Yes, daughter," she replied, "Hutash has sent a warrior to protect us. We need no longer fear."

A moment later, the woman called out to her people, "Come see the Great *Rhorhora!* The Herron! She has come to destroy the angry god!"

Villagers emerged from their huts or from where they were standing and gathered near to the mother and her child, many of them catching sight of me and pointing as Chihara had done so that others might look upon me as well. Their talk and their whispers turned into a din so loud that my male mirrored self again walked out of the hut he was in, naked and with a naked native girl trailing him, just behind.

"What the fuck is it this time?" he scowled. Then his eyes followed those of the onlookers and he saw me again. "This is just too much!" he grumbled to himself. He then phased into the air as Quantum Man to confront me face to face. "Don't you ever quit?" he said. "Or is that just the teenager in you?"

"Tell me something," I replied.

"What?" he said with a heavy, annoyed sigh.

"What color is your god-stone?" I asked.

"I think it's pretty apparent unless you're blind," he replied.

"Well mine," I said, "is green."

"And?" he replied with added annoyance in both his expression and his voice.

"It lets me do this!" I said and then merged *into* him.

All at once, I could sense the anger that was seething in him. I could feel him desperately trying to regain control. But it was me and not him who was the puppet master. I controlled his every move. Had I wanted to stop his heart I could have with but a thought. Instead, I only wanted one thing and that was the god-stone in his head. As I withdrew myself from him, I took it with me and left him to drop naked into the water below. The crowd of natives laughed uproariously at the spectacle of the once-god trying to regain his footing and falling flat on his face.

One man shouted to the others and all of them gathered up rocks or sticks and were about to murder him, when I shouted, "Stop!" in their native tongue. "You must not become like him," I said in a more gentle voice.

Each of them dropped the makeshift weapons they were holding. The man, somewhat shaken from the fall, stood up and tried to look godlike. Regardless, everyone's attention had turned to him. Everyone saw his weakness. Then one woman pointed at Peyton's member and shouted what roughly translates as, "Behold the flaccid god!" at which all of them looked and began to laugh. Ashamed, the man who once was all-powerful, covered his most private part with his hands, an act that brought about even more laughter.

"I shall take him back to the sky," I told them all, "to face judgment from the gods."

Then, using the purple god-stone that was now in my head, I phased us both back to the reality from which he had come—back to some random front lawn in the middle of the day. The woman, whose house it was, who stood watering her flowers, upon seeing a naked man only a few feet from her, began to scream and turned the hose on him. The male Peyton Herron, sopping wet, ran off into the distance, probably in search of clothes. Whatever—wherever—I didn't care.

As it turned out, I had phased us to Miami in 1956. I phased forward in time to 2025 to Santa Monica—well, Santa Monaco as it was called on Peyton's world. How glad I was, though, that the purple god-stone allowed me to phase back to modern civilization, albeit the wrong reality with no clue as to how to get back to mine. By the way, I learned afterward that the Chunwa people had adopted the heron as their sacred bird in honor of the goddess who had saved them all!

CHAPTER XLVI

Ophelia
(Auschwitz Concentration Camp)
(March 14, 1943)

To say that I wanted to die would be ironic, to say the least. It was not that I wanted my life to end but that I did not want to live the life that I had been dealt. I was humiliated and stripped, not only of my femininity but of my humanity as well. It didn't matter one way or another that I was not Jewish. It only mattered what they said. They were monsters, all of them. The Nuremberg trials would later indict twenty-four men—Nazis who had been in positions of authority. Twelve would be sentenced to death, nine to prison, with three acquitted. But there were roughly six million members of the Nazi Party, the same number as those Jews murdered in concentration camps. How I wished for Peyton to come to my rescue but she never did. I was lost in time in a world that knew nothing but selfishness and hate—the definition of evil.

The morning after my incarceration, I awoke to find Hannah lying on the cot next to me. She was staring at me with mournful eyes.

"Don't worry," she said. "I will help you find your place here."

Hannah was my only connection to this torturous new world. I spoke neither German nor Yiddish but my brave adopted Jewish sister would teach me both. The two languages were similar when spoken, though as far apart as could be imagined in written form. The German language, like English, was scripted in a Latin alphabet, while Yiddish was written using Hebrew letters. It was their accent, however, that betrayed many of the Jews who tried to pass themselves off as Germans when the Nazis began to round up those of Jewish descent.

Food was scarce. Prisoners were given a bitter drink in the

morning that tasted like bad coffee, a bowl of soup midday made from rotten vegetables, and a crust of bread that had been smeared with margarine before going to bed. If the rations ran out, it was too bad for those at the end of the line. On rare occasions, the last meal—a small bit of sausage, marmalade, or cheese—was added to the meal. Rat infestation was horrendous. Rats, which thrived on eating human corpses, would often crawl up and bite those who were sick and confined to bed. Lice infestation was also a problem. Talk was that there were billions of them which contributed to typhus among the prisoners. Those who fell ill were told to line up in front of the latrines and were brutally beaten. When sickness threatened to spread, prisoners were forced to give up their clothes while the barracks were being disinfected. As for clothing, everyone was forced to wear the same striped uniform day in and day out for four months until replacements were provided, many laundered after having been removed from the bodies of the dead. All in all, the barracks stank pretty bad between the stench of body odor and the smell of piss and shit from those too weak to make it to the latrines or hold it in that long. Pretty, young female newcomers like myself could hope to earn a small bar of chocolate if she let a guard fuck her in one of the tool sheds. I let them as often as they wanted. It was the only way that Hannah and I could survive. The threat of getting pregnant wasn't an issue. The guards knew better than to not wear condoms, but on the off chance that it did, there was always the Nazi doctor to perform a quick abortion during which time he made certain that the girl could never become pregnant again. Anyway, for me the trade for sex went on for around six months once or twice a week until I became too thin—skeletal would probably be a more appropriate word—for any of them to want me anymore. Things only got worse after that.

You cannot imagine the cold in the winter with only thin clothes for us to wear and a blanket to wrap around us. Hannah and I would huddle as close as we could at night, which helped a bit but, for the most part, our teeth still chattered and we would shiver most of the time.

It was just over two years later—March 5, 1945—when it was announced that many of us were to be taken to the showers. Hannah had perished from typhus eight months before. I had hoped to make it one more month when Germany would surrender, but that wasn't in the cards for me. I knew what the *showers* meant. Everyone would be told to undress in the barracks and then follow the guards to what was supposed to be the shower room. But it wasn't and only those in charge and I knew it. The fact was, though, that I was too weak—just bones with a bit of flesh—and I'd gone through so much that I just didn't care anymore. We were all led naked and barefoot, man, woman, and child alike, to a large, rectangular white building. Inside, it looked as though it might have been what they said. But when they locked the doors and there was the hiss of gas and the smell of bitter almonds, there was panic from everyone but me. I just stood there in the center of the room while most ran back the way we had come and began shouting and banging on the doors. I just stood there and thought about Peyton and Mom and Dad and about how much I loved them. And then I exhaled and took a deep breath of the poison gas. I felt my chest tighten. I was having trouble even taking in air. My head throbbed and I became nauseous and dizzy and confused. And then I dropped to the floor along with the nearly two thousand others in that massive extermination room.

CHAPTER XLVII

Quantum Girl Violet
(April 30, 2025)

When morning dawned, I was the first to awaken. Mark had had a restless sleep that woke me up at times. What we had done must have really taken a toll on him emotionally. Not that it was anything easy for me, but emotionally I was an adult. My life as a teenager was a do-over and so mentally I was better equipped. I could hear him mumbling, "Mom, don't leave me! Mom, come back!"

I turned toward him and gently rubbed his back to rouse him from whatever nightmare he was having. "What time is it" he asked sleepily.

I glanced over at the clock on the nightstand. "Eight thirty-six," I replied.

"I'm glad you woke me up," he said. "I was having a bad dream. I have them a lot."

I rolled over and spooned with him, wrapping my arm around him. "What was it about?" I asked.

"It was when my mom and dad were still together. They used to get into arguments all the time. She would yell that he didn't love her and that she wished she'd never married him, and he would yell back that she was just an ungrateful bitch and that he'd divorced his wife to be with her. Then one day, she was just gone. There wasn't so much as a note—not a kiss goodbye—not a word. The night before was the last time I ever saw her. He'd beaten her pretty badly. He used to beat her a lot. I think she was afraid of him because she never fought back. Dad started to drink a lot after she left and he'd get angry over nothing and, like I said last night, he used to beat *me*. I've never told anyone about it other than you. I was always too ashamed to say anything. People judge you, even for things that aren't in your control."

"I'm so sorry," I said. I hugged him and kissed the back of his neck. "I have a question," I went on. "Have you ever had a girlfriend before?"

"I once asked Melissa Crawford to the movies," he replied, "and we went together. I even brought her a rose when we met at the movie theatre. But then a bunch of her friends suddenly showed up including Tyler Larsen, who turned out to be her boyfriend. She ignored me, went over to him, wrapped her arms around his neck, and kissed him—I mean really kissed him, tongue and all—and then turned back to me and said, 'You are such a loser! What makes you think I would ever go out with you?' Then everyone laughed and walked away and I was left standing there still holding the rose."

My heart went out to him. "Roll over," I said and he did. I stared at him and he looked back at me. And then I kissed him, tongue and all. When the kiss, which had probably lasted a full minute, was over, I said, "We need to take a shower—together—and then have breakfast, pack some clothes, and go."

"Go where?" he asked.

"We'll take the car," I told him, "and head back to California to my home. We'll tell my folks that your dad passed away and that they were going to put you in a foster home. My Mama and Papa are both very understanding and compassionate and I'm sure they'll let you stay, only whatever personal happens or has happened between us has to stay between us. Mama is a Christian and she's very conservative about what goes on between a man and a woman outside of marriage. All hell broke loose when it came out last year that Phee had allowed a boy she was friends with to fondle her breasts."

"I understand," Mark replied. "Mum's the word."

"All right, then," I said. "Let's both get into the shower. I still feel as though I'm covered in algae from our midnight dip."

The two of us got out of bed. It was with some urging that I coaxed Mark into the bathroom with me. I literally had to take him by the hand and yank him there. That's how shy he was. I undressed myself and then I undressed him. He stared at my naked body with the wonderment of a blind man who had been given the gift of sight for the first time. To him, I was more beautiful than Aphrodite or Helen of Troy. I might have said Cleopatra but, truth be told, I *was* her. Embarrassed was only half a word for the look on his face when, in that he was only fifteen as was I, a part of his anatomy, shall we say expressed itself unintentionally. I glanced down at it and then smiled at him. I brought my arms around him and brought him up against me, his flesh touching mine. What became of his lower extremity I shall not describe other than that it was pleasurable for us both and his first experience. After that, I didn't need to ask whether he loved me. I know he would have given his life to protect mine. He already had in the future past. Some shred of obscure logic in me had me thinking that I had molested him that day. After all, the reality of it was that I had the mind of a grown woman that I had immersed into my fifteen-year-old self. But I loved him at every age, his or mine. We were star-crossed lovers, destined to coexist.

After breakfast and some small discussion, we decided it would be easier and cheaper to fly rather than drive and risk getting pulled over since neither of us had a driver's license and I was the only one who knew how to operate a car. We had one hundred twenty-eight dollars between us and a credit card from the wallet on his father's dresser. I changed my plane reservation for that afternoon and then booked a seat on the same flight for Mark using the card. We threw some bags of clothes along with various personal items Mark had, locked the doors to the house, backed the car into the garage, and then waited for the Uber I'd arranged for to take us to the airport. Once we were seated on the plane, I used my cell to message Phee:

Hey, Sis, sorry I've gone ghost for a couple of days but a lot's been going on. Needless to say, I'm about to hop a flight back to L.A. that will be arriving at LAX at 7:56 p.m., Spirit Airlines, flight

249. Please ask Papa to pick us up. Yes, that's right, us. Mark's coming with me. I'll explain all later tonight. Sorry to have been such a worry for all but there were things I needed to find out for myself. I think you'll like Mark. The two of you should get along like peas and carrots. He's a comic book geek like you. LMFAO! Please tell Mama and Papa I'm sorry for leaving as I did. I love you all so much. With bunches of kisses from your soon-to-return sister, Peyton P.S. Mark and I bought you a snow globe of the Statue of Liberty at a gift shop at the airport. I know you've never seen snow other than from a distance on the mountaintops. Now, you'll be able to see it every day!

Phee and I always had a special relationship. It was as though we were somehow connected. We would often finish each other's sentences or grab for the same bag of chips. We even came down with the measles at the exact same time, though I do believe it was because Derrick Hattersley gave it to us. Regardless, there was a closeness between us that was unbreakable by tide or time.

Mark and I managed to sit together on the plane even though it was crowded. An elderly man agreed to switch seats, probably because we were young and traveling alone. I sat next to the window. Mark would lean over me to look out. It was a long flight—more than nine hours. As the airline offered no food or snacks or drinks, we bought a couple of burgers and fries from one of the restaurants on the concourse as well as four cans of soda from one of the vending machines.

After we had finished eating, I gathered up my courage and asked Mark a question.

"If I told you something really outrageous," I said, "would you believe me or chalk me up as a nutcase?"

"How outrageous?" he asked. "On a scale of one to ten?"

"Probably about a hundred," I replied.

He looked me dead in the eye. "I don't think you're crazy," he said.

"There are a lot of things that most people know aren't real," I went on, "like ghosts and goblins and—I don't know—unicorns."

"Your point being," he replied.

"People know those are just made-up things," I said, "like Superman and Batman and Wonder Woman."

"And?" he replied.

"Well," I said, "If a man named Clark Kent said that he was Superman, since there *is* no Superman, people would know he's got a screw loose somewhere."

"Are you trying to tell me that Superman actually exists?" he asked.

"No," I replied. "I mean, yes. I mean, I don't mean Superman, but what if someone else with superpowers existed only something happened and she lost all of her powers and no one believed her, and everyone she told about it thought that she was batshit crazy?"

"Hypothetically," he said.

"Yes," I replied, "hypothetically."

"And what," he asked, "would that hypothetical superhero's name be, pray tell?"

"Quantum Girl," I replied with a pounding heart.

"Quantum Girl," he repeated.

"Oh, I know I'm probably going to regret this," I said, "but here goes. When I was fourteen, I was bullied a lot. It got so bad that I decided that I didn't want to live anymore and decided to hang myself. Apparently, the pipe that I suspended the rope from broke and I only succeeded in causing permanent brain damage. The thing is, I wasn't the first me because there can be alternate realities. There was a Peyton before me who had what she called a god-stone placed in her head by a being from the planet Rendenaaar called Dhraaal. The god-stone gave her all kinds of powers. She could phase through time or space or parallel dimensions or duplicate herself as many times as she wanted or create force fields. The problem was that the last time she went back in time she changed things and when she returned there was another reality that included me who was an alternate version of her only I never wound up actually killing myself and never received a god-stone to turn me into Quantum Girl like her. When she found me, though, I was little more than a vegetable and as her heart went out to me, she decided to try and heal me. The only way for her to do that was to will the god-stone from her head and into mine. That left her powerless. What she didn't count on was that with the god-stone in my head, even though it was able to fix me, I had no control and I wound up accidentally killing her. Afterward, though, when I was fully recovered, I took up her role as Quantum Girl."

I looked at Mark. "You're not going to run to another part of the plane, are you?" I asked.

"No," he said. "I'm listening."

"Anyway," I went on, "the original Peyton, the one who died, had met a reporter in New York a while before. The reporter kind of fell in love with her and so he quit his job and traveled across the county until he found her. Only it wasn't her that he found because she was already dead. He found me. But then he got hurt trying to protect me from a female from Rendenaaar. So, I phased us back in time and brought him to a hospital where he spent months recovering. I visited him every day and told him everything I'm telling you and he and I fell in love and when he got out, we got married. The thing is or was—I get kind of confused with all of the time traveling—that I wanted to meet him when *he* was younger and *I* was younger, so I phased back in time into myself when I was fifteen. Okay, here's the part that gets even more confusing if that's possible. As Quantum Girl, I was able to duplicate myself. So, one of me went to New York to try and meet up with him, while the other me stayed back home with Phee. Only, one morning, I woke up and all my powers were gone and no one remembered my ever having them. So, without telling anyone, I took a plane out to New York to find my other self and him. But when I got there, there *was* no other self."

"So, what about the guy," he asked, "your future husband. Did you wind up finding *him*?"

"Yes," I replied. "I did."

"I sure hope it wasn't Garrett Wentworth," he said, half wondering if it was.

"No," I told him. "It was you. Anyway, that's the story whether you believe it or not or think I'm some kind of lunatic. But Phee will corroborate that I said you were the one the other me went off to, to try and meet, though I don't know what happened to her—the other me, I mean."

Mark sighed. "It's a lot to take in all at once," he said.

"So, you don't believe me," I concluded out loud.

"I didn't say that," he said. "It's kind of hard to not believe someone that you're in love with." He stared at me and cocked his head a bit. "Quantum Girl, huh?" he said.

"Apparently, the reincarnation," I said, "of some bad-ass alien bitch from Rendenaaar, trillions of universes in the past. And I'm in love with you, too. Only don't mention that to my parents or they'll stick a chastity belt on me and lock me in my room."

Mark stared at me with concern.

"I'm joking!" I said. "But just *about* that last part. If you want, tomorrow I'll fill you in on all the details about my life as a superheroine." I shook my head to myself. "My parents refused to believe any of it. They had me go see a shrink."

"And what did the shrink say?" Mark asked.

"Blah, blah, blah," I said. "And then he wrote a prescription for some medication I refused to take."

"Did he actually say, 'Blah, blah, blah?'" Mark asked jokingly.

"He may as well have," I replied. "You know they say, 'Anyone who goes to see a psychiatrist should have his head examined.'"

CHAPTER XLVIII

Peyton
(the other one in Massapequa—
—the one with quantum powers)

It was a bit disconcerting to come face to face with another me who wasn't one of my split-offs. This was someone different from me entirely, a Payton Herron who was part of this reality. I use the term *reality* rather than dimension because there are distinct differences. Parallel dimensions are those that exist adjacent to each other but with different quantum signatures, meaning the space they are each in is slightly different from the one next to it. Alternate realities occur within separate universes. The first is like sheets of paper next to each other, while the second is like bubbles in a glass of soda pop. The original Peyton—the one who sacrificed her life for me—merged all of the parallel dimensions in this universe, but that still left an almost infinite amount of alternate realities which I like to call skews. Somehow, Mark and I had wound up in one of those.

"Do I have to repeat myself?" the other Payton asked, folding her arms in defiance. "I want to know, A: why you are in my bedroom, B: why you look exactly like me, and C: what the hell do you want?"

"We don't want anything!" I said back. "Something went wrong when I tried to phase us back home."

"And you look like me because…?" she demanded.

"Because I *am* you!" I said with a bit of frustration in my tone. "I'm just you from a different reality is all."

"And who is he?" she asked, again in a forceful way.

"He's my boyfriend," I said. "His name is Mark."

"Really!" she said. "Not on my world."

"Really!" I mocked back. "And who might your boyfriend be?"

291

"First of all," she announced, "I have a girlfriend. I'm not into dicks or Marks! And her name is Taylor Swift."

"Taylor Swift is like thirty-five years old!" I said. "That's technically old enough to be your mother!"

"I don't know what planet you dropped down from," she replied somewhat angrily, "but on this one she's sixteen!"

I was about to ask if this Taylor Swift wrote about break-ups, too, only with girls. My mouth started to open to project the words when another Peyton appeared. It was the older version of me. I never did get to ask the question. If they did break up I wondered what the lyrics would be.

"What is this," my skew exclaimed, "a fucking Payton Herron convention?"

"Sorry for the intrusion," older me said to her, "and hello again." Then she turned to me. "I remembered that I'd phased off with Mark on the first go-round, just as a solar flare hit that wound me up here, so I followed your quantum trail. I'll phase us back to our reality." She turned to Mark. "I'd advise you to exhale just before the phase. It'll help stop you from throwing up." She turned to me. "Ready?" she asked. I nodded. "Give my best to Taylor," she said to my skew, and then we phased from the reality that wasn't mine.

It seemed strange because we phased into what appeared to be the exact same bedroom, although there were two beds in it now. Mark, true to form, rushed into the bathroom and heaved out the dinner he had just consumed. Suddenly, there were sounds coming from downstairs. I heard the door lock being opened, the door handle turning, and a bunch of people walking in. I used my X-ray projection to see what was going on. We took it for granted that there would have been another me, but another Mark? That was *not* expected. As I followed everyone's path, watching them through the floor and walls, beyond Mama and Papa, we all saw my other self lead the other Mark to the guestroom as Phee proceeded upstairs, heading this way. I turned off the projection when she began to open the door. As it swung open, a puzzled expression appeared on her face.

"I thought the two of you were still downstairs," she said. "And who is she? She looks just like you only… older. And what happened to your black eye? What's going on?"

"We just phased here from New York," I said.

"I know," she said, "We just picked you up at the airport. And what do you mean 'phased?'"

"Reality overlay," older me said to me under her breath.

"Fuck," I said aside to her.

"What are you two whispering about?" Phee said.

"Do we tell her?" I asked.

"I don't think we have much choice," older me said.

"Tell me what?" Phee demanded.

It was at that instant that the other me burst into the room with, "Mama said to tell you to come back downstairs. Supper's about to be served." Then she saw me and said, "I tried to find you in Massapequa but you weren't there."

I just shrugged.

"Will someone please tell me what is going on?" Phee exclaimed.

"I told you I was able to divide myself," the other me said to her, "but you wouldn't believe me. I woke up with all of my powers gone," she said to me, "and no one remembered anything about our being Quantum Girl. They even sent me to see a head doctor!" She took a deep breath and then went on. "Can we please merge back? I don't have the ability to anymore."

I nodded and, once barefoot, she merged the two of us into one and then phased the few feet necessary to catch Phee after she fainted. After phasing Phee onto her bed and phasing out of one set of the two sets of clothes I found myself in, I went into the bathroom, dipped a bit of toilet paper in ammonia from the bottle that was under the sink, and then returned to the bed where I waved the pungent vapors under her nose. She came to with a start, stared and me, and then asked, "What happened?"

"You fainted," I said.

She craned her head up a bit. Mark and older me were standing near the foot of the bed looking on. "I know this is all a dream," she replied.

"No dream," I told her.

"I'm Mark," Mark said as she stared at him. "Mark Marsden."

"I know," Phee said. "We've already been introduced." Then she stared at older me. "And you are?"

"Your sister," came the reply, "twenty years from now."

"This can't be happening!" Phee exclaimed. She looked at me. "First you insist that you're some superhero called Quantum Girl and now I'm imagining future you!"

"I *am* Quantum Girl," I said and then phased into my costume at which point Phee fainted again.

Matters became even more complicated when the other Mark entered the room. "Your mom wants to know what the hold-up is," he said and then stopped in his tracks.

I didn't know which captured his attention and made him more confused—Quantum Girl, the older version of me, or seeing himself? As for me, I quickly phased off my cowl.

"Okay," he said to me, "I told you I believe you, but who are *they*?"

Older me looked at the two of them and then turned to me. "I think it would be easier if I just merged them," she said.

"You can do that?" I asked.

"There are a lot of powers that you haven't yet discovered," she replied. She looked at one Mark and then the other. "Would the two of you stand next to each other," she said. "And if one of you would take off your shoes it would be a whole lot better."

My Mark did as she asked, older me's eyes began to glow, and then the two Marks blurred into one solid form. Once there was only one of them, Mark let out a huge sigh and then stared at me.

"It's kind of strange," he said, "but I kind of feel like I'm in love with two of you." He glanced at older me. "Not you, though—at least not yet."

"Same here," I replied, at which point Phee began to come to again.

Seeing that happen, older me took her bow. "I think this calls for a quick exit," she said. "We don't want her passing out again." She stared at me and smiled. "See you in about twenty years," she said and then looked at Mark. "You, too." Then she phased out of sight and into the future with a pop from the air suddenly filling the void she had left.

I phased back into my street clothes as Phee opened her eyes. "I had the strangest dream," she said and then looked from side to side, "and I don't even remember lying down."

"Hello?" we heard Mama call from downstairs. "Supper's getting cold!"

Mark excused himself to go to the bathroom to take off one of the sets of clothes on him and then joined Phee and me at the table a few minutes later. There wasn't a whole lot of conversation. Mark and I had done a lot of explaining in the car, though we did leave out the part about all that had gone on with his father. As for Phee, she kept glancing at me as though she were expecting me to turn back into Quantum Girl or into identical twins.

CHAPTER XLIX

Quantum Girl Blue
(October 29, 1929)

From heroine to mentor, that's what happened to me. She had my powers—all of them—unskilled, untrained, and unable to be able to master any of them without my help. As for myself, I had gone to bed that night feeling helpless and lost.

"Okay," Mary said in a flurry of excitement, "what all can I do?"

"Well," I replied, "you've seen me duplicate and phase from one place to another. You can also use force fields to protect yourself or hurl them as a blast of energy. Oh, and you can see through things and allow others to see through them as well. I used to be able to time travel but I haven't been able to since I got here."

"Time travel!" Mary exclaimed. "That would be thrilling!"

"Yes," I replied, "but going into the past can change things, even into my past. Time could be altered so that I might never be born."

"Oh," she replied, "I wouldn't want *that* to happen! But how does any of it work? Do I say abracadabra or something?"

"No," I said, "you just have to concentrate."

She closed her eyes so tightly that blood rushed to her face. To be perfectly honest, she looked as though she were struggling on a toilet. Then, all at once, she disappeared.

"Uh, oh!" I thought to myself, but aloud I said, "Where did you go?"

"Down here!" she called out in a tiny voice.

I looked down to see her about three inches tall. "You need to focus," I shouted down to her, at which point she covered her ears. "Sorry," I said much quieter. "Concentrate on being bigger."

Suddenly, she became immense, bent over and filling up the room.

"I can't move," she moaned. "What now?"

"Just think about being normal in size again," I called up to her.

"Okay," she replied, and then she was, though in the same position she had just been in when gigantic.

"Whew!" she sighed. "That was an experience!"

"It takes time," I said, "though I didn't know the god-stones could cause anyone to change their size."

As the days and weeks passed, I taught her everything I knew about using the god-stone—everything but one and that was how to travel through time. Sadly, Great Granny passed away only two weeks after Mary got her powers. We had her buried at Rosehill Cemetery beside her husband and near her daughter, her son-in-law, and Mary's mom and dad. There weren't many people who showed up for the graveside ceremony—just two elderly women. Mary said Great Granny had gone to high school with them back in the day. After she was laid to rest, Mary and I went back home.

"Are you going to be all right?" I asked her after we had walked inside.

"Great Granny lived to a ripe old age," she replied.

"That's not what I mean," I told her. "I mean now that you're alone. She was the last family you had."

"But I'm *not* alone," she replied. "I have *you*. You're like a sister to me. I was thinking, though. You said you can't travel through time for whatever reason. But what if I can? If you teach me, I promise not to change anything."

"Phasing through time," I told her, "isn't really a lot different than phasing through space. It's just a matter of directing your thoughts to when you want to be in addition to where. It's important, though, to keep a grip on the Earth's gravitational field while you're time traveling."

"Because?" she asked.

"Because," I replied, "the Earth is moving through outer space at tremendous speed along with the solar system and the galaxy. You don't want to wind up lost in the middle of nowhere, not knowing how to find your way back."

"Understood," she said. "So, what do I do first?"

"I don't know if you *can* do anything," I replied, "but you need to start out small. Try going ten seconds into the future. Just clear your mind and think about just that."

Mary closed her eyes and a moment later, she disappeared. Ten seconds later, she was back in the exact same place.

"I guess it didn't work," she said with a frown.

"It worked," I replied, not knowing whether to be happy for her or not. "You were gone for exactly ten seconds. I checked my wristwatch."

"You're not just fooling me, are you?" she asked.

"No," I insisted. "Now, try it again, only this time phase through space as well."

"Phase where?" she asked.

I shrugged. "Maybe just outside the front door."

For a second time, she closed her eyes and then vanished. Ten seconds later, I heard the knob to the front door turn several times unsuccessfully and then the doorbell rang. I went and opened the door to find Mary just outside.

"I forgot my key," she said excitedly as she walked back in. "This is so incredible! My heart is just racing!"

Over the next few days, I got her to go further and further into the past and future but not so far that she could change anything. The last time, she went ahead nearly five years and came back with a sad expression on her face and a newspaper in her hand.

"What's wrong?" I asked.

She just shook her head with tears in her eyes and handed me the paper. I unfolded it and read the banner. "Death Takes Mayor Cermak." According to the article, on February 15, 1933, Chicago Mayor Anton Cermak was shot and killed while shaking hands with President-elect, Franklin Delano Roosevelt at Bayfront Park in

Miami, Florida. The mayor died of complications on March 6th, the date of the story.

"I could have saved him!" Mary wept. "But I promised you I wouldn't interfere."

"I told you the reason," I said.

"I know," she sobbed, "but do you know I went back to the moment it happened and I just stood there and watched as a man's life was robbed from him! Oh, Peyton, how can I live with myself after that—to be able to change history but just stand helplessly by?"

"You did the right thing," I replied. "Some things are just meant to be."

"But why would God give me the power to change things," she wept, "but not allow me to intervene?"

"I've asked myself that question a lot," I said. "but in my time there is a term called *The Butterfly Effect* where just changing one small thing can create a chain reaction that can affect countless lives that were not affected before."

"Let's go back to your time," she insisted. "There's nothing left for me here, what with Great Granny gone. Since I have the ability to time travel, I can take you with me like I did the newspaper."

"Why not?" I replied.

"What date should we go to?" she asked.

"How about May 1, 2025," I replied. "It's the last date I remember. Look into my mind for the exact location."

She nodded, wrapped her arms around me, closed her eyes, and then vanished, leaving me alone in the room, powerless, and stranded nearly a century back in the past.

CHAPTER L

Mary
(May 1, 2025)

I found myself in a bedroom with my arms stretched around open air. Peyton hadn't appeared with me. As I looked around, I could see the room that she had described with its twin beds. I could hear sounds outside the closed door. There were others in the house. There was a man's voice and a woman's—*Probably Peyton's parents*, I thought to myself. It was then that something strange happened. The naked body of a teenage girl appeared on the floor in a series of flashes. She was emaciated beyond belief—virtually a skeleton—and she was gasping for breath. I bent down to touch her and she convulsed somewhat and opened her eyes just a bit. I ran to the bedroom door and opened it.

"Help!" I called out at the top of my lungs. "Someone help!"

Almost immediately I could hear the patter of footsteps as Peyton's father and mother rushed up the stairs and burst into the room. Both of them saw what I saw with horror in their eyes. Peyton's mother knelt down near the girl.

"Ophelia?" she gasped. "Oh, dear God!" She turned her head back to her husband. "James, call 911! Get an ambulance! My God! My God! My God!"

The girl looked up at her mother. "Mom?" she said in a whisper of a voice.

"Don't try and talk, Baby," her mother replied. "Help is coming."

"They're on their way," Peyton's father said.

"James," Peyton's mother said, "get me her blanket."

The man rushed to the bed, pulled the covers off, and passed it on to her. The woman covered her daughter, who must have been trembling—if a skeleton can tremble.

The girl was still gasping for breath as approaching sirens could be heard.

"I'll go let them in," James said and then bolted out into the hall and down the stairs. I just stood watching, uncertain of what to do. A couple of minutes later, two men in white uniforms entered the room carrying medical bags. Peyton's mother stood up and backed away a few steps as the men rushed over to the girl.

"What happened to her?" one of them asked.

"We don't know?" Peyton's father replied.

The man then looked at me. I just shook my head. Then the girl mumbled something. The man bent down to hear her.

"What is she saying?" the other one asked.

"Cyanide," he replied. "She keeps repeating, 'cyanide.'"

The man next to the girl began speaking into the air but the sounds of another could be heard through a rectangular box attached to his belt.

"Nethercutt," he said, " we have what appears to be a teenage girl, who is emaciated like she came from a German concentration camp. Pulse is forty. BP is seventy over thirty-eight. Pupils are dilated with vague response. Respiration is lethargic. Patient mumbled something about cyanide. No indication as to whether it was inhaled or ingested. Over."

The voice through the box responded, "Administer one thousand micrograms of hydroxocobalamin and transport. Over."

"Roger that," the man said. "ETA in fifteen."

The man rose to his feet and then turned to us. "We'll be right back," he said. "We need to bring up a stretcher."

Both of them then left the room. Peyton's mother bent down and stroked the girl's forehead. A moment later, she stood up again and backed up out of the way when the men came back into the room. They carefully lifted the girl onto the stretcher and then took her out, down the stairs, onto a gurney, and into their ambulance.

"Which hospital are you taking her to?" Peyton's father asked.

"UCLA Santa Monica," came the one of them replied.

The men got into the vehicle and drove away. There was a fire truck there as well that followed them. By then, all three of us were standing on the street. Some neighbors had come out of their homes, understandably curious as to what was going on.

"I'll get the car," James Herron said.

Mrs. Herron turned to me. "I didn't get your name."

"Mary Lindsey," I replied. "I'm a friend of Peyton's."

"Have you seen her?" she asked.

"Yes," I replied. "She's been staying with me."

Just then, a car pulled out of the driveway with Peyton's dad. Mrs. Herron got in the passenger seat.

"May I come along?" I asked.

I drove with them to the hospital. For the most part, it was in silence. Then Peyton's mother spoke. "How could it have happened to her?" she said. "I saw her just a few hours ago."

"I don't know," came the stolid response from her husband. "Maybe the doctors can tell us." He paused for a minute or so and then, glancing in the rear-view mirror at me, asked, "So, how do you know Peyton?"

"We've been friends for quite a while," I said.

"She never mentioned you to us," he replied.

"Do you two know about her special abilities?" I asked.

He looked up at me again.

"I mean, well…" I began, "Well, what I want to ask is, does the name Quantum Girl mean anything to you?"

"She told you?" came Mrs. Herron's shocked response.

"We've been living together for close to a year," I replied. "And then she lost the god-stone and it went into my head and that's how I wound up here in this time."

"What do you mean, 'this time?'" Mr. Herron asked.

"I'm from 1929," I replied. "That's where Peyton and I met. Honestly, she's been like a kid sister to me. Then Great Granny died and we figured maybe I could take her back to her present because she wasn't able to time travel anymore. Only it didn't work and I wound up here alone. And that's when the girl phased in right in front of me."

"Her name's Ophelia," Mrs. Herron said.

"Wait!" I exclaimed. "That was Ophelia?"

"Peyton's sister," she replied. "Surely she told you about her."

"Yes, but I never imagined her to be like that," I said.

"Neither did we," she replied and then turned to her husband. "James," she said, "can't you drive a bit faster."

"Not and get there in one piece," he replied.

"I couldn't find Hannah," she said. "I called for her but she didn't respond. I'll phone Mrs. Sayles to look for her after we get to the hospital. I left the door open."

"Who's Hannah?" I said. "If I may ask."

"A little Jewish girl Peyton brought back from Auschwitz," she replied and then had a ghastly thought. "James," she said to him, "you don't suppose the two of them got pulled back in time? Oh, Dear God in Heaven! That would explain her condition!"

"We can't tell them that," James insisted. "No one would believe it."

Mr. Herron drove the car into the hospital parking lot, parked the car and then we all got out. I followed them into the building to an area marked *Intensive Care Unit* where it turned out Ophelia had been taken. Mr. Herron asked one man behind a desk about her and was told that she was being 'worked on,' and that we needed to wait. After a while, a doctor came out from in back and approached us.

"Are you her parents?" he asked.

Both of them nodded.

"Is she going to be all right," Mrs. Herron asked.

"We're doing all we can," the doctor replied, "but between the effects of the cyanide and her extreme emaciation, I'm afraid she doesn't have much time left."

"No!" Mrs. Herron sobbed as she fell into her husband's arms.

"Can we see her?" Mr. Herron asked.

"This way," the doctor replied with the three of us following him to her bed. "She has bouts of consciousness. If you want to say goodbye, now is the time to do it."

"But she's only fifteen," Mrs. Herron pleaded. "She's just a baby!"

"I'm sorry," came the response. Then he left, closing back the curtain behind him.

Ophelia lay on a bed in a small area that was closed off with curtains. There were wires that were hooked up to her that were attached to a machine with lighted numbers and moving lines and which made beeping sounds, and there was a bag of liquid that was dripping down a tube into her left arm.

"We can't lose her, James!" Mrs. Herron sobbed. "There must be something we can do."

Just then, the curtains were drawn back revealing a professional-looking couple.

"Are you the parents of Ophelia Herron?" the woman asked.

"Yes," Mr. Herron replied.

"I'm afraid the two of you are under arrest for child neglect. Please place your hands behind your backs."

"We need to stay with her," Mrs. Herron insisted.

"Ma'am," the officer, replied, "your fifteen-year-old daughter looks like she just came from a Nazi concentration camp. I don't know how she got that way, but it didn't happen overnight. She's been starved for months if not years. Now, I'm asking you politely. Please place your hands behind your backs."

"We'll get this all straightened out," Mr. Herron told his wife as he complied, urging her to do the same.

"I'll stay with her," I told them both.

The two were handcuffed and then led out of the building.

When they had gone, I pulled the curtain closed again.

Ophelia, Peyton's sister, was about as close to death as is humanly possible. I had no idea how she had gotten that way but I knew in my heart that I had to help. Peyton had taught me a lot about the abilities I now possessed. I had heard so much about *Phee* that she had become real to me, although I had never expected to meet her, especially not like this. I remembered how Peyton had been told the story of how Phee's later wife, Claire, had been on the brink of death but was brought back by a parallel version of her being merged into her. I thought, perhaps, I could do the same.

Wires be damned, I climbed on top of her and then phase-inverted me so that we were both facing upward and then phased off my clothes. I focused my will and then disappeared into her. I became a part of her and she a part of me. My flesh became her flesh. My organs became hers. Even my hair then flowed from her scalp. The indicators became louder. Her skeletal form fleshed out. At last, she opened her eyes. It felt very strange, at least to me, as we sat up. We pulled the needles from our arms and then pulled off all of the taped-on indicators. The machine flatlined as we climbed to our feet. We dressed back into the clothes I had taken off, pulled back the curtain, and walked out from the ICU. At the main desk, I asked the attendant where the police station was, got directions, and then phased there. Inside, I walked to the front desk and addressed the officer behind it.

"I'd like to see my parents," I told him. "I believe they're being questioned."

"Name?" he asked.

"Ophelia Herron," I replied.

A moment later, the male officer who had handcuffed Mr. Herron, now my father—our father—emerged from the back room.

"May I help you?" he asked.

"I'm here about my parents," I replied.

"You're Peyton?" he asked.

"No," I answered, "Ophelia—the one taken in the ambulance just a while ago."

"That's not possible," he said.

"Check for yourself," I replied. "I left the left the hospital. Call them. The bed I was in is now empty. Go to our house. There are photos of me all over the walls. And photos of Peyton as well. We're not identical. When you're satisfied that there was no child neglect, you can let my parents go. Make it happen before midnight and no one will press charges. Mistakes happen, even well-intentioned ones. Now may I see my parents to assure them that I'm just fine?"

The officer nodded and then led me to the examination room where Mrs. Herron sat. He opened the door and allowed me to go in. Then he closed the door behind me. The woman who had been besieged with tears looked up and saw her daughter.

"Hi, Mom," she said—we said.

Tears now flooded down Katherine Herron's face as she jumped up and embraced us.

"How can you be all right?" she wept. "You were like a skeleton half an hour ago."

"It's not just me, Mom," we said, "It's me and Mary. She merged with me to save me."

"I don't understand," she replied.

"You don't have to," we said. "But I'm well again and alive."

I was brought into Dad's room as well a few minutes later with a similar response. Then at ten minutes to midnight, having called the hospital, taken my thumbprint from my driver's permit, and, with Dad's permission to search the house, having seen the photos of Peyton and Ophelia, they let Mom and Dad go. I phased us all back home. The car could wait.

"I'd like to get to know Mary better," Mom said as the two of us sat at the kitchen table, milk for us, coffee for her.

"You will," we said. "You will."

Dad had already gone to bed. The day had been quite a strain on him—on all of us.

"So, Peyton is back in 1929 without her god-stone," Mom said. "How will we get her back?"

"I'll go find her," I said and stood up. "She may not be Quantum Girl at the moment, but I am." I paused for a moment and then said, "As for Hannah, you can stop looking for her. She died eight months ago—well, eighty-two years ago from now. She contracted typhus in the camp. There wasn't any medicine. I was a prisoner like her." I showed them the tattoo on my arm. "There was nothing I could do," I told them. "There was nothing any of us could do."

I split into two with one of me phasing into my costume in front of them and then that one vanished back into the past.

CHAPTER LI

Quantum Girl Red
(March 14, 1943)

I was at the studio, reviewing test prints from a recent shoot, when my other self phased out of nowhere right next to me.

"You've certainly been gone a while," I said. "I tried to make contact. I thought you might have been killed."

"You know there's no connection when we travel through time," she replied.

"So I've been told," I said with no small bit of sarcasm. "So, how was he?"

"He who?" came her response.

"The German," I said. "The one you fucked."

"Fine," she replied.

I turned to her, anger written all over my face. "And what about Mark?" I said. "No loyalty? I remember somewhere back up in time the words, 'Till death do you part.'"

"It's been more than a year!" she said defensively. "A person has needs."

"A person has honor and commitments," I replied. "Love means you wait for the one you've made promises to."

"Well, run my ass up the flagpole," she shot back, "for everyone to judge! Can we merge back now?"

"Not until you explain what all you were up to?" I demanded.

"Up to what?" she replied. "I did to Hitler what he did to all the Jews without altering the timeline. And I saved a little girl."

"And that didn't change the future?" I said.

"No," she said defensively. "No, it didn't! She was going to die and no one would have noticed."

"And you know this because…" I asked.

"Because I ran through a thousand outcomes," she replied, "until

I found the one that would effectually save her without any consequences."

"And so where is she now?" I asked.

"With Mama and Papa and Phee," she replied.

"What was so special about this one little girl that you had to risk all the potential consequences to the future?" I demanded to know.

"She touched me! All right?" she shouted. "She meant as much to me as Margaret has come to mean to both of us!"

"That doesn't explain the German," I said.

"Wilhelm," she replied.

"Wilhelm," I repeated.

"I went to Auschwitz," she said. "I witnessed all the horrors that I couldn't do anything about."

"Except for the little girl," I said.

"Hannah," she replied. "Her name was—is—Hannah."

"Except for Hannah," I said.

"I needed someone," she said, defending her actions. "I needed to be held by someone!"

"So," I replied, "out of all the millions of people in the world, you picked a Nazi!"

"Yes," she said, half shouting, "I picked a Nazi!"

"Why?" I asked. "Why would you do that?"

"Because," she replied, "because I still love Mark and I didn't want to fall in love with anyone else so I picked out someone I couldn't love!"

"To fuck," I said back.

"Yes," she replied. "to fuck! And he was damn good at it. After seeing firsthand what all was done in the concentration camps, knowing I had the power to change all of it but couldn't, I felt like going back into the closet and putting the rope around my neck again because I thought, *What good is it to have all these powers and not be able to use them to help everyone?* I—we—may as well be Harry Fucking Potter doing nothing with our abilities other than competing in tournaments in order to win trophies!" Tears came to her eyes. "Seriously, what good are we? What good is Quantum Girl and all the *god*-stones if we can't help anyone? I helped Hannah. That was the best I could do."

"Sorry to be so hard on you," I said in a conciliatory tone. "Hey, cheer up. I forgive you," and I reached out and hugged her.

"So, we can merge back?" she asked.

"Of course," I said.

But just as we were about to, Albert wheeled into the studio from his darkroom. He stopped in his tracks and stared at the two of us.

"I thought I heard voices," he said. "You never told me you had a twin."

"It never came up," I replied. "This is my sister…"

"Peyton," my other self said, extending her hand to him which he amicably took.

"I must have the two of you model together," he insisted.

"She's rather shy," I said, glancing at her.

"What is there to be shy about?" Arthur said. "If I've seen you, I've seen her. I insist! I'll even double your pay for each of you if you'll work together!"

"I guess it would be all right," my other self said uneasily at which point I gave her a sharp disapproving look.

"Fine, fine!" Arthur rejoiced, rubbing his hands together. "We can start tomorrow! Eight o'clock." He looked at this wristwatch. "I almost forgot what I came in here for! I needed to use the phone!"

He rolled his wheelchair over to the table on which telephone sat and picked up the black candlestick phone that was common at that time.

Once he was out of earshot, I turned to my other self with a scowl. "Now, we're stuck apart," I said.

"We can merge and then redivide again in the morning," she

suggested.

I shook my head. "Thank you, no," I replied. "I don't need to be distracted by the vivid memories of sex with Siegfried!"

"Wilhelm!" she corrected me.

"Whatever!" I said. "Let's go home and tell Margaret that she has two mommies now!"

"You're irascible!" my other self said. "Do you know that?"

"Yes," I replied, "and with good reason! Come on… *Peyton*!"

"Yes," *she* replied, "*sister*, Elise!"

And so we left—together—me and myself and I could never figure out what I did to deserve all this!

CHAPTER LII

Quantum Girl Black
(June 6, 2025)

We arrived in New York at 9:27 a.m. near the corner of 5th and Broadway on June 6, 2025, roughly one week after I had been whisked away by forces unknown. The streets were ablaze with vehicles and pedestrians. How Khattaaara was able to phase us back to my universe, let alone to the Earth and within days of my having left escapes me to this day, though I suspect it had something to do with either the god-stone in my head or quantum trails or both, but there we were. Manhattan is not like most other cities in that there is more foot traffic most of the time, I guess because parking is so restrictive that most would rather use public transportation. Anyway, people began staring at us in our strange attire, though more at Khattaaara with her different anatomy. No one ran off screaming, though. Most probably assumed that we were in costume for some science fiction movie that was to be filmed there. Khattaaara was a bit taken aback by it all. I could see that it made her uncomfortable.

"We need to find other garb," I said to her in Gaaalthaaaran. "especially to conceal thy *yaaargh* and *khalthraaam*. The problem stands, however, that we have no coin with which to purchase any."

She removed a ring from her finger that had a large diamond surrounded by rubies and emeralds, placed it in the palm of her hand, and stared at it. As her eyes glowed bright violet, a duplicate of the ring appeared next to it. She handed that one to me and then replaced the original.

Khattaaara stood invisible beside me as I showed the ring to the owner of the pawn shop I had taken her to. The man examined it carefully through the magnifier he had wedged in the orbit of his eye. Once he was done, he looked at me.

312

"This is quite a valuable ring," he said. "Where did you come by it?"

"I inherited it," I lied. "It belonged to my grandmother."

"What were you hoping to get for it?" he asked.

"Ten thousand dollars," I replied.

The man looked at me with a great deal of suspicion which probably was warranted, considering my age.

"How do I know it's not stolen?" he asked.

"Feel free to call the police," I replied. "It's not stolen. I just need the money. My mother died and I've been stuck with my creepy stepfather who wants to *do* things with me if you get my drift. I have an aunt who lives in Portland. I just need to be able to afford a place to stay until I can get in touch with her. She hasn't been answering her phone. Look, I know the ring's probably worth ten times what I'm asking. If you're not interested, I can go somewhere else."

"Do you have any ID?" he asked.

"I only have what I'm wearing," I replied, "and you can see what he got me dressed in. I need to buy normal clothes. I can't go around like this!"

"I'll still need a thumbprint," he insisted.

"Fine," I said.

I have always found it interesting how greed will motivate some people to do things that common sense insists they shouldn't. Within a few minutes, the exchange had taken place and I had ten thousand dollars in hand. And so we went shopping. Khattaaara stayed invisible while I tried on the clothes. The fact that it was summer made it infinitely more difficult to conceal her nonhuman anatomy. Fortunately, she was able to flatten her *yaaargh* and hold it against her back while a wide Ace bandage purchased at a nearby CVS helped to conceal her lower pair of breasts. As for her Spock-like ears, her hair covered them. The final touch was to carefully draw in her eyebrows. The fact that her eyes were violet just made her look exotic.

From our shopping spree, we went for something to eat and stopped at a hotdog cart near Central Park. I ordered two footlongs with ketchup, mustard, piccalilli, and chopped sweet onions, fries, and two Cokes, taking them to one of the benches to eat. This was all new to Khattaaara who had never even seen a straw before but she watched how I ate and drank and followed suit.

"Thy food is wondrous," she said to me in Gaaalthaaaran.

"Wait!" I said and then pulled a chocolate bar from the messenger bag I had also bought, and handed it to her. She looked at it oddly, not knowing what to do with it.

"Remove the covering," I said. "It is a special food."

Tearing off the wrappers, she brought it to her nose to sniff, broke off a small piece, and then placed it in her mouth. As she began to chew it, a strange look came into her eyes.

"Such is truly the food of the gods," she said.

"So, you like it?" I asked.

"Indeed!" she replied. " I must have more!"

"There is much of it in my world," I said. "It is called chocolate."

"Shuhkolaaat," she repeated. Her eye then caught sight of a man nearby walking a Doberman. "That is not a *goraaag*," she said. "What manner of beast *is* it?"

"It is called a dog," I replied. "People here keep them as pets."

As I looked from her to the dog and then back again, seeing the expression in her eyes, I thought, if wolves could be domesticated into dogs, perhaps Khattaaara could be *domesticated* into a human being. As things stood, she represented a danger to our planet and any other planet with intelligent life on it. I had no idea what had gone on in her past to turn her evil, but beyond my responsibility as Quantum Girl to prevent her from doing harm in this universe, there existed the fact that this was me in a previous incarnation and as such I had a duty to prevent this former me from upending my

314

present home.

While she was distracted, I froze time and phased back to April 30, 2015, to the house of a breeder in Redondo Beach, California, and rang the bell. This was a date and address I had learned from Claire. A woman in her forties answered the door.

"May I help you?" she asked.

"I understand you have a rough collie for sale," I said,

"I have two," she replied. "They're both female and are ten weeks old."

"Can I see them?" I asked.

"Of course," she said. "Come in and have a seat. I'll bring them out."

I entered and sat down. After a couple of minutes, she came back with two puppies. One was a sable and the other a blue merle[35]. She set both of them down on the floor near me. I smiled and picked up the blue merle.

"We call her Missy," she said. "She's the shyest of the litter."

"She's adorable. How much *is* she?" I asked.

"Fifteen hundred dollars," the woman replied.

"I have cash on me," I said. " Could I take her now?"

"Do you intend to show her?" she asked.

"Possibly," I replied, "but at the moment I need her to be a therapy dog."

"I'll draw up the paperwork," the woman replied. "I can mail you the registration and instructions on when she'll need her shots. I'll also give you some of the kibble she's been on and a leash."

My attention was taken up by the fur baby in my hands. I glanced up at her.

"Thank you," I said.

"Have you decided on a name?" she asked. "I'll need that for the paperwork."

---

[35] Where a sable collie has fur that is tan and white, a blue merle has a coat with mottled black, surrounded by gray, often with a tan muzzle and a white mane.

I set the puppy down, took out the money from my messenger bag, stood up, and handed it to her.

"Niska," I said.

After all was done, Niska and I phased back to the park. I set Niska down a few feet away, retook my position on the bench, and then unfroze time. As Khattaaara was still staring at the Dobermann, I looked down and exclaimed.

"Well, hello there!" I said and bent down and picked up Niska.

Khattaaara's attention at once turned back toward me, now with a pup in my lap. Her mood brightened at once.

"And what manner of creature is this?" she asked.

"Her name is Niska," I said. "She is also a dog—a different breed called a collie."

"Naaaghzkha," Khattaaara tried to repeat. "Khaaali."

"Yes," I said. "Wouldst thou like to hold her?"

Khattaaara nodded and I handed her the pup. She examined it with great curiosity.

"This dhaaagh," she said. "It has a *yaaargh*."

"No," I laughed. "It's called a tail. Her organs of reproduction are similar to mine."

The alien held up the dog to view its underside.

"And yet," she replied, "It has ten *khalthraaamig*. But it is a very pretty animal. We shall keep it. It shall be our royal dhaaagh. Naaaghzkha!"

"We need to find a place to stay," I told her. "We cannot rent anywhere. I'm too young to sign a lease and thou hast no identification. We can phase to my parents' house but thou must promise me thou wilt not harm anyone. My family is dear to me."

"It is agreed," Khattaaara replied.

I phased the three of us back home. We materialized in my room. Phee was there. It was late morning but she was still in bed. She turned and looked at us.

"Hello," she said in a tired voice. "What time is it?"

"Around ten," I said.

She rubbed her eyes and then saw Khattaaara, pressed her lids together, and then cocked her head. "What's up with the makeup?" she asked. "And why are there two of you?" Suddenly, her brain became alert. "I thought you couldn't time travel? How did you get back?"

"From where?" I asked.

"1929, silly!" She swung her legs over the edge of the bed and then saw Niska, whom I had set down.

"Oh, my God!" she exclaimed. "A puppy!" She looked up at me. "What's its name?"

"Niska," I said. "and *it's* a she. She'd been blind Claire's seeing-eye dog when there were other dimensions."

Phee bent down, as Niska walked up to her. She picked her up into her arms and pressed her cheek against her fur. "She's so soft!" she said. She glanced up at me. "Can we keep her?"

"I should hope so," I said. "I just paid a small fortune for her." I paused for a second and then asked, "And why do you think I can't time travel?"

"I tried to take you with me," she said, "or at least the Mary part of me did."

"Mary part," I repeated.

"Did something scramble your brain," she asked standing up. She handed Niska to me, sniffed under her right arm, and wrinkled her nose. "I need to jump into the shower," she said. "Mary may have her daily hygiene but more than a year in a concentration camp didn't work out well for Ophelia." She pulled off the nightgown she was wearing, let it drop to the floor, and then walked butt naked into the bathroom. Once there, she stared at her reflection in the mirror over the sink and forced a grin. "At least I have all of my teeth again," she said. Then she turned on the water in the tub, pulled up the lever for the shower, and got it.

Khattaaara and I just watched. Though as I glanced back at her,

317

she had a hold of her *yaaargh* and was sucking on the furred tip. I walked into the bathroom with Khattaaara just behind me and Niska close afoot.

As the mirror began to steam up, I began to lose my patience. "Who is Mary," I asked, "what do you mean 'a year in a concentration camp,' and what *about* 1929?"

"I'm still teared-up about Hannah," she said. "She died, you know, or maybe you don't, but there was nothing I could do to save her. I mean, I had to fuck half a dozen guards to get her food but it just wasn't enough. She died from typhus. 'No fate but what we make!' Fuck the Kyle Reese philosophy! You can't imagine how many days and nights I wept over her!"

I phased out of my clothes (which dropped in a pile on the floor) and got into the shower to face her, her back to the spray.

"Hey!" she said. "This is *my* shower time! And we haven't taken a shower together since we were like eight!"

"I'm not interested in lathering," I said.

"Then what?" she asked. She lifted her eyes toward Heaven and then looked back at me. "I guess you don't know," she said. "We merged."

"Who merged?" I asked.

"Mary and me or Ophelia and me," she replied and then shook her head. "Ugh!" she went on in exasperation, "Shower's all yours!" and then disappeared.

"What the hell!" I exclaimed and then, turning off the water, stepped out of the shower dripping wet.

I looked at Khattaaara wide-eyed. My attention, though, was turned by the sound of Phee's voice from the bedroom. Apparently, she had phased just outside the shower, grabbed her bath towel, and then gone back into the bedroom. I grabbed mine, began drying myself off, and followed her up to the closet she had gone into. I in turn was followed by Khattaaara and my newly purchased furry friend.

318

Phee turned to me, holding a red dress up against herself. "What do you think of this one?" she asked. "Claire and I are having lunch. I can't wait to tell her I'm Quantum Girl" Suddenly, she stared at me strangely. "I don't get it," she said.

"Get what?" I replied.

"If I have your god-stone," she asked, "how could you phase into the shower or duplicate or get here from the past."

"First of all," I replied as Phee slipped the dress on over her head, "I didn't duplicate. This is Khattaaara. You know, from Rendenaaar? Second, you don't have my god-stone. I still have it. And, third, what past are you talking about? I mean, Khattaaara and I just came here from the other universe but I was never *in* 1929!"

Phee froze and stared at me. "So, you're not the Peyton that I— or, rather, the Mary half of me—left back then?"

"I told you," I replied, "we just came from Rendenaaar. Well, from New York, actually, but from Rendenaaar like four hours before that."

She walked out of the closet, stared at Khattaaara, and then sat down on the bed. "I guess that means you're still stuck back there," she said. "Well, at least one of me went back in time, so at least you're not alone back there—then—oh, this is all so confusing!"

I then heard two stories. One began with one of me at a New Year's Eve celebration and the other when another of me—an older version—rescued a young Jewish girl from Auschwitz and brought her to 2025. That meant that there were at least two other versions of me out there, which somewhat explained why I now had a black god-stone instead of a violet one.

Khattaaara listened without understanding a word and then sat down on the bed next to Phee. The two of them stared each other in the face and then Khattaaara put her hand under Phee's dress and to her vag. Phee jumped up.

"Jesus!" she exclaimed as her gaze went back and forth between my former incarnation and myself. "Does she have any idea how inappropriate that is? And isn't she supposed to be evil?"

"Long story," I replied.

"I wish to have sex with her," Khattaaara said, eyeing Phee.

"I'm afraid thou wouldst need her consent for that," I replied. "This is not Rendenaaar. Besides, she is smitten with another female—or shall be some time hence."

"So, now you speak Rendenaaaran," Phee posited. "How long were you there? You do look a bit older."

"Nearly a year," I replied. "Well, not on Rendenaaar. I was stranded on another planet in that universe with another female named Laaadra-Taaagh. And the language is called Gaaalthaaaran."

"I sincerely hope you weren't intimate with either of them," she said.

"Well…" I replied, hedging the question.

"Eewe!" came the response. "They're, like, aliens!"

"They're not *like* aliens," I replied. "They *are* aliens. Well, Laaadra-Taaagh's obviously been dead now for trillions upon trillions of years."

"And just how are we going to break it to Mom that she's just acquired another *daughter*, albeit an extraterrestrial?"

"Mama's a Christian," I replied. "She believes that there's a reason for everything on God's green earth, though we're going to have to teach her—and by her I mean Khattaaara—to speak English."

Mama and Papa's reactions to Khattaaara were different from Phee's. Papa viewed her with curiosity, while Mama simply fainted. I must clarify that when she was introduced, Khattaaara had changed into one of my short silk dresses and so both her *yaaargh* and her double pair of breasts were quite apparent, not to mention her Spock-like ears.

Smelling salts brought my overwhelmed mother back to the world of the conscious. "Mama," I said, "you remember my telling you about Khattaaara, don't you?"

"Yes," she replied.

"And how I was reincarnated from her," I asked.

"Peanut," she replied, "there is no mention of reincarnation in the Bible."

"The Bible doesn't say anything about cell phones or television or automobiles either," I said. "Am I supposed to believe they don't exist either?"

"Point well taken," she replied. She stared at Khattaaara and Khattaaara stared back. It was almost hypnotic. She broke off the stare abruptly and then turned back to me. "So, you're expecting me to believe that your Katara…"

"Khattaaara," I corrected her with throaty intonation.

"Dear," she replied, "I'm afraid that my voice box is not capable of making that sound." She glanced once more at Khattaaara. "So, I'm to believe that she is actually you in a previous existence, brought here from the past by some device called a god-stone?"

"Something like that," I said.

"Well," she replied, glancing once more at Khattaaara, "if her soul and yours are somehow intertwined, then I guess it'd be our Creator's divine will that I should come to love her as much as my other daughters, though I never envisioned having one with pointed ears and a tail."

"What did she say?" Khattaaara asked me in Gaaalthaaaran.

"That she is prepared to love thee," I replied, "as were thee her own flesh and blood, born from the *yaaargh* she regrets she does not have."

Khattaaara looked at her curiously, tilting her head to one side while she did, appraising her. Then she folded her arms and said, "Tell her that we are pleased to accept her as our heyoooomaaan mother."

I turned back to my mother. "Khattaaara said she is honored," I told her, "to be regarded as your daughter and share a bond of love."

"Dear Mother of God," Mama replied as she stared once more at

Khattaaara, "the Lord most certainly moves in mysterious ways."

CHAPTER LIII

Quantum Girl Orange
(March 18, 1952)

The more I thought about it, the less I liked it—being in this body, I mean. It wasn't that living in the early Fifties was bad or anything. It was actually nice walking down the street in a poodle skirt and not seeing everyone—or anyone—being distracted by a cell phone pressed to their ear. Times were a lot simpler. There were no wars going on for the moment. I Love Lucy was the number one TV show, although only less than half of Americans owned television sets. Eisenhower was President, Nixon was his VP, and teenagers hung out at malt shops instead of malls. The only problem was that when I looked in the mirror it wasn't me who stared back. It was my then-teenage grandmother. I felt like Dr. Sam Beckett in Quantum Leap, only this quantum *girl* wasn't leaping out of the body she was in.

There wasn't even a clue as to where the mind of Margaret Fletcher was—not even a spark of her memory. And where was my body? Then there was the question of how it had happened or how my other self had been thrown back to 1941, though in her case, at least it was in her own body.

"I can't keep living her life," I told my older self who was and had been going by the name of Elise.

"What happens when you duplicate?" she asked me.

"I get two of *her*," I replied, "Margaret, I mean—no Peyton in sight."

"Try merging into me," she said.

I did as she suggested and, low and behold, Margaret's body was left behind. Margaret swooned and then caught herself. She looked around. We were in the living room but she had gone to bed when my mind had entered her head and that was five months ago.

"How did I get *here*?" she asked, totally confused.

I pulled out of Elise and faced her. She stared at the both of me and then focused on my older self.

"Mother," she asked, "what's going on? Why are there two of you and why is she... *younger*?"

So, we sat her down and told her all that had gone on, from the molestation to the drowning, and how her cheerleading instructor had been found guilty of multiple murders and subsequently executed.

"All that in just five months?" Margaret asked.

I shrugged. Elise told her that her coach had refused a defense lawyer. "I guess she knew there was no getting out of it," she said.

It was then that Margaret began to cry.

"What's wrong, Sweetheart?" Elise asked her.

"Babs was a really good friend of mine," she wept. "She didn't deserve to die."

Elise went over to her and held her.

"Can't you go back in time and keep her from killing herself?" Margaret sobbed.

"That would create too many ripples in the timeline," Elise told her, gently rubbing her back.

"I understand," she replied.

"But I have something that should cheer you up," Elise said. "Do you see that girl over there?"

"Uh-huh," Margaret replied as we separated and she wiped her eyes.

"Her name's Peyton," she said. "She's your granddaughter."

"How can she be my granddaughter?" she asked. "I'm not much older than her and, besides, I don't even have any children."

"And yet, here I am," I said and smiled. I extended my hand toward her which she accepted. "Pleased to meet you," I told her.

"The pleasure is mine, I'm sure," Margaret replied. Then she turned to Elise. "You two look a lot alike. Is she a Quantum Girl like you?"

I phased on my orange Quantum Girl costume.

"I assume that answers your question," I said.

"What happens to me in the future?" she asked.

"Well," I said, phasing back to myself, "you go to Smith College for two years where you study ballet, then move on to Julliard. Unfortunately, while performing in L.A., at the Shrine Auditorium, you have a bad fall and that ends your ballet career. But then you meet and fall in love with your physical therapist—Grandpa—and the rest is history, even though it hasn't happened yet. Oh, and after a miscarriage, you wind up giving birth to a little girl whom you name Katherine Elise. Katherine Elise Kimble, who in turn marries James Herron and winds up welcoming two beautiful baby girls named Peyton and Ophelia."

"What year are you from?" she asked.

"2025," I replied.

"So," she asked, "I'll be almost ninety by then. Am I still alive?"

I glanced at Elise. "Yes," I said, "but…"

"But what?" she asked.

"You're kind of in an old people's home," I replied.

"A convalescent home," Elise said, trying to soften the blow.

"That's not very comforting either way," she replied.

"Everyone dies sooner or later," I said.

"Do you?" she asked. "Do *either* of you?"

"We don't know yet," I replied. "I mean, I don't know if we can die of old age, but we're not immortal if that's what you mean. Other versions of us have already died several times if not more."

"Other versions," she said, parroting the phrase.

"Long story," I replied. "Other realities. Other dimensions."

"So, what now?" she asked.

"I guess I'll go back to my time," I said, "and get on with my life."

Margaret turned to Elise. "And what about you?" she asked.

"Will you be going with her?"

Elise shook her head. "You've been my little girl ever since I found you. I'm not going to leave you."

"But if I'm going off to college," she asked, "when will I ever see you?"

"I can visit you every day if you like," she replied.

"You promise?" she asked.

"I promise," she replied.

"Promises were made to be broken," a male voice said.

Our attention was suddenly turned to a violet Quantum Man in the room. Both Elise and I turned quantum ourselves but then, suddenly, neither of us could move.

The Quantum Man strolled around us, eyeing us, as Margaret cowered in fear. Then he shook his head to himself.

"You both think you're so brave, don't you?" he said in a voice that spewed arrogance. "You," he went on to Elise, "proud mother of the little girl you rescued from the rubble. And you," he said, eyeing me, "pretending to be her doting daughter, literally drowning in your role." He began clapping then. I can still hear the sound in my head to this day. It became louder and louder to the point that it was deafening and painful. I wanted to fight back but it was as though I were frozen. Then everything went black. The last thing I remembered was hearing Margaret scream.

CHAPTER LIV

Margaret
(September 24, 2025)

I was in the living room with my Mom and the girl who said she was my granddaughter when a costumed man glowing purple suddenly appeared out of nowhere. It was strange how he stared at me. I felt something hit my head like an icepick and then everything started flashing like I was in two places at once. I screamed and then I was just there in some kind of a large closet lit by a single lightbulb that hung from the ceiling. It was then that I saw her. She was hanging from a rope that had been tied into a noose around her neck. I couldn't see her face at first but then I guess the rope untwisted around and I saw that it was the girl I had just met— Peyton, who insisted that she was my granddaughter. My heart started racing. I tried to lift her body up so that she wouldn't strangle but she was too heavy. I let go of her and then tried the door but the rope was tied to the knob and the door opened out and her weight was pulling it shut. The rope was looped over a pipe that ran the length of the room. My first thought was to cut the rope but looking around I couldn't see anything to do it with. Then I thought, maybe I could break the pipe. There was a metal box near her feet. It looked as though that was what she had stood on before letting her body drop. I turned it on its side and got up on it. I couldn't quite reach the pipe so I jumped as high as I could and managed to grab hold of it. Then I kicked at the wall, trying to rock the pipe back and forth until, at last, it broke. Water came gushing out. Meanwhile, the rope became slack. I fell to the floor and Peyton, unconscious or dead, I didn't know, fell on top of me. I pulled myself out from under her, opened the closet door, and cried for help. As I heard the patter of feet and the sounds of a man calling out, "Peyton!" I turned back to her. I bent down to see if she was breathing, but then the flashing began again and in another moment I was back in the living room. The man was still there. My Mom and Peyton were frozen like statutes. I was soaking wet and still on my knees. I didn't know what was going on—only that there were purple rays that were aimed at my Mom coming from his eyes. I climbed to my feet and glared at him, filled with anger.

"Leave my Mom alone!" I screamed at him. "Go away!"

And then, suddenly, he was gone! I went to my Mom and shook her and she seemed to come to. I hugged her so tight. She looked at me and smiled and then shook Peyton to wake her up. I told them both what had happened. They weren't quite sure how but the running theory was that somehow, having been connected with Peyton for so long I had managed to pull the god-stone from her head and inadvertently phased back in time (that was the term they used) to the moment when she had tried to end her life, I guess so that I could save her..

As for the costumed man, I didn't know if I'd sent him into outer space or straight to Hell, but that didn't much matter. The three of us were safe and sound and it gave me comfort to think that even if way up in the future my fate was to be in some convalescent home, I wasn't there yet and I'd somehow managed to save the life of my future granddaughter, which was about the strangest thought a seventeen-year-old-could have. I felt good about what I had done—proud, actually. But then something happened. I felt a sudden pain in my head as, all at once—that same feeling as though an icepick had been stuck in my forehead. Then there was a flash of orange light that went from my head to hers—to Peyton's—and then Peyton disappeared. I turned and looked toward my mother for an answer but, to my horror, she had vanished, too!

CHAPTER LV

Quantum Girl Green
(Urth, November 18, 2025)

The Urth that my male counterpart was from was an upside-down version of Earth, a matriarchal civilization where all of the roles were reversed. What was most astonishing, though, was that everyone from the age of majority had a god-stone placed in their head. Thus, in terms of ability, I had reduced my counterpart to the empowerment level of a child. The god-stones were not divided into simple colors, but, rather, were created according to spectral frequencies, of which there were an almost limitless amount.

It was interesting to view a society where everyone has the same ability to phase through space and time, create forcefields and, in some cases, read minds and become invisible at will. There was, however, a police force that could extract a god-stone should an individual use it for unlawful purposes such as murder, theft, or sexual assault. Persons were also forbidden to travel backward in time in that it could and often would alter the present and might result in the uncreation of random individuals.

It was most curious when I phased to the door of my counterpart's home. I was surprised when a fifteen-year-old version of him answered. The even odder thing was that at this younger age, he looked even more like me with the exact same moles on his face.

"Can I help you?" he asked.

"You're Peyton Herron, I presume," I said.

"You presume correctly," he replied. "How may I help you?"

"My name's Peyton Herron, too," I said and then pushed my way through the doorway with an, "Is it all right if I come in?"

I looked around the living room which was pretty much the same as mine with a few exceptions. Then I turned around to face him again.

"Who are you?" he asked.

"I already told you," I said. "Peyton Herron. I'm your counterpart from an alternate reality."

"Why should I believe you?" he asked.

"You have micro-vision, don't you?" I replied. "Compare your DNA with mine."

And so he did.

"Fuck me!" he said afterward.

"I think that might be considered incestuous," I replied, "though I believe that my sister and her counterpart would adamantly protest."

"What do you want?" he scowled.

"Just to meet you," I replied. "'Know thine enemy.' Sun Tzu, *The Art of War*."

"I'm not at war with anyone," he said, defending himself.

"Not yet," I replied, "And it wasn't I who provoked it."

Just then, two adults phased into the room—a woman and a man. My jaw dropped as I realized they were the alternate reality version of my parents, except that Mama was a man and Papa was a woman—Cameron and Jane as it turned out!

Mr. Herron turned to my counterpart. "Peyton," he said, "we didn't realize you'd invited over a friend."

"I didn't invite her," Peyton scowled. "She just barged in."

I extended my hand toward him. "How do you do?" I said. "My name's Peyton as well."

"She claims she's from an alternate reality," Peyton said, "and insisted that I'm going to be an asshole in ten years."

Mrs. Herron looked at her son. "You *have* had your moments," she said.

"I checked her DNA," Peyton went on. "It's the same as mine other than the Y in twenty-three."

Mr. Herron turned to me. "We're about to have supper," he said.

"Perhaps you'd like to join us."

A severe frown expressed itself on Peyton's face. "I'd love to," I replied. "I actually just got here—to this reality, I mean. My intent was to phase back home but somehow I wound up here."

"They let fifteen-year-olds have god-stones in your reality?" Peyton said, aghast.

"I'm the only one," I said. "I call myself Quantum Girl," and briefly phased into my costume.

"Excuse me," Mrs. Herron said, "but you mean to tell me that no one else has a god-stone? However do they manage?"

"They just do," I replied. Then a thought hit me. "How is it that everyone is able to have a god-stone? In my reality, there are only seven—at least that I know of."

"We manufacture them," Mrs. Herron said. "The process was invented by a scientist named Tamara Drall about fifty years ago—founded a company called Quantech Labs, began selling the crystals at an affordable price, and, well, here we are."

"Come sit at the table, all of you," said Mr. Herron, "and I'll phase up the meal."

We went into the dining room and sat down. As we did, a handsome blond-haired teenage boy came in from outside and grabbed a chair. "Sorry, I'm late," he said. "Coach insisted we get in some extra laps what with the swim meet coming up next week." Then he saw me, did a doubletake, and shifted his gaze back and forth between Peyton and me.

"She's my alternate self," Peyton said to him. "So she claims."

The boy extended his hand to me. "Any alternate of Peypey has got to be an improvement," he said with a smile, adding, "My name's Orpheus, but you can call me..."

"Phee," I interrupted. "Same as my sister, Ophelia."

This Phee sat down and grabbed a breadstick to bite a piece off, as dinner was phased. "So," he began, chewing on it, "how did you wind up here?"

"It was an accident," I replied. "I was trying to get home, but I was using the god-stone from Peyton's—older Peyton's head, so it brought me here."

Orpheus appeared confused.

"I had a run-in with this older self from the future," I explained.

"Well, brother," Phee said, "I guess it appears you're going to survive into adulthood."

"Shut up!" Peyton said, frowning again as we all began to eat the casserole that was now on the table.

"How are you planning to get back," Mrs. Herron asked.

"I don't know exactly," I replied.

"Do you have any place to stay?" she asked.

I shook my head. "As I said, I only just arrived."

"Perhaps you'd like to stay here while you figure things out," Mr. Herron suggested.

"I'm sure she'll find a place," Peyton said, "what with her powers and all."

I glanced toward him and then turned to Mr. Herron. "I'd very much appreciate it," I replied.

"Fine, then," Mr. Herron said. "It's settled. After we finish eating, Peyton can show you to the guest room." He then looked at Peyton. "You *will* show her to the guest room and make her feel at home, won't you?"

"Yes, sir," Peyton replied and then laid down his fork.

"Are you finished already?" Mrs. Herron asked.

"I'm suddenly not very hungry," came the reply.

After supper was over, Peyton led me to the guest room—the same guest room as we had in my reality. "This is it," he announced. "I'd say make yourself at home but you probably won't want to stay for long."

I glared at him. "What is *with* you?" I asked. "You act like I'm Wednesday Addams or something!"

"First of all," he said, "Thursday Addams and he's a guy. And second, it's really creepy having someone who's not your twin but who looks like you and is the opposite sex!"

"Well," I said, "that's not the reaction Liam had when he first met my Phee."

"Who the hell's Liam," he asked.

"Liam was Phee's interdimensional twin," I replied.

"And what was *Liam's* reaction?" he asked.

"He fell in love with her," I said.

"Whatever!" Peyton replied. "I'm not Phee in either reality and I'm not Liam, so don't go expecting me to fall in love with *you*."

"I'm not!" I replied with a definite attitude. "Besides, I have a boyfriend—or I *will!*"

"Or you will?" he said mockingly. "What? Like you haven't even met him yet?"

"It's complicated," I replied.

Peyton just rolled his eyes and headed for the door. "The bathroom's just down the hall to the left," he said.

"I know very well where the bathroom is!" I replied. "This house is exactly like mine!"

"Then maybe you'll be able to go back there soon," he mumbled under his breath as he walked out, closing the door behind him.

"Grrrr!" I replied, grabbing the pillow off the bed and throwing it at the door.

CHAPTER LVI

Mary/Ophelia
(April 2, 1932)

After numerous attempts to make it back, finding myself in all the wrong places and times, the closest I could come was roughly two and a half years after I had left. My heart stopped at what I saw. The house—my house—was boarded up with a foreclosed sign posted on the door. All of the windows had been covered from the inside with newspaper that was yellowed and two years old. I phased inside to find it abandoned. The furniture was still all there but covered in a layer of dust. A rat scurried across the kitchen floor as I entered. Peyton was nowhere to be seen. *Of course not,* I thought to myself. *Where would she be after all this time? I* was the one who had powers. There would have been no way for her to have paid the mortgage. I had to find her, but how, I wondered. How does someone find one person in a city as large as Chicago?

I decided to start by knocking on neighbors' doors to find out if anyone knew her whereabouts. When that didn't result in any information, I went to the high school but it was shut down. I tried shanty towns and shelters, all of which were filthy and filled with those who were desperate with nowhere else to go but none of them remembered her having been there. I asked everyone I came in contact with if they had seen a pretty fifteen-year-old girl with light brown hair and gray eyes. The answer, time and again, was no. I divided myself into a thousand of me. I didn't need to eat or sleep. I was Quantum Girl. I just walked and searched for her, but in the end, after two months of searching, I had come up empty and just sat down on the front steps of what used to be my home when I was Mary and I wept.

CHAPTER LVII

Quantum Girl Blue
(October 29, 1929)

She was gone. Just like that, she was gone and my god-stone with her. I was trapped in the past with neither relatives nor friends and little money. If only I had the foresight to have transmuted more metal into gold, at least I wouldn't have had to worry, but the situation I was in had never even crossed my mind. I spent what little money I had on food. There were canned goods in the pantry, too, that I lived off of for a while but that supply eventually ran out. Heating was also a problem. The furnace in the basement used coal which, although I used it sparingly, was used up by mid-December when the temperature outside often dropped below zero. I shivered even under blankets at night. During the day, I would stand in bread lines, hoping to get something to eat. Then finally came the day when there was a notice nailed to the front door. It said that the house was being foreclosed for nonpayment and that everyone in it had to get out within thirty days. Four weeks and two days later, two sheriff's deputies banged on the door and told me I had thirty minutes to gather up my things and leave. I took what clothes I had along with a photo of Mary and Great Granny, piled them into an old suitcase, put on one of Mary's winter coats—the warmest I could find—as well as her galoshes and mittens, and left. I had begged the deputies to let me stay a while longer but even a flood of tears wouldn't convince them to give me a single extra day. It didn't matter to them how many people they committed to the streets what with the Great Depression. The banks just wanted their money and that was that. They couldn't care less that I was only fifteen years old.

I wandered the streets with my suitcase which was more of a burden than anything else. I would use it to sit on when I got tired which was often. There was snow everywhere which made it difficult to walk and froze my feet. People call Chicago *The Windy City*, but that wind wasn't much of a problem. The name came from an editorial that said there the local politicians were so full of hot air and empty promises that they ought to change the city's name.

Hot air, though, wasn't something that surrounded me. It just came from within. Every time I would exhale, a cloud of white steam would appear and then quickly vanish into the frigid air. I remember having read *To Build a Fire* by Jack London and how the man was so cold he could barely feel his fingers or his toes. I could relate. Sometimes I would pass by shanty towns where there were fires where I could briefly warm myself. Shantytowns were where a lot of homeless people had gathered together and built makeshift homes out of plywood or whatever else they could find. The towns were nicknamed Hoovervilles, blaming then-President Herbert Hoover for the conditions so many faced. All I knew was that I was hungry and cold with no relief in sight.

After three weeks of this life, with no hope that Mary would ever reappear with the god-stone, I made up my mind to try and make my way to California where, at least it was warm. Plus, I figured that maybe I could get some work there. Word on the streets was that, despite the depression, movies were still being made— talkies were now the thing—and I thought that maybe I could get a job acting in one. I didn't care about the timeline anymore. Hunger and cold do that to a person. I had no one in the world other than me, and I wanted to survive.

Like most hobos at the time—which I guess I had become—I hopped a freight train. Hopping into a boxcar was not an easy thing, especially when the train began moving, but it was the only way it could be done. The bulls or yardmen were always on the lookout for freeloaders until the train was on its way, and even then some of them would chase after you to try and pull you off. The cars could also be dangerous if the doors accidentally slammed shut and trapped you inside. Seasoned travelers would often place a board against the jamb to keep that from happening. Some less fortunate, who lacked the forethought to protect themselves that way, died from asphyxiation. Regardless, to make the jump you had to be both strong and quick on your feet.

I have to admit that before I left, I stole some man's cap at one of the shanties so that I could hide my hair and pose as a boy. The cars tended to be filled with men, some with disreputable histories— at least that's what I'd been told—*warned* is probably a better word.

Jumping on board was one thing but doing so with a suitcase was quite another. I had managed with no small effort to get it on board but then had a hard time grabbing hold to pull myself up into the boxcar. It was as if all the breath in my lungs had left me and I was about to say goodbye to both my luggage and the train when I felt a hand grip my right forearm and pull me up into the car. The man to whom the hand belonged turned out to be a bare-knuckles boxer who went by the name of Battlin' Bob Murdock. Battlin' Bob was from upstate New York, thirty-two years old, with a burly physique, short dark hair, and a cauliflower ear. And while he only had a grade school education, he was kind to a fault and would give you the shirt off his back if you needed it even if it was freezing cold.

"Thanks so much," I said to him as we both sat down. There were about fifteen other men in the car with us. None of them looked like the sort you'd have wanted to invite over for afternoon tea.

"Glad to be of help," he replied.

"Where are you headed?" I asked.

"San Francisco," he said. "I got me a manager who says he can get me a match with Jack Dempsey. 'Course Dempsey's not what he once was, but it's a way for me to make a name for myself. Only thing is I'll have to strap leather on my hands. No more bare knuckles, but I'll still be Battlin' Bob."

"I wish you the best," I said.

"How 'bout you?" he asked.

"Los Angeles," I answered. "I heard there are parts to be had making motion pictures."

Battlin' Bob looked at me. "Say," he said, "maybe you could get a part where you play opposite Greta Garbo."

"Who's she?" I asked.

"Yer puttin' me on," he replied. "Everyone knows who Garbo is! Why she's the most famous actress in the world! 'Course, I realize you're a might young for her. Shucks, I were just funnin' you. But you wantin' to be an actor and not know who Greta Garbo is, that's like bein' Catholic and not knowin' who's the pope."

"I'm not Catholic," I said, "and I just need to find a decent-paying job. I lost all my family."

"Me," he replied, "I never had none. Grew up in an orphanage. That's where I learned to defend myself with these," and he held up his fists. "If you wanna come with me to San Francisco," he went on, "I can teach you how to fight. They're always lookin' for lightweights."

"I think I'll stick to acting," I replied.

He looked me over. "Yeah," he said, "I suppose. No need to mess up that face of yours. By the way, I forgot to introduce myself proper. I'm Bob Mullins." He extended his right hand to me.

"Peyton Herron," I replied as I took his hand and shook it. "I'm pleased to make your acquaintance."

"Well," he said after the handshake, "at least we can travel together up until you make it to L.A. Then it's up to Frisco for me."

And that's how it went. Battlin' Bob Mullins and I became friends. Things changed a bit when a few days later we were changing trains in Oklahoma and the wind blew off my hat.

"Say," Bob said as he stared at me, "you're a girl!"

"I never said I wasn't," I replied.

"Oh, I get it!" he exclaimed. "You're wanting to protect yourself from all the men on the trains. Don't you worry, though. I won't let anything happen to you."

And so it was from then until Bob and I parted ways at the train station in L.A. I always wondered what happened to him, how he made out in the ring, and what happened after, but I was certain that he battled his way to victory to the very end of his days.

CHAPTER LVIII

Quantum Girl Red
(March 14, 1943)

There were two of me now. Margaret kept asking why we didn't phase together again. The truth was that we had become so different from each other that each of us abhorred the other's thoughts. While I had stayed home to take care of Margaret, my other self had gone to Germany and had betrayed the emotional and spiritual bonds we had with Mark. And on top of that, she had gained an attitude. I could not read her mind when she had traveled through time even a day but I could when she returned. I could read the memory of the intimacy she had shared with the Nazi named Wilhelm. I could feel him inside her, which translated to feeling him inside *me* and that sickened me to no small extent. She and I were at odds with each other. I was still who I was but she had grown into something else. Her words from when she was in Berlin echoed in my brain. "The Jews!" she said, "Filthy, disgusting creatures! One had the nerve to spit on me as I walked down the sidewalk with my husband. My husband had him dragged off and shot." How could those words have even left her mouth, acting or not?

"You've changed," I said to her when we were alone at home just after I had tucked Margaret in bed.

"How so?" she asked.

"You betrayed our vows with Mark for one thing," I replied.

"Mark won't even be born for another sixty-seven years," she answered.

"Should I have stopped loving him if he were a million miles away?" I asked. "Is there really a difference between space and time?"

"You're taking my little tryst way too seriously!" she shot back.

"I'm not taking it anywhere from where it was," I said.

"He didn't mean anything to me!" she screamed.

"Well, Mark *does*!" I screamed back.

"Mommy," Margaret said, sleepily coming from her bedroom, rubbing he eyes, "What are you arguing about?"

"Nothing, Sweetheart," I said in a gentle voice.

I took her by the hand and then headed with her back toward her room. I turned my head slightly in my twin's direction.

"We'll talk when I get back," I told her. "Calmly. We have a child."

As I tucked Margaret back in bed, she looked up at me. "Why are you two arguing?" she asked. "You're both the same person, aren't you?"

"She's a different part of me," I said. "She did things while she was away."

"Bad things?" Margaret asked.

"Do you remember when you told your friend, Gina, that I was Quantum Girl," I said, "and that I had superpowers and made her promise not to tell?"

"But she *did* tell," Margaret said, "only no one believed that it was true and then Gina got mad at me because she said I lied to her, and you got upset with me that I told Gina."

"Sometimes," I said, "even adults do things they shouldn't that they don't think are bad at the time or just don't care if they are."

"But you're both my mommy," she replied, "aren't you?"

"Of course, we are," I assured her, "and we both love you so much."

I tickled her and she laughed.

"It's just that she and I," I said, "are having differences just now. But we'll get over them. You'll see."

"I hope so," Margaret said and yawned.

"Now, you go back to sleep," I told her, "and in the morning we'll have crepes with blueberry preserves."

Margaret smiled. "I love you, Mommy," she said.

"I love you, too, Fair Margaret," I replied.

Back in the kitchen, I found my other self sitting at the table, sipping from a coffee-filled cup.

"We can't be arguing like this," I told her. "It's not doing us any good and it's not fair to Margaret."

My other self stared up at me over her cup. "Not fair to Fair Margaret," she said and smiled. "We need to merge back together. Whatever I did wrong, I apologize for but there were things I saw that drove me to it. Perhaps once when we're back together you'll understand."

I nodded. She stood up, phased off her clothes, and then merged back into me. For a moment, it was confusing—all the thoughts and emotions flooding into my head. But then I understood.

CHAPTER LIX

Quantum Girl Black
(June 6, 2025)

If I were to describe my mother in one word I would use the word *Christian*. She lives it, breathes it, and, if she were Catholic, would eat it and drink it as well. Katherine Elise Kimble Herron was a God-fearing woman who had read her King James Bible more than one hundred times in her thirty-six years at that time on this Earth. My father once said that she knew more Bible passages than John Calvin, the Sixteenth Century preacher who founded Calvinism that taught strict adherence to the Holy Books and that the glory and sovereignty of God must come before all other things. This was strange in and of itself because her mother, my grandmother, was something of a dreamer who adhered to scientific thought, who believed, not in the stories of Adam and Eve and the great flood, but rather in the timeless universe as seen by Einstein and Hubble and even spoke, during her final days, of a universe other than our own where men and women had tails like the Devil but were generally caring and kind. Papa said that Mama's fervent religious beliefs came after her father took ill of sepsis and died suddenly within just one day. He said she loved her father and clung to him and that when he had left her that way she searched for answers which she eventually found in both the Bible and the Scriptures. Thus, it was that when she first saw Khattaaara, she believed that one of Satan's own had been brought into her home.

Khattaaara , as perceived by my mother, possessed all the signs of one of Satan's minions. She had pointed ears and a tail, two pairs of breasts, and like angels, fallen or not, possessed no organs of reproduction—at least where she believed that organs or reproduction should be. This last she took notice of when Khattaaara had undressed right in front of her in the guest room Mama had taken her to, to show her where she was to sleep. Beyond all that, Khattaaara, when she spoke, appeared to hiss and babel in tongues. None of that mattered to Mama, though, who had the strength of the Lord infused in her veins and the determination of Paul. And so she decided there and then that she would save this miserable creature that had ascended somehow from damnation and traveled through the gates of Hell to stand before her. That I had told her that Khattaaara was my former incarnation gave Mama all the more reason and a steadfast and clear purpose to bring this alien being into the arms of Christ.

Even before Phee and I had taught her to speak English, Mama would sit beside her for hours, often taking hold of her hand or kissing her on the forehead, and read passages from both the Old Testament and the New. But while Khattaaara couldn't understand her words, she could read her mind and understand the good intentions of this woman and the love she felt for her as a strange and unearthly daughter. Mama saw the resemblance between Khattaaara and myself and so between the love the alien felt from my Mama and the heartstrings that slowly attached between the two of them, the monster, who was Khattaaara Gaaalthaaarana, Divine Empress of Rendenaaar, softened and became almost human.

Six weeks after her arrival, Mama took Khattaaara to Sunday church. Papa and Phee and I tagged along just in case anything went wrong. We drove to the Immanuel Church in Koreatown with its massive cathedral, stained glass windows, and fifty-foot ceiling from which hung large glowing chandeliers. Khattaaara took it all in with the wonder of a child. Her command of English was still remedial at that point in time but she could understand bits and pieces of what the minister spoke in his sermon.

"Jeeegaaahs," she repeated when she heard the word spoken. Then she stood up and shouted the name again. "Jeeegaaahs! Lowrd Jeeegaaahs!" She raised her arms up, her eyes glowed, and all at once thousands of butterflies appeared in the cathedral. Everyone stared at them in awe.

"It's a miracle!" the minister called out through his microphone. "The Lord has touched this child of Christ and worked his grace through her." He climbed down from his pulpit and walked up to her. "What is your name, my child?" he asked.

"Khattaaara," she replied.

"Well, Khattaaara," the minister said, "You are a blessed creature upon God's green earth." He turned and looked this way and that amongst his congregation as the butterflies continued to flutter overhead. "Her name is Katara," he called out "one of God's angels! Let us all shout out her name!"

And so there came the chorus of the more than a thousand parishioners who had come to worship that Sunday, each calling out, "Katara, Katara!" again and again until at last the minister held up his hands for them to stop. Then we walked back to his pulpit, turned some pages in his Bible, and said, "I shall now read a chapter from the Book of Revelations."

The ride home was interesting. Well, interesting is probably only half a word for it. Papa drove, as he had, going there. Mama sat in the passenger seat and Khattaaara was scrunched between Phee and myself. Mama didn't say anything at first. She just stared out the windshield.

"That was an excellent sermon," Phee said, breaking the awkward silence. "So much was revealed to me."

"I especially liked the part from Revelations," I added.

"And I especially liked the part where you two snuck off to go to the bathroom for fifteen minutes," Mama said sarcastically.

"We have very small bladders," Phee said.

"The size of a pea," I added.

"The size of a quantum pea," Mama replied. "Or perhaps the two of you believe that's the size of my brain! Did you not see what happened—either of you?"

"I saw a bunch of butterflies," Phee said.

"Thousands of them," I added, "just like the one the other day in our backyard."

"Monarchs," Phee said, clarifying the genus.

"I'm not talking about the butterflies," Mama replied. "I'm talking about how Katara found Jesus and how all of the congregation acknowledged that. You told me that in the past—which by the way I do not believe for one moment was before Adam and Eve—that our new daughter was an evil, wicked person. Well, now all that's changed because of the one man who died on the cross for her sins. Praise Jesus and praise the Lord!"

"Praaas Jeeegaaahs!" Khattaaara said.

"Praise Jesus," Phee mumbled.

"Praise the strangeness of it all," I thought to myself. Trust me, it was a Sunday to remember.

CHAPTER LX

Quantum Girl Orange
(A.D. 1,219,064,263)

One minute I was standing with Margaret and older me, the next, I found myself awakening on my back in what I could only describe as a forcefield coffin. I could see a stark brightness around me but I was trapped by whatever it was that I was in. I tried to break through. I projected a forcefield against the one that surrounded me but that backfired causing a buildup of intense pressure, so much so that it became difficult for me to breathe. Nor did my attempts to phase out of it succeed. At last, I decided to try and escape by traveling backward through time, figuring that there must have been a point *in* time where I was free of this. The forcefield, however, hindered the speed at which I was able to travel so that traveling back even a couple of years took hours.

As my journey progressed, strange-looking humanoids walked backward in and out of the room—hairless beings with enlarged craniums. I, however, remained invisible to them. Then, suddenly, I caught a glimpse of the unexpected—a version of myself glowing yellow! All at once, I reversed course and went forward until I saw her again and then stopped. It was necessary for me to move back and forth in time just a bit to capture her attention but then I did and watched as she became startled at what she apparently perceived as my first awakening. Immediately, she called out and members of that other species flooded into the room. In a few short moments, the invisible barrier that separated me from them disappeared. I felt the sudden rush of fresh air on my face and inhaled it into my lungs. I sat up, somewhat stiff from my imprisonment, and turned to my other self.

"Where am I?" I asked her. "You're not Red, are you?"

"Red?" she answered, shaking her head. "Red's still asleep if you can call it that. As for where you are—where *we* are—try more than a billion years in the future."

I stood up and looked around. The beings were staring at us both. "How did I get here?" I asked. "Did *you* bring me?"

Yellow shook her head. "I woke up here just like you."

"How long ago did you awaken?" I asked.

"Eleven months and three days," she replied, "though days now are roughly twenty-four and a half hours."

"Are there any other people like us," I asked.

"Not as far as I can tell," she replied.

"Great," I said. "Any chance we can travel back to our own time?"

"Maybe," she replied. "But for the moment, they need us to help them. The sun is going to expand and scorch the Earth. They need all of us."

"How many of us are there?" I asked.

"Seven," came the response.

"And the other five are in hibernation?" I asked.

"We've had no idea how to awaken them," she replied.

"We," I said, "meaning you and these future men? What do they want from us? Why have we been kept? How long have we been asleep?"

"About a billion years, I've been told," she replied.

"Jesus!" I said. "I didn't think humanity could last that long."

"Well," she said, "at least we're not alone."

"I still don't understand how this happened," I said, "or why we're divided."

"We each have a different one of the god-stones," she replied.

I stared at her. "Where were you when it happened? What's the last thing you remember?"

"I was at home," she replied, "taking a bath, and then I woke up here. I remember I was thinking about Mark."

"Self-pleasuring, no doubt," I said.

"I *am* human," she replied. "What about you?"

"Believe it or not," I said, " I was back in time. Nineteen fifty-three. I'd awakened in Grandma Margaret's body six months before that."

"Seriously," she replied.

"And you'll never guess who my mother—her mother—was."

"Thara-Klo?" she asked.

"Red," I replied, "only she was older than us—in her twenties. Did you know that Grams had been molested?"

"No shit," she replied. "Back then?"

"By her cheerleading coach," I replied. "And she wasn't the only one. The woman had a history. Murdered some, too. One of the girls I became friends with up and killed herself. And then she killed me when I was Grams. I didn't have any of my powers—not then—so I drowned. It was scary and painful. She knocked me out, tied me up, and threw me in the ocean. But then, after I died, my god-stone started working again and revived me."

"What happened to the coach?" she asked.

"Went to trial," I said, "was found guilty, and then executed. Gas chamber. I wish I could have watched. Bitch! I hope she was scared and suffered like I did—like all of the girls she murdered must have."

"A billion-year grudge," she replied. "That must be a record. Too bad Guinness isn't around anymore."

"What's with all these people," I asked, "if people's the right word? All of this looks more like a shrine than a burial crypt."

"We're their gods," she replied, "but it will take all of us and I don't know how to wake the others up. I've tried everything."

"Maybe I can help," I replied. "There are two of us now."

"I'm glad you're awake," she said and smiled.

"I think we should remain separate," I said.

"I agree," she replied. "At least for the time being."

CHAPTER LXI

Quantum Girl Green
(Urth, November 25, 2025)

I was standing hidden in the hallway near the entrance to the living room when I overheard them talking—my counterpart and his parents—perhaps squabbling is a better word.

"Why is she still here?" Peyton said.

"She seems to be a very nice girl," Mr. Herron replied.

"And quite pretty," Mrs. Herron chimed in. "She does look like a cunted version of our Peyton, doesn't she? I should think that if the two of them ever fell in love and had children they would be the spitting image of both of them."

"I do not intend to fall in love with someone who might as well be my twin sister!" Peyton ejaculated—though that might be a rather poor choice of a word, literary license be damned!

"We invited her to stay," Mr. Herron broke in, "and that's that!"

"For how long?" Peyton asked.

"As long as she wants," he replied.

"She is, after all, a Herron," *Mrs*. Herron added. "We can't just cast her off into the streets."

"She has a god-stone in her head," Peyton insisted, "though how she came by it is questionable, to say the least!"

"Do you know, Cameron," Mrs. Herron said to her husband, "I think it would be for the best if the two Peytons shared the same room so that they could come to terms with each other—or at least our Peyton could come to terms with her. I'm certain that Orpheus wouldn't mind staying in the guest room for a while. He's been begging for us to take him to visit Mars. I think the promise of a trip there would make an excellent carrot for him not to complain."

"I agree," said Mr. Herron as he rose from his chair. "I'll show our guest her new accommodations."

"You can't be serious," Peyton exclaimed. "There's just one bed!"

"That you and your brother have shared since you were small," Mrs. Herron said.

"But..." Peyton stammered

"You're going to have to learn to get along," Mrs. Herron went on, literally putting her foot down. "You know your father and I have the final decision as to whether you get your god-stone whether you are eighteen or twenty-one, so if you do not wish to wait an additional three years, I suggest you do as you're told."

As for me, I quickly phased back to the guest room before Mr. Herron had a chance to catch me eavesdropping on their conversation. And so, I just sat there on the bed, looking as innocent as the jewel thief awaiting trial.

And so it came to pass that, that very same night, Peyton and I shared the same double bed that he and Orpheus—his Phee—had shared since childhood. Never mind that Phee was gay and had seen his brother naked thousands of times and vice versa, but to the sad malevolence of Fate (with emphasis on the word, 'male') Peyton was heterosexual and was not only not turned on by his brother's anatomy but found himself quietly repulsed by it.

As we lay there on the individually spring-coiled, pillow-topped mattress, the lights having been damped twenty minutes before, I broke the silence that had occurred.

"You're just upset with me," I said, "because I'm a reflection of you—a reflection that owns tits—and a cunt as your mother put it, neither of which you have ever touched—or witnessed for that matter."

"I've seen pictures," he said.

"Not the same," I replied. "Is that why you hate me—because I have what you have always wanted?"

"I don't want to have them a part of me," he said, "breasts and vaginas."

351

"But you want them regardless," I replied, "to see—not in just a photograph—to touch and fuck and perhaps even to taste. I can read your character like tea leaves. I mean, you're all prim and proper—breasts instead of tits, vagina instead of cunt. You're fifteen with all those pent-up hormones racing through your veins and into your cock and that makes you angry—so angry that you…"

"That I what?" he asked.

"I don't know," I said. "I suddenly forgot what I was going to say. I remember being near the ocean with you and that there were natives around and that you were angry about something. I can't even remember how I got here." I stared at him in the moonlit room. "Anyway, you can't go on angry like this because you've never been with a girl."

"And so, what am I supposed to do?" he said. "None of the girls at school like me that way. Most of them are into other girls."

"Guys!" I said and then got out of bed and stood facing him. "Their legs are all like Jell-O when it comes to someone of the opposite sex they really like."

I shook out my hair and let the nightgown his mother had lent me drop to the floor. Peyton reached over the bed to the lamp on the nightstand next to where I had been, turned it on, and then stared at me. I turned around, faced him again, and then climbed back onto the bed on my hands and knees over him. His eyes fixed themselves on my breasts.

"Go ahead," I told him. "Touch them."

He did, one and then the other. Then I shifted my balance to my left arm, and with my right hand, I took his and guided it to my vag. I could hear his head start beating a mile a minute. Then I felt down to his equivalent. There was no doubt in my mind that he was aroused. I reached into his jams and grabbed hold and then guided it into me. I did the work. I did the rest. When it was done and I laid down beside him, he turned his head to me and asked, "Why did you do that? I thought you said you had a boyfriend."

"I do," I said. "I will. And I know enough not to confuse sex with love. But I need you to promise me something. Whether we do this just this once or a hundred times, I want your word that you will do your best to be a good person, god-stone or not—power or not."

"I promise," he said, and reading him like a human lie detector, I could tell that he meant it. Then I kissed him and he kissed me back. That was the first time but it wasn't the last. We never mentioned it to anyone else and feigned animosity toward each other in front of everyone else.

I stayed there for nearly half a year with no clue whatsoever as to how to find my way back home. Then, out of the clear blue sky, another one of him appeared—another older version—one of the split-offs from the one I had left in the past of this world. When he saw me, he used a forcefield to hurl me into a wall. Peyton lunged at him but the older one became incorporeal for a split second and Peyton went right through him.

"Leave her alone!" the young Peyton shouted.

The older one laughed. "Was I ever that pathetic?" he said and then turned to me. "You have part of our stone," he went on. Then he focused hard, his eyes began to glow, and the purple god-stone flew from my head. Once it was back in his, his expression changed. His face seethed in anger. He hurled a forcefield at me that enveloped me and I passed out.

CHAPTER LXII

Quantum Girl Blue
(October 29, 1929)

Having arrived in Hollywood, I walked the streets during the day and slept on park benches at night until I got my bearings. I found some extra work at United Artists on a movie called *What a Widow!* which was a romantic comedy starring Gloria Swanson, who thirty years later played Norma Desmond opposite William Holden in Billy Wilder's *Sunset Boulevard*. During a lunch break, I was spotted by Charles Chaplin—actually, he hit on me—but wound up casting me in the lead female role in *City Lights*. It seemed that he had been about to cast another actress named Virginia Cherrill, but the two of them didn't get along. Despite that she was twenty and I was only fifteen, Charlie had the makeup artists add on a few years.

Most everyone who worked with Charlie couldn't help but admire his talent and how he threw himself into his productions. He was writer, producer, and director and acted in the film as well. *City Lights* was still silent when *talkies* were coming out. I spent a lot of time with Charlie. I know that he had a crush on me despite my age but our friendship never evolved into anything more. He's had a really bad divorce a few years back and it takes time for a person to recover. Sometimes, I'd get depressed, mainly over not being able to go back home to Phee and my parents and I missed Mary, but he was always there to cheer me up with one of his Little Tramp routines. With the pay I got, I had rented a small bungalow near the studio. Charlie helped me furnish it, he told me, with furniture he had snuck out of the prop department but I suspected that he bought it somewhere and didn't want me to feel obligated to him.

There weren't any lines to learn for my part in the movie. I played a blind flower girl that Charlie as the Little Tramp falls in love with. Somehow, my character comes to the mistaken belief that the Little Tramp is rich. Going through a series of incredible hardships to keep her and her grandmother from being evicted[36] and to pay for surgery to help her regain her sight, the Little Tramp sacrifices himself to help her. After the operation, with her vision restored, the girl is able to own her own flower shop. While talking to a friend inside it, the two of them see the Little Tramp and laugh at how funny he appears. When she goes out to give him a flower and a coin, she touches his hand and then reaches up to feel his face. Suddenly, she realizes that this was her benefactor and tears start to well up in her eyes.

In my time, everyone was so caught up in movies about superheroes, physical disabilities, discrimination, and social conflicts. This, though, was a movie about self-sacrifice and love. It was a beautiful film.

I think that my presence made a difference in Charlie. In some ways, he was like a father to me, and in others he acted as though he were still twenty years old even though he was forty at the time. Charlie had a penchant for girls around my age and it was all that I could do to maintain my *dignity*, to put it mildly.

"Charlie," I said while we were having dinner at the Brown Derby, "would you still like me if I was closer to your age?"

The Brown Derby was a popular spot for movie stars, including Gloria Swanson who came by our table to say hello and congratulate me on my performance, never recognizing me from when I worked as an extra on her film. The building was in the shape of an *actual* British derby and, of course, painted brown.

"I would love you if you were a hundred years old," Charlie replied. "I would love you if you were old and wrinkled and your breasts scraped the floor."

"Yeah, right," I replied.

---

[36] How coincidental, I thought, thinking back about Mary and Great Grams and how I had intended to help them keep their home.

Charlie's expression turned to one of perplexity.

"What is the meaning of, 'Yeah, right?'" he asked.

"It's an expression," I replied, "that means I don't think so. It will be in vogue around the time when *you're* one hundred years old."

"Age," he said, "is a relative thing as Dr. Einstein once proved."

"Well," I replied, "then it's a good thing we're not related."

Charlie just shrugged his shoulders and sighed. "For all sad words of tongue and pen," he quoted, "the saddest are these, 'It might have been.'" Then, with his chin resting on his hands and his elbows on the table, he stared at me like a boy who had just lost his dog and said, "I know. 'Yeah, right.'"

Anyway, things went along swimmingly as they used to say. Charlie and I attended the premiere together. It was at the Los Angeles Theatre, January 30th, 1931, four months after my seventeenth birthday. We walked down the red carpet that was lined with reporters and newspaper and magazine photographers, each armed with flashbulb cameras that exploded in bursts of light. The façade of the building had four Corinthian columns and a garishly ornate wrought iron marquee. Charlie wore a black tuxedo and bow tie. I was in a sheer pink floor-length dress with a matching cape, decorated with beads, custom-designed in Paris by Elsa Schiaparelli at Charlie's request.

"Mr. Chaplin," one reporter called out, "is it true that you and Miss Herron are engaged?"

Charlie stopped and turned to the man and said in a calm voice, "As with the rumors of my death," he said, "any talk of our relationship has been highly exaggerated." Then he whispered to me, "Just smile baring teeth, and wave to the reptiles."

When the evening was done and the crowd at the reception afterward had worn thin, Charlie walked me back to my bungalow. We made small talk along the way, but when we came to my front walk he suddenly became morose.

"Ordinarily," he said, "I'd do a pratfall to impress you but I'm afraid I'm not as supple as I used to be."

"Oh, I think you're perfectly wonderful," I replied.

"But..." he interjected. "There is always a but."

"Charlie, dear," I said, taking hold of his hand, "I told you I have a beau."

Charlie turned and looked me in the eye. "An invisible one, no doubt," he said. "Neither flesh nor blood nor bone and yet he exists to stonewall my affections."

"His name is Mark," I said.

"Truly a fortunate man," he replied, "to have captured the heart of Helen of Troy." As it was wont to do, his mood suddenly changed. "I'm planning a new picture," he said. "It's called *Modern Times*. It concerns the Tramp, struggling against industrialization with the help of a homeless woman who remains faithfully at his side. I would like to have you in the lead role."

"I know what it's like to be homeless," I said.

"Excellent," he replied as though our previous conversation hadn't gone on.

"Charlie," I said, "I *do* love you. It's just that my heart is already spoken for."

"Think nothing of it," he replied.

Then I kissed him on the cheek, bid my farewell, and went into the small house that now was my home. After I had closed the door and was about to press the button in the wall to turn on the ceiling fixture, a man's voice startled me.

"Hello, Quantum Girl," the man said.

Startled, I wheeled around to face him though I couldn't make out his face in the darkened room.

"Who are you?" I said in a voice that trembled.

"Quantum *Man*," he replied.

"What do you want?" I asked.

"You," he replied. "I want *you*."

I saw his eyes glow bright violet, my head began to spin, and then, I guess, I blacked out.

CHAPTER LXIII

Ophelia (Lia)
(the alternate reality)

I was placed in an adult facility. Other than when I was arrested, I'd never even been to jail before. It was beyond humiliating. I was brought to the prison in handcuffs. Once inside, they were taken off and I was brought to a small room and told to undress. The room was cold but that didn't seem to matter to the female guards who were all warmly dressed. After I had my clothes off, my arms held down trying to cover myself as best I could, one of the officers looked in my mouth, ears, and nose and then told me to bend over and spread my legs. I remember at the time thinking that it felt as though I was being raped. I've always tried to be a strong person but I remember starting to cry. That didn't matter to the guards, though. I assumed that they had seen a reaction like I was having so many times that they had become desensitized to it. After the strip search was done, I was handed a bundle of clothes consisting of dark blue pants with an elastic band, a light blue pullover blouse, underwear, socks, and slip-on shoes. It was the second time I had been put through this routine. The first was when I was first arrested.

I was placed in a cell with another girl around my age, probably to protect me from the other prisoners *due* to my age. I mean, despite that I was only fifteen years old, I had been charged as an adult and sent to an adult prison. That was CIW or the California Institution for Women, which was located in Chino. The compound was surrounded by two fences with barbed wire. Chino is in a somewhat rural area. I remember when I was being transported there, I could smell the horses or, rather, their excrement. It must have been close to an hour's drive on the bus from the L.A. County women's jail which was down in Lynnwood.

In the cell were two beds that were steel projections from the walls with thin mattresses on them. On my bed were a folded sheet, a blanket, a pillow, a washcloth, a body towel, and various hygienes as they were called, meaning toothpaste, a toothbrush, a hairbrush, deodorant, sanitary pads, and soap. There were no iron bars like in men's prisons. There were just steel doors with small windows in them, not so that we could see out but so that the guards could see in. You cannot imagine how I felt the first time that door clanged shut. My whole body trembled. It was the one pivotal moment that I truly wanted to die and would have taken my life there and then if I'd had the means.

My cellmate was named Kimberly Williams. She was pretty with shoulder-length straight dark hair and hazel eyes. Like me, she was arrested when she was fifteen and also charged as an adult. That was two years before I arrived. She had been convicted of murder in the first degree and sentenced to twenty-five years to life. The victim was her stepfather, whom she claimed had sexually molested her since she was six years old when he and her mother got married. Growing up she had been a problem child, probably as a result of what had been going on in the home. She told me that she had finally had enough. After her stepfather had beaten and raped her for what turned out to be the last time, she took a kitchen knife while he was asleep in bed and stabbed him eighteen times. But as there had never been any allegations of wrongdoing by her stepfather, the prosecution painted her as a willful child and the jury bought into it, as did her mother who refused to believe her stories of all of the horror she had faced at the hands of her supposedly loving husband. So, for all of the time she was there, Kimberly had neither support from the outside nor visitors. She viewed the world as upside-down and hated, not just her now-deceased stepfather, but all men from the prosecutor to the judge to her ineffectual public defender and every other one of their sex.

As for me, Mom and Dad and Peyton would come and visit me every weekend without fail. Visitation hours were 8:30 a.m. until

2:00 p.m. We met in the visitation room with everyone else and sat at our own table. You couldn't bring anything in other an your ID, one car key, and dollar bills[37] but there were vending machines and free games and playing cards. There was also an outdoor area. I really looked forward to the visits I had. Mom and Dad always tried to put on a happy face for me but I knew that they were torn up inside. Peyton was ever cheerful, filled with stories about the outside world. Dad, though, had hired a lawyer to appeal my case to try and get the conviction overturned. I didn't hold out a lot of hope. Hope in me was a thing of the past. Looking around the room each week, I thought of myself as the sanest one there. Peyton still tried to convince me that she was some sort of superheroine called Quantum Girl. She said that she's going to write a book about it entitled, *Quantum Girl, a Tale of Reincarnation.* When I asked her how it would end, she just smiled and told me I'd have to wait until it was published.

The prison was institutional. There were few if any creature comforts. The guards could be friendly or not depending on their moods. CIW was not without its reputation. A year before I was sent there, Leslie Van Houten, one of the Manson family, was released from there, having spent fifty-three years behind bars. She was nineteen years old when she was arrested, charged, and convicted of two counts of murder. Like me, she used a knife, but unlike me, her victims were innocent of any wrongdoing.

After I first arrived, I would cry myself to sleep every night. This went on for two weeks until one night. Kim climbed into bed with me and held me. My bed became hers as well from then on. My world and my future were within the prison walls. I had nothing to look forward to other than the repetition of each and every day. I had my weekend family, of course, but Kim became my family the rest of the time. More than that, she became the closest thing to a soulmate that I could ever hope to imagine in my now-confined

---

[37] $70 for each adult and $40 for each minor visitor.

existence.

As time wore on, intimacy broke out between us. I had had boyfriends in the past but never a girlfriend—at least not in that way. And, despite that I had put on airs that I was all that and sexually experienced, I was a virgin when I had come to prison. How ironic it was that it was a prison guard who robbed me of that during the strip search. At least, when I was arrested, the guard at the county jail was more kind. So, there it was, I, Ophelia Elise Herron, who had been the diehard sparrow, was now a resolute sapph. I fell in love with Kim and she with me. How strange, I thought, the turns in life. Peyton, who had declared her love for Theresa Martinez, suddenly fixated on one boy named Mark, who appeared as much a figment of her imagination as Quantum Girl. But Peyton was on the outside looking in and I was the one being looked in at.

Love, though, comes in all forms. Mom, who touts herself as a devout Christian, had scorned Peyton at the time for her homosexuality. But with me it was different. When I told her about Kim and introduced her at long last, she smiled at her and said, "Thank you for loving my daughter." I don't know if my mother believed that Jesus would be unforgiving in the afterlife, but she recognized the loneliness and hopelessness I had felt until Kim had settled the tearing of my heart just a bit. It was her unconditional love for me that placed it before her love of God. Jesus may have been her Savior, but I was her child.

No one is innocent in prison. Some are just more guilty than others. Things can be rough, especially if you're young. It's not that you can't defend yourself. It's just that you have a pretty pink target on your back. If you're young and pretty, you get cross-haired by the bull dykes. If you're just young, you get things stolen from you from food to underwear to shoes. Fortunately for me, I had a violent reputation. I was in the news and on TV. Kim wasn't so lucky when she first got there. For her, it was a matter of out of the frying pan and into a bed of hot coals. But she endured and survived. That's what you have to do in prison. It's survival of the unfittest—at least as far as the normals on the outside are concerned. As far as I was concerned, my life was over, although I wasn't quite sure how to make it end. *Even if I slit my wrists,* I thought, *I'd be found in a short enough time to save my life and all I'd be left with would be scars and pain.* How I wished that Peyton was her imaginary Quantum Girl. Then she wouldn't have gotten raped and I would never have done what I had to do. I didn't regret what I had done. Hell isn't a destination for those who have sinned. It's a place that people go through while they're waiting for things to change.

Three years and four months in something miraculous happened. I became pregnant. There was a long investigation as to how it had happened. All of the male guards and staff were questioned but when an amniocentesis was performed after twenty weeks, it was determined that the female fetus carried only my genes with just a slight variance. Presumably—and according to my mother—this had happened only once before in recorded history and with earth-shattering consequences. But as I had no visions of any god impregnating me, I had to assume that it was the result of some genetic fluke. When the baby was born, I named her Jordan. They wouldn't let me keep her, though. Mom and Dad assured me that they would shoulder the responsibility, but Peyton said she would take her. *And why not let her?* I thought. I trusted her more than anyone and she had just recently turned eighteen. So, that's what happened. Peyton became the mother of my baby girl.

None of the appeals worked. I resigned myself to the fact that I would more than likely grow old and die where I was. Perhaps, like Leslie Van Houten, I'd finally get paroled when I was in my seventies. Then, I'd be able to see the night sky again. I prayed for Peyton and Jordan. I wondered if there really was a God who would take me in his arms after my journey ended. I doubted it, though—not after all I'd been through.

CHAPTER LXIV

Peyton
*(the alternate reality
March 15, 2042)*

It had been Jordan's seventeenth birthday the day before. It was a Saturday. It was just me and her who went to the prison to visit her mother. Lia and I were both thirty-one years old but Lia seemed older than her years. Papa had taken to drinking and died of cirrhosis nearly six years before, and Mama had to be placed in a mental institution. She had lost her religion and decried Jesua as a false prophet. Then the visions came. She claimed to be an angel sent by the *true* god, whom she said was called Khii, and that her name wasn't Katherine Herron, but, rather, Tara Cloverfield, and that she had been abducted from a world that circled the sun opposite the Earth. She had been a princess there, she claimed. No medication appeared to help but as with Lia, I visited her at least once a week.

I had raised Jordan from when she was only three days old. She grew up to be a beautiful girl with pale blonde hair and blue eyes, so like her mother. The fact that she was conceived through Parthenogenesis was not made public. It was just assumed by any and all who gave it thought that the father was someone who worked at the prison. I never did hook up with Mark. Try as I might to find him, it appeared that he did not exist in this reality and so I remained single but not alone. I had Jordan ever in my life.

It wasn't until the night before, per Lia's request, that I told Jordan the truth about who Lia and I were to her. Whenever we had visited in the past, Jordan had always greeted Lia like the aunt she thought she was. We were in the living room on the sofa when I told her. She stared at me, uncertain what to say.

"I know this must be difficult for you to take in," I said to her, "but I swore to your mother that I wouldn't say anything until today."

"I don't know what *to* say," she replied. "I can't just suddenly not think of you as my mother. You've raised me since I was born."

"I *am* your mother," I assured her, "but so is she—not just biologically but in her heart. She's wanted to tell you so many times but was afraid you wouldn't be old enough to understand."

"It makes sense," she replied, "why you always brought me with you when we went to visit her—why there were always tears in her eyes. But I don't understand one thing. I get that she's my mother. But who's my father?"

"You don't have one," I said. "You're the billion in one virgin birth."

"How is that possible?" she asked.

"The way I understand it," I replied, "is that two of her eggs fused together, fertilizing each other. Don't ask me how. It can happen in some birds and sharks and lizards but only rarely in humans and, according to what I read, those who are born this way can never themselves reproduce."

"So," she said, "I can't have children—not ever."

I shook my head. "I don't think so," I replied.

"I guess the Herron name," she said, "ends with me."

I took her hands in mine. "You can always adopt," I replied, "but I recommend falling in love first."

"Strong words from someone who never took her own advice," she said with a smile.

"You were always more important to me," I replied, "than any love I might have wished to have had."

I guess this was our nine-hundred, thirty-sixth visit to the prison together. When Lia entered the visitors' room she looked first at me. I nodded to her and then she looked at Jordan.

"Hello, Mother," Jordan said as she came up to us.

Lia took her in her arms and hugged her, tears streaming from her eyes. Then she broke away and their eyes met.

"I didn't know how you'd react when you were told the truth?" she said.

"That I have two mothers who love me?" Jordan replied. There were tears in her eyes as well.

"How about I bring us all some hot chocolate?" I asked.

Jordan and Lia both nodded, so I went off to one of the vending machines. When I returned both of them were at one of the tables, talking and laughing as though nothing had happened.

"I'm going off to college next fall," Jordan told her other mother. "I got the acceptance letter two days ago."

"Are you excited?" Lia asked.

"Ecstatic!" came the reply. "I intend to major in theoretical physics. I think all of Mama's Quantum Girl stories inspired me."

"I'm so proud of you," Lia said to her.

Jordan smiled. "That means a lot to me," she replied and then added with emphasis, "Mother."

I too smiled but with the truth out, a weight had been lifted off my chest. Jordan had run the gauntlet of truth and come out, not only unscathed but somehow better as a result. These two were my family and all that I needed to have made my life complete.

CHAPTER LXV

Jordan
*(the alternate reality
October 25, 2071)*

I had earned my PhD at Eastern Michigan University after which I began research at Quantech Labs, a company in which I eventually became a partner. My mother, Ophelia, had taken her own life in Sixty-three after her partner had died from breast cancer. Quantech was headquartered in Constance, Arizona, basically an isolated community that was chosen due to the classified nature of its work. I had my other mother come there to live with me. She was sixty years old, about to turn sixty-one. I was forty-three and had been divorced from my husband, Michael for a little over eight years. There was an apartment on the top floor of the facility. I lived there. I found it necessary due to the amount of research I was doing at the time.

My mother had aged gracefully. Her light brown hair was streaked with gray, there were crow's feet at the edges of her eyes and there were lines on either side of her mouth. I wanted her with me because she needed me. The physicians had diagnosed her with Parkinson's disease which was apparent by the trembling of her hands. She tended to stare and didn't blink very much. She'd been placed on a new drug called *Sentraxitol* but it didn't appear to be affecting her affliction. Adding to that were her nightmares where she envisioned herself, in this battle or that, as the imaginary Quantum Girl she had once claimed to be. How serendipitous was it that I came to work at a corporation called Quantech, though perhaps I had chosen that place because the name was so pronounced in my mind?

Breakthroughs in the field of quantum field theory had come a long way in the past decade, ever since Acharya from New Delhi discovered what he named the Acharya Interdimensional Barrier or AIB that appeared on its surface to be spacetime's line of defense against the convergence of multiple dimensions. Once penetrated, however, only one extraneous existence was found which scientists here had labeled the quantum fabric that appeared to undergird our universe. Acharya's breaching of the AIB had been repeated only once six months after its discovery but remained a mystery until I and another of our team, Adam Lockridge, were able, not only to duplicate the results but also maintain an open portal between the two realms of existence. A critical turn in our research came when I placed eight 10mm synthetic diamond spheres into the portal and then irradiated them with a prismatic laser, each at a different frequency. The result was that each sphere took on a different color while exhibiting a unique radiation similar to what had been detected within the quantum fabric. After ten minutes and forty-seven seconds, however, the spheres all disappeared into the portal. I repeated the experiment with a single sphere and subjected it to a laser set to 750 THz which is at the violet end of the spectrum. After *dipping* it in the rift for thirty-seven seconds, I pulled it back and then closed the window between the dimensions. Minutes and then hours ticked by but the sphere remained in our universe. I sat in my lab coat, sitting on a stool, staring at it when my mother walked in.

"You've been down here all night," she said. "You need to get some rest."

"In a moment," I replied.

"What have you been working on?" she asked.

"It's a bit complicated," I told her. "I irradiated several diamonds and then briefly placed them in the quantum fabric. I just lost half a million dollars' worth, but I still have this one—not that it's good for anything. But I'm curious as to where all the others went."

My mother came over the to table and looked at the glowing gemstone. "Dear God!" she exclaimed. "It's a god-stone!"

"From one of your stories…" I replied.

She reached down, picked it up, and held it up close to look at.

"Mama," I said, concerned. "you need to be careful."

I had barely gotten the words out when the gemstone began to shrink and spin. Then, all at once, it flew out of her hand, up to her forehead, and then disappeared. And then she changed. She became younger—no more than twenty-five—and all signs of her disease were gone.

"What's happening?" I exclaimed.

Mama smiled. "I told you," she said. "I told everyone. No one would believe me. 'You dreamed it,' they all said. Even you." She looked up at me. "Dream this!"

Suddenly, she turned into what I knew from her drawings was Quantum Girl. I got up from my stool and took a step back. "I don't understand," I said. "How can this be?"

"I've always wondered where the god-stones came from," I replied, "but all the time it was you." She stared at me. "You need to end your experiments, though. The stones are just too dangerous. No doubt the ones you lost are on their way back to Rendenaaar where they will wreak havoc."

"How can I live with the fact that I caused that?" she said.

"Accept the fact that it's part of the history of a universe that died trillions upon trillions of years ago."

"But even if that's the case," she replied, "My actions here and now were the cause of it all."

"What you did," she said, "was already done. The past created the present and the present created the past." There was an intense look that overtook her then. "I want to go back home—to my home—my reality. I'd like you to come with me."

"My place is here," I told her. "I still need to visit Grandma."

"Well," she replied, "I'll come visit *you*."

I hugged her tightly and she hugged me back. Then she vanished from my arms and the air seemed to snap.

"I love you, Mama," I said softly to the empty air.

How strange it was, I thought to myself, that no one had believed her all those years. I let out a chuckle. My mother had been a superhero all along—Quantum Girl, Guardian of Everything There Was—*And, to think,* I thought to myself, *that it was my discovery that had caused her powers to exist!*

CHAPTER LXVI

Quantum Girl Violet
(April 30, 2025)

I wasn't certain what had happened to the Phee I originally had left when the one of me had phased off to New York to try and hook up with Mark. I wondered whether it was possible that alternate realities kept splitting off whenever I did anything. In that case, the other Phee would have been left without a sister. It was all very confusing and I had no mentor to ask questions of.

As we all sat down to supper, Mama, as usual, had us join our hands and bow our heads in prayer.

"Thank you, Lord," she said, "for the food we are about to receive, and bless us who are about to partake in this bounty. Amen."

Mama had prepared meatloaf that came with a side salad and ice tea. We then began to eat with Phee staring at me between bites.

"What?" I finally blurted out to her.

"Just waiting," she said.

"For?" I said back.

"Waiting to see what you turn into next!" she snapped back.

"What's *that* supposed to mean?" I replied.

"I don't know," she said. "Maybe you'll turn into Supergirl or Captain Marvel or some alien with pointed ears and a tail!"

"Been there. Done that," I replied.

"Should we be concerned?" she asked.

"About?" I replied.

"You," she said, "with your quantum powers."

"May I say something?" Mark said.

"No!" Phee and I replied to him at the exact same time.

"Children," Mama said in a calm voice, "this is our supper table where we do not discuss politics, religion, or superheroes. Oh, and

371

by the way, Reverent Hollister called earlier to inform me that the church was having a bake sale a week from Saturday and asked for my participation, baking a cake and then sitting at the welcoming table."

Phee, when no one was watching, stuck out her tongue at me. I stuck mine out back at her. Unfortunately, Mama had caught a glimpse of it.

"That will be enough of that!" she exclaimed.

"Ugh!" I replied, "I'm out of here!" I set down my fork and phased up to my bedroom from where I heard Mama scream in terror. I could hear everything with my quantum hearing.

"Where did she go!" Mama exclaimed.

"She's a superhero," Phee replied unenthusiastically.

"What do you mean she's a superhero?" Mama said, her voice shaking. "There are no such things as superheroes."

"So I thought until up in the bedroom a while ago," Phee replied. "There is actually more than one of her."

"Dear Lord Jesus in Heaven!" Mama exclaimed.

"I thought you're not supposed to use the Lord's name in vain," Phee said calmly.

"I am not using the Lord's name in vain," Mama shouted. "One of my two daughters just vanished into thin air in front of me! How am I supposed to react? Ophelia Jane Herron, do you know where your sister is?"

"I'm up in my bedroom!" I shouted. "Jeez!" That last to myself.

Thump, thump, thump, thump, thump! came the marching of feet in a frenzy up the carpeted stairs. A moment later, Mama burst into the room, followed by Papa, Phee, and Mark in that order. As for me, I was lying on my back in my bed, my legs spaced apart, my knees up in the air.

Down went my knees in an instant so as not to produce any further shock to my mother in that I had taken upon myself of late to go commando. My mother screeched to a halt once inside the room like Roadrunner at the edge of a cliff. "*Hmeep, hmeep!*"[38]

"Young lady," Mama said, with her hands emotionally folded across her chest, "I would like an explanation!"

Wearily, I sat up, at first propping myself up on my elbows and then scrooching up to a full sitting position.

I shrugged. "I have superpowers. I've had them since when I'd just turned fourteen when I found out that I was the reincarnation of some alien woman named Khattaaara who, by the way, had pointed ears and a tail," at which point I sneered at Phee.

"How is this possible?" Mama exclaimed. She turned to Papa who just shrugged, like, *How am I supposed to know?* "Our faith in God," she went on, glancing toward Heaven, "does not allow for reincarnations! Even Our Lord and Savior, Jesus Christ, will be coming back as Himself."

"I just know what I know," I said as I climbed out of bed. I stood in the center of the room, caused the lights to become strobe-like, phased in and out of my Quantum Girl costume, and began to dance to *I've Got the Power* by Snap phasing in and out, creating multiples of myself and then merging back. When the song was over and the lights in the room were restored as were my street clothes, Mama just stood there, frozen like a statue, and then fainted dead away. Papa caught her in his arms and then laid her on my bed.

Phee glared at me. "You didn't have to do that!" she said. "A simple explanation would have sufficed!"

"She asked," I replied.

"We've been through a lot," Mark added. "You can't imagine."

"Our mother is lying on the bed unconscious!" Phee exclaimed.

I shook my head to myself, phased into the bathroom, and then phased back with a washcloth that I had wetted with ammonia that I waved under my mother's nose. She stirred back into consciousness and stared at me.

"Tell me that was all a dream," she begged.

---

[38] Forgive my spelling, but that's how it sounds.

"I wish that I could," I said every so gently. "I love you, Mama, but there are things in the universe beyond what the Bible has to say. Please try and accept me as I now am."

"I'll love you any way you are, Sweet Pea," she said in a weak voice, "but reincarnated from an alien? Jesus, Mary, and Joseph, how on earth did my poor uterus go so wrong?"

Something happened just then, though. I heard a man's voice say, "Loved the moves," he said smugly. I quickly turned toward it to see a man in a costume similar to mine. As I glanced around, everyone else was frozen.

"Who are you?" I asked.

"Quantum *Man*," he replied.

"What do you want?" I demanded to know.

"I'm here for you," he said, "Peyton Elise Herron aka Quantum Girl."

Then his eyes glowed brightly and I felt myself growing faint. As I looked down at my arms, they became transparent and began to waver as though I had started to duplicate but couldn't. That was the last thing I remembered.

CHAPTER XLVII

Quantum Girl Green
(billions of years in the future)

I had awakened on an earth that was devoid of life. There were no oceans. There was no atmosphere. A ring of debris from what had once been Earth's moon encircled the plant and reflected the dim light from the sun which had turned into a white dwarf star.

I had awakened on the ground on my back, staring at a nearly all-black sky, my quantum vision revealing that most of the galaxies were gone. I stood up and looked around. The Earth was barren. No matter where on the planet I phased to, there was nothing around me but hard silicate rock. This was the Earth's mantle, the crust having been torn away when the sun had become a red giant, engulfing the inner planets. How it was that I was still alive on a world without air I did not know but I assumed it was from the god-stone in my head that somehow continued to oxygenate my blood. I had no urge to breathe. There was no gasping for breath. But then each of us survive for nine months in our mother's womb without the need for air.

I had no idea how far into the future I had gone, though my guess was, from the look of things, about six billion years. Looking upward into the far distance, I saw that Jupiter had lost its giant red spot and that Saturn had lost its rings. I was alone on this frozen planet with nowhere to go other than backward in time. As I was about to try, I felt myself being pulled. That is the best way I could describe it. The world around me turned into a swirling mass of light until, at last, I found myself in a room *filled* with light. But there was more than that. There were others around me, most of them humanoid but not human. I awoke lying down on some sort of a pedestal. It was when I sat up that I first saw *them*—other versions of myself—other colors of Quantum Girl. There was red and blue, yellow and orange, and violet.

"What's going on?" I asked.

"We brought you back from when you awakened," the yellow Quantum Girl explained. "You were the last because it took you so long to revive."

I climbed down from the bed where I sat and stood facing her.

"Where am I?" I asked. "Where are we and why are there so many of us?"

You ask too many questions, one of the humanoids said telepathically as I found myself being pulled into my other selves until there was just one of me.

"I don't understand," I replied.

The answer lies within you, Faaah telepathed as she and the rest of the caretakers dissolved into thin air. A moment later, the brilliant light that filled the room dimmed into blackness.

I awoke in my bedroom. It was night—winter from the snow outside frosted the window panes, and Phee was in her bed fast asleep. Somewhere beneath the soil were there six versions of me who would sleep for a billion years or were there not? How strange it was, the dream I just had that I had been in Egypt and in Rome, that I had battled a Quantum Man, and that I had led so many different lives. But *was* it a dream? I wondered. Was any of it? Throughout the hours until dawn, I questioned whether all that I had gone through was real. I had to know.

When morning finally came, I phased to Chicago, searched through official records, and was led by them to Rosehill Cemetery on the North Side. There I found two graves, side by side with a monument at their head. The graves were overgrown with weeds but I phased the weeds away. The grave on the left read, "Robert McGuire, Beloved Father and Husband, 1902-1944." The one on the right was the one I had come there to find: "Mary Jane Lindsey McGuire, 1906-1959, Beloved Wife and Mother." But there was more—a message from the past—for while many of the monuments there had marble angels atop them, this one, strangely enough, had a life-size bronze statue of Quantum Girl, head held high, cape appearing to billow in the wind. The base on which the statue stood was covered in new-fallen snow. As I brushed it off, I saw the inscription that read, "To my long-lost friend. You were never forgotten. I only hope that you found your way back home."

I have never learned what set me on this series of adventures, though I suspect it was the one who guards the threads of eternity. Perhaps it was done to teach me human suffering so that I could truly meet the measure of what a superheroine should be. I have the ability to turn into a billion of myself and my heart can hear a billion prayers. I wondered if I could answer all of them; after all, I have all the time in the world.

I do not know whether the God of the Hebrews exists or whether Christ will return to the Earth. I only know that there must be a reason for my having been given these powers and there must be some great purpose beyond that. Lord Acton once said that absolute power corrupts absolutely. Lord Actor may have been right most of the time, but not where I am concerned. My name is Peyton Herron. My name is Quantum Girl. There is a road that lies before me and I choose to walk the righteous path for that is how I was raised. That is how I was taught. And that is how I choose to live.

AFTERWORD

The Quantum Girl Saga deals with a lot more than aliens and superpowers. They touch upon bullying, self-harm, and suicide. These are issues faced by young people today. As a teenager myself, I strongly encourage anyone twenty-five or younger, who is facing those issues or others such as sexual assault or date rape, substance abuse, child abuse, sexual trafficking, anxiety or depression, or if things are bad at home and you are considering running away, please call the Thursday's Child hotline at 1 (800) USA KIDS from a landline, or (818) 831-1234 internationally or from a cellphone. Phone lines are open 24/7 and are confidential and free. They care. I care. I'm Peyton Herron, Quantum Girl, and spokesperson for Thursday's Child. Their website is www.thursdayschild.org, where you can also get help.